PRAISE FOR KATHERINE DEAUXVILLE AND *ENRAPTURED*

"A superbly written Regency romp. A rare delight . . . utterly captivating."
— Virginia Henley, *New York Times* bestselling author

"Pure entertainment from page one!"
— Connie Mason, bestselling author of *Gunslinger*

THE MOVE

Suddenly, sitting in the duke's library, Marigold had the most astonishing sensation. Westermere's big, masculine body, even though he was at the moment ignoring her, was sending her the most peculiar, wildly sensual message. It was so strong that her own senses positively quivered in response. Her whole body tingled with it.

She felt dizzy, and she recognized that the evening's chess match was a failure. Worse, she had hardly convinced Westermere of the importance of mutual respect and intimacy that Mary Wollstonecraft had taught superceded marriage. She certainly had not enhanced her character in his eyes. But she could say that her own feelings toward Westermere had somewhat mysteriously improved. Perhaps there was hope yet.

Perhaps, Marigold thought, it was time to go on to the next step.

"There's no mention of the Malay chess move—" the duke began, turning to her with an open book in his hand. He stopped abruptly when he observed her staring at him.

"I think," she said, before he could speak, "now is the time to progress to ah—uh, physical intimacy. Would tonight, Your Grace, be convenient for you?"

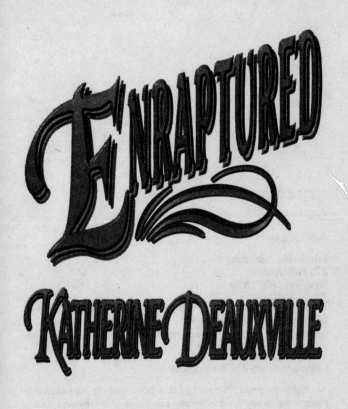

ENRAPTURED

KATHERINE DEAUXVILLE

LEISURE BOOKS   NEW YORK CITY

*To my editor, Christopher Keeslar, with great admiration
and many thanks.*

A LEISURE BOOK®

June 1999

Published by

Dorchester Publishing Co., Inc.
276 Fifth Avenue
New York, NY 10001

ISBN 0-8439-4540-0

The name "Leisure Books" and the stylized "L" with design are
trademarks of Dorchester Publishing Co., Inc.

Printed in the United States of America.

Chapter One

1819

"An absolute snot," the Honorable Hubert Tonsley-Pryce said from the depths of his wing chair in his club, the prestigious Brown's. "Westermere was sent down from Eton, you know. *Eton.*" Here the third son of the earl of Malmesbury could not repress a shudder at such a hideous happenstance. "Sent down for being impertinent to every master he had. The whole family's insufferable; there isn't a peer in England who doesn't know that about the Westermeres. This insubordinate sprig considered himself better than the entire school, no master was spared his upstart views of the curriculum—in fact, he had the audacity to correct old Clacksmather on one of his pet logarithms—and be right!"

As his audience looked up from their game of whist and the pages of *The Tattler*, impressed in spite of themselves, the Honorable Hubert nodded vigorously.

"The shock to poor old Clacksmather was irreparable, alas," he went on. "The old boy had been teaching his bag of mossy logarithms for years, and it never occurred to him that one day he'd be called on it. Never recovered, either. From the day young Westermere so rudely confronted him with his error, Clacksmather's body has trembled so's he can barely hold a glass of port. Now they tell me he has a permanent tic in his left eye."

The marquess of Newbury, who seldom followed these club conversations due to disinterest and advanced age, was nevertheless intrigued now by the expressions on the faces of his fellow members. He looked around keenly, then lifted his ear appliance and quavered, "Snob? Did you say snob, Halsey-Rice?"

"Snot," Tonsley-Pryce repeated rather testily as he leaned forward to project the word directly into the marquess's ear horn. "God knows I'd never condemn a man for mere snobbishness, Percy," he shouted. "A healthy fastidiousness is a necessary part of every gentleman's character— only plebeians term it snobbery. But being an utterly obnoxious little snot, as Westermere was, is quite another thing."

The marquess nodded. "He's not that now," he

squeaked. "A little snot, I mean. Grown man, isn't he?"

Before Tonsley-Pryce could answer, a deep voice from behind *The Mail* rumbled, "The Eton thing didn't keep him from going up to Oxford. Quite brilliant there, from all accounts. Took a first in any number of things." The duke of Carlyle lowered *The Mail* and surveyed them all craggily. "Didn't young Westermere start some archaeology club? Or was that theology? Damned if I can remember, they all sound so much alike."

Heads swiveled back to the Honorable Hubert, who said somewhat thinly, "Archaeology, your grace. You may have read some accounts in the London digests of the excavations young Lord Westermere did in Egypt, repairing Bonaparte's devastation of various ancient tombs."

The duke's eagle eye suddenly bent on the Honorable Hubert and he stared for a long moment, ruminatively. "Filthy little beast, Boney," his lordship said finally, retreating once more behind *The Mail*. "Might have known we'd have to send an Englishman out to set things right."

The marquess of Newbury tugged at Hubert's sleeve. "What's the point, Stilsley-Tice?" he squeaked. "Young Westermere sounds solid enough. A good member of Brown's, isn't he?"

Somewhat flushed, the Honorable Hubert leaned into the marquess's ear horn to speak as confidentially as he could at the top of his lungs. "The point is," he bellowed, "Westermere is not only rude and insufferably arrogant, he's much too—eccentric—for Brown's. I tell you, after the outrageous business over that impossible numerical system he developed to win at whist, I believe we should have a committee to look over his membership."

The old marquess gasped outright. The others stirred uncomfortably and looked around. A committee of inquiry was a drastic step; one could lose one's membership in Brown's as a result. Worse, one's reputation.

"Tut, man, I tried to buy his system from him," the subdeacon of St. Archibald's said, "but Westermere only laughed and said it was an experiment, to see if the laws of probability could be manipulated." He shook his head. "Too bad, too. As far as I know, young Sacheverel's thrown his notes away, destroyed them completely. Damned fine system—it wiped out half the club in only one evening. Charlie Fotheringill stripped himself bare—had to borrow a half a crown from me to get a cab home."

"And the business of his idea of a metropolitan police," Tonsley-Pryce persisted. "Scientific inquiry, indeed! I tell you, in some ways we were better off with Westermere's experiments in gambling, scandalous though they may have been, than these bottles and boxes of decayed specimens, as he labels them—although they're no better than rags and balls of hair and other offal— that he's having the porters store downstairs."

"I say," one of the younger members said, licking his lips nervously, "that *is* carrying things a bit far, rubbish in the basement and all. I didn't know about that. Bones and rags and hanks of hair, did you say? Perhaps we could have someone speak to him."

The members looked around. All except the duke of Carlyle, who was muttering to himself behind his paper about some disappointment in the shipping news.

"I've heard Westermere's stood up in the ring with Gentleman Dan and Mr. Simpson, the pugilists," the youngest member said hesitantly. "They say Westermere's quite good."

After that, they sat in silence for a while, waiting for the voice of the first volunteer for the committee.

A few blocks away, the subject of this conversation, Sacheverel de Vries, the twelfth duke of Westermere, was studying a tray he held in his lap. It was divided into plush-lined compartments filled with bits of lint and fibers. As his rather old-fashioned leaf-springed coach rolled through the streets near Covent Garden the vehicle lurched several times to avoid collisions. Which made the duke grab tightly at the box of specimens he was studying, and scowl.

Plainly, it was an effort to concentrate. After one particularly violent jolt the duke extended a muscular arm, picked up his walking stick and banged on the roof of the coach.

"Easy up there, Jack," he shouted to the coachman on the box outside, "or I'll spill all my collection. What the devil's going on?"

The trap door in the roof opened and a broad, hearty face appeared. "Appears to be a demonstration, sorr," the duke's coachman shouted, "in the city market. Women protesting about bread for the poor. But it won't hold us up, Your Grace, you can be sure of that."

It was spoken too soon, for in the next instant the great coach wallowed from side to side like a ship of the line changing course. The door on the duke's right was wrenched open and a body hurtled inside, landing on all fours with an audible *oof*.

The body—and it could be seen it was that of a very young woman—scrambled up into the opposite seat with all haste.

Peering at her through the gloom of the gilt and gray velvet interior, Westermere saw a female, unattractively disheveled, with her bonnet knocked back and hanging by its strings, clad in equally unappealing dun-colored clothing. Hers was the sort of apparel worn by impoverished elderly aunts, governesses, and superannuated parlormaids on their day off.

The dreariness ended there, however. Luscious brown and gold ringlets poured out from the crooked bonnet and the exquisite face was that of a ravishing Helen of Troy. Her complexion was the creamiest silk, her features a marvel of symmetry, and the whole of London's ton would pay homage to thick-lashed, cobalt-blue eyes if they could but see them.

She was as imposing in size as beauty: Half-sprawled on the seat and still gasping from her leap into his coach, she was possessed of the most superbly enticing female figure Westermere had ever seen, even encased in all that depressingly well-patched attire. Tall, with full, round breasts, a tiny waist and legs that could only be guessed at, this vision of lovely sensuousness was definitely Junoesque.

For a moment she stared at him, panting; then her eyes dropped to the tray. Sacheverel took a cautious grip on his specimens.

"Lord Westermere?" Her voice held a note of wildness. "You are Lord Westermere?"

When he didn't answer, she looked quickly around the coach, then back at him. She stared at his long legs stretched out in Hessian boots, his broad-shouldered body in fawn britches and perfectly-tailored ebony twill jacket topped by the *dernier cri* of white silk cravats, and finally Westermere's face with its scowling black brows.

The amazon beauty's eyes widened.

"It *is* you," she breathed. "I had thought you older and uglier, a monster sinfully withered in age, but no—it is you, I am sure of it!"

As Sacheverel growled some vague denial, she hitched herself forward on the seat and, raising a hand to point at a spot just under the duke's ruby-studded gold stickpin, cried in a ringing voice, "Do you know why I have thrown myself into

13

your carriage in this way? I am your nemesis, bold Lord Avarice, you cannot escape me! You are a brutal exploiter—yea, even murderer! I have seen the evidence, wasted bodies of the children who work in your mines, and the gaunt despair of their pitiful mothers."

For a moment Westermere warily eyed the uplifted hand, sure that she meant to strike him. But the blow never fell. Instead, the young woman took a deep breath and went on, "I have come in the name of Christian justice to beseech you to release those suffering women and children you hold prisoner in your mines and vile places of torture called spinning mills, and try to provide care for them and more healthful employment."

Westermere had been studying her lush, rosy lips as she spoke, her admirably white, even teeth. But now he closed up his specimen box with a snap. Whatever her babbling about mines and neglected tenants, this intrusion had gone far enough.

"I assure you," he said, "I am not the proprietor of any mines or other objects of your imagination, mademoiselle. I want you out of my coach this instant. Jack," he shouted, banging again with his stick on the coachman's trap door, "pull up and stop!"

"Nay!" At his words she jumped to her feet, promptly hitting her head on the upholstered ceiling. "I would be betraying those dear sisters who support me in this purpose and the very memory of our leader, Mary Wollstonecraft, if I stop now. I *will* save those oppressed souls you hold in poverty and serfdom in your villages, even"—she held up one hand dramatically, and those azure eyes flashed—"if it means doing so at peril to my own body!"

At the words *Mary Wollstonecraft*, the duke of Westermere had straightened in his seat, his eyes narrowing.

By damn, this wild beauty appeared by her own words to be an apostle of that crackbrained prophet of women's equal rights and so-called social justice—the lunatic Wollstonecraft! He should have known what she was about when he first laid eyes on those damnable clothes: They were straight out of a penny-pinching parsonage somewhere or he was a turbaned Turk!

The twelfth duke of Westermere considered himself enlightened, a modern man of science. But he was convinced that institutions such as female academies, and particularly parsonages, fulminated with the subversive machinations of spinsterish females who read all sorts of inflammatory books, mostly from the continent, that undermined the morals and good sense of English life. Even the drab physical attributes of these unfortunates emphasized all that which was pernicious, contrary and unpleasant in their sex.

In addition, some of these husbandless females were audacious enough to form societies with so-called "social purpose" that did little, actually, in Sacheverel's opinion, but stir up the working class and foster in the women themselves those strident, masculine traits which made them so unnatural.

God rot it, he didn't want this Wollstonecraft apostle in his carriage a moment longer!

He reached over to open the door of the coach, which had come to a stop at the curb in front of the Crown and Scepter inn, and he fished in his vest pocket for a piece of silver to give her for a cab, or food—or whatever she lacked.

But the young woman bent over him, so close that he could feel her warm, excited breath on his face. "Oh no, you're not going to get rid of me, sir," she cried, "until you have agreed in some way to right your terrible wrongs! I need to talk to you. I need your promises, preferably on paper!"

"Blast," Sacheverel said. He slipped the coin back into his pocket. He reached up to take her by both arms and forcibly eject her, just as the two Westermere footmen jumped down from their perch and into the street.

She managed to slither out of his grip. "I see you do not intend to take our demands seriously, sir!"

"Damned right," Sacheverel said, making another grab for her as she climbed onto the seat cushions opposite.

Outside, a crowd had gathered at the front of the Crown and Scepter, among them several young women in coal scuttle bonnets and frayed, unstylish dresses. One wore a particularly ugly yellow-and-black-checked traveling cloak.

Perched on the cushions of the seat opposite, the girl cried, "You force me to more drastic tactics, sir!"

The crowd heard her and cheered. She lifted her chin, bravely.

"If you do not agree to close the mines and provide more healthful and prosperous employment for your sick and starving tenants, I swear that I will set up a cry that all outside this coach can hear—and—and—tear my clothes!" At these words her azure eyes met his almost desperately. "With these people looking on as witnesses, I-I will call the authorities and—and—declare you have attempted to rape me!"

It took Sacheveral a moment to digest all this. Then, he realized the situation had an unpleasant, albeit familiar, cast to it. He'd heard about these things. He was being threatened. Blackmailed, actually. The amazon beauty had leaped into his coach determined to pull off this very stunt!

His next thought was that if he didn't agree to this nonsense she was spouting, she really was going to claim he'd assaulted her.

The duke lost his hold on what was left of his composure. "*Attempted* to rape you?" he bellowed. "In front of this riffraff? Mademoiselle, I assure you, if such a thought were in my mind, I would not indulge in any such feeble, inept exercise! I do not *attempt* things. I do them!"

Temper or not, it was an unwise thing to say. The crowd outside, even the footmen, gasped.

Disgusted, the duke rose from his seat with the intention of throwing her into the arms of his servants waiting outside. He was totally unprepared for the way she launched herself at him, knocking him flat on the floor of the coach.

There wasn't much room to maneuver. Clutching her as she lay sprawled on top of him, Sacheverel heard her breath close in his ears, felt the enticing softness of her breasts against him, her soft body struggling in his arms. This was followed by the distinct sound of ripping fabric.

Instantly alert, he dragged the young woman up into a sitting position. The faces of his coachmen and the crowd filled the open coach door.

She was, Sacheverel had to admit, a sight to behold. He was sitting on the floor of the Westermere state conveyance holding, in a loose embrace, this woman who had somehow managed to rip open the front of her jacket, pull down her under bodice and expose a magnificent pair of creamy, incredibly flawless breasts.

The crowd outside got enough of a view to emit shocked gasps and small screams, as well as a sprinkling of male sounds of awed appreciation.

She made no move to cover herself. Her thoroughly nude bust was the cynosure of all eyes. Sacheverel saw she pointedly did not look at him; her cheeks were blazing.

By God, she's done it! he thought, with something like admiration.

"He attacked me," the beauteous vision croaked to their audience.

18

"The hell I did! That's a damnable lie."

In the next breath Sacheverel shouted to the coachman to whip up the horses at once. He could no longer toss her out onto the street; she'd undoubtedly raise the rabble out there to a frenzy. But when he tried to haul her up onto the seat, his hands encountered warm, tempting flesh, and he jerked back. "Gad, cover yourself!" he barked.

She paid no attention. On the outside, his footmen were struggling to close the door against the fascinated mob. Sacheverel was astounded when her next move was to lunge to the window, one hand flung across her bosom, and cry out to some young women there to be steadfast and not to worry for her. The young girl in the checkered cloak ran alongside, shouting encouragement.

Gnashing his teeth, Sacheverel yanked off his jacket and threw it around her shoulders. It didn't fit across those generous breasts. She promptly tore the jacket off, anyway, and threw it back at him.

The coach leaped ahead. Now that they were alone, the girl sat back, both hands clutching her nakedness, glaring at him.

He glowered back, speechless. Angry blood pumped at his temples.

By God, she wanted to flaunt herself! It was part of the scheme to intimidate and blackmail him. He saw her bonnet was lost and that her hair had come tumbling down in a brown-gold shower. With that mesmerizing, naked flesh she

19

looked like a mermaid or a goddess—or a wanton. To her credit her cheeks burned, defiant red flags.

Well, she'd chosen to carry off this fool stunt, he told himself grimly, so there was no need for her to look so confoundedly shamefaced. He half expected her to rant at him about the poor and downtrodden as the coach careened into a commercial street and headed for the banks of the Thames, but she remained silent.

As they turned into Dabney Court, one of the young footmen hung from the roof at the side window and shouted, "Jack presents his compliments, your grace, and wants to know, where we are headed?"

The duke of Westermere flung himself back against the gray velvet tufts of his seat, his expression like granite.

"Brown's," he barked. "Damme, take me to my club! I need a moment to think."

As it turned out, Brown's was a poor choice. It only showed how ragged the duke's temper was.

Old George, the club's ancient head porter, tottered to the duke's carriage just in time to get caught in the melee as Westermere and his two footmen struggled up the steps with a half-naked young woman. To make matters worse, the young woman had begun to denounce the duke at the top of her lungs to anyone who would listen. A small crowd of the curious gathered almost immediately. Old George wrung his hands.

"Your Grace," he wailed as he followed the duke and his footmen and the young woman, who had finally been buried under a hastily found lap robe, "ah, forgive—I cannot bring myself to mention it but—"

George dodged the club's front door as it was flung open and the bundled figure carried through.

"Your Grace, with all due respect, allow me to say the rules of Brown's are strict about females being forbidden from any part of the premises, under any circumstances!"

"The cloakroom," the harried duke rasped.

Seeing them coming, the cloakroom attendant dove for safety as the three men dumped their burden over the mahogany counter and closed and locked the cloakroom door. After only a second, the lap robe flew through the air, followed by the duke's jacket and one of the footmen's livery coats.

"Covering me up is not going to keep me from denouncing you, sir," the disordered female vision cried. She looked as though she would attempt to vault over the cloakroom's counter at any minute. "Now you have attacking me to add to your sins!"

That was not true at all and she well knew it. The duke of Westermere, furiously resentful of such an arrant attempt to gull him right there in his own club, turned away, so angry that he was unable to look at her.

Everyone else did.

The entire membership assembled in Brown's reading room, lounge and game rooms, upon hearing the noise, trooped out into the downstairs foyer to see what the rumpus was about.

They found themselves staring at a ravishing young woman standing behind Brown's cloakroom counter, hatless and coatless, with long, tangled brown-gold hair come loose from its moorings. The front of her dress was ripped open and although she struggled to hold it together with trembling hands, it was plain she was naked to the waist, and she gave occasional glimpses of delectably heaving breasts.

There was absolute silence for at least—it was agreed upon later by those who were there—two whole minutes.

Then the earl of Stackston and Digby, the membership chairman, said in a hollow voice, "I'm afraid you've done it this time, Westermere. This will never pass the committee."

Chapter Two

The duke's butler, who was a very tall man, as butlers should be, with gray hair, a large nose, and a countenance stern to the point of balefulness, entered the duke's library with a pretty young woman in an ancient yellow-and-black-checkered traveling cape.

"Miss Penelope MacDougal," he announced in a voice that portended the invasion of an army of barefoot Highlanders brandishing claymores.

However, Miss MacDougal was, despite the butler's expression, a petite, irresistibly pretty blond young thing, who threw herself into her friend's arms with a cry of gladness. "Oh, Marigold, how relieved I am to see you!" For a moment, tears threatened to get the best of melting brown eyes in a heart-shaped face. Penelope wiped them away, hastily. "I knew that your father had been summoned to London and had met with the duke. The village was on its ear when the news reached there. Jail and public humiliation—even the possibility of a horrid assault upon your person by the duke, was what the gossip expected! Even I feared the worst when your dear father returned to Stokesbury Hatton without you."

"Sit down, Penny dear," Marigold told her, pulling her toward a table where tea in an enormous silver service had already been set out. "I am quite all right, as you can see, although I have doleful news for you. I haven't achieved any of my objectives. Here I am, living in Westermere's house, totally ignored, and with little or no way to meet or address him! I don't even know where he is. He has been traveling; when I ask the servants they seem to know no more than I." She sat down beside her. "Do you take your tea with one sugar, or two?"

Penelope looked around, taking stock of their surroundings for the first time.

The room where they sat, the duke of Westermere's library, reached through to the second floor of his London mansion and featured an upper gallery that ran around all four sides. The walls were lined with shelves of books except for when the French windows reached almost to the ceiling. Books were piled against the walls and spilled across parquet floors covered in the finest Turkish carpets. Large tables held more books and the stacked trays of the sort used for butterfly collections or botanical specimens. For all its vastness and clutter, the library had the look of a busy place.

"Oh lud, Marigold, this was not what we planned, was it?" Penelope whispered. "We were so worried, the cause was so desperate when we set off to London, that we had prepared ourselves for any martyrdom that you, as our leader, might have to suffer. We expected to see you thrown in jail or at the least carried off to the duke's bed to be rav—" She dropped her eyes, modestly. "Well, you know. And now look at you. You say you haven't even seen him!"

Marigold Fenwick looked equally glum as they sipped their tea. They could admit it now. Their great, daring plan had, in most ways, come crashing down around their ears.

The three cavaliers, they had called themselves since childhood: Sophronia Stack, whose father was Stokesbury Hatton's doctor; Penelope MacDougal, whose father was the local schoolmaster, and Marigold Fenwick, the vicar's only child. As they'd grown up in the grimy little town owned by the dukes of Westermere, they'd read the same books, been educated in music and arithmetic by schoolmaster MacDougal and, when they discovered the writings of Mary Wollstonecraft, were instant, enthusiastic converts of that great woman. Together they took solemn vows to be independent, true to honor, justice, and themselves. And being intelligent, good-hearted girls, it was inevitable that they could not ignore the condition of England's poor in the mills and mines around them.

Now, both were thinking, perhaps they had gone a little far in their zeal, coming to London for this bold confrontation with the duke. It had been Marigold's idea—she was always the most fearless—but the adventure had produced little of anything but the worst sort of gossip.

As for Penny MacDougal, Marigold's dearest friend, she didn't have to comment on Marigold's appearance; Marigold knew how she looked. She had lost one of her major battles over the matter of her wardrobe. And all the while she still hadn't even set eyes on the duke.

On this, the fourteenth day of her stay in Westermere's London mansion, she was wearing a black silk faille with empire waist and the new, larger puffed sleeves and slightly fuller skirt, with a white lace collar and matching cuffs that fell gracefully over the elbows. Her hair was piled high and held by streamers of black velvet ribbon, and a black velvet ribbon with ivory and onyx cameo was around her throat. The sunlight falling from the tall library windows lit her glossy golden brown curls, her startling eyes and full pink mouth, to make her a glowing portrait of beauty and elegant serenity.

Which, at least inside, she certainly wasn't feeling at all.

"I have seventeen frocks," Marigold said gloomily. "The first were made for me almost overnight and brought to me willy-nilly, while my poor old serge was taken away and burned." She sighed. "Now, thanks to this forced robing, the results of which you see before you, there are dresses for morning wear and afternoon wear, and for going about in open carriages, although I have yet to use any of these as I have not left the house, and dresses for dinner at home—if you can call this my home. The situation is most bizarre. All this attention to my wardrobe baffles me. But dear Papa told me that he sat in this very library and listened to Westermere rant about wild women in ugly clothes throwing themselves into his coaches for a good hour. As though that was more important than anything I had said to him!"

Marigold looked down at her hands clasped tightly in her lap.

"In fact, if you wish to know the truth of it, dear Penny, I dread the thought that we are facing defeat, but it is a conviction I cannot escape." She grew somewhat perplexed. "What shall I do? I don't think the monster heard anything at all I said to him when I threw myself into his carriage! And except for dear Papa's visit, I think he intends to forget all about me!"

Her friend looked at her in horror. "Marigold, don't say that! You can't give up now!"

The other set her jaw as she poured another cup of tea. "He denied everything to Papa, that he owns mills or workhouses, and countered with accusations of his own—that this is a plot by bluestocking females against all men and the basic propriety of English life. He seems especially to hate educated women. And as you know," she said, handing the teacup to Penny, "education for women is the very foundation of our beliefs as put down by the great Mary Wollstonecraft."

They were both silent for a moment, thinking of England's towering defender of women's rights, who had supported herself by her writings in books and journals, particularly on the subject of the importance of justice for women, their dignity in society, and that they not be treated like men's chattels. Mary's brilliant daughter, Mary Wollstonecraft Godwin, was now married to Percy Shelley, the famed poet, and living in Italy, and had written novels of her own.

"I have come to the conclusion that the duke of Westermere is quite mad," Marigold said, breaking the silence. "Only a madman would deny that, since he is rich as Croesus, he does not own most of the cotton mills and coal mines of northeast England! I asked Papa if the Westermere family line had a history of lunacy, but my dear father was forced to tell me he didn't know. It's something to think about, however."

Her friend looked thoughtful. "Perhaps you had better come home, Marigold. Our plan was always dangerous for you, trying to shame a great magnate like Lord Westermere into improving the lot of his people. But now here you are, and have been for almost a fortnight, and you admit he does not even see or speak to you."

Marigold bit her lip. "Yes, it galls me every moment to think how many are sick and without food, while I stay here, vainly trying to catch Westermere's ear. How is young Johnny?" she said anxiously. When the other girl looked downcast, she paled. "Dear God, our sweet little lamb is not—"

The other girl shook her head. "Marigold, there is so much lung fever among the miners' children, and it carries them off at an early age when they are not strong, like little John Cobb. Surely you should be resigned to that fate by now. Johnny lives, but even Dr. Stack does not hold out much hope for the child in that dank little cottage, with five brothers and sisters sharing that most pitiful ration of food that is all his widowed mother can provide."

Marigold stood up, blue eyes blazing.

"You see, from what you're telling me, I cannot leave! The gauntlet has been thrown down, Penelope. I admit my plan has faltered and worse— instead of holding Westermere up to public humiliation, he has responded with a diabolical tactic of his own." She hesitated, then blurted out, "The scoundrel actually told Papa he intended to marry me!"

While Penelope sat frozen in surprise, Marigold went on, "Oh yes, well I haven't told you this part, but listen to the gracious words with which the duke announced his intent to his would-be betrothed's father! 'Well, damme, she's ruined me at Brown's and before half of London, and made me out for a fool even at court, so she might as well share in the blasted gillimaufry. I have to get married sometime, and this seems an arrangement, with an empty-pocket parson's brat, which is no more forged in hell than any marriage of my friends that I've witnessed!' "

Penelope held her teacup poised, unable to move. "Good heavens," she choked out, "what does that mean?"

Marigold scowled at her. "I tell you, Papa was quite offended, especially about the slur to men of the cloth, as of course he is one himself. 'Empty-pocket parson's brat,' indeed! Papa said he didn't blame me for not considering an offer made in such vile, grudging terms." She poured her friend more tea. "Besides, who'd want to marry Westermere? From the look I had of him that day in his coach he's a bad-tempered, beetle-browed, overgrown lout who no woman would have cause to bestow her affections upon in the way Mary Wollstonecraft wrote about, much less chain herself to him in marriage! I can't think of a worse fate."

"He wants to marry you?" The schoolmaster's daughter wriggled a moment, then nearly screamed, "Oh, Marigold, think of all that money! Oh, dear blessed heaven, the money—what marvelous good we could do with it!"

Marigold frowned. "Penny, it was this sort of outrageous scheme that brought us to London, wasn't it? Now look where we are. Haven't we entertained enough follies?"

Her friend's enormous brown eyes were shining. "No, listen to me! Nobles settle money on their brides when they are married, often a great deal. I'm sure Westermere would settle thousands of pounds on you as a matter of course." When Marigold opened her mouth to protest she went on, "And if for some terrible reason Westermere denied you a proper bride gift you could could, ah—anything, negotiate, I mean—oh, confound it, seduce him so that he would be your absolute slave! Marigold, you are so beautiful, the best looking among us. *You* could do that!"

Penelope was so carried away she spilled a bit of tea in her lap. "And if he still resisted giving you a part of his fortune," the blond girl went on eagerly, "you could somehow enslave him with your body and then deny him his marital rights until he begged for them and agreed to anything we asked!"

It was Marigold's turn to look amazed.

"Westermere? Are we talking about icy-cold young Scratch himself? You mean bewitch the devil's own so that he would grovel on his knees for a chance to bed me regularly?"

Her friend nodded. "You could do it," Penelope insisted. "Oh, Marigold, we have talked of sacrifice for the poor people suffering so at home. Think of what you were planning to do when you jumped into his coach—blackmail Westermere and wreck your reputation as well. But for a just cause! Think of what the village and the mine could do with a proper surgery for Sophronia's father! And a new schoolhouse for Pa! And the workhouse torn down!" Her hands fluttered. "Oh, I wish I knew more about sex! It's terrible to be just eighteen and not having had anyone tell you anything substantial. But the physical part—I mean letting him do . . . what he would want to do to you—wouldn't be all that bad, would it, Marigold?"

Her friend's face reflected not fear but scorn.

" 'All that bad?' I swear to you, Penny, I don't think the hulking brute has the finesse for refined conjugal relations. Marriage, even of the most affectionate sort that you and Sophronia and I agree, after our studies of *A Vindication of the Rights of Woman*, is the ideal, would be wasted on him. I mean, have you seen him?" she hissed. "He's—he—he has a revoltingly big—I swear to you he does, I observed him in tight fawn britches in the coach! It is quite in keeping with his—his big feet—and all that. Fagh!" she said, turning away, "Westermere reeks of muscle and lust. He would never beg me for physical passion. I'm sure coarse actresses and street drabs are more his style!"

When Marigold looked up she could see she had lost her friend's attention. Penelope's eyes had widened. She was sitting quite stiffly holding her teacup askew, looking past her even as Marigold handed her a linen napkin to wipe up the spilled tea.

"Penny, do help me with this," Marigold said, trying to push the linen napkin into the other girl's hand. "And hold your cup up. Look at what you're doing; you're spilling even more!"

But Penelope continued to gaze fixedly over her friend's shoulder at a tall figure in a voluminous black travelling cloak.

"The d-duke," she choked in a barely audible voice. At that moment Penelope was so frightened she could hardly think. But Westermere had, apparently, been standing in the doorway for some time, listening to all they had to say about a plot to get some part of his fortune, Marigold's possible matrimony, and, dear God, all about denying him his conjugal rights!

"Besides, I wouldn't know how to go about such a thing," Marigold was saying, as she scrubbed vigorously at Penelope's lap. "That is, how to use sensual arts to get money from a man." She stopped, and looked pensive. "I should think merely taking off my clothes and showing my naked body and—um, walking around the room, you know, or lying on the bed in various lascivious poses, whatever they might be, would hardly be enough. Not to raise the sort of unbridled lust that would so madden a man like Westermere that he would hand over enough of his fortune for a new surgery for Dr. Stack, and a schoolhouse, and food and all else the village needs."

"Perhaps," Penelope breathed, her eyes pinned to the tall figure who was now advancing quietly but purposefully across the library's Turkish carpets, "a l-loving, self-respecting, virtuous woman could make him s-see the error of his ways, and cause him to give money freely and ch-charitably."

Marigold sighed. "That is the ideal, of course. But as Wollstonecraft's book points out, even true love is free love. Remember, where there is mutual respect and friendship, matrimony is hardly necessary." She dropped the tea-stained napkin onto the great silver tray and reached for a bread and butter sandwich. "But where to find a man that perfect?" she murmured between bites. "One would look long in this world for a paragon like that."

Sacheverel de Vries, Duke of Westermere, had reached a point close enough to Marigold's chair so that he could bend over and take her quite by surprise, even as a horrified Penelope watched.

He put his mouth to her ear and growled: "Free love, fraud and thievery, ladies? Is this what you've been hatching while I'm away?"

Both women screamed and jumped to their feet. Marigold dropped her bread and butter, and teacups shattered on the parquet floor. There was a moment of mayhem that reached a peak when the duke caught sight of Penelope's yellow-and-black-checked traveling cloak.

For a moment he looked somewhat unhinged. "There it is again," he shouted.

He scooped the garment up in both hands and strode to the hearth and dumped it on the fire. For good measure he picked up the poker and jammed it in among the coals until it burst into smoky flames.

"Goddammit," Sacheverel bellowed, brandishing the poker as he looked heavenward. "I am besieged! Is there no end to this?"

At that, poor Penelope fainted.

Chapter Three

It had been a long and miserable ride from Bristol, and Sacheverel's favorite mount, Waterloo, who'd been given to him by Arthur Wellesley himself on the battlefield of the same name, went lame in Swindon.

It had been pouring rain by then, a good forty miles from London, and all too apparent that he would have been better off to have taken the lumbersome Westermere coach rather than make the journey by horseback. But all that was hindsight, Sacheverel told himself. It didn't put him in a better temper to have to stable Wellington's gift at a rundown inn, and hire a hack to ride the rest of the way. He tried not to dwell on the thought that there was no telling what condition he'd find Waterloo in when he sent one of the coachboys back for him. Tired to the point of raw irritability, Sacheveral reached London, burst through the outer hall of Horton Crescent without even stopping long enough to hand his rain-soaked cloak over to old Pomfret, the butler, and strode toward the partly open library doors in search of a much-needed bottle of French brandy and a fire to warm his weary backside.

What the duke of Westermere encountered, instead, was the low murmur of female voices. The sound brought him up short. The library was already occupied, he realized. He could make out on a table across the vast room the glimmer of his mother's George the First silver service and cups laid out for tea.

He stopped just inside the doors. As he did so, Sacheveral was able to catch more than a few words that, after he had carefully considered their source and content, made sudden, pounding streams of outrage run through his already aching head.

Seduce him? He couldn't believe his ears.

These young female voices, chattering on with a *sang froid* that amazed him considering that they were sitting in his house, warming themselves before his fire and calmly drinking his tea, were discussing how to render him more or less helpless by judicial doses of sex.

And steal his money!

By thunder, that took gall! Yet as he eavesdropped, they were going over the details of just how this—after he had been stupefied by lust—was to be best achieved!

There were other interesting points, but Sacheverel had heard enough.

He entered, stepping noiselessly on the thick pile of the Persian rugs, intending to catch them at their scurrilous game.

He didn't recognize the blond girl; he was too intent on his house guest, who he had made a point of avoiding these past weeks. The pestiferous vicar's daughter.

Just as she attempted to wipe some spilled tea out of her companion's lap, he slipped up behind her and grated, "Free love, fraud and thievery, ladies? Is this what you've been hatching while I was away?"

The effect was instantaneous. And enormously gratifying. They sprang to their feet, their teacups flying, squeaking in horror like terrified mice in a church loft.

Unfortunately, at that moment, even as he was cold, wet and suffering a surfeit of aggravation from a trying day both in Bristol and on the road, Sacheverel's bloodshot eye fell on the garment the blond girl was wearing—a hideous yellow-and-black-checked traveling cloak whose appearance brought back all the unbearable mayhem of the day he had first seen it, when his coach had been attacked by these very females outside the city markets.

The twelfth duke of Westermere had always been extremely sensitive to anything ugly, even as a child. A gross lack of beauty had always seemed to upset the order and aesthetic sensibility that was so much a part of even his early character. Often he responded violently, although as he grew older he had learned to curb his more overt reactions.

However, this ugly damned cloak had become a personal affront. Almost as much as the females themselves.

Sacheverel pounced upon the offending garment, yanked it from the blond girl's grasp, then rushed over to hurl it onto the fire. He picked up the poker and stabbed the black-and-yellow checks until tongues of flame burst through the cloth.

He would have stamped wrathfully on the hideous thing, but even he could see there was no room to stand upright on a coal fire in the library fireplace.

When he got his bearings, and the yellow-and-black-checked cloak had forever been removed from the world of the living, Sacheverel saw the small Scottish girl lying on the floor in a swoon, and the tall beauty had thrown herself between them, arms spread, to defend her friend to the death.

"Don't you touch her!" she screamed.

"Don't be stupid," Sacheveral rasped. The onset of what felt like a bout of quinzy from fatigue and the long ride was working on his voice. "Calm yourself, I have no designs on the rest of her clothing." As he took a look at the slender figure so gracefully reposed on the floor he growled, "Although from what she's wearing, I'm tempted. Tell me, why do they make women's frocks out of horse blankets in Scotland?"

The parsonage girl drew herself up, eyes shooting blue fire. "Oh, you are impossible, sir! Is assaulting women all that you can bring yourself to? Now you speak ill of of dear little Penelope, crassly criticizing her dress! My friend may be poor and not attired in the latest mode, her father but a lowly schoolmaster, but she is the sweetest, truest companion one could have! I could not have managed so far without her."

Sacheverel's scowl deepened. It was as he'd guessed: The unconscious Scottish sprite was another female conspirator.

He had already shed his wet cloak, flinging it on the brass fender before the fire. As Sacheverel bent and lifted the unconscious guest in his arms to carry her to the sofa, Pomfret appeared bearing a large silver tray with an assortment of bottles and glass goblets. The butler was discreetly followed by Jack Ironfoot, the coachman, carrying the duke's saddlebags and a black leather object about the size of a hatbox, but much more sturdily built, which he set down carefully by the library table.

"Smelling salts and other restoratives, your grace," the butler intoned, setting the tray within reach.

Brusquely, Sacheverel nodded his thanks. Old Pomfret had a sixth sense about these things.

Years spent in his father's autocratic service had developed an ear so keen that the butler could hear a female form drop to the floor in a swoon from as far back as the servants' quarters.

One of the "restoratives," Sacheverel saw, was a small decanter of Malvaux brandy. While Pomfret and the Fenwick female stretched the partially-revived girl out on the couch and administered drops of spirits of ammonia, he quickly poured himself a shot of the Malvaux.

He deserved it, he told himself. Let the others take care of the Scottish lass. It was his guess the swoon wouldn't last long.

He was right. At the second pass of the smelling salts under her nose, the girl sat up abruptly and in an anguished voice announced that she didn't know what had overcome her, but she must leave.

With a signal from the duke, Pomfret fetched a sturdy black wool cloak with an arctic fox fur hood from a hall closet, and persuaded the girl to borrow it for her journey in lieu of the black-and-yellow remnants of her former garment now reposing in the library grate. The blond girl pulled the gray fur around her face, buttoned the catch under her chin, and pulled the long sweep of the black cloak about her threadbare skirts. Peering at her, even Sacheverel had to admit the cloak and gray fur framing her piquant features made her quite attractive.

"He must give it to you as a gift, Penelope," Marigold cried. "I see no reason why you should

41

return it, when he has completely destroyed your other!"

"Yes, take it," Sacheverel said, feeling magnanimous. He herded the girls out of the library, and old Pomfret pattered ahead of them to the front door. Jack Ironfoot had gone to bring up the coach.

"Penelope, you can't go back to Stokesbury Hatton tonight," the Fenwick girl was saying. "It's late, and even with Westermere's footmen and outriders it might be—"

"She can, and will," Sacheverel interrupted. He was not happy with the conversation he'd overheard, and there was unfinished business he had to attend to regarding the parsonage girl and her father. A lot of nonsense to be gotten out of the way. In addition, the day had been hellish; he looked forward to spending some time thinking on what had happened—or not happened—and what he could do next.

Last but not least, the condition of his throat bothered him. Rain and cold on the way to and from Bristol had not helped, and unless he was mistaken he could possibly be laid up in bed with the croup, an evil to which he was sometimes prone. It took some time, though, to get the MacDougal girl on her way. Twice she entered the coach, only to come bouncing back out again in a flood of tears, and declarations that she could not leave her dearest friend, Marigold. And to embrace the Fenwick girl yet again and plead that she give up her plans to stay in London and come back to Stokesbury Hatton with her.

From the doorway, Sacheverel said nothing. The girl could come or she could stay; he knew she was mindful of the offer he had made her father.

Each time Miss MacDougal changed her mind and came out of the coach, the young footmen, always anxious to be of help to a pretty young girl, fell all over themselves opening the door and assisting her inside, and then back out again, until Jack Ironfoot, the coachman, who had grown impatient with all the tears and foolishness, cracked his whip about their ears and sent them to their seats high in the rear.

That settled it. The duke slammed the door, the horses were whipped up and they were away.

In an hour, Westermere was taking a solitary meal by the fire in the library, the Fenwick female having gone off to have hers wherever she was in the custom of taking it.

Mrs. Cawdigan, the housekeeper, had brought up a tureen of a hearty beef and barley broth for Sacheverel's supper, accompanied by a bottle of the London house cellar's best claret, and a crusty loaf of bread with salted butter. Like Pomfret, Mrs. Cawdigan had a sixth sense about the Westermere household and could judge, uncannily, when hot beef soup with chunks of onions and potatoes was needed to subvert one of the dukes attacks of croup.

She also called in her nephew Charles, the assistant porter, to unpack "the machine," as the staff usually referred to it, from the leather box Jack had brought, and put it up in its regular place on the marble-topped table in front of the central window.

Before he sat down to take his supper, Sacheverel took a moment to look it over carefully, unwrapping the yards of clean linen packing to make sure it had not suffered on its journey.

Then he sat down at the small table and ladled beef and barley soup into his bowl, dipping in a piece of bread, chewing it morosely as he regarded the item on its stand.

A few days earlier he had traveled to Bristol to get Sir Rowland Sackville, one of the magistrates there, to at least look at the instrument and see what it could demonstrate.

Thinking about it, he sighed.

It hadn't seemed to matter to Sackville, an extraordinarily fatheaded official, that a man's life hung in the balance; that was the damnable part of it. The magistrate, who held his position because he was the second son of an earl and not because he had any talent for the courts of justice, was so dense between the ears that Sacheverel had to spend the best part of an hour explaining the basics of this particular science.

The earliest, most primitive microscopes had used drops of water in a small hole in a glass plate as a magnifier. Which was interesting but hardly reliable; it was an arrangement that could be regarded only as a curiosity. By the 1600s Antoine van Leeuwenhoek of Amsterdam, using the glass-grinding techniques of the incomparable Netherlander spectacle makers, had been able to make a fairly efficient machine that was promptly used for botanical purposes.

Sacheverel had been able to tell by Sackville's face that the man had only vaguest idea of what "botanical purposes" might mean. As for microscopes—Bristol's chief magistrate had thought the whole idea inordinately funny.

"Looking into a peephole, is it, to make something small look bigger?" Sackville had guffawed. "I've known people trying to do that for years, you've only to ask them what peephole they're trying to look up into, haw, haw!" After he'd choked merrily on his wine he went on. "Come now, Westermere, the Dutch are always fiddle-faddling with this sort of thing, aren't they? Lens makers, spectacle makers, they ought to put their time to better use, what? I'd tell them to invest in New Amsterdam land on the Hudson, that would be my advice to them. Slow coaches, the Dutch; they're better suited to farming than—"

Sackville pointed a portly finger at the precious cargo Sacheverel had carried in his saddle bags all the way from London and set up in his study.

"—making doojiggers and folderol like that," he finished.

Sacheverel had felt his stomach clench in anger and disgust. The doojigger and folderol—usually known by its more precise name of achromatic

45

microscope—was one of a particularly advanced design, and worth a small fortune. It was twin to that owned by Sacheverel's friend and prominent English scientist, Joseph Lister.

Watching the magistrate pour another round of port, the duke barely managed to keep his temper in check; after all, what could one say to a man who believed the Dutch still owned New York? The microscope had not, as Sacheverel had fervently hoped, roused the slightest curiosity in Sir Rowland Sackville.

"It's not a doojigger, milord," Sacheverel said, managing to keep a genial smile. "On the contrary, if you will let me demonstrate, I will prove to you the microscope's effectiveness in identifying evidence more accurately than can be done by any other agency."

He spoke slowly and carefully in an effort to get his message through the other man's fat skull. His mission was all-important. Some months ago a former soldier, a drifter named Oris Ludberry, had come to the rescue of a man being robbed and severely beaten by thugs in a Bristol alley.

Unfortunately they had been three against one, with the victim unconscious and unable to help. Ludberry had finally beaten off the attackers, in the process sustaining some injuries himself. But by the time the patrol had arrived, the man was expiring in Ludberry's arms and suspicion had fallen upon Ludberry himself, who was charged on the spot as the robber and attacker. Chief evidence against the former soldier was that he had picked up the man's gold watch that one of the robbers had dropped and still had hold of it. And there was a fistful of reddish hair locked in the victim's hand that he had apparently pulled from the skull of one of the men who had killed him.

"Now if you put a strand of this hair under the microscope," Sacheverel had told Sackville, "and compare it with strands of Ludberry's own hair, the difference is plain. The hair wrenched from the attacker's scalp by the dying man is six-tenths gray. The gray strands themselves have quite a different texture, more wiry, actually, as is normal with gray hair. Whereas Ludberry is still a young man, and his carrot-top is thick and silky. Put side by side, one cannot ignore the evidence, milord. Ludberry is not the attacker, as he has steadfastly maintained. But at least one of the murderers is a redheaded man with some gray hair. And a search needs to be begun at once for him."

"We're not looking for anyone else," Sir Rowland had told him loudly. "Use your head, Westermere! Damned fool was standing over his victim when the patrol came with the loot in his hands. They saw him with their own eyes. That's good enough for the courts, sirrah!"

Sacheverel had made one last attempt to invite the magistrate to take a look at his carefully arranged specimens on their glass slides, but the other waved him away.

"No, no, take the damned thing away, Westermere," the magistrate had huffed. "Can't get my eyes to scrunch up like that, anyway, and if I did, what would I see? Hairs, that's what I'd see. Damned little difference since they're both red. Bah, you'd never convince another magistrate! The culprit was caught dead in the act, clear as day, with the watch in his hand."

That had been yesterday.

Sacheverel pushed away his empty plate and poured himself the rest of the bottle of claret. The flames in the grate were dying down; he hadn't been in the mood to poke up the fire. His face felt unusually flushed.

The sense of utter defeat over the business of the microscope gnawed at him as much as Ludberry's current peril. The three Bristol magistrates, no doubt egged on by a cheerfully perverse Sackville, had rendered a swift verdict: guilty as charged, and death by hanging at dawn on Saturday.

But how good it would have been, for once, Sacheverel was thinking, to have introduced some new and enlightening criminal science into England's hoary courts! He'd had many a long night's discussion about changing the court system with Bobbie Peel, a fellow officer and long-time friend from Wellington's peninsular campaign. And Sir Robert was as dedicated to reform, particularly to do something about the police, as he, Sacheverel, was about the courts.

Now the exquisitely-crafted instrument sat on the marble table where he could see it and wonder if it would ever be used in the way he had come to long for.

He was about to ring for another bottle of claret when there was a tap at the doors and Pomfret ushered in Jack Ironfoot, the coachman.

"What the devil are you doing back?" Sacheverel said, waving the empty claret bottle at the butler as a signal to bring him another.

The coachman walked to the fire, poked it up with a proprietory air, then lifted his heavy skirts and backed into the warmth. "I was able to catch the schedule of the Yorkminster Flyer at Luton," he said, "and put the young lady on the public conveyance so's not to make too much of a night's journey of it, in case your Bristol trip should make you need me." A devilish smile flashed in his ruddy face. "I put young Harold on the Flyer to take the little lady the rest of the way to Stokesbury Hatton. Riding atop, o'course," he said quickly, seeing the duke's face, "not inside. But gives the lad his bit of heaven for the rest of the year, sitting up there, dreaming about how he'd brawly snatch her from highwaymen if such like should come along the York road tonight. And Dennis, what had to come back with the cross old bear that's me, had his bit of torment."

Sacheverel could not hold back a smile as the coachman helped himself to a glass of wine without waiting for permission.

Damn Jack. His old sergeant kept the footmen in a state of torture, much as he had with their rifle company's green recruits in the war. But

Ironfoot molded good soldiers then, just as he made superior Westermere coachboys and other staffers now.

Jack Ironfoot wiped the wine from his lips with the back of his hand and sighed. "Ludberry's had it then," he said.

Sacheverel scowled. "I was not able to budge that stupid ass of a magistrate in Bristol, if that's what you mean. Evidence means nothing to him, much less the immutable science of logic."

Jack lifted his brows, philosophically. "I did not think it would, sir, if you'll pardon my saying so. As for Ludberry, poor lad, a war is needed to keep him busy. He's a fine soldier, but when there's no fighting about he falls apart with the drink."

That had not been apparent in Spain. Then, young Oris Ludberry had been one of the steadiest in Sacheverel's tight-knit company of riflemen, the pride of Arthur Wellesley's operations behind French lines.

The duke poured himself another glass of claret, somewhat unsteadily. He hadn't had all that much to drink, but he was not feeling up to par. His throat was on fire, and there was an ominous grating in his chest.

His coachman's expression, though, irritated him. "Don't look at me like that, Ironfoot," he growled, "we're not going to let any of the Ninth Rifles hang, as you well know. I have written down the times that the guard changes at Bristol prison, when they take Ludberry out of the cell on Saturday and up to the scaffold in the prison

yard. It took me two days of discreet inquiries—
and believe me, they were the soul of discretion
since Magistrate Sackville was at my elbow the
entire time I was in the city. But I finally found a
prison turnkey who is eminently bribable." He
leaned back in his chair, drained his glass, and
looked up at the ceiling as he drawled, "Now let
us see—I had thought you, Merce Coffin, and
Mortimer, if you can get him away from his wife
and brats at Chester—"

Pleasure broke over the coachman's face like
the bright dawn light. "You let me take care of it,
Captain dear, and never give it another thought.
Since the magistrate there in Bristol is on to you
and know you've paid a visit to the city, being
interested in Ludberry's trial, they'll think of you
first off if anything was to happen to interfere
with the prisoner's execution."

The big coachman gave a gargle of harsh laughter.

"Not that we don't intend to see that interfer-
ence does happen, God bless us all and Wellington, too, may the lord forever love him! Yes,
Merce and Mortimer and me should be able to
handle this little business in Bristol most nicely
while you are here in London, Your Grace. And
if you don't mind me giving you a bit of advice,
right away you should be making yourself known
at the balls and the routs, as usual. In a very public way."

Sacheverel winced. He felt as though he could
well do with a couple of days in bed, nursing his

damned malaise, but Jack was right. He had to be highly visible while Ludberry was relieved of his date with the Bristol gallows.

He said, "You're right, Jack, and I'll do it. But getting Ludberry out of Bristol jail may not be as difficult as getting him a ship out to Sydney or Boston. This time he must be sent far enough to fight his demons where he can't put any one of us in jeopardy. I won't have him here in England or on the Continent. The war's over, but there are still old enemies about."

"And Oris's enemy is the bottle," the coachman agreed. "Aye, he'll be better off in a far country, to start a new life. But Captain, something tells me the cost for passage and silence is going to be more dear than cheating the Bristol gallows."

"No doubt, no doubt," the other said wearily. "Come to me in the morning, Jack, and I'll see what gold I have here in the Horton Crescent house strongbox. We want to use coin of the realm, not money drawn on any bank where the draft can be traced."

Pomfret came in to get the soup tureen and the bottles. The coachman took his leave noisily with a heavy tread, slamming the door in back to the servants quarters in a way that shook even the big London house.

Sacheverel sank back in the wing chair, staring rather blearily at the fire that Pomfret, in passing, had once again poked into new life.

It was getting late, several hours after midnight he guessed, and he knew he should go up to bed.

But the heat of the blaze kept him by the hearth.

So what it came down to, Sacheverel thought, was that they would rescue Ludberry by the tricks of war they had excelled in as Wellington's riflemen. And not, as he had hoped, by the deductive science of the microscope. He couldn't help being damned disappointed.

He had great faith in Merce and Mortimer with Jack to lead them; the odds were against Ludberry having to stretch his neck Saturday morning in Bristol. But Sacheverel wished that his original plan had worked. The problem was that he needed a magistrate much smarter than Sackville, if such an animal existed. He was beginning to wonder if one did in England's current system of courts.

He must have dozed off. He came awake slowly when he realized there was someone else in the room. At first Sacheverel thought it was Mrs. Cawdigan come to see if Pomfret had taken the supper things away. Or one of the footmen prowling around to see what was about after the noise Jack Ironfoot had made going out.

He opened his eyes and started to speak, but in the next instant a strange, hair-raising sensation kept him silent, glued to his chair.

It was the late hour, of course. And he'd had a good bit to drink that played tricks on his eyes. Several of the candles had gone out, and the library was lit mostly by the fire.

However, that was not what jolted his nerves.

53

A white, wraithlike figure like a ghost or a spirit moved silently, a shawl over its shoulders, stopping near the marble-topped table.

Sacheverel blinked feverishly. Then he saw it was no ghost but the confounded Fenwick girl, hovering much too close to what was, at the moment, his most prized possession.

"Don't touch—" Sacheverel all but shouted. To his dismay his voice had dwindled to a monstrous croak. He wanted to warn her at the top of his lungs not to put one destructive, careless female finger on his instrument.

The girl jumped at the rasping sound of his voice, but in the next instant she turned to him, smiling, her eyes gleaming, her hands clasped in pure joy.

"Oh, Westermere," she cried, "it's a microscope, isn't it! An achromatic microscope, and I have never seen one so fine!"

Chapter Four

"Croup is really a form of laryngitis," young Dr. Reginald Pendragon said, leaning over the better to peer down into the duke of Westermere's throat with the aid of a wooden spatula. "Nasty stuff, but rarely fatal," he added, cheerfully. "Worst part, Satch, old boy, is having to give the voice a complete rest. So mum's the word for at least a couple of days." As he spoke he probed vigorously with the wooden tongue depressor, ignoring the gagging sounds coming from his patient. Satisfied, he straightened up and wiped his hands on a hot towel that Tim Cruddles, the duke's valet, held ready.

Dr. Pendragon was in his mid-twenties and looked even younger as he was slender, of medium stature, and poetically handsome with his

"Roman" forward-brushed crop of flaxen hair and thickly lashed hazel eyes. However, he was a former army surgeon and veteran of the peninsula wars, a graduate of the University of Edinburgh Medical School—generally considered the world's best—and used modern terms like "laryngitis" and "bronchitis" rather than the familiar, old-fashioned "quinsy" and "croup."

Also, as Marigold, Mrs. Cawdigan and the household staff gathered around the duke's bedside could see, the young doctor's breezy manner indicated he had been a close friend of the duke for some time. Certainly no one else would dream of addressing the six-foot-four-inch, glowering ducal body sprawled under a steaming croup tent and clad only in a pair of lawn underbritches, as "Satch."

"Well, that's it," the doctor said. "Keep the spirit kettle going under the croup tent, Mrs. Cawdigan." His gaze, however, lingered on Marigold. "Umm, moisture's important, you know, especially for that hard cough that seizes up from time to time."

The housekeeper fairly wriggled with pleasure. "Oh, I know the marvelous good a croup tent can do, doctor," she said, failing to mention that Marigold had been the one to rig the sheet over the head of the bed and set the kettle boiling under it. "I always like to keep a tiny drop of spirits of coal tar in the lip of the kettle, I do, to mix with the steam. In my humble experience, there's nothing like tar essence for breaking up the phlegm."

"Is that what that odor is?" Dr. Pendragon was watching Marigold's admirable derriere as she bent over the bed to adjust the duke's pillows. "Pungent, yes, very pungent, Mrs. Cawdigan," he murmured, also eyeing Marigold's shapely ankles as the hem of her skirt hiked up, "I'll say that for it."

They watched as Marigold adjusted the kettle again so that a jet of steam drifted into the scowling face of the twelfth duke of Westermere, who on top of his impatience with doctoring, was obviously uncomfortable, breathing with a loud, grating rasp.

The young doctor finished packing his black physician's bag as he said, "Had bouts of this since you were a child, haven't you, Satch?"

An irritable croaking noise was his answer. Dr. Pendragon put his hand on his patient's wrist and took his pulse. "Damned nuisance, croup. Most of us look forward to growing out of these childhood ailments. Had the chicken pox? The mumps? Mumps are a real danger in an adult male," he said with notable relish. "Mumps get into the gonads and wreak havoc, sheer havoc. A tragedy in a grown man, they'll leave any poor devil a veritable impotent shell."

The doctor was interrupted from under the croup tent by an ominous rumbling. Both the valet, Mr. Cruddles, and Mrs. Cawdigan started, visibly.

"Oh dear doctor, sir," the housekeeper cried, "don't mention dire consequences like mumps to His Grace, if you don't mind. You can see such talk upsets him so that, sure as I'm standing here, it'll not put him in a proper frame of mind to get well and healthy!"

They heard a wrathful "gronk" from under the croup tent.

"We mustn't provoke him to use his voice, either, from what you just said." Mrs. Cawdigan wet her lips nervously, looking at the valet for support. "What Lord Westermere is trying to tell you is that he had the mumps, bless him, right and proper, both sides, when he was but eight years of age. I was here then, assistant housekeeper for the old duke, his grandfather, and I'd swear to his mumps on me life, I would! I saw him all swole up myself, poor little chappie!"

But Dr. Pendragon had lost interest in mumps. His attention had drifted again to Marigold, who was tidying up glasses, spoons and washcloths and passing them to the servants to carry away.

Reginald Pendragon had been introduced to the ravishing but mysterious young lady residing in the duke's London house when he'd arrived, but he was baffled as far as to her true place in the order of things. Except of course that, like virtually the whole of London, he had heard the astonishing stories regarding the duke's arrangement. Which he could barely credit. An engagement? And the usually unassailable Satch had already talked to her father?

Nevertheless, there she was, living in Satch's house, and without, apparently, any visible chaperone or relation, or like arrangement. On the other hand, he had to admit, anyone as powerful as the duke of Westermere made his own rules; there was hardly anyone in Britain outside the king who would dare challenge him.

One could hardly blame Satch, Reggie told himself. He was the attending physician and even he was having a difficult time taking his eyes from her. Lucky devil, he thought with a sigh. Talk of heaven! Whatever the reason for her being in de Vries's London mansion, the prospect of spending a few days in bed with Miss Fenwick at hand to solicitously spoon hot tea and honey into one's lips, to place cool cloths upon one's fevered brow with a touch of those exquisite fingers, to have her bend over so that those incomparable breasts breathed their warm sachet almost into one's nostrils—

"Gronk!" came a fractious command from the croup tent.

The doctor brought himself back with an effort. His Grace had been watching with narrowed eyes, and was obviously not pleased with his admiring contemplation of the luscious parson's daughter.

"Yes, well," he said, hastily, "you have excellent care available, Satch. Couldn't do better. There's your housekeeper, Mrs. Cawdigan, and your—your—"

"Fiancée!" Torn by a barking cough, the duke

59

grimaced. "Fiancée, damme!" he rasped, more carefully.

"House guest," Miss Marigold Fenwick corrected sweetly. "I am the duke of Westermere's house guest, doctor, with the permission of my father, Dr. Eusebius Fenwick, the vicar of the parish of St. Dunstan's Mere church in Hobbs, Yorkshire." She fixed those glorious azure eyes on Reggie and went on, "In return for His Grace's hospitality, you may be sure I will, with the help of Mrs. Cawdigan and Mr. Cruddles, see that he receives the best of nursing."

Reginald Pendragon could only stare at her, thoroughly enchanted. Whatever was going on, Sacheveral de Vries was in good hands with his army of servants and angelically beautiful "house guest," as she called herself. There was, unfortunately, he realized with a sigh, no need for him to linger further.

"Stay in bed, Satch." He dug in his bag for several jars of ungents that the duke's nurses could apply to their master's throat and chest. "Let your—ah, Miss Fenwick, read aloud to you and all that. Marvelous stuff to pass the time, what? Hot soup, brandy and honey," he added, making his way to the door, "sponge baths, too. No exertion. And oh yes, give him paper and pen and ink so he can scribble messages. I'll call again in the morning."

As the doctor took his leave, the valet was already making preparations for the duke's bath.

Footmen had arrived with silver bowls of steaming water and large linen towels.

"Now we'll make you comfy in a wink, Your Grace," Mrs. Cawdigan said, moving briskly into position at the duke's knees, while the valet dropped a small towel discreetly over the area covered by the duke's revealing small clothes.

"Here you are, miss," Mrs. Cawdigan said briskly as she slapped a hot, wet washcloth into Marigold's hands, "you can make yourself useful and do His Grace's feet."

Marigold looked down at that part of the duke of Westermere's anatomy assigned to her by Mrs. Cawdigan. Westermere's feet were bare and, she supposed, as feet would go, definitely aristocratic. Large and well formed, they were rather pale—from wearing boots for most of his life, she supposed—but the skin was smooth, the toes not overly hairy, and soles free from corns, calluses, deformed nails or other rather usual imperfections.

Even his feet, Marigold couldn't help thinking, looked assured.

At the same time, she was aware that she and Mrs. Cawdigan and the others made a strange tableau there in the huge bedroom. At least six footmen and assorted porters, the housekeeper and valet, were in attendance, holding bowls and pots of hot water and soap and towels, all with their eyes fixed on the object of their attention, who was stretched out, virile and almost naked, in his massive bed hung with red velvet curtains and embellished with the Westermere coat of arms.

And good heavens, she, Marigold Fenwick, had by some inexplicable stroke of ill fortune been assigned the ducal feet to attend to! At that moment she looked up and caught the duke's black eyes through the cloudlike vapors of the croup kettle.

As always, that big, masculine body sent the most peculiar message. She'd once said the duke of Westermere oozed muscle and lust. Now her nerves positively quivered in response.

Phagh, Marigold promptly told herself, where was her head? She was a spineless ninny to agree to be any part of this!

She turned and took Mrs. Cawdigan's bowl and towels away from her before the housekeeper could protest. She seized the woman by the arm and steered her toward the door.

"Sponge baths," Marigold said loudly, "are really not in our domain, Mrs. Cawdigan, I'm sure you will agree. No properly run household would ask such a task of gentlewomen, so I suggest we make our retreat and leave this to Mr. Cruddles and those already attending His Grace."

She had hardly finished speaking when there was a burst of angry rasping from the big bed. Marigold kept on going.

"Tell the duke," she said, raising her voice, "that I shall return this afternoon after he has bathed and had his nap, and read to him from that excellent work by Mary Wollstonecraft, *A Vindica-*

tion of the Rights of Woman." With that she
pushed Mrs. Cawdigan out into the corridor, and
closed the door.

After the duke of Westermere had his sponge
bath and had drunk his lunch of half a bottle of
Madeira and a bowl of beef bouillon, he was in
no mood to sleep. On the contrary, his enforced
silence, not to mention the inactivity due to his
slight fever, made him both irritable and restless.
Pulling across his lap the writing desk that Cruddles had brought, Sacheverel fired off a series of
querulous inquiries, peremptory orders, acerbic
comments and ill-natured complaints to his staff
in such quantity that within a very short time an
extra supply of paper and another bottle of ink
had to be brought from the library.

By the time Marigold arrived at three o'clock
with a copy of *A Vindication of the Rights of
Woman* under her arm, there was a stack of these
messages waiting. A fine little tapestried Queen
Anne side chair had been drawn up next to the
bed, awaiting her.

The duke's servants had dressed their patient
in a linen nightshirt under a wine-colored silk
robe that matched the bed's satin coverlet worked
in gold and silver thread. The effect, especially
since the duke was newly shaven, was quite attractive. However, when he saw Marigold, Westermere gave a croak of impatience and, hiking
his big body up in bed, couldn't wait to signal her
with a forefinger stabbed in the air to sit down at

the small table covered with handwritten messages, and begin.

Marigold was attired in a russet afternoon frock, cut low in front in the current fashion to display more of her breasts than she really found comfortable, and she wore a small lace shawl over her shoulders. She looked very composed with her hair pulled up on top of her head à la Grecque and tied with velvet ribbons. She gave a cool look to the duke's furious gesturing, but she did sit down.

Ignoring all the grunts and stabbing motions, Marigold put her book beside the pile of scrawled notes.

"I had thought I would begin reading to you," she said calmly, opening Mary Wollstonecraft's tome, "to put you in a more restful frame of mind before we attempt any sort of . . . communication. Certainly you must agree ordinary conversation is out of the question. Dr. Pendragon has issued orders that you are not to use your voice at all. But it has occurred to me that if I read to you for a while—"

The duke had been scribbling furiously on the note paper on his writing desk. Now he balled up a note and sent it through the air to Marigold. It landed on the carpet beside her foot. She looked down at it, but did not pick it up.

"I will now read from *A Vindication of the Rights of Woman*, Your Grace," she announced, opening her book, "on the subject of women and their relation to men in love—if one can use such a term in regard to the male gender—and marriage."

The duke opened his mouth, but before he could utter a sound, she began:

". . . if they are really capable of acting like rational creatures, let them not be treated like slaves; or, like the brutes who are dependent on the reason of man when they associate with him; but cultivate their minds, give them the salutary, sublime curb of principle, and let them attain conscious dignity by feeling themselves only dependent on God. Teach them, in common with man, to submit to necessity, instead of giving, to render them more pleasing, a sex to morals."

At first the duke looked as though he could hardly believe his ears. Then he grabbed several sheets of note paper and gashed each with his pen, splattering ink, to write *STOP THAT!* several times. He then balled them up and hurled them like missiles in the direction of the reader.

As the furious communications flew around her and landed on the floor, Marigold continued:

"Further, should experience prove that they cannot attain the same degree of strength of mind, perseverance, and fortitude, let their virtues be the same in kind, though they may vainly struggle for the same degree; and the superiority of man with me be equally clear, if not clearer; and truth, as it is a simple principle, which admits of not modification, would be common to both. Nay, the order of society as it is at present regulated would not be inverted, for woman would then only have the rank that reason assigned her, and arts could not be practiced to bring the balance even, much less to turn it."

The duke hurled the last of his notes at her and, flushed with aggravation, gave into a fit of painful coughing.

Marigold went on serenely:

"These may be termed utopian dreams.—Thanks to that Being who impressed them on my soul, and gave me sufficient strength of mind to dare to exert my own reason till, becoming dependent only on him for the support of my virtue, I view, with indignation, the mistaken notions that enslave my sex."

She paused. "This is Mary Wollstonecraft herself now, of course, who is speaking."

The duke was no longer listening. He sat up in bed, his back rigid against the bed pillows. On the red silk coverlet his big hands contracted convulsively. He uttered a painful "Gronk!" in dire warning.

Marigold calmly turned the page. "Let me remind you, Your Grace, that Dr. Pendragon urged me to read to you as a means of promoting mild entertainment and a restful atmosphere. As Mr. Cruddles tells me you have not yet had your nap, why don't you lie back down among your pillows and compose yourself in a manner more conducive to sleep, and let me go on? As Wollstonecraft says, 'I love man as my fellow, but his scepter, real or usurped, extends not to me, unless the reason of an individual demands my homage; and even then the submission is to reason, and not to man.'"

The duke groped across the table at bedside, and his hands closed around the water carafe.

"'. . . females have been insulated,'" Marigold read on, "'as it were; and, while they have been stripped of the virtues that should clothe humanity, they have been decked with artificial graces that enable them to exercise a short-lived tyranny.' I shouldn't throw that if I were you," she said, calmly. "If you toss that bottle at me it only proves Mary Wollstonecraft's thesis—that brute opposition will not obliterate the essential virtue of feminine reason."

"But damme, it will shut you up!" All that remained of Westermere's voice was a thin, ghastly rasp.

Abandoning thoughts of tossing the carafe at her head, he tore back the satin coverlets and, in a flurry of bare, hairy legs and thighs, bounded out of bed, seized Marigold and dragged her from her chair, at the same time managing to grab up most of the notes that were still on the table.

With Marigold in one hand and a fistful of his notes in the other, Sacheveral de Vries hauled her to his big bed, dumped her upon it, and flung his communications at her.

"Sir!" Marigold said, fending off the flying pieces of paper while hastily scrambling to a sitting position and adjusting her hiked-up skirts. "That was hardly necessary!"

Sacheverel jumped onto the bed, making it bounce, and reached for the writing desk.

Necessary, otherwise I'd have you prating at me all afternoon, he scrawled on a piece of paper. *You are not going to read damned lunatic Wollstonecraft at me, by gad. Not in my own house!*

Marigold's eyes flashed as she drew herself up. "I assure you, Westermere, this is no frivolous fancy. I am deeply devoted to the teaching of this incomparable woman, and have been for years! If you infer that I do not have better sense to know what I am doing, then I fear you are the deluded one!" She tossed her head. "Or mayhap you think that I have deliberately chosen to read to you for the express purpose of raising your temper and goading you into manhandling me! Pray, I assure you, sir, I would never elect of my own free will to bring about such an odious event!"

The duke had been rummaging through the papers, setting out his notes in piles on the bedcovers. He'd written all since lunchtime, but some he did not seem to remember. He straightened out a balled-up scrap of paper to Marigold that said, *How tall are you?* and then, frowning, hastily crumpled it back up.

He seemed to find the one he wanted. Smoothed out and handed to Marigold, it read; *How do you know achromatic microscope? You don't, do you?*

Marigold calmly closed her edition of Mary Wollstonecraft's tome and placed it slowly and deliberately on the embroidered bedspread beside her.

Then she folded her hands in her lap and, lifting her eyes to a point in the middle of the red velvet swaths of the canopy of the great bed, she said, "Milord, the achromatic system gives images practically free from extraneous colors, which is most important to virtually anything one wishes to study under a microscope. As explained to me, the achromatic lens is made by combining lenses of different glasses having different focal powers, such as crown glass over flint glass, so that the light emerging from the lens forms an image practically free from color distortion." She shifted her gaze rather coldly to the ducal coat of arms above his head. "I know that you know all this, milord, since you yourself own such a fine microscope. So I can only assume you are taking some perverse pleasure in testing me."

When the duke quickly reached for a piece of paper she told him, "Nay, please do not exert yourself, Westermere! Remember Dr. Pendragon's instructions to remain calm and not exert yourself. You do not have to write more questions. I will freely tell you that I have never had the opportunity to do more than glimpse, much less use, a microscope of any sort, but I have studied several illustrated catalogues owned by the father of a dear friend of mine, Dr. John Stack of my home village of Stokesbury Hatton. Many late evenings my friends and I—Sophronia, his daughter, and Penelope MacDougal, whom you have recently had the privilege of meeting—have sat up in Dr. Stack's surgery and pored over his wondrous books, many of which contain the latest equipment he would so dearly love to have in his work."

A rasping growl greeted this last statement.

It was obvious the duke did not want to hear any appeals on behalf of impoverished villages or their equally impoverished medical clinics. He bent his dark head, his long, slightly wavy hair, unclubbed since he'd bathed and shaved, and scrawled out another note, which he held out to her.

When she took it and read it, it was Marigold's turn to raise her eyebrows.

Chapter Five

"B-botany?"

Sacheverel saw that delightfully rounded lower lip hesitate. He was so distracted that he almost lost track of his question.

She looked down at the note again that he had tossed to her. "What do I know about botany?"

Westermere nodded, eyes narrowed.

In the past few minutes, especially with her explanation of how she had come to know about achromatic microscopes by studying catalogues in some village doctor's library, he'd found himself drastically revising his prejudice against overeducated women. For here, by God, unless he was totally deluded, was one of that unseemly tribe who seemed to have some use after all!

Cannily, he told himself the task of the moment

was to find out just how useful she could be.

Now, sitting perched on his bed, she certainly didn't look like the harridan who'd accosted him in Covent Garden a few days ago. She wore a russet dress that showed a devilishly attractive bit of creamy bosom, her hair was most fashionably done, and her skirts were hiked up enough to show a length of shapely ankle, a bit of slender leg.

That, Satch reminded himself, was what had recommended her to him from the moment he'd set eyes on her: that despite her unrestrained behavior and idiot notions—obviously the result of an unfortunate bluestocking parsonage upbringing—her truly astonishing physical beauty and glowing good health made her a prime specimen to breed into any noble line. His father and his grandfather would have heartily agreed with him.

From the time of William the Conqueror, the family of Westermeres had all been fine physical specimens by virtue of a judicious selection of mates. It was not unknown for a Westermere to turn down heiresses whose fortunes had dazzled others because of some rumored family history of weak lungs, crooked teeth, or even in one case, webbed feet.

Gad, Satch thought, gazing at her as she bent her gold-brown head to reread his note, Miss Marigold Fenwick would produce a superb line of children! Handsome Westermere offspring would outshine those of any titled family in the entire north of England!

"I have some knowledge," she was saying, "of schoolmaster MacDougal's collection of *Vegetable Staticks* by Stephen Hales, which I gather is an excellent work, although I confess I found his propositions on the movement of water in plants more than a little confusing."

Perhaps she already knew how to file and catalogue, he told himself as he watched the gentle rise and fall of her pillowy décolletage as she bent forward to place his note with the others.

The saints knew Satch was desperate for a clerk for his specimens and papers. His search over a number of years to find candidates to meet his exacting requirements for an unassuming, orderly and skilled assistant had led to the appearance of an astonishing number of dolts whom he hadn't been able to tolerate for more than twenty-four hours. A few of the miserable bunglers he had thrown bodily out of the house himself.

"Linnaeus," the beauteous Miss Fenwick was saying, thoughtfully. "Schoolmaster MacDougal won a priceless copy of the great master's work, circa seventeen hundred fifty-three, as valedictorian's prize when Mr. MacDougal graduated from university. It's his most beloved possession—besides Penelope, of course. I confess, Sophronia, Penelope and I have had wondrous hours together in the schoolmaster's library examining pages of these beautifully illustrated plants."

Sacheveral was all attention now. He scribbled off a flurry of notes and tossed them at her.

" 'How many plants can I identify from the first volume of Dr. Linnaeus' *Species plantarum*?' " she read. "La, sir, aren't there some six thousand in all? From all over the world? I would have to be a prodig—"

GET IT! Satch told her, gashing the paper with the quill point as he wrote. *Big book, green binding, across room, third shelf to the left!*

When Marigold was a little slow in deciphering the ink-splattered message, the Duke of Westermere gave her a hearty prod between the shoulder blades that propelled her from the bed and halfway across the room.

"Really," she told him over her shoulder, "how many times must I tell you how much I dislike being so rudely handled? After all, I am *not* one of your servants!"

Her protest was answered by a flurry of violent gestures, which partly displaced one side of the croup tent and apparently indicated she was to hurry up, find the books and return as soon as possible.

It was not so easily done. One whole wall of the bedroom was covered with the duke's scientific books of every conceivable genre, plus several bound collections of specimens.

After some searching, all the while being bombarded with balled up notes of instructions from the duke that flew about her like miniature hailstones, and which Marigold, much to His Grace's annoyance, did not bother to pick up and read, she found the volume he wanted. It was a specially illustrated translation of Linnaeus' botanical works, but so big and heavy Marigold could hardly stagger back to the bed with it.

With a fine disregard for his condition, the duke reached up a big hand and pulled down the rest of the croup tent to make room. He then scribbled a note that he gave to Marigold that said, *Turn off damned kettle! Steam warps pages*!

Marigold bent to take the little croup kettle off the hob. The next thing she knew, he had seized her by her arm and unceremoniously pulled her into the bed with him.

For a startled moment, Marigold lay rather stiffly against the duke of Westermere, the enormous botany book braced across their bodies. When she turned to give him a reproving look, the duke's black eyes were close to hers.

"Don't make me talk." He spoke in a whisper that was painful even for her to hear. "Hold up your side of the book," he croaked. " 'S'too heavy."

The look that passed between them asked a question. Would she cater to his whim, for whatever strange reason he had in mind? Or would she serve him as rudely as he had treated her for most of the afternoon, and flatly refuse?

Marigold sighed. Why was it the woman, with all her virtuous instincts, as Mary Wollstonecraft pointed out, was always so vulnerable to an appeal that was not without its pathetic overtones? Because, of course, even though he was a crass, grasping monster who stood for all the things she detested, Westermere was sick and in some pain: One had only to listen to his voice to know that.

"Ah, well, let me see," Marigold said, resigned, as she propped the huge book against her stomach. Fortunately, more-than-equal weight was also borne by the duke's much stronger, muscular midsection. "I gather you want me to read to you?"

A violent shake of his black-haired head. Then a message, scrawled with a hand braced against the middle of the big book.

SAINT-JOHN'S-WORT. MILLET. FOXGLOVE. VETCH.

He thrust the paper with the words into her hand. "You want me to look up these plants?" They lay side by side in the bed with the heavy book propped across them. "Is that what we're doing this for?"

Staring right into her eyes, the duke gave a vehement nod. As he did so, some of his long, unbound hair fell across the bridge of his nose. Without thinking, Marigold reached up with her free hand and tucked the strand behind his ear, thus prompting him to give her a particularly piercing look.

It took her several minutes to find *vetch*. The big illustrated book was almost unmanageable in that position, held by two persons lying flat on their backs, but the man next to her was adamant. Also, Marigold felt compelled to stop from time to time to admire some of the exquisite drawings in carefully done watercolor wash, even delicate oils on inserted vellum sheets.

"Here we are: *vetch*," she said, finally. " 'Any of a genus *Vica* of herbaceous twining leguminous plants for fodder.' It's very good for the soil, too," she added. "The farmers around Hobbs grow it when they rotate their crops, as it enriches the ground, they say.

"Oh, Saint-John's-wort!" she cried as they viewed the next drawing. " 'Genus *Hypericum* of the family Guttiferrae. Herbs and shrubs with showy pentamerous yellow flowers.' I love them, the little darlings, aren't they pretty? They're also good for babies with colic."

A rather heavy finger suddenly reached across the page as the duke poked at the word *pentamerous*.

"Five," Marigold murmured, not looking up, "in bundles of five. Come, your grace, don't you remember your Greek?"

For a moment his hand hesitated, lingering inches from the top of her head. Sacheverel found he was so pleased with her he had almost patted her. He let his hand fall.

She could be a gem, a treasure! he told himself, inordinately pleased. He was sure she had a phenomenal memory. Sacheverel had picked the subject *vetch* thinking of the tiny seeds as they might be found on the boots of a cattle thief. It had been just so in a recent case, when the culprit had sworn that he had never been in his neighbor's vetch field, when in fact the botanical evidence had placed him in the field at the same time as the herd had been raided.

"Foxglove," she said, turning to a magnificent watercolor and ink rendition of half a page of *Digitalis pupurea* with their showy racemes of dotted white and purple tubular flowers.

Satch slapped his hand over the deadly plant. She'd had less than a second to look at them. *How many?* he scribbled.

She looked at him, realizing for the first time that she was not merely amusing him with his books as they whiled away his bedridden afternoon. It *was* some sort of test.

"Four," she said. "Two of each color, and a purple bud."

Sacheverel leaned back among the pillows, shaking his head when she offered to readjust the croup tent. He didn't want any more of the damned croup treatment; he wanted to think.

By George, she could memorize so rapidly! She was bright, brighter than almost anyone—male or female—he'd encountered in some time, and observant. What an assistant in his research work she'd make!

When they were married, he would set up a nicely equipped laboratory for her where she could work in tidy, controlled, scientific surroundings. A sudden picture of her superb body, nicely rounded in pregnancy and clad in some sort of smock-like laboratory covering drifted through his mind. Sacheverel imagined her bending over the latest model of a Düsseldorf-made microscope he'd been reading about. Or sitting at a laboratory table, taking the tedious work of cataloguing British earth and clay samples off his hands.

Considering such a prospect, he allowed his thoughts to meld in an eminently warm and satisfactory way. Satch lifted a lazy hand and scrawled on his note paper, *Go ahead—read* Fungi *until you come to the end*.

She gave him an inquiring look from those blue eyes, but dutifully, she found the section on toadstools and mushrooms and began to read.

Satch settled down in the pillows and let his head move comfortably to her warm shoulder.

Some time later, as Marigold was reading the distinction between the fungus family Boletaceae, which bear spores in an easily detachable layer on the underside of the cap, and are not to be confused with their close relatives, the hydnums, or hedgehog mushrooms, which have teeth, spines or warts on the under surface, she noticed that the duke had fallen asleep. Not only asleep, but he lay so heavily against her that his body pinned down most of her frock.

She put the big book aside carefully and gave him an experimental push, but nothing happened. She realized the weight of the Italian botany book had concealed the pressure of the duke's body as he'd rolled, or even, one might say, snuggled against her as he slept. However that situation was apparent now, much to her annoyance.

Worn out with his malaise, Sacheverel de Vries slept deeply, a large, muscular figure immobilizing most of her shoulder, hip and leg on the left side. He was virtually squeezing her out of the bed.

Making an impatient sound, Marigold reached for the bell pull, which, fortunately, was within reach. After giving the tapestried length a few sharp tugs to summon whomever might be on duty downstairs, she suddenly hoped it would be Cruddles, the valet, who answered. A gentleman's gentleman could be counted on to be discreet. And she was beginning to be unpleasantly aware of the picture they presented lying side by side—even somewhat tangled together—the duke clad only in his night clothes.

Perhaps, she told herself, she should try to dislodge him before anyone got there. Just in case it was one of the footmen, or even Mrs. Cawdigan, and not Cruddles.

Using her left foot braced against his knee, Marigold took the skirt of her dress in both hands and gave it a hard pull. The duke, his face buried against her shoulder, promptly muttered something, but remained as immovable as a granite boulder.

"Oh, you beast," Marigold hissed. She gave him a rather vicious pinch on a bare patch of skin on his wrist. "Wake up!"

She could hear footsteps in the hall. If it was

Cruddles, he had brought at least two footmen with him. Perhaps Mrs. Cawdigan, too.

Frantically, Marigold braced both her feet against the duke's side, and seized her skirt with both hands. There was a sudden ripping sound and Marigold was free. Not only that, but the momentum of her release as the gown tore loose sent her over the side of the bed. She landed on the floor on top of the remains of the croup tent just as Cruddles and two footmen entered.

The footmen were carrying candelabras, as the afternoon was waning and the duke's bedroom was almost in twilight. As they came through the door Marigold could see the young footmen's eyes widen, and those of Mr. Cruddles, too.

And no wonder. She had, she realized as she got to her knees on the soggy sheeting, lost most of one side of her skirt and petticoat when she'd ripped loose from the duke. What was left of her gown was little more than a scarflike panel waving lasciviously down her front.

Hastily grabbing what little there was left, she felt around to the rear. Not much there, either, she found with a shudder, although her petticoat kept her from complete indecency.

The servants' eyes, taking in the sprawled, unconscious figure of the duke in the big bed, and Marigold's dishabille, were wide as dinner plates. They had undoubtedly heard all the rumor and innuendo that had surely kept London buzzing from top to bottom. But none of it, Marigold knew, would match what they were seeing now.

The duke's fiancée/house guest looked as though she had done battle and lost. And the duke, flopped over on his back now in the middle of the disordered bed, looked alarmingly dead to the world.

A feeble thought that there might be some way to explain passed through Marigold's mind. But even as it did, she caught a definitely cautionary look from the duke's valet. Cruddles' message said quite plainly: *In our world one never, ever explains.*

Marigold caught herself in time.

Cruddles, true to his training, now moved his eyes to the coat of arms above the headboard of the duke's bed.

"You rang, miss?" the impervious Cruddles asked.

Chapter Six

"I want you to know that I will have no part of this," Marigold cried.

She backed out of the way of two footmen carrying the duke's white satin formal coat at arm's length. In doing so, she trod on the skirt of the ball gown that two seamstresses on their knees were desperately trying to hem.

Marigold's protests were drowned in the general noise. There were perhaps thirty or even forty people crowded into the duke's bedroom. Two young footmen were waiting to put on the duke's satin pumps, and a few moments before, the hairdressers, plus the powderer with his giant horn, had arrived to do the duke's hair. But they'd left at a run when his grace indicated by a few thrown objects and a hoarse croak that he'd be

deviled and damned if he'd be crimped and powdered with his throat in its present condition. It
was all to please his aunt, anyway, who clung to
her old-fashioned notions of formal dress.

Marigold had witnessed the whole incident,
which confirmed her opinion that what was to
take place that evening was a venture in utter
madness. She reached out to grab the arm of Dr.
Pendragon.

"Doctor, I appeal to you," she cried. "Surely
only the most hopelessly addicted of London's
ton will be out tonight in this weather! It is not
only bitterly cold, but raining and sleeting, too. I
hope your common sense, if not the wisdom of
your considerable scientific training, will convince you of the unreasonableness of the duke's
intention to attend the duchess of Sutherland's
ball, make a visit to Almack's, and even go to
some stupid rout!"

She held on to Pendragon as the doctor looked
longingly at the other side of the room where the
duke was being dressed by his valet and several
footmen. "You have attended Westermere's condition for the past two days," she pleaded. "To let
him go out in such weather is nothing short of
murder!"

At the word "murder" the physician seemed to
flinch.

"What?" he said, finally giving her his attention.
"Ummm, not to be alarmed, dear Miss Fenwick,
the prince regent himself will attend the Sutherland affair, and Saturday is the regular night for

routs—half of London will be in the streets. Besides," he said, giving her hand a hurried pat, "Satch will only stay a moment at Almack's. I can swear to you, he hates the place."

"Sir, you miss the point!" Marigold attempted to follow the doctor as he moved away, but the women on their knees around her pulled her back.

"Mademoiselle," one of the seamstress reminded her, "If you will stand still this will not take so long, as it will not have to be done over and over again!"

Marigold looked down. The women were basting a decorative band of crystal beads and pearls to the bottom of the gown to make it longer, a last-minute alteration that would hopefully adjust it to Marigold's considerable height. The reason this work was being done in the duke's bedroom was that Westermere himself was supervising from behind a screen on the other side of the room. The Kensington couturiere stood receiving and sending notes as the duke advised her.

It was difficult to realize that up until four o'clock that afternoon the duke of Westermere had still been confined to his bed, although no longer under the croup tent, following his physician's advice to rest and avoid unnecessary exertion. He'd enjoyed his lunch of a hearty mixed grill and an excellent port and had been reading, on and off between naps, a book in German on a series of unsolved 16th-century Silesian ax murders.

But on the stroke of four, he had risen from his bed, Cruddles had thrown open the bedroom doors, and an army of household servants had marched in to begin preparations for what was announced as the duke's scheduled evening out in London.

Marigold had been astounded to hear of this turn of events. She'd taken it upon herself to ring for Cruddles to ask him to come to her room and tell her if what she'd heard was true. But Mrs. Cawdigan had come bursting in instead, to tell her to hurry as the dressmakers had arrived with her partly assembled gown. Marigold was expected to accompany the duke that evening.

Nothing could have horrified her more. "Lud, have they all taken leave of their senses?" she had cried.

Mrs. Cawdigan's only answer had been to push her out into the gallery and toward the duke's suite of rooms. The hall had been crowded not only with the Horton Crescent mansion's domestic staff, but a leading London ladies' hairdresser, a cobbler with boxes of the latest Paris shoes, and Madame Rosenzweig and company, introduced as haute couture dressmakers from Kensington, carrying two partly finished ball gowns from their regular stock.

Madame Rosenzweig seemed familiar with the duke's aesthetic eccentricities. The gowns were carried across the room for his critical inspection while Cruddles and two footmen clubbed his dark, wavy hair and secured it in a peruke with a white silk bow. After some silent examination, the duke had lifted a finger and chose the tight-skirted, cream-colored satin gown, rejecting the more girlish flowing white tulle.

When Madame Rosenzweig would have demurred in favor of the simpler frock, the duke scrawled fiercely, *Damme, everyone knows she's a virgin, just look at her! The thing's too milk-white—we might as well give her a harp to carry!*

The couturiere rolled her eyes heavenward. "Ah, he is mad, but a genius," she muttered under her breath. "*Un vrai homme viril* who must have the clothes *parfait*, just so! Not only *his*, but everyone else's!"

The duke pointed out that his choice, the cream satin gown, was not long enough. "But your grace, a little glimpse of ankle is the rage now," the dressmaker protested.

He wrote, *Not for her. She is no scrawny schoolgirl.* In a flurry of scribbling he demanded a band of Belgian crystal beads and pearls to extend the skirt, and a scrap of an Empire bodice, barely enough to cover the breasts, in the same beads and pearls.

Madame Rosenzweig moaned and clutched at her hair. But an apprentice was sent to the Kensington shop to fetch the last piece of the pearl and crystal trim on the bolt.

While Cruddles smoothed him into tight white

silk hose with a double band of garters, Sacheverel examined the selection of dance pumps the Italian cobbler had brought, elegantly wrapped in paper tissue, and found a pair decorated with rosettes of freshwater pearls.

When she saw them, Marigold was indignant.

"Am I to have nothing to say about my shoes, either?" she fumed. "May I remind the duke I am being dressed for a social evening I have hardly agreed to?" She glared down at the shoemaker as he struggled to get the knife-narrow shoes on her feet. "If you would have the courtesy to ask me, sir, instead of listening to the dictates of Westermere behind his dressing screen, I would tell you these things *do not fit!*"

No one paid any attention. On the other side of the room, Reginald Pendragon took a last look at his patient's throat with a tongue depressor and shielded candle.

"Still can't talk much, can you?" the young doctor said sympathetically. "God's teeth, Satch, relent and let me come with you! It's going to be a long, miserable evening if you intend to show yourself to most of London's sociables. I hate to send you out in filthy weather with only a notepad and pen and ink to stave off pneumonia."

Sacheverel scrawled off a message and handed it to him. *The girl can talk enough for both of us.*

The doctor looked down at the paper with a doubtful expression. "Oh yes, Miss Fenwick is rarely at a loss for words or doughty spirit, I'll say that. But Satch, consider that your very manner and rank put you at the center of avid speculation, more so since London has heard that Miss Fenwick is your—ah, um, fiancée. Her appearance by your side will create a storm of interest. You'll undoubtedly find yourself answering questions."

The more interest the better, the other wrote. *Whole idea*.

Sacheverel pushed Cruddles away and, seated on the edge of the bed, shrugged into his silk shirt himself. The valet then proceeded to carefully wrap an elaborate white silk stock around his throat. Meanwhile, Mrs. Cawdigan's nephew, Charles, had just finished smoothing the duke's silk stockings to wrinkleless perfection.

Sacheverel stretched both legs and felt the tightness give, but just enough. No problem having the things bag about the knees halfway through the evening. Many of the Ton's dandies stood the entire night to avoid just such a ruinous effect.

He picked up the notepad. *Duchess of Suth, my late father's oldest sister*, he wrote. *Aunt Bessie civil to anybody I bring*.

"Hmmm." Reggie Pendragon was remembering his last meeting with Satch's relative at one of her soirees. The formidable dowager duchess was nearly six feet tall with a piercing eye and stentorian voice, a bastion of intimidation—as Satch himself could be when he wanted to. "It's not just that," Reggie began.

A wave of the duke's hand cut him off.

Gesturing for Cruddles to hold the lap desk steady, the Duke of Westermere wrote, *Dammit, don't want you with me, Reggie, do I make myself clear? So far no one implicated Oris's affair but me. Went to Bristol on my own to plead Ludberry's case, damned cretin magistrate Sackville will swear only me involved. Whatever happens elsewhere I will be safely in London on Sat. escorting notorious parsonage fiancée for all to see.*

His friend shook his head. "It's dangerous. I don't like it. Let me remind you, Satch, you have enemies other than a thick-headed magistrate in Bristol."

The duke raised a sardonic eyebrow. He wrote, *Undoubtedly*, and handed the note to Pendragon.

The valet moved the writing desk aside. Sacheverel signaled the footmen to bring his glittering coat. He slipped his arms into it and settled it about his shoulders, the valet fussing with his elaborately wound stock and his black, unpowdered hair. Sacheverel de Vries, Viscount St. Osbert, twelfth Duke of Westermere, stood back to see himself full length in the long mirror.

Except for the rather high set of white silk, which was intended to protect his throat more than meet the dictates of fashion, his grace's turnout was impeccable, and dazzling. He was a fine, strapping, black-eyed figure of a man, several inches over six feet, a fine horseman, swimmer, and distinguished amateur challenger of Gentleman Dan and other well-known pugilists. For all his notorious meticulousness about clothes and art, the current skintight formal fashions of the prince regent's court set off Westermere's physique superbly.

He wore a coat emblazoned with various military decorations, including the Wellington Star and Wreath, a Dnieper Sunburst of Valor from the Tsar of Russia with thirty diamonds and rubies, and a rather curious gold filigree Hand of Fatima from the Bey of Egypt, featuring dangling pieces of jade.

The duke nodded in the mirror that he was satisfied. He had hardly to turn to look for Marigold: The dressmaker and her assistants were already bringing her forward.

Here was the critical moment, their faces said. The duke's selection of the cream-colored satin rather than the white gown had been just right, that was apparent. So had been his insistence on a trim of crystal beads and pearls around the hem and across the high Empire bodice. The tight, tube-like cut of the ball gown emphasized Marigold's regal height and her slimness, yet subtly outlined her shapely bosom and hips.

Sacheveral de Vries's eye fell on Madame Rosenzweig's artistic triumph, a demi-turban of ribbons, loops of pearls, and white ostrich plumes. He quickly reached for his pen and Cruddles' outstretched hand holding the notepad.

What is that? the duke scrawled thunderously. They all knew what he meant. He was glaring at the headdress which, to give Madame Rosenzweig credit, was a reasonable reproduction of a similar ornamentation admired only last week by the Prince Regent himself.

The couturiere looked at her assistants for support, but the women gathered around her seemed about to faint.

"Your Grace," she faltered, "it is the very latest—"

"Do I have any say in this?" Marigold interrupted, rather peevishly. "I rather like it." She bent to get a better look at herself in the pier glass. "From what little I've seen this year, feathers are very elegant and the gold ribbons do lend a nice touch. Let me remind you, sir, since I am a very unwilling participant in this extraordinary evening, the purpose of which has yet to be explained to me—"

A typhoon of scribbled notes took to the air. *Get that thing off her head!* one said as it was pitched at Madame Rosenzweig. And another, to Cruddles: *Burn the damned feathers, she looks like an Irish chicken!*

A seamstress bent and picked up the third ink-splattered note from the carpet which said simply, *Leave pearls*.

"Milord," Cruddles reminded his master, "I fear there are ink spots now on the front of your coat."

The only reply was a snarl. The duke watched with a scowl as the Kensington modistes hastily removed the offending plumes and gold ribbons, leaving ropes of pearls twined in Marigold's looped and braided hair. With an abrupt gesture he signaled for Marigold to be brought to stand beside him before the pier glass.

The duke, resplendent in glitter and creamy satin with a few almost imperceptible ink spots on his waistcoat, was a towering, handsome figure, marred only slightly by a preoccupied scowl.

Next to him, Marigold stared at her reflection in the pier glass with a feeling of wonder and shock that was entirely new to her.

She rather numbly told herself she did not know which affected her more: the duke of Westermere in formal clothes that suddenly and quite overwhelmingly brought home the full implications of his arrogant wealth, power and rank—or the stunningly beautiful, aristocratic beauty by his side.

She hardly recognized herself.

It was as though one of the storybooks of enchanted princesses and fairy godmothers that she and Sophronia and Penelope had so loved when they were children had suddenly come alive. This reflection in the glass by the duke's side was a ravishing, enchantingly lovely young woman so perfect she could not possibly be real.

The next moment a feeling of guilt swept over her. Marigold could not help but think of Penelope and Sophronia, her dear "cavaliers" devoted to improving conditions in the village, and what they would say if they could see her now. Or worse, her poor father—that gentle, kindly, quite impoverished man of God.

With a sense of embarrassment she realized the

pearls she wore looped in her hair were worth enough—to take just one instance—to pay her father the vicar's modest living for several years. With that foremost in her thoughts, Marigold had a thoroughly stubborn resistance to all this splendor rising within her.

It was all very well to play out this charade in Westermere's house in the hopes of getting him to do something to aid the village. Stokesbury Hatton was, indeed, in dire straits, or she would not have agreed to place herself in the midst of all this London farrago. But Marigold did not see that this extravagant display, or ridiculous evening with the ton, was going to accomplish anything.

"I'm sorry," she said in a loud voice that made everyone but the duke start in surprise. "It is as I explained before. I really cannot lend myself to something which, on the surface, seems utterly without sense or purpose. Nor on the other hand, will I agree to acquiesce out of sheer ignorance."

The duke turned his stare on her. Marigold fearlessly went on: "Let me paraphrase that excellent social philosopher, Mary Wollestonecraft, when I say, as I said before this evening, I love man as my fellow, but Westermere's scepter, real or usurped, extends not to me, unless the reason of an individual demands my homage. And even then the submission is to reason, and not to Westermere himself."

Her words fell into the shocked silence of the room. Several of the younger footmen, their eyes on the duke's face, began backing toward the safety of the bedroom doors. The poor couturiere and her seamstresses had the stunned air of those victims of the Terror about to be marched away to the guillotine. But while Marigold was declaring that she had no intention of accompanying the duke of Westermere that evening, the duke's valet had come up and draped a full-length marten fur cape with hood about her shoulders.

As for the duke, the explosion that the others so obviously expected did not appear to be forthcoming. Instead, he was busily writing another note, which he gave to a footman to deliver to Marigold just as Charles brought up his great black traveling cape.

"Your Grace, I am quite serious, I beg you to listen to me!" Marigold tried to get the voluminous fur out of her way so that she could read Westermere's scribbled message the footman handed her. "No matter what arguments you may think to present, I really will not surrender to—"

She stopped abruptly, her eyes widening. Westermere's choppy scrawls in black ink across the paper were the last thing, perhaps in her whole life, that Marigold had expected to find.

Please cooperate, his message said simply. *I need your help*.

Chapter Seven

No appeal could have been more unexpected or affected Marigold more. Her first thought was: How could any decent, compassionate person have refused Westermere's plea?

But alas, it was all a trick. She discovered it some hours later as a plump youth, who had introduced himself as Viscount Something or Other, whirled her down the length of the duchess of Sutherland's ballroom to a rather strenuous galop.

"I need your help," the duke of Westermere had written quite poignantly.

And she'd been a naive, silly goose, Marigold scolded herself as she dodged the remarkably inept feet of the viscount. She should be convinced by now that if there was one person who was capable of getting his self-serving, devious way, it was certainly the duke of Westermere. Just as he had persuaded her several days ago because of his illness to read to him from the botany book—indeed, to actually get in bed with him!

Now he had once again successfully played on her sympathies and enticed her into an evening of socializing for which she had no heart, and certainly no inclination!

Oh, how wise Mary Wollstonecraft had been, Marigold thought bitterly as the fat youth seized her about the waist and attempted, unsuccessfully, to lift her in a small jeté, when that noble woman had written about the vulnerability of women's generous nature!

On the surface, she'd felt she had to respond to Westermere for the obvious reason that he needed someone to speak for him when communication through pen and ink grew tiresome or even—as in the case of his aunt, the dowager duchess—nearly unmanageable.

When they'd arrived at their destination they'd found what seemed like hundreds of coaches surrounding the mansion near Green Park, testiment to the fact that all of privileged London vied for an invitation to the Sutherland balls. When they'd entered the marble halls, Marigold had seen Maria Theresa Elizabeth, Duchess of Sutherland, at the top of the stairs at the center of a building resembling a less homey version of the House of Lords, greeting her guests.

Don't shilly-shally, the duke had just written in

a note that he slipped into her hand at the last moment, *hold your own. Aunt Bessie no dragon.*

Marigold found that difficult to believe.

Flanked by a butler shouting the names of arriving guests and several pages in powdered wigs, the duchess gave Marigold the most desultory of inspections before she turned to her nephew, who was trying to hold his paper tablet inconspicuously.

The duchess saw it at once. "Don't tell me you can't talk, boy!" she boomed. "Croup, again, isn't it? Phagh, this is no way to present yourself for a social evening, sickly and voiceless! Is that ink on the front of your weskit? Can't dance, can't flirt, clothes in terrible condition, you should be ashamed of yourself! And stay away from the Prince Regent—Mrs. FitzHerbert is deathly fearful of infections."

The duke of Westermere, who disliked the dissolute monarch and made no secret of it, wrote, *Then why doesn't she leave him*?

The sally was lost on the duchess, who lifted her quizzing glass and turned back to Marigold.

"Hummm, nice frock," Maria Theresa Elizabeth trumpeted, "picked it out yourself, didn't you, Sacheverel?" She focused the glass on Marigold. After a long, critical appraisal she declared, "Hah, rather large gel, no doubt about that, but the dress does her justice."

Marigold remembered what the duke had told her. "Your Grace," she said firmly, "the duke of Westermere has asked me, by your leave, to speak

98

for him since he has, as you can see, a malaise of the vocal cords that the physician has diagnosed as laryngitis. With your gracious permission, Westermere wishes me to—"

"Hah, wishes you to do lots of things, gel, I have no doubt," the duchess interrupted, ignoring the growing line of her guests waiting on the stairs. The large, not-unhandsome face with its big nose and sunburst diadem of diamonds and emeralds peered closely at Marigold. "Don't preen, gel, you're passably pretty," she commanded, rapping Marigold's knuckles rather sharply with the handle of the quizzing glass. "And stand up straight. Tall gels can't slouch."

There was an interruption as the butler had to announce several guests, including the Belgian ambassador and his wife, and the duchess of Luxembourg, and let them go by.

The old lady rather absently gave them a nod and returned the Luxembourg ruler's bow. She immediately turned and boomed at Marigold, "So you're the fiancée, hmmm? I'm told you're the parson's daughter of St. Dunstan's Mere Church in Yorkshire. I'll have you know I give five shillings a year to that living, gel, plus three dozen beeswax candles, five bushels of wheat and two altar cloths. It's all there in the parish records, look it up yourself. King William's clerks set it down in ten-seventy-four."

Marigold was so taken aback, it was a moment before she could say anything. Then she felt bright color flooding her face. What the duchess had said was downright humiliating. The guests waiting behind them had not missed a word.

"I am sure my father thanks you for the five shillings, Your Grace," she finally managed. "And the beeswax candles—and—and the rest." She was surprised that the old duchess knew so much about her father's parish. Or more likely, she'd had her administrators look it up. Then she saw the duke's black eyes watching her.

She tossed her head. Obviously Westermere was enjoying the whole thing. Of course her father received various parish gifts for St. Dunstan's Mere Church, none of them lavish, most ancient in origin, but those from the duchess of Sutherland were not all of it. To quote just five shillings and several bushels of wheat was unfair, and made the living sound even more poverty-stricken than it already was.

It was plain, Marigold told herself, that she was being put down at the duchess of Sutherland's ball to entertain London's Ton. The faces watching on the stair, and above them on the balcony, were avid with interest. Thanks to the duchess, by morning half of London would be repeating that her father received token wages, three dozen candles, baskets of grain and two altar cloths as his annual stipend! Even now several simpering dandies could not hide their grins.

Westermere would have pulled Marigold away and up the stairs, but the old dowager still held her nephew by the arm.

"Odd smell," the duchess said, her big nose

sniffing the air. "Sacheverel, tell me, boy, what is that? Some sort of new scent?"

Marigold and the duke exchanged glances. After two days under a croup tent with a touch of Mrs. Cawdigan's famous coal tar remedy bubbling away in the kettle, the duke still carried some of the essence with him. In fact, Marigold thought she had detected some faint, wafting odor in the coach, but could not quite place it.

It took her but a second to locate it now. When she did, her ever-rebellious spirit rose up, and she was seized by a totally irrepressible kernel of revenge.

"I can explain, Your Grace," she said quickly. "It is, after all, what I am here for, is it not?"

Ignoring Westermere's black-eyed look of warning, she went on, "His Grace is wearing a scent from the East, a *parfum* that is very new. No, actually it's very ancient." She was making up all of this hurriedly, encouraged by the expression on Westermere's face. "They call . . . ah, myrrh. And frankincense," she added, inspired. "Myrrh is all the rage in Constantinople. It's a very potent . . . um, ah, aphrodisiac. Sometimes it is even used for . . . embalming of, ah, mummies!"

The duchess's mouth dropped open.

The duke's face now wore a grim smile, but his hand took Marigold's arm above the elbow in an iron grip.

"Aphrodisiacs? Lud, boy," the old duchess cried, "dissipation will destroy your health—take note of the effect it's had already on your voice! And damme, you're not planning on being fixed up as a heathen mummy, are you?"

Shaking his head no, the duke steered Marigold up the steps and toward the ballroom so fast that her feet hardly touched the ground.

He drew her to one side at the entrance, put his mouth to her ear and whispered, hoarsely, "Don't start the rumor that I use aphrodisiacs."

She jerked her arm out of his grip.

"Hah, sir, and what will you do about the rumors you and your aunt have set in motion about me?" Marigold cried. "That I am your rustic fiancée from an impoverished parsonage family that lives on five shillings a year, a handful of candles and a bushel of wheat, and that our clothes are, presumably, made of altar cloths that your good aunt provides us under charter from William the Conqueror?"

The duke glared at her a long moment before he rasped, "Control yourself. S'all true, no insult intended."

"Nay, sir." Marigold was so angry she stamped her foot. "I shall not be silent when in addition to all that I have mentioned you also have the temerity to flaunt me in public as your fiancée, a disgusting condition to which I have never—never—agreed. Nor has my father! If you persist in this, it is my intention to announce to one and all that your declarations of betrothal to me are all a dastardly fraud!"

At that moment the earl of Desmond, a lanky

youth seemingly not intimidated at all by Westermere, as they had gone to Eton and Oxford together, had come up to claim Marigold's hand for the promenade. The duke, not able to put his voice to anything more, let her go.

"My dear Miss Fenwick," the earl said after he had properly introduced himself, "tell me, has Westermere's Egyptian travels given him a taste for Eastern immortality? Surely you must know the whole room's abuzz with the news that at the appropriate time old Sacheverel intends to soak and tar his remains into a mummy!" The earl smiled down at her devilishly. "I fear Aunt Bessie would detest that. All the Westermeres are very vain about their looks."

Marigold had hardly been listening as they glided through the figures of the French promenade, but "Egyptian travels" caught her attention. The duke of Westermere had visited Egypt? That was interesting.

"It's not something he looks forward to, mummification," she said gravely, as with clasped hands she and the earl formed a "four" with another couple, turned and then glided to the end of the line. "But yes, he may be considering it. Of course, he does not speak of the blinding light of his conversion at Thebes—it is a delicate subject. But whether anyone except his very closest friends realizes it or not, the spiritual revelation changed him greatly. Especially after nearly losing his life when he was thrown into the Pasha of Sudan's pit of crocodiles."

"I say," the earl murmured, impressed. "Pit of crocodiles turned old Satch into a Musselman? You must tell me more."

Marigold did, to the best of her ability. She was relating the duke of Westermere's daring rescue of a Frenchwoman from an Ethiopian harem when the promenade ended, and the earl reluctantly surrendered her to a horde of young men all eager to dance with her and hear the revelations of a Westermere history of which the world had never dreamed.

Now, as the viscount lumbered to the end of the galop, still agog at her account of the Siamese twins joined at the hip that the ninth duke of Westermere had so successfully hidden in a tower, Marigold surveyed the line of partners waiting to claim her for the next set.

Each had a list of burning questions to ask; some looked as though they were bursting with impatience to quiz her about the lofty Westermeres. By now everyone had heard of Sacheverel de Vries's fiancée. At least he claimed that she was his betrothed. She denied it, an unusual enough circumstance in itself. And all were eager to meet her in person. Young Miss Fenwick seemed privy to all the Westermeres' secrets. The duchess of Sutherland's ball had made the duke's lady friend quite the most sensationally original young woman in London.

Beyond the line of eager would-be partners, Marigold could see Sacheverel de Vries watching her, downing glasses of brandy that the duchess's servants were bringing him in relays.

Hah, he had a right to glower, Marigold told herself, and swill all the liquor he wanted! No doubt some of the stories that had so entertained her dancing partners had finally gotten back to him. For a while he'd gone off to the gaming rooms, but apparently the strain of having to communicate through notepaper and pen and ink had driven him out again.

At that moment she saw a group of young men, among them the earl of Desmond, approach Westermere and begin a quite animated conversation. It was so animated that Marigold, watching them, nervously concluded that their talk must have been about Westermere's religious conversion. She was beginning to feel a little apprehensive.

The feeling grew as she viewed his blackbrowed, now perfectly expressionless face as someone clapped him on the shoulder, evidently congratulating him on his newfound spirituality. Or perhaps on his courage in fighting his way out of a tribe of Bedouins' vicious pit of cobras. All the young blades of London's ton were full of admiration.

The duke's expression did not change. Once or twice young Desmond turned and flashed Marigold a cordial smile. Hurriedly, Marigold signaled for one of the duchess's servants to bring her cloak.

She was not sure where she was going; the

duke's house in Horton Crescent, probably. It seemed a good moment to leave.

Unfortunately, just as a footman brought her the long fur cape, Westermere broke away from his friends and swiftly made his way through the crowd to her.

He helped her put the cloak around her shoulders without a word. Ah, Marigold thought a little dizzily as he took her arm, how many tales had she put in circulation that evening, anyway? She couldn't remember.

Perhaps, she told herself, she had gone too far with the hidden Siamese twins and the murder of the seventh duchess suspected of witchcraft. She suddenly did not feel as confident as she had a few hours ago.

Marigold tried to tell herself that she was justified in her imaginative re-creation of Westermere history. It had been only to retaliate for the old duchess's arrogant, mean-spirited way of speaking of her family. And Westermere's continuing humiliation of her.

She faltered as the duke guided her to the wide marble stairs. She knew she might as well broach the subject and get it over with. "You see," she blurted out, "I heard for the first time tonight that you had traveled extensively in . . . um, Egypt."

He did not bother to turn to her. When one was close one did notice a very faint but pungent odor of coal tar. It really was no worse, she tried to tell herself, than some of the pomades many of the dandies wore.

Sacheverel de Vries, twelfth Duke of Westermere, steered Marigold down the mansion's still-crowded stairs. The duchess was not in sight; the Prince Regent and his mistress, Mrs. FitzHerbert, having arrived but a few minutes before, but the butler still shouted the names of the line of guests.

As they waited outside under the marble portal, while frenzied coach boys ran screaming for the duke's carriage to be brought up, Westermere pressed a note into Marigold's slightly trembling hand.

It said simply: *On to Almack's.*

Chapter Eight

"Satch will stay only a few moments at Almack's," Reginald Pendragon had said. "I can swear to you, he hates the place."

Marigold could almost see why. The famed institution consisted of three rooms and plainly looked to be a commercial venture, in spite of its reputation as the gathering place of the standard-setters of London society.

She knew, as did practically everyone who had ever heard of it, that in order to use Almack's, one had to be reviewed and accepted by the owners and pay a yearly subscription of ten guineas, just as in any other London club. Drinks and other refreshments could be had, although the food was said to be notoriously bad. There were gaming rooms, and a ball was held once a week.

Almack's fame rested on the patronage of the elite of London society. It had been a favorite haunt of Beau Brummel, the Prince Regent's great friend and the world of fashion's undisputed authority on dress, manners and snobbery. The autocratic, often cruel Brummel had remained the favored companion of the roistering "Prinny" until their famous falling out.

A governing board of Lady Patronesses set the rules and standards at Almack's. They'd made a terrible scandal when they refused to let England's great hero, the duke of Wellington, enter because he was wearing trousers and not knee breeches. Many thought Almack's had carried its power too far with that high-handed incident. Some of Arthur Wellesley's friends, like the duke of Westermere, had deliberately shunned the place for the remaining months of that year.

But Almack's remained "the" place for the Ton to go and be seen. Prinny brought his latest mistresses there as well as the ever-reliable Mrs. FitzHerbert, and a good many of his cronies followed suit in their liaisons with London's most famous beauties. Still, at the other end of the scale, young girls of reasonably good family who had come "out" were also brought to be displayed by their sponsors looking for good marriage connections.

With all this, Almack's could not help but be a great, seething whirlpool of social activity and gossip. Everyone who was anyone, Beau Brummel had proclaimed, went to Almack's and told everyone else what they'd heard and seen there. One met the high and the low, magistrates and admirals and government ministers and celebrities of dubious means and reputations, including Brummel himself, and even the dissolute members of royalty, beginning with the regent, Prince George of Hanover, and his brothers.

Yet Sacheverel de Vries, Marigold thought as she looked around, in spite of his rumored dislike of Almack's, had a purpose in being there. She was sure of it.

The gossip that had begun at the duchess of Sutherland's ball had swept quickly on to Almack's. If Westermere detested both the place and the rumors that had been set in motion, why were they here, she wondered, right in the midst of it?

Her question went unanswered for, with a nod to the patronesses whose faces reflected both the horror of the stories that had already been carried to them, and avid triumph that the exalted subject himself had shown up, the duke gave Marigold his arm, and they entered through the double doors.

Every head in the room turned their way. The orchestra was not playing. There was a startled silence. In the next moment, voices burst forth with enough volume to make the chandeliers rattle.

Instantly, there was a crush of people around them. Actresses and actors, current beauties, distinguished members of the bar, fops and dandies, dowagers with bashful young ladies in tow, they rushed to the duke of Westermere, all talking—shouting, actually—at once.

Keeping a grip on Marigold by his side, the duke fended them off. She did what he'd told her to do. "I am instructed by His Grace," Marigold said, raising her voice, "to ask that he be excused due to the condition of his throat, which has been attacked by a bout of quinsy that has rendered him quite mute."

Even while she was speaking, Westermere was pushing Marigold none-too-gently toward Almack's buffet room.

"Ah, no," she said in answer to a question from a large man in a hussar's uniform, "the duke of Westermere has not been to India that I know of, nor do I think he has studied Buddhism. He has instructed me to tell you that he will address the subject of eastern religions at such time as he regains his voice."

Something he will never do, Marigold added to herself. A series of scribbled notes in the carriage had given her the duke's opinion of her role as Westermere family historian in no uncertain terms.

I'll cut out your tongue if you do anything like it again, had been one of his milder threats.

Marigold was becoming put off by his manner. In fact, the whole evening had become a strain. As she tucked a strand of pearls back up into the intricate curls of her coiffure, she told herself bitterly that Westermere, when he regained his voice, would no doubt have little trouble persuading London's ton that he had *not* had a religious conversion and become a Musselman, and did *not* intend to be interred as an Egyptian mummy. As for the more exciting episodes of Westermere family history, as related by his guest, Miss Marigold Fenwick, at his Aunt Bessie's ball, these stories had been misunderstood, if not actually misrepresented.

After all, it was his word as a peer of the realm against hers, Marigold told herself with a sigh.

Perhaps the most aggravating thing was that he still insisted on referring to her as his fiancée, a word that grew more hateful to Marigold's ears every time he uttered it. On top of that, who in London after this disastrous evening would not believe that she was the ragtag "parson's brat" from some tumble-down parish in Yorkshire? No, London's Ton would take the word of Westermere and his old dragon of an aunt, no matter how much Marigold insisted on the truth!

And the truth, she quickly had to admit, was not all that impressive. Because for instance, St. Dunstan's Mere *was* little, and the parsonage *was* poor.

More than a little dispiritedly, she allowed herself to be pulled along to Almack's buffet where the duke got himself a brandy and Marigold a fruit tart and a pot of lukewarm tea. Although a curious crowd trailed them, and several well-dressed people tried to introduce themselves, Marigold's role was, as directed by Westermere's flurry of notes, to see that no one lingered by offering the obvious excuse that Westermere could not talk.

He had also commanded her, after the duchess of Sutherland's ball, not to encourage any conversations on her own.

A curious episode, Almack's, Marigold couldn't help thinking as they took their leave a quarter hour later and the duke led her down the stairs to the waiting coach. She wondered if the next stop, at a rout, would be even more mysterious.

It was but a short ride through dark streets. Then the big coach stopped in what Marigold, peering through the windows, guessed to be a shabby part of London near Chelsea that had once been quite fashionable. They could hear the noise of the rout in second-story rooms above them, even before the coach boys flung open the doors.

Marigold looked up at the brightly lit French windows. The curtains were pulled back so that anyone in the street could see there was a goodly crowd inside, an effective form of advertisement. Up there was one of London's famed parties where no food or drink was served, and where there were no orchestras for dancing, nor even, most times, any gaming tables. In most cases one discreetly paid a certain sum at the door and visited with the intention of meeting people.

And what people, she saw as the duke took her arm and they ascended the narrow stairs to the hall above. A crowd had even spilled over outside on the landing. Officers of the cavalry and the militia flirted with young ladies chaperoned by older women who, oddly, did not seem quite the type to be aunts or mothers. A young man in black, surrounded by other attentive young men, was reading a poem to them from a somewhat frayed piece of paper. The sound of so many voices, all talking at once, made Marigold's ears ring.

It was more crowded inside. The rooms were sparsely furnished and looked as though they had once been elegant but that some hard necessity had stripped them of all but a few chairs and settees. Yet they were packed with people. Westermere pushed their way to a swarthy, pretty woman in a dark dress, wearing black plumes with sparkling paillettes in her hair, who seemed to be their hostess.

"Amelia." This was a new Westermere, who bowed gallantly as Marigold stared. He managed to whisper the name with his damaged voice. He lifted the woman's hand to kiss it, then turned and shot Marigold a prompting look.

She knew what he wanted her to do. "Madame," Marigold said, and curtsied, "the duke of Westermere has asked me, by your leave, to speak for him as he has, as you can see, a malaise of the vocal cords that the doc—"

"Ah, Sacheverel," the woman said, and burst out laughing. "Are you still assailed by your one bedeviling weakness? Ah, you proud, lofty devil, you don't know how much your plebeian attacks of quinsy endear you to me!"

She threw her arms around his neck and hugged him, causing people to turn and stare. Releasing him, she turned to Marigold.

"I am Amelia Bentinck, my dear," she explained, "Captain de Vries and I are the dearest of friends. Not too long ago he would come to me when he had an attack of bad throat in the commandant's quarters my husband, General Bentinck, had in Zaragosa. I would dose him with brandy and honey and let him play with the children for an hour or two. Then he would be off again in pursuit of his duty in the rain—lud, it was usually raining in that dreadful place—and the terrible cold, all the while not able to croak a word, you understand. I tell you, the croup was his saving grace. Otherwise he would be too perfect for the likes of mere mortals!"

The war, Marigold thought with an odd sense of relief. After all, even though she was pretty, the general's wife was almost old enough to be his mother.

The duke had been scribbling rapidly on his notepad. He tore off a sheet and handed it to Amelia Bentinck.

Reading it, her smile faded. "It is kind of you to ask. Yes, the children are here, with me, in London, all except Richard, my oldest, who has joined his—his—father's old regiment. And we are making do, as you see," she said, lifting a hand to indicate the crowded room.

When Westermere took out his notepad again, Amelia Bentinck put her hand over it to stop him.

115

Several people pressed around them, waiting to pay the fee to get into the rout.

"We have quite a crowd tonight," she said, hurriedly. "I am promised I will have Lord Byron; some friends have sworn they will bring him and his latest paramour. You can't know how much that will help."

She smiled brightly at two men, who handed her pound notes and slipped inside. She turned and said in a low voice, "It was really too much to keep up the house in Sussex, and I had to let it go. It's Jack we miss, though, sorely, sorely. You know what a good man he was, and what a fine soldier." She blinked as she patted his arm. "Come and see me when you have your voice, and we'll have a long talk."

Mrs. Bentinck abruptly stood on tiptoe and kissed the duke on the cheek and murmured so that Marigold could barely hear, "Satch dear, is this *the one*? Ah, she's lovely and fine, you scoundrel! I hope what I've heard is true, that you are betrothed."

At that moment some guests wanting to be admitted engaged Amelia Bentinck's attention. The duke pulled Marigold away.

"Her husband, the general, is dead?" Marigold tried to keep up with him as they pushed through the crowd.

He nodded. Marigold would have liked more details—the affection between them made her curious. Wellington's soldiers, even those of high rank, lived on very small pensions since Napoleon had been defeated. Unless they were privately wealthy, their families struggled—as it was obvious Amelia Bentinck was doing.

In the larger room, the descriptions she had heard of London's routs were accurate: no food available, no drink unless one stealthily brought one's own, no dancing, no gaming. Instead, there was a crowd of people interested in meeting celebrities and making interesting and influential social connections. Plus a large representation of military officers, who seemed to be doing their best to support their old commander's widow. They greeted the duke of Westermere loudly, then teased him unmercifully when they discovered he was having an attack of his famous affliction. One group of somewhat shabbily dressed young men arguing politics turned out to be writers and journalists. There were several well-known musicians, a smattering of dandyish London bucks, and the usual young girls and their eager relations. Everyone except the famous poet, Lord Byron, who the general's wife hoped would materialize.

Marigold hoped so, too.

She had seen artists' drawings of George Gordon, Lord Byron, in *The Tattler* and other magazines, and he was said to be one of the handsomest men in England, although he suffered a chronic problem with his weight, and was inclined to be chubby in spite of his off-and-on diets limited to draughts of vinegar and water and very little food. Then there was his lameness, as

117

he had been born clubfooted. It had made his life a torment in the past, but now aided Byron in being an even more romantic figure to his many admirers. His scandalous affairs with women were known all over Britain. Some whispered an even more scandalous story, that Byron had even had a child by his half-sister, Augusta.

Marigold had read Byron's "Corsair" and other poems and privately thought his friend, Percy Bysshe Shelley, was the better poet. But Lord Byron was glamorous and greatly admired; if Amelia Bentinck could get him to attend her rout even for an hour it would be a coup, and doubtless attract other "names" in the future.

Some officers who had known the duke in the war came to engage in a one-sided conversation with him. Westermere nodded, wrote a few notes, and even smiled at their stories. But as word circulated through the crowd that Lord Byron and his party were just coming in, Westermere suddenly scowled, grabbed his cloak and Marigold's and took her by the arm.

"Where are we going?" she demanded, as he dragged her toward a small door at the rear of the hall. "We can't leave now! Mrs. Bentinck has had a great triumph; Lord Byron the poet has just arrived!"

He made a growling noise. Evidently the twelfth duke of Westermere had no more admiration for Lord Byron, England's great poet, than he did for the prince regent.

Beyond the door they found themselves in a

back hall where a startled kitchen girl pointed to a flight of steps. Dragging Marigold by the hand, the duke led her through a scullery and out into the street.

At curbside several conveyances were waiting for their owners. The rain had stopped, and a cold wind was blowing. In the east the sky was faintly pink.

"Let go of me!" Marigold cried, pulling her arm out of Westermere's grip. She really didn't want to miss seeing London's great celebrity. "I thought we were out for the evening! Phagh! I shall never allow myself to be cozened and deceived in this way again!"

The duke signaled for his coach parked at the end of the street. Marigold yanked her cloak around her against the chill pre-dawn air. "This has not been a refined social evening on London town, but some sort of mockery, sir! A barefaced jape! For you have dragged me in and out of your aunt's ball, then that dreadful place they call Almack's, and finally a rout held, I gather, for much-needed money by an impoverished military widow, with no sense or purpose. All I have to show for this evening are my dancing slippers, trampled to shreds, half a fruit tart and a weak pot of tea, and a missed opportunity to meet one of England's finest literary figures!"

As usual, Westermere was paying no attention. As the coach drew up, Manuel, who was substituting for Jack Ironside, jumped down from the box. He helped the duke off first with his evening cloak, then his satin coat and weskit. They swapped cloaks, Manuel putting his heavy benjamin with double shoulder capes about Westermere's shoulders and followed it up with his coachman's hat and long woolen scarf. Their eyes met, and both men grinned.

Manuel turned and shouted, "Down, down," to the others on their front and rear perches. To Marigold's surprise, the duke's men jumped down and scrambled into the coach's interior, slamming the doors.

"Lud, what are they doing?" she cried. "Where are we going to ride?"

The young Spaniard took Marigold's elbow to assist her. "*Señor* present now nice drive for milady," he said, soothingly. "He very good driver four-in-hand. Muy excelente!"

Marigold had no idea what the coachman was talking about. But she gasped as he deftly boosted her up over the wheel and to the high driver's seat. She found herself sitting by Westermere's side, looking down at the backs of his coach horses, four powerful, gleaming, matched grays.

Marigold's hands automatically sought the small iron rail that ran around the side of the narrow seat. It was exactly as though she were sitting on the top of a huge, top-heavy mountain, slightly leaning over four giant horses.

The coach was standing still but she could almost feel it swaying. As it surely would as soon as they started up. And oh, dear God, Marigold realized as she turned her head very, very carefully to look at the man beside her, the duke of Westermere was going to drive!

For a moment her mind went blank. Then she heard Manuel joining the others safely inside the coach. "Please, please let me down," Marigold whispered.

She was not at all interested in finding out if driving a coach four-in-hand was one of the duke of Westermere's many talents. He had jammed Manuel's wide-brimmed hat on his head, twined the rein for each horse about his fingers, and taken his foot off the brake. At his whistle the horses started off with a clatter of hooves through Chelsea.

"What are you doing to me?" Marigold cried, as the full motion of the coach from the high driver's seat picked her up and swung her from side to side. Her fingers were frozen to the bar, which was the only thing, she felt, that kept her from being flung off into the air.

At her cry, the duke turned to her. She saw the flash of white teeth from under the brim of the coachman's hat before he turned his attention back to the team.

Picking up speed, the Westermere coach flew down through London, heading south toward the Thames. The weather had broken and a cold wind filled the pre-dawn sky with scudding clouds under pinprick stars. But the streets, except for an occasional lamp post, were still dark.

Unfortunately, at a corner near the Tower of London, the speeding coach came upon a dray going to market and squeaked past it without slowing, with a hairbreadth to spare.

The duke's men inside cheered their driver's daring and skill. Marigold, speechless with terror, hung on to the seat with both hands. When she opened her eyes they were past the wagon, although the driver's enraged curses hung in the air behind them.

Westermere turned the plunging horses toward the southbound road that ran along London's docksides. He seemed to be enjoying himself thoroughly. The wind had torn at the satin tie on his peruke and his black hair had come loose, giving him a gypsyish look. He looked like a working man making his living as some noble's coachman.

The highway along London's docks was paved with wooden blocks, ballasts taken from ships they could see as dark shapes at anchor in the great river. The surface of the wood block road was, compared to the city's rutted streets, smooth and even. They headed southward toward Greenwich.

Expecting, correctly, that the duke would open up the team on the straightaway, Manuel leaned out the window below and blew a blast on the coach horn. The instrument the Spaniard used was not the famed "yard of steel" of the commercial conveyances that linked England, but a fine brass instrument from France, decorated with the Westermere coat of arms.

Manuel blew several blasts, although at that

hour there appeared to be no one on the road to warn. As the mellow tootling penetrated the river mist, the men inside the coach cheered anyway.

Marigold's cloak blew open, but she was afraid to let go of the rail long enough to catch it and pull it around her. The wind blew from the river, and the wild speed of the coach created its own gale: She could feel the loops of pearls in what was left of her elaborate coiffure rattling and coming loose.

With her cloak open and the hood blown back, she was unbearably cold. But there was nothing that could be done about it. The coach careened at maddening speed down the highway, propelled by the duke's reckless humor. Was he trying to frighten her? she wondered wildly. Was this his idea of revenge? Or was Westermere merely giving vent to a wish for freedom, leaving the constraints and frivolity of London's elite, the boredom of the evening, far behind?

Marigold told herself that she should be accustomed by now to these eccentric outbursts that seemed so much a part of the duke of Westermere's lifestyle. Since they had turned onto the river highway, she had been praying rather raggedly under her breath. This was not some nobleman's half-drunken whim. Nor was it the action of some brash dandy of the ton indulging himself as his own coachman, with horses and coach boys and servants, after a roistering night on the town.

"Awwk!" Marigold screamed as the coach left

the wood-paved highway with a jolt that lifted her several inches from her seat, its wheels dropping down to a dirt surface. They were passing long wharves now near the pool of London, and the sky had lightened considerably. Through fog drifting on the Thames they could see ocean-bound sailing ships in the process of being loaded. Some of the dockhands stopped work to watch the Westermere coach fly past, and raised a cheer.

By now Marigold had stopped praying for her immortal soul, leaving that task for the time being with the vicar, her father. She was grimly determined not to have Westermere give her a fatal heart attack if she could help it. She took a deep breath, but just as she did so the duke's foot moved to the brake as he began to rein in the sweating, blowing grays. They were slowing down!

I want to get down, Marigold thought desperately. But she had enough strength left to clamp her teeth together. She would never give in. Westermere deserved her tales at the duchess's ball. She was not sorry at all that she'd punctured some of the famed Westermere arrogance. After all, look at the way he had treated her! This whole excursion into London, the duchess's ball, Almack's, the rout, had used her for some dastardly, humiliating purpose, she was sure!

With a grinding of the brake, and Westermere's shouts to the horses, they came to a stop.

"Here," Westermere called, pulling off the

coachman's hat and jumping down from the high seat, as Manuel ran around to take the horses' heads. The duke's voice was a still a hoarse rasp but the cold air had restored some of it.

They had drawn up in the cobblestoned courtyard of a seamen's inn, the Oar and Anchor, somewhere south of London. The rest of Westermere's men piled out of the interior of the coach, marveling at the speed with which they had made it there. Some sort of record had been set, apparently. There was praise for the duke, should he ever give up the peerage and want to take work as a coachman. He'd be the best in England.

Westermere handed the benjamin back to Manuel and retrieved his own cloak, then gave the other a handful of coins with instructions to buy everyone a half-yard of ale, a brandy for himself, and with extra hurry, a mug of tea, very hot, for Miss Fenwick.

Ostlers from the inn swarmed around the coach, unhitching the steaming horses. The duke himself climbed the wheel, pried Marigold's fingers loose, and lifted her down.

As Westermere disentangled her grip from the rail, carried her over the wheel and set her on her feet, she told herself that by all that was holy Westermere knew exactly what he had done, scaring her half out of her wits with a wild, reckless ride down the Thames where, several times, she was sure he had skillfully avoided disaster. Each time, those idiot men of his in the coach had roared and cheered!

But instead of lashing out at him, Marigold slumped against the duke's tall frame with a woeful lack of dignity, and clung to him with a sound that was distressingly like a moan of relief.

Hold me, she wanted to say. *Just hold me and never put me back on that dreadful conveyance!* It was a good thing her face was pressed tightly into the front of his cloak and she could not utter the words, for he seemed to be smiling.

"Come, come, call on your indomitable feminine spirit, Miss Fenwick," he rasped, "and do not do anything so lacking in integrity as to faint in a public place." But his fingers gently tucked back her windblown hair and the disordered, dangling strands of pearls. "Surely you know that liberated ladies of independent spirit ride the coaches every day without swooning afterward into the nearest gentleman's arms?"

That did it.

Marigold pried herself away from him, eyes flashing. "You, sir," she said, fully restored, "are—"

She didn't have time to finish. A familiar figure came toward them, making its way across the Oar and Anchor's courtyard. "Cargo all safe and accounted for, Captain," Jack Ironfoot said when he reached them. The coachman's eyes slid to Marigold and he grinned. "And on its way to Buenos Aires, the good Lord willing, and all the rest well and safe, too. A good couple of day's work, sir, if

126

I do say so myself. Just like the old days."

They clasped hands. Nothing more seemed to be required. Then Jack turned toward the coach to go check what the others were doing. "It's a heavenly dream, it is, to be able lay my head on a soft pillow and catch up on my sleep at last," he muttered. "As it's little I've had since I left Your Grace."

"Here's your tea," the duke of Westermere said to Marigold, taking the steaming mug from Manuel and handing it to her. "Drink up. You'll find it hot enough this time."

Chapter Nine

After one heard the story it made sense, Marigold supposed, as she lifted the filled tray full of specimens labeled: ROPE, HEMP, FIBERS OF, and set it to one side with other trays that were stacked on the big library table.

Jack Ironfoot, the coachman, and Reggie Pendragon, coming in and out of the cavernous library to discuss various details of the adventure's aftermath with the duke of Westermere, had made no attempt to lower their voices or try to conceal anything from her. So it was not very long before Marigold was able to put together the account of that extraordinary evening that encompassed the duchess of Sutherland's ball, Almack's, Amelia Bentinck's rout, and the daredevil ride down to the docks south of London to pick up Jack Ironfoot.

Now, as though she had somehow become a part of his regular schedule, the duke gave Marigold no further explanation, but left her an accumulation of work each morning before he left for his ride in nearby Rotten Row.

He never invited her to accompany him on the bridle path that was the gathering place for London's elite. Which was just as well. Marigold did not consider herself an accomplished horsewoman. The vicarage had only one small gig in need of repair and had not been able to afford the upkeep of a horse for years. Consequently, Marigold's childhood experiments in trying to ride the unpredictable village nags and ponies with Sophronia and Penelope had been highly unsatisfactory, if not actually dangerous to life and limb.

Every morning the duke came to the library exactly at the stroke of eight, looking big and handsome in highly polished Hessians, tight riding coat and even tighter riding breeches, to sit down beside her at the big table to explain why it was important to catalogue various fibers so that, if left at the scene of a crime, each would tell its own story.

Before she'd begun sorting out Westermere's rather odd collections, Marigold had never known there were so many varieties of rope, made in so many different ways. Some were plain, ordinary hemp twists, thick as hawsers. Some were made of silk or horsehair and as intricately knotted as macramé, the craft work sailors did at sea.

The rope samples she'd been working on lately were taken mostly from sailing ships, but a few came from other places, such as stables and farms, and one from Reading jail. Marigold tried not to think about the hemp pieces she was neatly folding, labeling and storing that might once have been part of a hangman's deathly kit.

With a voice that was still faintly hoarse from his bout with laryngitis, Westermere carefully explained that a rope could be a very damaging piece of evidence in criminal cases. Rope could pinpoint what sort of ship it came from, for instance, or even the ship's nationality. In England, one could often identify the district where the rope was made. Fibers under the microscope, if the British courts could be persuaded to accept such evidence, would help convict criminals, he was sure of it.

Listening to him, one could not miss how deeply he felt when he spoke of the use of the microscope in England's courts.

They sat side by side at the big table. Often their knees touched as the duke reached across to bring a sample tray within reach. Watching him, Marigold could not help but note somewhat wearily that Westermere was so good-looking, so confident of his enormous privilege, that he wore it like his own skin.

The thought made her quite discouraged. She knew Westermere would not listen to anything she might say on the subject of the villages and factories the Westermere dukes had held in thrall for centuries, and so ruthlessly exploited. Yet he was so eloquent in his arguments for the use of science in the cause of justice. Those bold black brows drew down over his nose as he uttered convincing, condemnatory words about incompetent magistrates on the bench. He even had, Marigold couldn't help noticing rather dreamily, remarkably satiny skin where most men, she had observed, were inclined to a little roughness, sometimes even the remains of the pitting of adolescence.

Now he seemed to feel her scrutiny, for he stopped, looked at her, and then asked if she was paying attention.

From then on she made it a point to watch him more discreetly. In fact, she was changing her mind about the duke of Westermere, and it puzzled her. For one thing, his men loved him. Passionately. Jack Ironfooot, Dr. Pendragon and men named Merce, Mortimer and Walters had gathered in the library before the fire with their mugs of ale to discuss the events of that memorable evening in London. And they'd disclosed that Westermere had been their company commander in the duke of Wellington's army in Spain. Specifically, a detachment of riflemen sharpshooters, those envied technicians of the infantry.

It was plain that his war comrades considered Westermere the nonpareil warrior. One often told anecdote fondly followed another. There was the story of Westermere rescuing a bewildered cat stranded on a barricade at Badajoz by dashing out in the face of a fusillade from Napoleon's troops, only to have the ungrateful animal deliver itself of a batch of kittens on the floor of his tent that evening. There was also one of Westermere leading a raiding party of his ragged, hungry men on the supplies of some of the prince regent's dearest cronies who'd been luxuriously touring the war with servants and baggage for some entertaining sightseeing, coming away with several roast chickens, a ham, and a barrel of wine. The duke had been carrying a severely wounded Merce Coffin, a big man who weighed almost as much as Westermere himself, on his back for four miles through enemy lines to safety.

From what his old army comrades said, more than once the duke of Westermere had turned down promotions to major, even higher rank on Wellington's staff, to remain and fight with his men.

The reason for that, Westermere had retorted jokingly, was that he did not trust them to do a damn thing right on their own. He'd had to keep an eye on them even if it meant staying a lowly rifle company commander the entire war.

The ex-soldiers who had rescued one of their old comrades from the Bristol jail did not stay long in London; with the exception of Jack Ironfoot and the doctor they were eager to return to their homes and families. But listening to them, Marigold began to understand more of what had happened that night of the duchess of Sutherland's ball.

While Westermere was in London, very visibly squiring Marigold through an evening of entertainments, Jack Ironfoot, the rifle company's old sergeant, had led the others in a daring breakout at Bristol jail. With the help of a few well-bribed bailiffs, Oris Ludberry had been led through an underground sewer before the appointed hour of his hanging, stuffed in the bed of a victualer's wagon, taken from the city to a fishing boat in a cove some miles up the coast, and from the fishing boat transferred to a ship bound for Buenos Aires. There, it was assumed, he could look forward to a free and happy future.

While this was going on, they'd made sure no suspicion could possibly fall on the duke. For although Westermere had previously pleaded with the magistrates at Bristol to consider further evidence in Ludberry's case—and therefore was under suspicion in any successful escape attempt— it was plain the duke was in London attending a ball at his aunt's, an assembly at Almack's and a rout that night in the company of his fiancée, who, witnesses would attest, was a stunningly handsome vicar's daughter from a small village in Yorkshire.

It was just like the old days, Westermere's men said, laughing and congratulating themselves.

Just as daring, by God, as some of the tricks they'd played on old Boney behind his lines.

After a few shy glances at Marigold across the room, they offered a toast to the very good health of the young miss who had lent her gracious presence to the adventure.

And not only that, Merce Coffin added, grinning, this young lady was a proper sport to endure the captain when he had a whim to be on the box of a four-in-hand. The whole world knew that when Captain de Vries fancied a spell for himself as a coachman, good Christians fled for their lives.

They all laughed uproariously at this. Marigold pretended to ignore them. She remembered that ride on the high coachman's box coming down the Thames all too well; Westermere had been working off the peculiar mood of the evening—she understood that much now. But she also understood that the hair-raising exhibition of driving had been aimed at her, too, to pay her back for the stories she'd told at the duchess's ball.

As she carefully laid samples of rope fibers in their little slots, she told herself that she refused to feel guilty. Of course Westermere had used her. He could not have gone out alone. What would he have done without her with his case of laryngitis that kept him from doing little more than write on his paper pad and make a dumb show? She'd had her suspicions about their "gala evening" from the time she put on her ball gown until the hour they returned to the Horton Crescent mansion.

And his "parsonage fiancée" indeed! She saw now she'd quite simply suited his plans.

"The banns," Reggie Pendragon, who was quite gleefully tipsy, reminded them. "Got to have banns. She's a marvel, Satch, the most beautiful woman I've ever seen, but one can't have a fiancée in one's household like this without posting the banns. Must make everything proper and legal."

"Oh, I intend to," the duke said, his black eyes surveying Marigold over the rim of his ale cup. "I intend to take care of that shortly."

Marigold heard him, but said nothing. She had her own schemes, she told herself. At the moment she was busy thinking about them, and sorting them out.

The former members of the duke's company of riflemen were not the only visitors to Horton Crescent. Westermere entertained at dinner once a week with notable acquaintances such as Sir Robert Peel, who'd also fought in the Peninsular war, and who was now devoting his energies and considerable influence to the reform of the Bow Street Runners. Most of Peel's interests had to do with crime, and the duke was deeply interested.

London's constables, who were the only police force for most of the city, had become as corrupt and unmanageable as the criminal element they were supposed to control. By contrast, periodicals such as *The Observer* pointed out that the problem could have a positive outcome. The Thames River Police, created by the West India Trading company a decade earlier to curb the thefts that plagued the world's largest port, was a notable success. Patrick Colquhoun, hired to be director of the Thames police, had a permanent staff of eighty, and an on-call staff of over a thousand. The Thames River officers had regular patrols, which tended to suppress crime, and received salaries, a big improvement over the Bow Street Runners' stipends that had led to so much bribery and general dishonesty.

Another regular guest was the duke's longtime Quaker friend, Joseph Jackson Lister, a London wine merchant whose experiments had played an important part in the development of the non-color-distorting achromatic microscope.

There were others, too: journalists and writers, solicitors and barristers, and politician friends of Bobby Peel, who was planning soon to run for the House of Commons. At the duke's request, Marigold took her place as his hostess, but regularly retired soon after the last course was served and the brandy and cordials brought in. Everyone seemed to accept her role as the duke of Westermere's fiancée, although she was sure a few of them thought the title merely a substitute for "mistress."

However, as Marigold had been told over and over again, the Westermeres were a law unto themselves. Their eccentricities were known all over England. Rich and incredibly powerful, they expected to be taken at their word. "Fiancée" seemed good enough, at least for those who gathered in Horton Crescent.

Besides, they were gentlemen: Marigold was never treated with anything but the utmost respect.

Dinner, she thought, was seldom boring. Free speech was indulged to an almost scandalous extent. Most of those who came to Westermere's table were not admirers of Prince George of Hanover, the son of King George the Third, now prince regent. At one rather boisterous gathering of young peers down from Oxford, the earl of Salisbury's son stood up and recited Percy Shelley's attack on the royal family from memory.

"An old, mad, blind, despised and dying king—
Princes, the dregs of their dull race, who flow
Through public scorn—mud from a muddy spring,
Rulers who neither see, nor feel, nor know,
But leech-like to their fainting country cling,
Till they drop, blind in blood, without a blow,
A people starved and stabbed in the untilled field,
An army, which liberticide and prey
Makes a two-edged sword to all who wield,
Golden and sanguine laws which tempt and slay;
Religion Christless, Godless—a book sealed;
A Senate—Time's worst statute unrepealed,
Are graves, from which a glorious Phantom may
Burst, to illumine our tempestuous day."

Even before young Salisbury had finished there were calls for order from the guests around the table, some laughter, and a growl from someone not to talk treason. The young man was pulled back down into his seat. His fellow students, sons of the highest peers of the land, were cheering him loudly.

Marigold had listened, fascinated. She knew some of Shelley's poetry but never dreamed that he espoused such revolutionary ideas. It was plain that the verse was an attack on the royal family and critical of England's condition. The poem did speak in its closing lines about a "glorious phantom."

Who could that be? she wondered. Most of the wealthy men at the table looked uneasy at the brash recitation. Except Robert Peel. But then the reformer had already made his ideas on political change well-known in speeches and in the press.

For the most part, the duke of Westermere seemed indifferent to political talk unless it concerned his pet interests of science and the systems of justice. Now he was signaling to Marigold that he wanted her to call Pomfret to have the table cleared and the brandy brought in.

Catching Pomfret's eye and setting the process in motion, Marigold stood up, ready to leave the men to their tobacco and their port. But as she retired to the parlor and a book she had been reading, she was thinking about the mission that had brought her to London.

Marigold had not forgotten the reason she was there. How could she, when she'd received letters that past week, from both Sophronia Stack and

Penelope MacDougal, gently chiding her about her overlong stay in the duke of Westermere's London house? Without, seemingly, any progress to report?

Marigold told herself somewhat unhappily that the two of the three cavaliers who remained in Stokesbury Hatton would surely hear accounts, or read of them in such papers as *The Tattler* and *The Observer*, of Miss Fenwick's appearances at balls and routs, escorted by her "betrothed" and one of London's greatest catches, the duke of Westermere. With, of course, the usual descriptions of her gown and jewels.

Marigold put down her book and frowned. It was useless to try to read when worrisome thoughts intruded. She wouldn't blame Sophronia and Penelope if, lacking the true facts, they came to the conclusion that the monster Westermere had won her over, probably seduced her, completely deflecting her from what had once been their sacred cause—to persuade him to come to the relief of their suffering, poverty-stricken village.

Marigold closed her eyes, remembering that afternoon she'd sat in the library with her dear friend Penelope. And Penelope's astonishment at the idea of the duke's wanting to marry her.

When Marigold tried to explain the circumstances of the duke's marriage offer, there had been Penelope's abrupt about-face, and her pragmatic suggestion that, since they could not move Westermere through public scandal and humiliation as per their original plan, they should conquer by feminine guile!

At first Marigold rejected the idea. Its deceptions sounded as though they incorporated all that Mary Wollstonecraft so eloquently denounced in her writings.

Yet the more she saw of Westermere in his everyday surroundings, as she helped him do his scientific studies and experiments—and particularly as she noticed how much his men still worshipped him—the more her opinion of him changed. He seemed to have an admirably open mind, as evidenced by his enlightened, influential London friends who came to his house and gave free exchange of liberal ideas around his dinner table. This gave Marigold the feeling that their plan might not yet be lost.

As she stared down at the book in her hand, she entertained the thought that if Westermere could not be blackmailed into charity and responsibility toward his villages, perhaps he could be converted!

Of course, she also remembered Penelope's outrageous talk about seducing the man, and arousing such feelings of passion in him that he could not deny her smallest request. Her smallest requests were, naturally, a clinic for Sophronia's father, a new schoolhouse, and so forth.

That would take a lot of unbridled passion, Marigold thought, biting her lip; she was hardly sure she could rise to the effort. But perhaps there was another way.

Suddenly she remembered Penelope stammering, just as Westermere sneaked up on them in the library. *Perhaps a loving, self-respecting, virtuous woman could make him see the error of his ways, and cause him to give his money freely!*

Loving, self-respecting, virtuous.

Marigold thought it over. Mary Wollstonecraft herself would have no trouble with that.

First came "friendship" between a man and a woman, Wollstonecraft had written. And respect for each other's God-given intellectual rights.

Then after "friendship" and "respect" came the final expression—physical intimacy.

Marigold sighed.

She didn't want to dwell on the difficulties. If she could change Westermere into a great and altruistic peer, what a wonderful accomplishment that would be! With his wealth and power he could alleviate such suffering, bring about so much good, beginning in one small place—Stokesbury Hatton! It made her giddy just to think of it.

Well, first must come friendship, she thought, looking around the drawing room. They'd hardly had time to cultivate that so far. Being adversaries seemed to come more naturally.

To achieve Mary Wollstonecraft's friendly accord between equals, they should spend more time together. The trouble was, Marigold had hardly seen the duke the past few days except when he entertained at dinner, and at their morning sessions over his scientific work in the library.

141

He did play whist, she remembered. It was too bad that vicarage life did not encourage such frivolous pastimes as cards. She had no knowledge of the game, and whenever she played other games with Sophronia and Penelope, her friends invariably trounced her.

Yet it would undoubtedly stimulate the duke's friendly feelings to beat her at whist. Men, she had been told, loved that sort of thing. It made them feel quite superior and—well, friendly.

However, Marigold also knew she played so miserably, she was sure arrogant Westermere would grow tired of it. She wanted to woo his friendship, not antagonize him. Then her eyes fell on one of the drawing room's small tables with a chessboard and pieces.

Chess, she thought with delight.

She often played with her father. Chess was an excellent game.

Marigold suddenly knew, with as much certainty as she had ever known anything, that this was where the first stage of friendship with the duke of Westermere would begin.

Chapter Ten

"The bishop has read the banns," the duke of Westermere said as he seated himself at the drawing room chess table on the side of the "blacks." "Last Sunday in the Church of—"

He paused and looked up at Pomfret, who was bringing in a tray with glasses and a bottle of Bulgarian apricot cordial. They had come into the drawing room after dinner and the duke had agreed to play a game.

"The Church of St. James Viterbius the Lesser, Your Grace," the old butler murmured. "You will remember your great-uncle, the marquess of Dolby, endows the choir school there."

"Ah, yes, that one." Westermere settled himself in his chair and looked down at the chessboard. He was attired in a very handsome white silk shirt, loose-belted lounge jacket and, in the popular new style, tight-fitting long trousers. "Nice little church, near Cheapside. Has a Norman or Saxon something or other."

"Bell tower, Your Grace," Promfret supplied in an undertone as he set the tray with a cordial bottle and glasses on a nearby marble-topped table. "Saxon, circa 966. And a Roman vault with intact sarcophagi."

Westermere picked up his ebony king to examine it. "I told the bishop to get a hurry on and read the banns and get them out of the way. Then we'll have a nice short marriage ceremony."

Marigold, who had just seated herself opposite the duke on the side of some beautifully carved ivory chess pieces, bit back the retort that sprang to her lips. Her first reaction was thorough annoyance that she hadn't been consulted about any reading of the banns. Nor had she agreed to a public announcement of any betrothal, read by the bishop or not. It just showed that, with his usual high-handedness, Westermere was choosing to ignore everything she'd said to him on the subject.

When Pomfret offered her a glass of the apricot liqueur, Marigold shook her head.

Westermere was perfectly aware that, as a follower of Mary Wollstonecraft, she believed in true freedom of love between a man and a woman. That is, once she was certain in her own mind, the formality of marriage to him or anyone else was totally unnecessary.

She could see that he didn't seem to be able to grasp that idea. Or more likely, she told herself, he didn't want to.

Marigold sighed. She knew if she challenged the duke of Westermere on the subject of having the banns read without even telling her about it when they were about to spend what she hoped would be a convivial evening over the chess table—the first step in her plan to develop trust and friendship—it would only bring about an unpleasant confrontation. And Westermere's confrontations could be very wearing. As it was, he was scowling down at the ivory and ebony pieces on the chessboard as though he already regretted agreeing to spend the evening this way.

"Damme, are you sure you don't play cards?" he growled. "Chess is a slow, picky game. Waste of time, if one's looking for entertainment."

Marigold waited a moment before she answered. Even then she couldn't keep a certain waspish note out of her voice. Chess was her father's delight; she'd spent many wonderful, exciting hours over the chessboard with him. She might have known someone like Westermere wouldn't appreciate it.

She managed a thin smile. "La, it would pain me deeply to think I have influenced you to squander your time, Your Grace, when you are convinced you might be better amused elsewhere. However, I would not have suggested chess if you had not assured me you knew how to play."

Katherine Deauxville

He gave her a bland look as Pomfret handed him a glass of the cordial. "Oh, I know how to play." His black eyes lingered on Marigold's hair, which was piled in curls anchored with a Spanish tortoise-shell comb, and dropped down to her bared shoulders and the creamy curves of the deep décolletage revealed by the green velvet gown. "Chess is just not my passion, that's all." Still regarding her thoughtfully, he put down his glass. "Shall we begin?"

Marigold was not going to ask what his passion was; she was determined to maintain a mood that would lead to something resembling Mary Wollstonecraft's ideal of friendship.

But the duke had been honest when he'd admitted his talent was not great at chess. She soon found he was an aggressive though not very skilled player who got into trouble almost at once, losing a bishop and two knights to her. However, Marigold could not help but admire the way he concentrated more carefully after that, finally gathering his scattered forces to put up a slashing, if somewhat unnecessarily reckless, attack.

It was a shame to put his king in check, but the vulnerable position of his pieces practically forced her to do it.

When she did, the duke of Westermere sat for a long moment looking down at the chessboard, a peculiar expression on his face. "Is the game over when you do that?" he said finally.

"Not if you can find a way to rescue your king," Marigold replied gently.

146

He did not look at her. With one hand he swept all the pieces together in the middle of the board and said flatly, "Then you win, Miss Fenwick, and we will start over again."

Something in all this made Marigold begin to regret that they had agreed to play chess after dinner. One game, actually, was all she'd had in mind. A leisurely affair, punctuated with good, sociable talk. With the duke's declaration of a second game, she sensed they were somehow not going to achieve that level of promising civility.

All her life Marigold had heard her father compare chess to a miniature war, with its kings, queens, knights and bishops doing intricate battle across the board. From the moment the second game started she wondered if whoever had originally made the comparison had not had the opportunity to observe Sacheverel de Vries, twelfth duke of Westermere. The man had been in a real war and was capable, once he put his mind to it, of turning a game of chess into something resembling the real thing. Knights did not advance, they charged. Castles thundered, rooks deployed like infantry. The table shook every time he moved a piece.

Marigold was completely aghast. Her little ivory chessmen were being used for moves no experienced chess player would ever attempt. It was chaos. And he was winning!

In an amazingly short time the duke of Westermere checkmated her, taking the second game. "That's more like it," he said, looking satisfied.

Marigold watched him set up the pieces for a third game. "You can't play chess like that," she protested. "The object is not to—to—capture all your opponent's pieces in that way, for goodness' sake! In fact, it is evidence of a skillful game to be as economical in your moves as possible and leave some—"

He gave her a glittering look. "I'm sending for Madame Rosenzweig to make you a gown for the marriage ceremony. Something in pink."

She could see that, in addition to the barbaric way he was playing, the duke wished to provoke her to some argument about marriage. She was just as determined to resist it.

Marigold moved her rook and said, "If I—and I only—should determine that our friendship, mutual respect and affection, Your Grace, should eventually bring us to physical intimacy, it will not be necessary for us to be married."

He promptly captured her pawn *en passant*. "Don't be a ninny. And don't quote me that subversive Wollstonecraft drivel. Every damned female in London wants to marry me. Mothers practically lay their daughters on my doorsteps in the morning for me to trip over when I go out. Besides, I have no desire to take you as a mistress. It's legitimate children I'm interested in, not a houseful of handsome bastards."

Marigold gasped. She immediately captured one of his knights and put his king in check.

"Sir," she spluttered, "you are certainly not doing much to impress me with our potential for friendship, respect and affection to speak of me in such proprietary terms! Handsome bastards, indeed! And—and mistresses. How coarse!"

"Coarse? Hah," he shot back, "how damned refined is your idiot idea you just proposed, of diddling me without benefit of clergy?" He bent his head to the board, viewing the checkmate suspiciously. "What did you do just then?"

"It's called a Malay conversion," Marigold said, more calmly. "It's one of the many moves my father and I—"

"The devil you say!" The duke of Westermere bounded up from the chess table, overturning his chair, his expression wrathful. "A Malay—what?"

His reaction was excessive; Marigold refused to respond to it. Instead she said calmly, "There are many forms of chess, Chinese, Korean, Japanese, and Malay, where chess, as we know it, originated. As well as the western form we have been playing. However, certain moves have been accepted—"

"The devil take damned Malay whatever-it-is," the duke snarled, making for the door to the library. "Here in England we call it cheating!"

Marigold jumped up and followed him into the big room. He had already moved the library ladder and was climbing it, obviously searching for something on the upper shelves.

Marigold went to the ladder and took hold of one of the lower rungs with both hands. "How dare you accuse me of such a vile thing as cheating?" she cried, looking up.

He was several feet above her, pulling out books on the subject of chess and letting them drop a half-story to the floor.

One almost hit her as he barked, "Miss Fenwick, your outraged virtue amazes me, considering that when you threw yourself into my coach in Covent Garden you were prepared to stage a false assault on your person and blackmail me as a consequence, claiming that I had tried to rape you. I will skip over your display of public nudity that followed," he went on, "and remind you that you further stated to one of your insurgent female comrades wearing hideous clothes in this very room that you would consider enticing me into a witless state of lust and then seducing me." She stepped aside as he climbed down the ladder with an armful of books and dumped them on the library table. With his back to her, he said, "Now tell me why you would object to my observation that you also cheat at chess."

Marigold opened her mouth, but no words came out.

Westermere was going through the books, tossing them across the table, looking, she supposed, for verification of the ill-fated Malay chess move. She was sorry, now, that she'd used it. It was a valid move, but it would take him all night to find it. Or he might not find corroboration at all if the books were out of date.

She regretted, too, that she also had to admit

that nearly everything Westermere had said was true. She had jumped into his coach and bared herself to all the world and tried to blackmail him. There was a good reason behind all her actions, the welfare of suffering people, but the way the duke put it she felt a sudden, certainly undeserved, feeling of shame.

Lud, after that recital of a list of all the things she'd done, no wonder he thought she would cheat at chess.

She sat down at the big table and watched him rummaging through old books on games of all kinds. Her hopes for a companionable evening were just about destroyed, thanks to this awkward dispute. And her goal of an affectionate, mutually respectful friendship that would change Westermere and guide him to a better appreciation of his duties to his poverty-stricken people seemed far, far away.

"I don't see anything about damned Malay chess," he was muttering, putting another book aside. "Nor yet a damned thing about Chinese or Japanese versions."

There was not much she could think of to say. Marigold propped her chin on her hand and studied the line of his jaw, noting once again his remarkably silky skin, the thickness of his long eyelashes.

Suddenly, sitting right there, she had the most astonishing return of the feeling that had attacked her in the duke's bedroom when they were gathered there for his sponge bath. That big, masculine body, even though he was at the moment ignoring her, sent her the same peculiar, wildly sensual message. It was so strong that her own senses positively quivered in response.

Marigold had an irresistible desire to reach out and touch Sacheverel de Vries. To stroke his smooth-shaven cheek, actually, with the back of her hand.

The next moment she realized that what she was experiencing was a vastly affectionate emotion. Her whole body tingled with it.

She felt dizzy. And she recognized the evening over chess was a failure. Worse, she certainly had not enhanced her character in his eyes. At least she could say that her own feelings toward Westermere had somewhat mysteriously improved. Perhaps there was hope yet.

Perhaps, Marigold thought, it was time to go on to the next step.

"There's no—" the duke began, turning to her with an open book in his hand. He stopped, abruptly, when he observed her staring at him.

"I think," she said before he could speak, "now is the time to progress to ah—uh, physical intimacy. Would tonight, Your Grace, be convenient for you?"

In the hallway just outside the library the old butler, Promfret, had paused with the silver tray with its glasses and bottle of cordial, having gone into the drawing room a few moments before to tidy up.

After some fifty years and more in the household on Horton Crescent, most of them spent as an eminently trusted retainer privy to the most confidential Westermere family happenings, Pomfret was a master eavesdropper. Even as he lingered by the open library door he gave the impression, tray in hand, of still being in motion. But Pomfret had heard every word that was said between the duke and young Miss Fenwick in the library, and some of the conversation before that, in the drawing room, over chess. None of what he heard surprised him, although all of it was interesting.

However, when Pomfret saw the tall figure in a black cape looming suddenly in the rear recesses of the downstairs hallway, he hobbled away from the library doorway and went to meet it.

The figure was Jack Ironfoot, standing in the shadows at the door to the back stairs and servants' quarters.

"Well, Pommy," the coachman asked in a low voice, "is His Grace in for the evening, or will he go out?"

The old butler moved past him, tray and hand, through the door to the back staircase. The odor of onions and roasting meat drifted up to them from the kitchen. Only when the door closed behind them did the butler answer.

"I would say it appears that His Grace," Pomfret said in his usual sepulchral tone, "will be sleeping in tonight."

"Hah! The captain's working late with the

young miss, is he then?" Jack winked hugely, which the older man ignored. "Well then, if the captain is safely in to stay, I'm out in the streets to do my business. And a dangerous business it's getting to be, I'll tell you, after Bristol."

With that, Ironfoot turned and went down the stairs.

At the same hour, forty miles away in the township of Swindon, the rain was still coming down in chill, wind-driven bursts that buffeted anyone sprinting from the kitchen door of the Red Knight and Sword to the entrance to the stables. Puddles had formed in the quagmire behind the inn's outbuildings that were almost ankle deep, and the footing was treacherous. But the head groom, Barry Durston, plowed through the mud with considerable haste. He'd had an urgent summons to come examine a particularly fine gelding, property of the duke of Westermere, that had been left at the Red Knight to recover from lameness. The young groom who'd come on duty at seven o'clock had sent a message up to the inn that, in his opinion, the horse appeared to have been tampered with.

Propelled by a final gust, Barry stepped through the stable doors and tossed his dripping cloak onto a peg over the feed bins.

"What do we have here, now?" he inquired briskly of the groom. "The duke's throughbred's been tampered with? Nonsense, Tim me boy, nobody's allowed in the box stalls but the proper identified patrons, you know that."

The young groom looked uncertain. "See for yourself. I don't want to tell you what I think, not until you've seen it." He led the way down the aisle past the box stalls where the inn's patrons had left their mounts. The horses stuck their heads out over the stall doors to watch the two men as the groom continued, "I was bedding down the animals as usual, sir, the first thing I do right off in the evening, and when I get to the stall, this horse here, the big roan what the duke left with us to recuperate from his lameness, he was backed in his stall with his head down like he was feeling poorly. So of course I went in and looked him over."

They reached the stall door at the same time. The younger man unlatched it and stood aside for Barry to pass. The horse in question, the Duke of Westermere's thoroughbred gelding named Trafalgar, stood rather listlessly, hipshot because of his lame leg, at the back of the enclosure.

"Here now," the head groom said. He grasped Trafalgar's bridle and the horse turned his head to nuzzle his shoulder. "What's your complaint, old man?" Barry murmured as he examined the horse's neck and withers. "Haven't we been treating you fine enough with a dry place and a bit of grain with your hay since you come limping in here with the duke, hard-ridden and all splashed with mud and—"

He stopped with an oath. "What's *this*?"

"That's the way I found him," the younger man put in quickly. "When I asked Sally and the pot boy from the kitchen, they said there was a stranger around at the back door there wanting to buy some soup or a bit of bread, and looking for a place to spend the night. When he asked about the stables they told him no, 'twas only the inn's patrons what put there horses there, and no one was allowed to sleep on the hay or such like. Sally remembers she couldn't see him as he wore a cloak with the hood up against the rain and kept to the shadows. She says she gave him bread and a piece of mutton and he paid for it proper in silver coin, but then he was gone."

Barry swore again. He ran his fingers along the horse's sides and the big horse trembled, then shied. "Beaten with a whip?" he muttered. "A bit of rope?"

"A crop sir," the other answered. "A riding crop, one taken from the rack by the door. It's still there, lying in the corner. I haven't moved it nor picked it up for I knew you'd want a look at it. But that's what was used, the riding crop, I'd swear, for there's blood on it."

The head groom held the horse by his bridle and ran his hand down his flanks. The horse whinnied in pain.

Barry cursed again. "Ah, poor brute, he's torn up for fair. It'll be some time before those strokes heal. It don't make no sense," he growled.

"Some villain roaming the roads comes into me

stables and beats a horse—the duke's horse, mind you. It's a devil of a thing. I don't know, lad—maybe it *was* the devil!"

The young groom gave him a strange look. "That's what Sally said. That he looked like the devil himself, hanging back from the light like that, and covering his face with the hood so she couldn't get a good look at him. He asked about the duke. That wasn't too odd as he said he was a courier carrying a letter and trying to catch up with His Grace. So Sally told him that Lord Westermere was gone, that his horse was lame and he'd had to leave it here, and he'd hired another to finish his journey to London."

Now the head groom was staring at him. "Lord help us, boy, the girl in the kitchen told him the duke's horse was here, in the stables?"

The other nodded. "Sally kept trying to see what he looked like, and stepped out into the yard even with the pouring down rain to do it, but she said he only laughed and slipped off into the shadows. It was a dreadful laugh, Sally said. At first she thought the man was having some sort of fit. It didn't sound like no proper laugh. And then she says he told her something before he disappeared."

"Told her something?" The head groom let go of the bridle and looked at his hands, streaked with blood from the horse's wounds. "What in God's name did he say?"

The other reached over and pulled a clean currying cloth from a peg outside the stall. "He said, sir, that he was sorry he'd missed the duke, but that he'd find him. And that he'd leave him a message."

Chapter Eleven

"Your nightshirt, milord," Cruddles said, holding up an Irish linen sleeping garment with lace-trimmed collar for the duke's approval.

Sacheverel, who was wearing nothing at all as the last bits of soapy foam were scraped from his jaw, turned and gave the nightshirt a quick appraisal.

His first thought was that the night wear looked too damned conjugal. Something one would sleep in after six months of a delightful honeymoon, at about the time one's bride was blushingly whispering in his ear that she was expecting their first child.

That whole issue, betrothal and marriage, had become a sore point. One he hadn't counted on facing that night.

"No nightshirt," he said to his valet, turning back to the shaving mirror, "just the robe."

A dressing gown with only one's nude body under it was, as every dandy in London would agree, the traditional attire for seduction. But Satch was finding himself more than a little disappointed that he was not going to spend his wedding night, as had his father and grandfather and generations of dukes of Westermere, gently instructing his virgin bride in the tender delights of married bliss.

No, by all the saints, he thought irritably, they had to do it now, thanks to the pernicious influence of some crackpot woman of loose morals who'd spent her life writing subversive tracts that attacked the very foundations of English life.

Free love, indeed.

What Sacheverel had learned, and had heard repeated that very night from the lips of his intended bride, was that according to Wollstonecraft's thesis, young, uninstructed females could decide, with what pathetically little they knew of the world, to make connection with any man they chose to believe had developed "respect, friendship and affection" for them.

It was utter rot. And furthermore, it led to social chaos, as any thinking person knew; for instance, in the inevitable appearance of an uncontrolled population of children and infants who could not account for their fathers—if their mothers even knew who they were—who would clog the workhouses and no doubt contribute in years to come to restless, insurgent mobs in the city streets.

Fortunately, it was within his power, Satch knew, as Cruddles helped him on with a handsome maroon silk dressing gown and tied the sash about his middle, to reverse this process, at least as far as his betrothed was concerned. He just hadn't planned to do it so precipitously.

He hated making preparations on the spur of the moment, he told himself as he stepped in front of the pier glass. However, thanks to prompt organization by the Horton Crescent staff, things were pretty well in hand and everything in place for the next move.

Mrs. Cawdigan had seen to a rather elaborate display of lace-trimmed sheets and pillows and royal blue velvet bedspread embroidered with the Westermere crest in gold. A cozy fire of oak logs burned in the marble fireplace. Pomfret had brought a selection of sparkling white wine and an excellent claret from the cellar. The white had already been placed in a silver bucket of crushed ice that stood on a stand beside a small table of refreshments consisting of pastries, cheeses and cold meats. And after a few moments spent searching the upper reaches of the shelves in the library, Sacheverel had Cruddles carry up a few books he'd selected.

They were all-important books, he was reminded, as he took a glass of claret from the valet.

Virgins were a damned tricky proposition; there was no telling how much they knew about anything. And he was no expert. He'd had only one encounter with a virgin, when he was fifteen; the daughter of the Westermere gamekeeper. A thoroughgoing disaster, both the act itself and the aftermath. At fifteen he could not remember who had been the aggressor, but the gamekeeper, highly regarded by the duke, his grandfather, had gone storming to that worthy person demanding reparation, claiming his family's honor had been besmirched and his daughter ruined. An argument with which, surprisingly, his grandfather had agreed.

The girl was married off—happily, Satch later heard—and he'd received the last birching of his life at the hands of his grandsire. The man's final words to him about it were that his next adventure would be better served by someone more experienced. The old duke had promptly sent him to visit a well-known actress.

He looked at himself critically in the pier glass. He had decided not to wear the lounging slippers Cruddles was holding, but go rather engagingly barefoot so as to appear less intimidating. And not to club his hair, too, for the same reason. It would come down later in the throes of passion, anyway.

"A little scent, milord?" the valet suggested, holding up a cut glass bottle of Italian essence for him to see in the mirror.

Sacheverel gave Cruddles a frowning, preoccupied look. He was not totally happy with the effect of his bare feet as he viewed them in the looking glass. Perhaps they were a bit too casual.

On the other hand, he'd theorized his bare feet would give her an opportunity to familiarize herself with his body while not being too indelicate. Feet were fairly mundane. Besides, he remembered, she'd glimpsed them when he was sick in bed.

"No scent," he said, waving the bottle away. With all the other arrangements, scent would be rather overreaching.

With one last piercing glance at himself in the mirror, he moved away to sit on the edge of the bed, where Cruddles had placed the books. He picked up a rare illustrated volume showing Persian shahs and their companions of pleasure in an oriental garden, disporting themselves in positions of sexual delight on pillowed couches, swings, and by the banks of a stream. Satch had picked the book from the shelves because the jeweled kings and their concubines were prettily and colorfully presented, and the unknown painter had made them all unswervingly cheerful: Every almond-eyed Persian face was smiling, no matter what improbable erotic contortions their bodies were engaged in.

He'd brought other books up from the library, including a medical book on anatomy, but discarded the idea of using the latter as the drawings were rather stark. The third was a pillow book, designed to enlighten Japanese brides. Unfortunately, he found the Japanese artist had typically presented the male genitalia as huge, and drawings of the act itself resembled nothing much short of assault. Under the circumstances, it was not unusual to find none of the Japanese figures smiling.

The Persian book, definitely, he decided.

Some hours ago, with the forethought of a self-trained man of science such as himself, it had occurred to him that his betrothed might not be acquainted with the sight and characteristics of the male sex organ. Nor indeed, of the entire male body. Many gently raised young women weren't. The Persian book should give her a pleasant first view of all that, as well as an opportunity to study the depiction of somewhat acrobatic but lively sexual contact.

The whole idea, Satch told himself somewhat impatiently, was to take her to bed and make her his. Demonstrate that she was truly betrothed to him. On her way shortly to be married. A night of passionate lovemaking would certainly convince Miss Marigold Fenwick once and for all of the inevitability of his intentions.

Nevertheless he found himself a little edgy when Cruddles went to the door to let her in.

She was accompanied by two footmen with candelabras. For a moment he couldn't see her clearly for the flickering lights and shadows.

"Your Grace," he heard her say. She gave him a deep curtsy. "Good evening."

Satch returned a stiff bow, suddenly conscious of his bare feet. It was too late to think of that now. "Good evening," he told her.

The young footmen immediately retired, closing the bedroom door. He was somewhat disappointed to see the luscious Miss Fenwick wearing rather prim, striped wool dressing robe and high-necked nightgown. Evidently he had given orders about her wardrobe but had forgotten her sleeping attire; the striped dressing robe looked like something Mrs. Cawdigan would purchase.

However, in all other ways her tall, voluptuous form was eminently pleasing. Satch felt a decidedly anticipatory warmth in his veins as he gazed at her.

The maids had seen to her toilette, brushing out her marvelous hair so that it cascaded in brown-gold waves over her shoulders, and not forgetting to attach a rosy ribbon that pulled a part of it back from her brow and secured it at the back of her head, the ribbon ends trailing flirtatiously. The azure eyes, framed in the thickest of lashes, sparkled with what he could only suppose was subdued excitement. That enchanting mouth had been bitten, no doubt on the chambermaids' direction, to a ripe, irresistible pink. He felt his body react immediately as his temperature rose.

"Were we not supposed to wear bed slippers?" she said forthrightly, staring at his feet. "I can take mine off, if you wish."

"Yes, by all means do that," Satch said. At least that was one article of clothing disposed of. He lifted his hand and signaled for Cruddles to serve the wine.

That evening he'd gone down to the wine cellar with old Pomfret and selected the excellent French sparkling white himself. Several glasses, he reasoned, should put Marigold Fenwick at ease without bringing on an unmanageable intoxication. He suddenly decided to have not the claret, but a shot of brandy.

He saw her turn away to take a seat in one of the bedroom's small Louis Quatorze chairs. Satch moved quickly to take her by the arm and steer her toward the bed.

"Sit here," he told her, patting the side with the books. He downed the brandy Cruddles handed him in a gulp and gave back the glass, then signaled for Cruddles to leave them. "Now," he said, seating himself on the edge of the bed beside her. A head-spinning odor of flowers distracted him for a moment. She was wearing a scent. He was glad he had wisely decided to forgo his own; for both of them to have worn it would have been too much.

Now was the time for their conversation, he told himself, as he picked up the Persian book.

Satch was aware that he had better proceed with caution. Sudden, vivid pictures were flashing through his mind of Miss Marigold Fenwick's naked breasts as they'd been displayed that first day in his coach, her delightful legs glimpsed in that same vehicle, and lately the exquisite shoulders and arms and tantalizing décolletage revealed to him every evening as they dined. He'd thought of all that many times. Naturally each time he did it had an effect on him. As it was having now.

He curbed his thoughts with an effort. He couldn't give in to ill-managed passion—he wanted to make this an exquisite evening for this beautiful if headstrong girl to whom he was now quite satisfied to be betrothed. He was not unaware of the difficulty of steering her innocence through the dangerous shoals of first-time sex.

He picked up the bottle of white wine that Cruddles had placed beside the bed and, signaling for her to hold it up, refilled her glass.

She drank it down a little too quickly. "Thank you, I was quite thirsty," she said, licking her upper lip with the tip of her pink tongue. "It has a delightful flavor. Is it wine?"

Satch cursed himself for not guessing she'd never tasted spirits before; after all, she was a country vicar's daughter. He tried to take the glass away from her, but she held on to it.

"It's quite delicious," she said, dazzling him with a look from heavenly blue eyes. "Do you mind pouring me a bit more?"

He certainly did, but she wouldn't let go of the glass. Rather than have a tug of war with her over the thing, he poured her a little less than half. While he did so, she studied him thoroughly, including his maroon silk dressing gown. It was she who first noticed the garment had slipped to one side at the knees, exposing his bare legs and feet, and her eyes widened.

It was just as he had suspected, Satch told himself. She'd never been this close to a man before. At least not one who was naked under his bedroom attire.

He saw her look around. Her eyes fell on the books on the bed.

"Is this yours?" She picked up a book and held it in her lap, holding it open with her elbow while she rather carefully lifted the French wine to her lips.

Satch realized she'd picked up the damned Japanese pillow thing. It was open to a kimono-clad warrior climbing onto a doll-like woman, his buttocks and gargantuan genitalia completely exposed.

"Good heavens, are they Orientals?" She bent her head with some disbelief to examine the page. "Surely their—his—I mean he can't truly be that—er, generous!"

"Wrong book," Satch said, as he snatched it away from her. In doing so he jogged her arm, making her spill what was left of the wine in her glass onto the bedspread.

As she wiped up the spilled wine with the sleeve of her robe he explained hurriedly, "Japanese men are not—ah—what you see in the book is a compensatory exaggeration by the illustrator." Her eyes opened even wider. He said, "That is to say the Japanese male organs are actually rather small compared to—"

Satch had a feeling he was on perilous ground. He meant to say "males of northern European stock" but realized that was best avoided. After all, the whole point of this was to treat her gently and not alarm her.

She bit her lip, looking puzzled. "How odd. Could I ask, Your Grace, how many nude Japanese men you have seen to make this comparison?"

Now it was he who stared back at her.

"God's blood, woman, I do not go about studying nude Japanese men! My information came from a book. As you know, I own and read a great many books." Something else occurred to him. "I am constrained to ask you not to add nude Japanese men to your repertory of wild-eyed stories, as you have already spread the rumor at my Aunt Bessie's ball, if you remember, that I use damned aphrodisiacs! These accounts do little for my reputation."

Her beautiful face managed to look contrite. "I'm sorry, Westermere, for what I did at the ball. True friends do not treat each other that way. I have little enthusiasm, now, for spreading any stories, you must believe me." She hiked closer to him on the edge of the bed. "What is it you wish to read to me?"

He glowered at her. The Persian book of erotic art no longer seemed like a good way of introducing his betrothed to the reality of soon-to-be-married sex. But he doubted he could turn aside her curiosity now that he'd stirred it up.

The devil with all of it, he told himself. "My desire is not merely to read to you," he growled, "but to—ah, enlighten your virginal innocence before we do what we are about to do. As a consequence, it occurred to me that you may not have ever seen a male form—ummm—aah—*au naturel*."

She had been looking into his eyes, following every word. Now she impulsively put her warm hand over his.

"Oh, Westermere, you have been most sparing of my sensibilities to arrange for me to view your books before any . . . fleshly encounter. But I am not frightened. On the contrary, I quote Mary Wollstonecraft when I say: 'Women as well as men ought to have the common appetites and passions of their nature.' Indeed, 'nature, in these respects, may safely be left to herself.' "

He stared at her, wondering what her opinion would be if he unleashed the "common appetites and passions" nature was providing him in abundance at that moment, and threw her back on the bed and kissed her soundly.

"The book," she reminded him.

Simply overwhelming her with passion seemed a lost cause. Satch lifted the Persian book and opened it at random. She immediately moved closer to see, bracing her arm behind him on the bed so that it touched his back. He felt the warmth through his dressing gown.

Satch quickly saw it was not the sort of illustration he would have picked if he had been more careful. Perhaps it would have been better to have started with the medical books on anatomy after all; he was beginning to suspect they'd skipped over several subjects basic to the business at hand.

He heard her muffled gasp.

Before he could do anything she turned to him. "Westermere, is it really possible to do this? That the woman in the picture in the garden swing—I mean, that when the ladies of the harem or whatever it is propel her toward—the er, man—that he can stand there a distance away and—uh, good heavens, hit the target?"

"The damned Persians think so," he growled, quickly turning the page. Personally, he thought it was another gross exaggeration, like the male genitalia in the Japanese pillow book.

The next illustration, even though it was a man and woman engaged in a fairly uncomplicated sexual position, failed to convey, in his opinion, the delicacy and emotion of the sensual act. Particularly as it related to marriage.

Perhaps, he thought, it was because the naked shah wore a turban and a huge, drooping black mustache, which made it difficult to liken him to any Englishman. And the illustration of the dusky, wasp-waisted beauty he was in the act of penetrating wore the same indefatigable smile as the others. No woman Satch had ever had ever made love to had grinned so relentlessly, or he would have thrown her out of the bed.

The girl beside him seemed to sense his dissatisfaction. "Your Grace, this is all very interesting, but I wish to tell you I am not exactly—er, unenlightened." When he whirled to stare at her, black eyebrows raised, she said quickly, "Oh, no, not that. I am still quite certifiably virginal. But my dear friend Sophronia Stack, whose father is our village doctor, has several of his books on this general subject, although they are medical books and not so imaginatively illustrated as yours. We—my friends and I—in the way of young, intelligent women possessed of a normal curiosity, have perused them thoroughly."

She stood up and slipped off the striped robe. This left her in her nightgown, which was more sheer than Sacheverel had expected. In spite of its high neck and long sleeves, it did not take much imagination to follow the exquisite shape it concealed.

He watched the fabric of the nightgown move gently across the curves of her bottom as she padded across the room to the table with bowls and plates of refreshments.

"Oh, strawberry tarts," he heard her say in tones of real delight. "Strawberries at this time of year! How nice of you to provide them! And cold chicken!"

Satch jumped up from his seat on the bed and reached her in time to take away the plate she was filling.

"Afterward," he murmured.

He could not help himself, he ran his fingers around the back of her neck and was rewarded by seeing her shiver slightly. When she looked up at him, his fingers moved to the front and began on the small pearl buttons at the neck of the gown.

"Do we begin now?" she whispered, her eyes on his face. The expression on her face tore at his heart.

"Yes, sweetheart," he muttered. "We begin now."

But the infinitesimally small buttons on her nightgown proved resistant, much as he punched at them. He knew he was taking too long, for she sighed.

"Let me do this," she told him.

He dropped his hands, and in a trice she had the pesky buttons unfastened. Then, without stopping, she seized the hem of the nightgown with both hands and stripped it over her head.

"There, that's done," she said.

It took Satch a few stunned seconds to realize what had happened. Miss Fenwick—Marigold—his bride-to-be, now stood before him naked, the most dazzling sight he'd encountered in his life.

No woman that he had ever known could come close to her. Tall, with magnificent waves of golden brown hair cascading over her shoulders, she was perfectly lovely in both face and form. Those beautiful breasts were high and firm, her rib cage long and graceful, followed by a tiny waist and rounded hips. Her legs were exceptionally long; she looked like the heavenly huntress Diana.

A slight flush had risen to her cheeks as he stared at her, but he could see she'd had just enough wine—and doses of Wollstonecraft—to make her audacious.

"I hope, Your Grace," she said, lifting her chin, "you will not require me to join in any—er, diversions—such as we've seen in your books."

"No, no," Satch said hoarsely, "I have no swings. What sort of an idiot do you take me for?"

She made no answer. Instead she turned and walked toward the bed. The sight of her sauntering naked across his bedroom made real all of Sacheverel's wildest dreams. He was right behind her.

She sat down on the edge of the bed, totally entrancing in her nakedness, and smiled at him.

She patted a place beside her. "What do we discuss now?" his future bride wanted to know.

Chapter Twelve

Marigold had heard about drinking wine, so she knew it accounted for her lightheadedness. But in all truth she felt as though she could do with several glasses more, as she was not feeling quite as composed as she had even a few minutes ago.

Being completely naked certainly had something to do with it, she thought, as did the burning look on Westermere's ordinarily impassive face. He could not seem to take his eyes from her.

He sat down on the edge of the bed. "There's no need for more—ah, discussion, is there?" he asked, huskily.

He was sitting so close to her, and the presence of his body under the silk of the dressing robe still had on her the same heart-pounding effect. Marigold could not make up her mind whether she liked it or not.

"Unless you have questions you have not yet asked." he murmured.

Did she have any questions? She didn't know. She found she really could not think properly when he was so close beside her. Out of the corner of her eye she saw that the front of his silk robe had gaped open again, revealing not only the duke's slightly hairy legs and knees, but also a length of very muscular thigh. And above that—

Above that was the hidden presence of male virility she'd seen in the books he'd shown her. The realization was sobering.

It was really going to happen. That "ultimate physical intimacy" between man and woman to which, as Mary Wollstonecraft taught, all respect and friendship invariably led.

"No, Your Grace," she heard herself answering in a low voice, "I think not. I—I have no questions."

Still, she could not hold back a little shiver as he picked up her hand, his bold black eyes searching hers, and kissed it. Then he drew her into his arms. For a moment the awkwardness of the position, sitting on the edge of the big bed and having to turn in order to reach each other, filled her mind. Then his arms were around her, his lips touched hers, and all coherent thought fled.

It was not the friendly, familial peck she'd been used to since childhood. For one thing, she had no knowledge of what mouths were supposed to do in this sort of kiss. Secondly, there was the shock of him, strong and hard and purposeful, his big body pressed against her, holding her. And then an even bigger surprise, his tongue parting her lips.

With a gasp, she drew back at once. She knew she was on her own now. Mary Wollstonecraft in her advice on intimate relationships had never dwelt on details.

"Westermere, is this customary?" she cried. "To open one's lips in an—er, embrace?"

He didn't answer her, for his mouth had quickly descended to her shoulder and arms, dropping hungry caresses. She could feel him trembling. Both his hands covered her breasts, his fingers stroking and lightly pinching the nipples into tight buds. Then she felt his mouth there, teasing and tugging.

For a moment Marigold was so assailed she was breathless. What he was doing made fiery, shivery lightning run through her entire body. She could not hold back a squeak.

At the sound he stopped at once, raised his head and looked down at her. "My love, I did not hurt you, did I?" he said quickly.

She stared at him. He looked wild and passionate, a totally different sort of person. His dark hair tumbled about his face, the slash of his mouth was wet from the caresses he had lavished on her shoulders and breasts. Yet it was very exciting. She still wanted to explore the sensation;

as far as she was concerned it had all passed much too quickly.

"My angel," the duke groaned, "have I overwhelmed you? I'm sorry. Perhaps I had better begin by taking off my robe and restoring us to the unfettered equals nature intended."

The idea sounded reasonable, but the reality was something else. For if Westermere's ardor was somewhat overpowering, what he revealed when he shrugged out of his dressing gown and threw it on the floor was undeniably prodigious.

He was a big man, yet beautifully, gracefully muscled. His abdomen was a rippled washboard of well-contained power, as well as his arms and chest. Particularly the biceps and pectorals. His long, well-shaped legs were magnificent, and for a dark man, he was not too hairy. Even the mat of curls on his chest was comparatively restrained. But what drew the eyes was that he was fully aroused.

"Good heavens," Marigold blurted, "are you always that way?" It looked positively painful.

He looked somewhat confounded for a moment. Then he climbed into the bed beside her and lay back. "Not always this way, my darling," he said somewhat hoarsely. "My body is reacting to a notably irresistible desire to have you, that is all. That was the point of acquainting you with the pictures in the books I showed you, remember? That is, that you would be familiar with the visible aspects of an aroused male. Come," he told her, holding out his arms, "lie down with me."

Marigold considered all this as she stayed just out of his reach. "But Westermere, you don't resemble those Persian kings at all! And you said the pictures of Japanese men were exaggerated. But now that you—"

He half sat up, propped on his elbow. "I don't wish to discuss pictures of Japanese men again," he growled. "I thought we had finished with all that."

"Nevertheless—" Marigold bit her lip. "Would you give me just a moment to look at you? I really am not fully acquainted yet, as you mentioned, with the visible aspects of—well, you." She hesitated. "May I—may I even—touch you?"

The duke gave her a black, piercing look. Then he lay back, and lifted one arm and placed it over his eyes, resigned. "Be gentle, sweetheart," he muttered, "and don't poke about. Watch your fingernails."

"Oh, thank you," Marigold said sincerely. "How considerate you are!"

She stroked the length of his great, straining shaft with the tip of one finger, noting that it was both hard and hot and the skin silky-soft. Beneath it the scrotum was taut and slightly damp. When she ran her fingertip under it, exploring, she was amazed to hear a loud groan burst from his lips.

"Oh, Westermere," she cried, jerking her hand away, "does this cause you pain? If so, I certainly will not continue!"

To her amazement he seized her hand and put

179

it back. "Not pain, precious," he rasped. "I groaned because it was actually an amazing surfeit of feeling. Just wrap your fingers around, if you don't mind, and caress it as you were doing."

"I don't know," she said, uncertainly.

She couldn't remember what she was doing, actually, when he seemed seized by such a paroxysm of agony. But she was curious about the size and shape of his big sex.

As she stroked her fingers over him, especially around the tip, which caused his body to visibly shake and brought more fervent moans from him, Marigold was sensing something of her own mounting excitement. She was warming and moistening in her most intimate places where she had developed a rather generalized ache. At times, as she allowed both her hands to play with his taut, ruddy flesh, her own response was that of an unsatisfied burning, making her lower extremities squirm.

Nevertheless, the duke's obvious distress, and in particular his convulsive twitching, was beginning to worry her.

"Westermere," she whispered, "I am capable of help, if this is growing too much for you. Remember, I have studied in Dr. Stack's books what we are about to do, and am not uninformed."

He took his arm down from his eyes and looked at her, his expression one of disbelief.

"Yes," Marigold told him. She was struggling to get the feverish clamor in her own body under control. "I am beginning to have some rather ungovernable response myself, and while it is obviously not as painful as yours, if you will just lie still I believe it is possible for me to move over you and straddle you, and—and—accomplish the task."

It took a moment for him to digest that. Then the duke jerked up from the bed with an oath.

"Damme, woman, are you saying you're going to deflower yourself while I lie under you like a damned barber pole?"

Marigold had to grab at his arms to keep from falling off the bed. "Your Grace, my intentions were only of the best!" she cried. "Believe me, I have only the utmost sympathy for you in your current tormented state, and desire only to lend my assistance!"

"Tormented, that's right!" he shouted. "And you've only yourself to blame, you innocent, seductive, virginal Circe! I've been enraptured and rendered witless by some confounded female spell for the first time in my life." His black eyes blazed at her. "But God's blood, woman, to insinuate that I am incompetent in bed and cannot deflower my own betrothed—"

"I am not your betrothed!" Marigold screamed as he reached for her.

"You soon will be," he muttered as he pulled her under him and trapped her. "Before you get out of this bed," he told her, kissing her until he left her breathless, "you will be as claimed, possessed, and betrothed as any woman has ever been. And I will do it all, every bit of it, without any help, do you understand?"

"No," she protested, as his legs moved between hers and pushed them apart. "Westermere, I warn you—this must be done with m-mutual friendship and respect, or I refuse to go any further! Oh!"

It had been done so quickly. First his fingers in her soft cleft, finding her moist and ready for him, then the touch of his body invading her throbbing flesh. She could feel the muscles in his arms quiver as he held her.

He looked down at her, breathing hard. It was so strange to be joined in this way, Marigold thought wildly. As though after all that had passed between them, all their disagreement on so many important things, they had nevertheless become one. A fiery, passionate one. She lifted her arms and put them around his neck.

"Oh, Westermere, what have you done?" she moaned.

"I have made you mine, sweetheart." He kissed her again as he pushed into her slowly. For a long moment there was nothing in the world but that, the feel of his mouth caressing hers, his body possessing her.

"There will be a little pain," he whispered against her lips.

She knew that. When he thrust against her virginal barrier it was not too bad, for he was very gentle.

"Marigold," he murmured shakily, "I have the

utmost respect and love for you. I want you to be my wife."

The softly whispered words rang in her ears, for after that there was nothing but paradise.

Their bodies twined and moved, tangled in lacy sheets, and she sensed dimly that he was holding back, leashing his desire. When at last she closed her eyes and cried out, reaching her peak of ecstasy, he followed her, almost lifting her from the bed with the violent thrusts of his own release. After it was over he was careful not to let his weight down on her. He held himself up, hands and arms braced, looking down at her until Marigold opened her eyes.

It took a few minutes before their hearts stopped racing madly and they could catch their breath.

"Oh, Westermere," Marigold managed. They were still joined; she could feel him throbbing within her. "That was the most sublime experience! Why do people not talk about it more?"

"They do, love." He smoothed back her wet hair with one hand. "Some of them most vulgarly, I regret to say." The look in his black eyes was devilish. "Sweetheart, I am glad that coupling with me meets with your approval."

"Approval? Oh, surely you know that it was wonderful!" Something strange was happening. He was slipping out of her. He rolled over beside her, sat up and put his feet over the side of the bed. "Where are you going? Surely you are not going to leave me now?"

"Shhhh, I am going to get you a towel," he told her. "This is your first time, there may be a sign of virginal blood."

Marigold was afraid he was right. There was warmth and stickiness between her legs. When he came back with a linen serviette she pulled back the covers and, fleetingly surprised at her own lack of embarrassment, slipped it between her thighs.

It seemed beyond belief that in just a matter of hours, ending in the past few passionate moments, she had given herself to him in the most private of all embraces. Now she had the most amazing, comfortable feelings about her body and his. It was true, they had become one. She had adored watching him stalk across the room and return with the linen napkin, giving her a full view of his magnificent body. Surely they had achieved their reward, she thought, sighing. Like most everything else, Mary Wollstonecraft had known surpassingly well what she was writing about.

He slid into the bed and gathered her in his arms. "There is nothing you need or want?" His black eyes studied her. "Strawberries or a slice of roast pheasant? Would you like more wine?"

Marigold shook her head, and snuggled against him. She could not keep her hand from stroking his arm and moving on to explore his muscular chest. In reply, his arms gave her an affectionate squeeze.

"Oh, I am so happy," she whispered.

He had said that he had love and respect for her. And he wanted to make her his wife. For a moment Marigold indulged in delirious thoughts of what that would be like. They worked well together, she would continue as his partner in his research and studies. And then there would be glorious evenings spent playing—she hastily changed the perilous idea of chess to a card game, perhaps whist. And then the sweetness and love and passion of going to bed together. What bliss!

It didn't end there. Having Westermere's children, beautiful babies and lovely little girls and boys, with enough wealth, Marigold thought dreamily, to provide for them nicely and send them to England's best schools.

Her thoughts came to a sudden, screaming halt. Somewhere deep inside her a warning voice had cried *Stop! Beware! Think what you are contemplating!*

In answer, Marigold stiffened in the duke's arms. Good heavens, passion and emotion had led her to indulge in fancies about what was, after all, still the enemy!

Not only that, but she seemed to have capitulated completely. All virtuous intentions of converting Westermere to the noblest model of an enlightened peer, her great plan of winning him over with friendship and intimacy, had fled from her mind and, apparently, her character. The best schools in England, indeed! Oh lud, what had she been thinking of?

She'd been thinking of him, Marigold told herself as she lifted his heavy arm from her waist and turned to him.

She saw he had fallen asleep. He looked so handsome lying there against the lace-trimmed pillows, almost boyish with his long tumbling hair and thick eyelashes against his smooth cheek, that she choked back a sob.

Oh, the worst had happened! It could not be, but she had fallen in love with him! Friendship and respect and physical intimacy, she saw now, was an illusion. She had just made a dreadful discovery. When she loved, it was apparently with her whole heart and soul!

Worse, the power of this emotion had shattered her devotion to her ideals and loyal friends, and filled her mind with traitorous, frivolous thoughts. She could not believe that a few minutes ago, as she lay in Westermere's arms, she had thought with satisfaction of providing her future children with the ill-gotten wealth of the Westermere dukes!

Why had she imagined, even in the aftermath of glorious desire, that she could possibly be the duke of Westermere's wife?

Her father, out of the goodness of that fine man's heart, might understand and accept. But as for the village of Stokesbury Hatton that, without ever speaking of it openly, expected so much from her, its inhabitants would surely rise up and stone her! And she would not blame them.

As for Sophronia and Penelope, she could not even bear to think of them.

She had gone to London with a desperate plan that she, Marigold, had assured her two friends would promise much if only she could do it right. But now, instead of having all-powerful Westermere at their mercy, she, the would-be heroine of their great scheme, had become his love-struck slave!

She dared not even look at him. If she did she would surely give in to shameful idolatry, and lavish his face with kisses to wake him in the hope of making love a second time.

Choking back tears, Marigold put her legs over the edge of the bed and looked for her robe.

Timothy Cruddles was somewhere about, she was sure. It seemed to her that the man never slept in his devotion to the duke. If she met the valet in the hallway she doubted he would think anything of her slipping away from the duke's bedroom to discreetly return to her own quarters. That is, if she could keep from bursting into tears at the sight of anyone with an even mildly sympathetic face!

But she could not remain in London, in Westermere's power. In his arms she blindly desired only his love and his children and the happiness he could give her. She had to hold back a shudder, realizing she had almost traded the terrible suffering of others for her own future.

Her mind moved quickly, her will stiffened by new resolve. It was early morning. With any luck she could dress herself in one of her more subdued ensembles and take any serviceable cloak from the downstairs coat room, and thus attired make her way through London's streets to the coaching depot. It was a long walk, but country living had accustomed her to walking.

She would not take any luggage, Marigold decided. She had come to the duke's mansion in Horton Crescent in her old worsted dress, and she would leave with as little of Westermere's property as possible. Only a walking gown, underclothes, shoes, bonnet and a traveling cloak. Nothing in the world would prevail upon her to take any more.

Marigold put her hand on the doorknob of the duke's bedroom and stood, her head bent, feeling more desolate than she'd ever thought possible. He had been so gentle and kind in his lovemaking and, since he was experienced, careful in seeing that he lifted them both up to ecstasy. None of that had been lost on her. To leave him now wrenched at her soul. She heard a soft snore from the great canopied bed.

She could not look back to where Sacheverel de Vries, the twelfth duke of Westermere, lay sprawled, taking up most of the bed. For if she did, her heart would surely break.

With a sob she turned the knob softly, swung open the great door to his bedroom, and went out.

A bare half-hour later, a visibly distraught Pomfret came down the front steps of the mansion in Horton Crescent and stepped into the street, wagging one arm to flag down a familiar figure as it approached out of the darkness. The clock in the nearby bell tower of St. George's had just struck twice for the hour.

"God preserve us," the old man cried, "you're late! Where have you been? You've just missed her. She's left—Cruddles and I saw her go from the house in the middle of the night! Quick, man, I'd say she's on her way back to the vicar, going to catch the coach to the north."

Jack Ironfoot stopped in his tracks. "And His Grace? How is it with him?"

"His Grace is in his bed," the other answered, "blissfully content and asleep."

The coachman gave a grunt of relief. "It was never my thought that she was any danger to him, Pommy, for all your worry. Still, with all the clever games the young miss has played from the moment she jumped into the coach in Covent Garden, one could never be sure."

"This may be another," the butler warned.

Ironfoot shook his head. He hitched his cloak around him and pulled the hood forward to hide most of his face.

"Nay, she's gone to the Bird in Cage, I'll warrant," the coachman said, "that's the closest stop to catch the Northern Flyer. Since she's on foot, I'd best follow her, considering the hour and the byways she'll choose to go passing through." He gave a great, rumbling sigh. "God help us all, as sure as you 'n me is standing here, his grace will want to know everything if she's just slipped away

189

like that to go home. And telling him, Pommy, by God, ain't something I'm looking forward to."

With that, the big man turned and swiftly strode down the cobblestones of the dark London street.

Chapter Thirteen

Sophronia Stack, carrying a wicker basket covered with a neat white cloth, quickened her steps as she entered the shady confines of Soldiers' Wood.

There had once been a battle there in the forest, some said during the great war between the noble houses of York and Lancaster; some said much later, between the forces of the Lord Protector, Oliver Cromwell, and the cavalier supporters of King Charles, with great slaughter on both sides. Whatever the truth of it, the wood was a darksome place.

As a consequence villagers from miles around believed the wood on the west side of Stokesbury Hatton to be haunted. Most did what Sophronia was now doing: They quickened their pace and hurried along under the low-hanging branches of the great oak and beech trees, keeping their eyes on the path for the three miles or so they had to travel before they could see bright sunshine on the miller's oat fields ahead.

However, the woods were not deserted. Sophronia, in particular, knew that.

In it poachers from the town hunted rabbit, wild pig and even deer in spite of the dukes of Westermere's harsh game laws. Gypsies often camped there, away from the eyes of townsfolk, on their travels to and from the north and Scotland.

Now and then a few ragged outlaws, and sometimes an escaped prisoner from the assizes at Hobbs, took refuge in the dim forest until the militia was called, usually by the duke's bailiffs, to flush them out. There were even, the country folk believed, wolves still in the wildest parts, although there had not been a wolf sighted in northeast England for two hundred years.

Sophronia made the trip on foot through Soldiers' Wood twice a week. Each time the tall, dark-eyed doctor's daughter went to pay a call at the Widow McCandlish's cottage on the road to the next village, Wickham, and take a cup of tea with the old lady and tell the latest news from Stokesbury Hatton. She returned with the widow's donation to the poor: a half-dozen fresh eggs from Mrs. McCandlish's own hens, and a small sackful of biscuits that was the widow's specialty, a type widely consumed in that part of

Yorkshire mainly because it was rockhard and dry, and would keep a hungry child busy for hours.

In late winter there were still patches of old snow in the places the sun never touched, and the ground was thick with fallen leaves, muffling all but the sharpest sounds. Ordinarily Sophia was too proud to show her unease by looking over her shoulder, but now she did so, several times. Since she'd entered the deepest part of the woods she thought she'd heard noises, like those of something following her.

Probably the wind, she thought, as she shifted the sack of bread to her right hand in case she should have to protect herself. Which was not as foolish as it sounded: The hardtack biscuits inside were as heavy as rocks.

She quickened her pace to something just under a run, but after a few yards she slowed. Bolting down the path in Soldiers' Wood would only make her disheveled and breathless, and would upset her father when he saw her. He didn't like the weekly trips to the Widow McCandlish as it was.

There were few people, actually, who had ever seen Sophia minus her ever-present calm exterior. A dark, close-mouthed girl, was how most folks thought of her; standoffish, careful of her dignity. She was well aware few in the village would have warmed to her if Dr. Stack had not been, by virtue of his position and education, so respectable a part of the county gentry. And she was, after all, his daughter.

Now, looking around, she wondered about the spot in the woods where the gypsies camped. You could not see it from the path, but it was said the Rom used the same place year after year, leaving mysterious marks on the trees that showed where water or grazing for the horses was to be found, and, rumor had it, identified certain unsuspecting houses and shops in Stokesbury Hatton where gypsies could usually steal a little without bringing the whole town down on them.

It was to the hidden gypsy encampment in Soldiers' Wood that young Dr. Thomas Stack, fresh from medical school in London, had been brought many years ago to attend to a gypsy "king," a huge, unwashed man in a hat with multicolored plumes, his chest decked with gold crosses and rosaries obviously on leave from their pious owners, and with gold and silver coins tied in his greasy locks. He told the young doctor he was Miguel of Hungary, greatly suffering from a painful attack of the gout.

Dr. Stack alleviated the king's pain, and left him several bottles of medicine. The grateful monarch was generous. When he left the encampment that night, the young doctor took with him two suckling pigs that he suspected had been someone's property in a nearby town, and Alida, the gypsy king's daughter. She would be his housekeeper, Miguel of Hungary assured him. At least until the gypsies came south again to claim her.

Who could turn down the gift—or loan—of a flashing-eyed, grimy, but quite beautiful gypsy king's daughter? Not young Dr. Stack, whose contact with women had been almost nonexistent because of a medical student's killing workload and chronic poverty.

He had installed the gypsy king's daughter as his housekeeper. And when the gypsies came back in the spring, Tom Stack had married her, and their daughter, Sophronia, was on the way.

The new Mrs. Stack was hardly the sort of wife for a learned young doctor, the village gossiped, but she had a haughty, if gypsyish way about her that commanded respect. When the dreaded typhoid carried the doctor's wife off several years later in spite of all he could do, Tom Stack was heartbroken. The villagers of Stokesbury Hatton opened their hearts and did the best they could for the doctor and his child, who was as much of a close-mouthed, black-eyed gypsy beauty as had been her mother.

Someday, Sophronia told herself as she strode along, the bag of hardtack banging against her leg, she was going to leave the path and go look for the gypsy campground. There had been gypsies there that winter; she'd smelled the smoke of their fires as she passed by each week, and the temptation had been strong to go into the woods in search of them. Would they remember her? Was her grandfather, Miguel, or any of the gypsies who knew her mother, Alida, still alive? At times, on errands like these to the widow McCandlish's, feeling the wildness of the woods around her that seemed to call to her, she was certain they were.

At the moment, though, it was not the sounds of the forest she was hearing. Someone was approaching on horseback. Had been, in fact, for quite a while. It was the faint sound of the horse's hooves on the path that her sensitive hearing had picked up for the last half-hour, if not her conscious mind.

Sophronia stopped, and turned around to face the rider. She was not surprised to see who it was.

For some fifty years the dukes of Westermere had employed a firm of agents, Parham & Parham, out of Edinburgh. Jeremiah Parham had been the first to open his office in the town at the order of the Old Duke, the present duke's grandfather, who had first built the mill, dammed the river for power, and imported men from Wales to develop the coal mine.

Jeremiah was succeeded by his son, now known as Mr. Parham Senior, who was semiretired and had turned over most of the Parham business in the Westermere villages to Robinson Parham, his son.

Sophronia did not have to peer far into the dim light under the trees to see that it was the younger Parham now on his fine, spirited horse, a glossy chestnut named Spanish Pete that he often entered in local races.

Robinson Parham, Jr., was an excellent rider. Of all the men in the county, one could recognize him at once by his hard, slim body, the ease and grace with which he and his mount moved together. "There comes Parham," hunt people would say, when in twilight they could do no more than identify him and his horse by their silhouette.

Parham played the flute, had a passable voice, and danced beautifully. As a consequence he was invited to all the minor gentry's parties and balls for miles around, as he was also fairly wealthy, handsome, and a bachelor. It must have been galling to him that even possessed of all these gentlemanly attributes he was not recognized by the county nobility. He was not invited to the marquis of Beaulieu's estate, High Tor, when the house was open and the marquess in residence, or the duchess of Sutherland's receptions when she visited her castle.

In fact, he only occasionally had entree to Mrs. Horsley Blount's affairs and then only when there was a shortage of men—even though the lady was only the niece of a baronet in far-off Wiltshire. For all their money and airs, the ambitious Parhams were considered to be only the Westermere dukes' agents. It was a condition most did not distinguish from being "in trade."

Sophronia knew him as a dangerous man. The people of Stokesbury Hatton who worked in the mills and the mines had told her what the Parham family was like. Some said that in all the years the Parhams had been the dukes of Westermere's agents, the youngest Parham was by far the most oppressive.

He reined in as Sophronia turned to face him. "Hello, gypsy girl," he greeted her, smiling. "Looking for your friends? They broke camp weeks ago."

She knew that he wanted her to protest that the gypsies who camped in Soldiers' Woods were not her friends. That she had never seen them, and knew nothing of them in spite of the stories about her mother. But Sophronia only lifted her chin haughtily and stared at him, saying nothing.

The smile slid from young Parham's face. He jerked at his horse's reins, making it toss its head in surprise.

"Sullen bitch." There was no one in the woods to hear; Parham's expression said he could use what language he pleased to the doctor's daughter. "Still saving that precious hot nook you keep so safe under those skirts? Tell me what you do at night, gypsy, to keep those animal fires stoked. Do you caress yourself, touch yourself—"

Sophronia tried to close her ears to his words, but he seemed to have thought a great deal about meeting in the woods like this, and about what he would say to her.

The pictures he painted of Sophronia naked and in bed, pleasing herself, were astonishingly vivid. As he indulged in his spoken fantasy, Robinson Parham rested one arm on the pommel of his saddle, reins slack, stripping her of her clothes with his stare.

Sophronia wanted to get away. But she knew better than to turn her back on him and start down the path to Stokesbury Hatton.

Had young Parham waited somewhere in the woods for her, she wondered. Waiting to pounce? Or had he followed her all the way from the widow's house, biding his time until he reached a lonesome place to confront her?

Whatever it was, being alone with him like this put her at a great disadvantage. If only someone would come along! Some hunter, someone on foot making their way to Wickham. She could not outrun a man on horseback. But she had never in her life had to stand like this, forced to listen to an obscene outpouring about her person.

Still, Parham would be a fool to do more than bully and harass her. She was not afraid of him. Since he was so fond of mentioning her gypsy blood, she could show him what a gypsy's wrath was like! He would have to kill her, first, to touch her.

He was not going to do that, she knew, staring at him steadily. He wanted to terrorize her. But she was not just some poor mill girl who had no defenses against the duke's powerful agent and had to submit to whatever he wanted. Sadly, she knew there had been plenty of those.

"—wrap those beautiful long legs around my neck," he was saying, "and plunge into you, stupid gypsy trash, until you beg me to stop."

To her own surprise, Sophronia burst out laughing. It was absurd. His desire to frighten her had the opposite effect. Parham was a degenerate wretch for all his dazzling looks. He might just as well have been a dirty-minded old codger, slobbering over the village maids from his seat on the bench in front of the tavern.

The man on the horse was so intent on spilling out his lurid words that it was a moment before he realized she was laughing at him. He stopped and glared at her.

Sophronia was unaware of the effect she had when she laughed. It transformed her from a slender young girl in a prim gray woolen dress, her dark hair pulled back into a spinsterish bun at the nape of her neck, to a vivid, mocking beauty, all fire and magic. The sound of her laughter rebounded in the woods, wakening the birds with its echoes.

Parham looked dumbfounded. Then his face turned red with rage. "You laugh at me?" he choked. "Bitch, you laugh at me?"

He kicked the big chestnut toward her. Spanish Pete shied, not wanting to charge the girl clutching her sack of hardtack biscuit and the basket of eggs. The horse danced and sidled away as his master shouted curses at him and applied his whip to Spanish Pete's neck and head.

Sophronia could not help it, she winced. One did not treat a beautiful horse like that; anyone could see the poor stallion was alarmed and confused. But Parham was determined that the horse should do her bodily harm or at least make her take to her heels and run.

She held her ground, but he forced the horse closer. Sophronia had to grab the stirrup to keep the chestnut from crowding her off the road and into the ditch.

This was too much, she decided.

She lifted the sack of hardtack and swung with all her might. The Widow McCandlish's donation to the poor hit the stallion with an audible whack right on a particularly tender spot below his tail.

Spanish Pete reared, almost dumping his rider from the saddle. Then, with a loud whinny, the horse stuck out his neck, gathered his body like a giant spring, and bolted down the forest path with Robinson Parham, that excellent horseman, fighting madly to keep his seat.

They would reach, Sophronia realized, the edge of the woods and the miller's oat field long before she could make her way there. But she doubted the agent would stop unless Spanish Pete managed to throw him.

He will make his way back to the town, she told herself. And when his temper had cooled, no doubt Parham would take up his wicked daydreams about her again.

She laughed contemptuously as she picked up the basket of eggs. Young Parham was a man who amused himself by thinking vile thoughts about women who hardly knew him—and who certainly had not encouraged him. She would not let him start this again no matter how many times

Katherine Deauxville

he waylaid her! The next time, Sophronia told herself, she would bring a knife from the kitchen.

She frowned. Parham had done his damage. She could see some of the eggs had not survived their encounter; they'd probably cracked when she'd almost dropped them. For the first time that day, she was really angry.

Ah, how they needed those eggs! The Cavaliers fed them to sick mill children, beaten and sweetened with treacle and mixed with the vicarage's precious supply of milk. The potion seemed to wonders, more than anything else they'd tried, even soup and pottage of dried beans. She was afraid to lift the yolk-stained cover and count how many were left.

Sophronia swung the sackful of hardtack purposefully as she started down the path. She would definitely bring a knife next time. The big steel one with a notch at the tip that her father used to carve meat was what she had in mind.

Almost two hours later Sophronia knocked on the back door of St. Dunstan's parsonage, and let herself in. Marigold was waiting for her, seated at the kitchen table wearing a big patchwork apron, sorting food she'd collected from St. Dunstan's parishioners and a few village shopkeepers.

"I'm afraid donations are not generous this week," she sighed. She got to her feet to greet her friend and take the basket. "It's the end of winter. Everyone who usually gives freely is as short as—" Marigold gave a small scream. "Holy saints preserve us, Sophie, who threw dirt all over the front of your gown?"

" 'Tis a contribution from Robinson Parham and his horse. A gift I hadn't expected!" There was a smoldering look in the other girl's eyes. "They met me in the darkest part of Soldiers' Wood. Don't look that way—it would have been worse if he had managed to back me into the ditch. Just think, Marigold, then I would have not only lost the eggs, but soaked Mrs. McCandlish's dainty biscuits in ditch water as well."

Marigold didn't laugh. "Well, who's to say a little ditch water would not improve them? It takes hungry children hours to gnaw away even a mouthful." She studied her friend for a long moment, then clapped her hand over her mouth to subdue a burst of giggles. "Oh, forgive me, dear Sophie, but you should see your face! I would not want to be in Parham's boots when next you meet. Your expression is most murderous."

"Murderous?" The other girl shrugged out of her cloak and draped it over a chair before the kitchen fire. "When we meet again I shall be carrying a knife," she said between her teeth. "If he says vile things to me as he did today in Soldiers' Woods, I shall find a way to make him most assuredly miserable." She sat down at the table and moved two loaves of rather stale bread to one side. "If that man is stupid enough to try to attack me I shall take my knife and not try for the heart and chance hitting a rib, but go straight for Parham's belly. It's an easier blow and, Papa tells me, is usually just as fatal if one punctures enough of the vitals."

Marigold stared at her. "Heavens above, you've been thinking about it!"

Sophronia lifted her chiseled, impassive face. "He called me gypsy trash, Marigold. And all at once I thought of the knife. You see, he was right." She smiled softly. "Blood will tell, especially the blood of gypsy trash."

Marigold lifted the tea cozy from the pot in the center of the table and poured her friend a cup. "Phagh, you give me the chills when you look like that, dear Sophie. Here, hot chamomile tea will tame your black spirits. What was Parham's intent, do you think, accosting you there in the woods? Is this his twisted way of paying you court?"

Sophronia sipped her tea, frowning. "Paying me court? Nay, not that. He wants to make me afraid of him. Terrorize me. That is most of his pleasure."

"But Sophie," Marigold protested, "he wouldn't dare! Your father is Stokesbury Hatton's doctor, university trained. You're not some poor village girl he can abuse."

The other laughed. "La, Marigold, he likely thinks I have a terrible taint in my gypsy blood, that it brings me down to the level of the poor girls that work in his mines."

Marigold had gotten up to fetch a plate of buttered toast kept warming on the hearth. Now she sat down abruptly and stared at her friend.

"There are women in the Westermere mines? I cannot believe it!"

Her friend nodded. "It is widely known, although no one in the village will talk of it directly. Women and little children, poor creatures, some as young as Johnny Cobb, pick coal, mind the animals and even drag the coal carts out of the mine themselves."

"Oh," Marigold burst out, "what terrible evil has set this in motion? Coal mines are deathly places for children, surely!"

Sophronia shrugged. "They are unhealthy places for anyone, my father will tell you that. He's tended many cases of sick and injured that work in that dangerous place. It's been only two years since the black damp gas came out of the coal seam and struck down fifty-eight men, do you remember? And before that, the number twelve gallery collapsed, and all those working down there drowned or starved to death when the diggers could not get to them."

Marigold shuddered. "I know of the coal mines' misery. I have lived with it all my life through dear Papa's ministry. But Sophie—women and little children! I have heard some of those galleries are so far underground that it is so hot the miners strip naked to endure it while they work. How can Parham—"

Sophia interrupted, helping herself to a slice of toast. "Marigold, remember the heath past the mills, on the other side of Stokesbury Hatton? It's at the bottom of the slag hill where the poorest miners and their families live in little better than lean-to's. The Cavaliers have never brought food there because we barely have enough for the mill's tenements. But my father used to be called to the heath when the miners had accidents. The heath is a hell, he will tell you that. There is no water, it must be brought up half a mile from the river, and the road has a ditch in the middle of it which drains away the waste and filth. That ditch breeds noxious airs which Papa is sure causes much of the disease, but the Westermere mine company, which owns all the lands upon which this paradise rests, will not spare a penny to put in proper drains."

"Why is your father no longer called there to tend the sick and injured?" Marigold wanted to know.

Sophronia's eyes still held a smoldering light. "When the mine supervisor, Mr. Hatfield, started offering the heath's women and children jobs in the mines, they began bringing a doctor from Hobbs. An unsavory soul, my father knows of him, it is not known if he has had any sort of formal training. Half the time the Hobbs doctor does not come, which is looked upon as good fortune by these poor souls, for his doctoring kills as many as it cures. Some of the heath miners slip away to Papa's surgery, especially to bring their sick children, for otherwise they would get no doctoring at all. But the supervisor will punish them if they're found out."

"It cannot be," Marigold cried. "Is there no way

to stop this spreading injustice and oppression by the Westermeres and their hirelings? Something must be done!"

Sophia put her hand over Marigold's. "Dear friend, consider that the heath's miners are desperate for the few farthings their women and starving children can earn. They do not want to be rescued. Go down and speak among them and try to get them to tell their secrets as the Quakers have tried to do, and they will tell you nothing."

"But do they not see they only increase their misery by being so shut mouthed?" Marigold cried. "Sophie, the Cavaliers must expose these exploiters of human misery! The mine manager, at least, can be brought to account for his acts!"

"Oh Marigold," the other girl said with considerable resignation, "what the mine is doing is not unlawful. Women and children may work naked in the depths of a coal mine in England just as they may work from dawn to dark in the spinning mill. Our monarch and his government of nobles sees nothing wrong in oppressing the poor." She picked up the loaves from the table. "Here, do you want me to cut this bread before Penelope gets here? And where is the treacle to mix with the milk?"

Marigold sat silent, biting her lip. They could not ignore the fact that the poor Cavaliers were not so well regarded as they once had been. If they had been dismissed before as young girls of good family with a misplaced idea of social justice, begging food and distributing it to sick chil-

207

dren, at least they had been regarded as capable of doing no great harm. But that was before Marigold's scheme to go to London, to confront the duke of Westermere and force him, if necessary, to do something about the plight of his impoverished villages.

Now Marigold had found that she was not so welcome when she went to solicit weekly donations. And it was not much better for Penelope and Sophronia. Everyone had heard the remarkable gossip that had been carried back from London about Marigold's adventures. Some of the stories were so exaggerated and unfair that Marigold's friends had refrained from repeating them to her, as they knew she would be greatly upset.

As far as Stokesbury Hatton was concerned, no one in the village knew quite what to believe. The rumor that the vicar's daughter had been betrothed to Sacheverel de Vries, the current duke of Westermere, seemed to be true enough. The Stokesbury Hatton miller's cousin who worked for an ostler close by the dukes' mansion in Horton Crescent said it was widely known the banns had been read twice by the Bishop of London at the Church of St. James Viterbius the Lesser in Cheapside.

Before that, young Mistress Marigold's father, the vicar, had gone all the way to London to pay the duke a visit. No doubt to find out what was going on, the gossips added. Prior to the vicar's visit to London the worst sort of stories had come back, that she and her friends had staged a riot

A Special Offer For Leisure Historical Romance Readers Only!

Get Four FREE* Romance Novels

A $21.96 Value!

Thrill to the most sensual, adventure-filled Historical Romances on the market today...

FROM  LEISURE BOOKS

As a home subscriber to the Leisure Historical Romance Book Club, you'll enjoy the best in today's BRAND-NEW Historical Romance fiction. For over twenty-five years, Leisure Books has brought you the award-winning, high-quality authors you know and love to read. Each Leisure Historical Romance will sweep you away to a world of high adventure...and intimate romance. Discover for yourself all the passion and excitement millions of readers thrill to each and every month.

SAVE AT LEAST $5.00 EACH TIME YOU BUY!

Each month, the Leisure Historical Romance Book Club brings you four brand-new titles from Leisure Books, America's foremost publisher of Historical Romances. EACH PACKAGE WILL SAVE YOU AT LEAST $5.00 FROM THE BOOKSTORE PRICE! And you'll never miss a new title with our convenient home delivery service.

Here's how we do it. Each package will carry a 10-DAY EXAMINATION privilege. At the end of that time, if you decide to keep your books, simply pay the low invoice price of $16.96 ($19.98 CANADA), no shipping or handling charges added.* HOME DELIVERY IS ALWAYS FREE.* With today's top Historical Romance novels selling for $5.99 and higher, our price SAVES YOU AT LEAST $5.00 with each shipment.

AND YOUR FIRST FOUR-BOOK SHIPMENT IS TOTALLY FREE!*

IT'S A BARGAIN YOU CAN'T BEAT! A Super $21.96 Value!

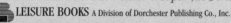 **LEISURE BOOKS** A Division of Dorchester Publishing Co., Inc.

GET YOUR 4 FREE* BOOKS NOW—
A $21.96 VALUE!

Mail the Free* Books
Certificate
Today!

Get Four Books Totally
FREE* —
A $21.96 Value!

(Tear Here and Mail Your FREE* Book Card Today!)

PLEASE RUSH
MY FOUR FREE*
BOOKS TO ME
RIGHT AWAY!

Leisure Historical Romance Book Club
P.O. Box 6613
Edison, NJ 08818-6613

in Covent Garden, that she'd assaulted the young duke and was being held prisoner in his house, where all sorts of nefarious goings-on had taken place. Anyone could a hazard a guess as to what these might be if the father had to insist on a betrothal as a result!

On the other hand, much could be forgiven when one of Stokesbury Hatton's own gentry had been clever enough to make such a great alliance with the purpose of becoming a powerful duke's wife. One could wink at the circumstances that had brought that about.

However, when Marigold returned from London with nothing but the clothes on her back and unwed, and the duke of Westermere nowhere in sight, there was general shock and dismay. Speculation was not kind. Where was the betrothal? Where, indeed, was the marriage?

The vicar's daughter had let her big fish slip from the hook, was the uncharitable conclusion. After all, one could not have much sympathy for a female who, after things had gone as far as everyone had heard, had still failed to get the man to the altar.

Now what would she do? the village wondered. Especially since it was plain the vicar had forced the betrothal in the first place, going down to London to confront the young duke and demanded that he do the honorable thing.

Sophronia must have read Marigold's thoughts, for she asked, "Did all go well enough when you were collecting this week?"

Marigold lowered her eyes. "Well, as you can see, we don't have as much as people usually give." She sighed. "Oh Sophie, I've told myself that it's because winter's ending and there's always a shortage just before spring, that at this time of year even the most generous hold back."

Sophronia scowled. "Marigold, was anyone rude to you when you went to collect?"

"Oh no! The St. Dunstan's people say nothing to me, of course, even if their manner positively reeks of Christian charity. Fat Mrs. Bosthwaite even patted my hand! I tell you, their 'forgiveness' is almost as difficult to bear as the miller's pinching my bottom before he would give me a stingy bag of flour! But whatever one can say about this dreadful mess, it is obvious I am in all eyes a fallen woman."

"Now, Marigold," Sophronia protested, "not all are like that! Mary Wollstonecraft says—"

Marigold put both hands over her ears. "Dear Sophie, don't speak of Mary Wollstonecraft just yet! I swear to you, I wallow in a sea of confusion as to what our leader and spiritual guide meant when she wrote of a woman's intimate connection with man. It was all so clear to me before," she moaned, "and now it is not. Not after London!"

Sophronia poured the vicarage's jug of milk into a bowl and added the stone cup of treacle, watching her friend out of the corner of her eye. Marigold had not been very forthcoming as to what had happened in the duke's house in London. Certain parts of the story that she'd told to her dearest friends, Sophronia and Penelope, had been most honestly detailed. Marigold had claimed that, following the initial collapse of their scheme to blackmail him and the duke's failure to respond either to Marigold's sincere appeals for help for Stokesbury Hatton or to her tearing off her clothes in public, she had decided—partly because of the difficulty of dealing with Westermere's overbearing masculine nature—to cultivate his potential virtues with overtures of friendship, respect, and affection. Up to that point, it sounded as if the Three Cavaliers had achieved their goal.

But now she was back again, and it was obvious something had gone wrong.

One rainy afternoon when they were all having tea in the vicarage's parlor, Marigold had confessed that the friendship, affection and respect that she had offered to the duke, qualities that had seemed so promising after their remarkable chess game, had, yes, led to the ultimate physical intimacy of Mary Wollstonecraft's teachings.

It was something about which Penelope and Sophronia had been burningly curious, but hadn't wanted to press her. Yet they confessed they were consumed with excitement. So it was true, then! First they wanted to know what "the ultimate physical intimacy" was like. And second, why it hadn't worked. Penelope reminded Marigold that this was, after all, what she, Penelope, had first suggested several weeks ago, when they were taking tea in the duke's library.

"If I remember rightly, that was a different sort of proposal," Marigold said stiffly. "Really, Penny, you wanted me to somehow mesmerize Westermere with sensual physical acts that would enslave him—your very words—so that he could be persuaded to do something about his oppressed villages."

Sophronia had looked from one face to the other. "Was this the conversation the duke overheard when he came in and threw Penny's cloak in the fire? That you intended to render him helpless with lust, after you had already threatened rape and blackmail?" Before her friend could answer she went on, "Marigold, you told me it was his intransigent masculine nature that made Westermere so difficult, and accounted so much for our lack of success! But surely the man had some reason to feel, after he heard you so openly discuss seducing him with Penelope, that you—we—were troublesome and treacherous and not to be trusted!"

"How can you say that?" Marigold burst out.

"And you *did* succeed," Penelope put in, "because after all, he promised to marry you! Why, Westermere even went so far as to see you properly betrothed!"

Sophronia dropped her voice. "Come, Marigold, tell us, was having physical intimacy with someone like Westermere a sublime experience as Mary Wollstonecraft assures us—although in not so many words? Or was he brutal, inconsiderate, and the act itself something you would rather forget?"

Marigold squared her shoulders, her face flushed. She felt she looked the picture of guilt and embarrassment, but she could not bring herself to tell even her dearest friends what it had been like to achieve Mary Wollstonecraft's ideal in Westermere's arms.

Physical intimacy—drat the term—had made her completely vulnerable to his sensual power, and was no doubt due to some hitherto undiscovered, miserable fatal flaw in her moral character. She'd found these last few days that even staying in the same city with him would have been madness if she wanted to continue to call her soul her own. Even now her heart ached, and she could not sleep for thinking of him.

Marigold realized she had made a sacrifice she could not bring herself to explain, for she feared her friends might think her the worst kind of fool—not to be able to stand up to a mere man and maintain her independence and integrity just because—just because she'd slept with him.

"Whether it was a sublime experience or not," she said, her voice trembling, "is hardly relevant to what is happening now that I have returned. I know you are my dear friends, Penelope and Sophronia, and will always support me, as indeed I will support you, too. In whatever we do. But my . . . foray—to London, if we can call it that, has changed nothing. What we should be discussing is that conditions on Westermere's lands are even worse than when I left."

Marigold's words, spoken as the Three Cavaliers sat in the vicarage parlor, had been: "I left London because I had failed. You do not think I would do otherwise if there remained any hope, do you?" She wanted them to understand that the duke of Westermere could never be converted to the ideal of an enlightened, compassionate peer.

Sophronia was opening the egg basket. Now she gave a dismayed exclamation. "Oh, Marigold, only two eggs are intact. The rest is egg soup!"

Marigold quickly stood up to see. She put her arm around her friend's shoulder. "Oh well, all is not lost," she sighed. "At least the Widow McCandlish's dainty biscuits are still with us!"

At that moment the kitchen door flew open and Penelope, wearing a bright new plaid woolen cloak, stood there, looking triumphant.

"Dear friends, all is not lost," she crowed. She was carrying string bags of bread, and food in cloth-wrapped parcels, and kicked the door closed behind her. "We're blessed with good luck! I have the remains of Mrs. Horton's dinner virtually untouched because the family was too indisposed to eat, as most of them have the grippe. The children will love it. There's a fine piece of roast pork we can slice thin so that nearly everyone has a taste, and a ton of boiled potatoes."

"Little Johnny Cobb," Marigold breathed. Their consumptive, five year-old angel needed good food; he and his mother, Molly, and her hungry brood were always on her mind.

Penelope put down the bags on the table and drew an excited breath, her blond curls bouncing under her bonnet. "And there's more."

"Where?" Marigold said, looking over their windfall.

"Not there, you dunce! It's not food, it's in the town!" Penny grabbed Marigold's and Sophronia's hands. "Sing the praises of the Three Cavaliers!" she cried. "Winston Lane is full of drays and servants, so crowded no one can get through. And all the windows have been opened up and they are scrubbing everything. People are saying The Elms hasn't been open for twenty years or more; no one remembers what it looks like inside. But it will be grand, I know, for the furniture and things that I saw are most elegant. And an army of servants, all in uniforms and livery, even the porters!"

"Stop, stop," Sophronia cried, disentangling her hand. "What are you talking about, Penny?"

"The old Westermere house, The Elms! Have you forgotten it's there in Winston Lane but back up in the trees so that one can hardly see it from the road?" She whirled on Marigold. "Oh, sweet friend, you have not failed! All will be repaired now that he's coming, you'll see!"

Marigold stared at her, dreading to hear. "Who?" she whispered.

"The duke!" Sophronia and Penelope shouted together. "The Elms is the Westermeres' house,"

Penelope said, doing an Indian war dance about the kitchen. "He's coming here, he's coming from London! The duke knows now that he owns Stokesbury Hatton, what else could it be? Marigold, you must take up your good work again!"

Chapter Fourteen

Pomfret the butler ushered Sir Robert Peel into the library, where the duke of Westermere was sitting hunched over his achromatic microscope at the great marble-topped table.

Sir Robert could not help noticing the library's latest addition, a very large brass telescope mounted on a tripod nearly four feet tall, and positioned at the library windows so that the instrument pointed up at the winter sky.

"What a beauty, Satch," Sir Robert said, going to the telescope and putting his eye to it. "Trying out another perspective, from the ridiculousness of the microcosm to the submlimity of the cosmos?"

"The microcosm is hardly ridiculous," the other muttered, not looking up, "it's damned fascinating or I would not spend so much time exploring it. Look at this."

Sir Robert came over to the library table, and threw himself into a chair. He wrinkled his nose. "Something stinks," he said, looking about him.

The duke grunted. "Blood samples get a little ripe after a while. I've noticed Mrs. Cawdigan has grown somewhat gingerly mopping up in here."

"Blood samples?" The peer hastily put down a flask he'd been examining. "Odds fish, my friend, what are you up to now?"

The duke looked up from the microscope, then sat back in his chair and rubbed his eyes with thumb and forefinger. Robert Peel thought he had seldom seen him looking so haggard. The fact that Sacheverel de Vries was also unshaven at that hour, and rather carelessly dressed in trousers and lounge jacket and wrinkled cotton shirt was unusual, too.

"God take it, Bobby," he said irritably. "The maddening thing is that, as always, no one will give a farthing for the idea, in spite of the fact that it well may revolutionize the field of criminal law."

The other stroked his chin. "Blood samples," he murmured.

The duke raised an irascible eyebrow. "Yes, blood samples. We know there are incompatible differences between animal blood and human blood, it is plainly seen under the microscope. That is why Denis's experiments a hundred and fifty years ago in France using lamb's blood to transfuse humans produced such disastrous results. And why ten years later our own English Parliament prohibited hemolytic transfusions. Unfortunately, there has been no serious scientific study since. However—"

He paused, scowling as Sir Robert, still maintaining an air of interest, took out a handkerchief from his sleeve and held it to his nose. "Sorry, Satch," the peer murmured, "you haven't killed anyone in here lately, have you? My senses are responding to the subtle miasma of the abbatoir."

"I don't see what you keep complaining about. Haven't I just explained it to you? Pomfret!" the duke shouted.

The old man appeared almost instantly, carrying a tray with brandy and glasses, followed by a footman with a spray bottle of light floral essence. While Pomfret quickly poured Sir Robert a glass of spirits the footman covered the four corners of the room, squirting the flowery scent into the air.

"—in comparing animal to human blood," the duke went on as if there had been no interruption, "I have made a discovery. Human blood, too, from one individual to another is quite different. Although I confess the components are so numerous and unknown to me, I scarce know what to make of them. I can identify red cells, which is about the sum of what is known, I am sorry to say, but there are others which seem of similar construction, yet bear only superficial resemblance to the red."

Sir Robert downed his brandy as the butler and

footman noiselessly withdrew. When he put aside his glass he took the opportunity to study his friend for several long moments.

As all his friends and acquaintances were well aware, the young duke of Westermere had been gifted with an acerbic nature to accompany his undisputed genius. But the change in him now was quite apparent. There was something there—a bitterness?—that Sir Robert could not quite fathom. And no one had explained yet the disappearance from Horton Crescent of the extraordinary Miss Fenwick, the fiancée; it was certainly an important factor in Westermere's current mood.

"What are you doing, Satch?" he said, softly.

The duke rubbed his eyes again. "You think me mad, Bobby," he said, tiredly. "But I am only trying to find a scale of difference that will enable the forensic scientist to identify both victim and criminal by their blood. Come now, think how important that would be to a reformed division of police. In place of the bullies and extortionists we now find keeping the peace under the guise of constables, we would have an enlightened, educated, scientific agency of trained men to inquire into criminal cases, and enforce the laws."

"Hmmm. It is an excellent idea, brilliant, but then I would expect that of you."

Even as he spoke, Sir Robert knew that for some weeks, from the date of Miss Fenwick's departure to be exact, Satch had shut himself up in the Horton Crescent house on the excuse of doing research, keeping faithfully to a skeleton of his former schedules such as the morning ride in Rotten Row, and visits to his club—where it was said, he was still negotiating his way out of some infraction of Brown's rules.

But for many who knew him there had been a change in Westermere. When he was not in the library pursuing experiments carried out with the microscope, he was conferring with his solicitors and managers. One of Sir Robert's acquaintances in the banking exchange had told him that the duke of Westermere had been making inquiry into every piece of property, every Westermere investment both in England and overseas, that the vast family empire claimed.

It was unlike Satch to express any interest in the sources of his money, Sir Robert thought as he studied him; since the war his obsession had been only with things scientific. This sudden interest in his holdings was a curious development. And so far, not one word from him about the delightful young woman who had prompted Sacheverel de Vries to do what had heretofore been regarded by his friends as the impossible: announce his engagement and his desire for an expeditious marriage. Had that fallen through? he wondered.

Sir Robert said, "Tell me, Satch, when was the last time you slept?"

The other gave him a burning look. "Last night." He hiked himself up in his seat and looked into his microscope again. "Don't cluck over me,

Bobby, is that what you came for? Well, this is not Spain, and you are no longer my superior officer."

Pomfret hovered over Lord Peel with the brandy bottle, but he waved him away. "I came to pay a friendly call," Peel said evenly, "that is all, and to inquire after your health. Which seems a mite debilitated. You look, as my mother used to say, quite peaked. Has Reggie Pendragon seen you?"

His response, as the duke peered into the microscope, was something resembling a snarl. Sir Robert decided there was nothing like taking the bull by the horns.

"Not worried about finances, are you?" he asked. "Come, Satch, we've been friends a long time. If money reverses are the trouble, I want to put delicacy aside and offer my agents to you, Strothers and Darnworthy, excellent chaps, I have every confidence in them and they have brought me enviable returns on my investments. If you—"

"Desist, Peel," the other said abruptly. "No matter what you may have heard, I am not impoverished!"

"I have hardly heard that," Sir Robert said. "And if I did I would not believe it. I have heard only that you've been closeted with managers and solicitors for weeks, delving into the particulars of your fortune. Which is not like you, Satch. To speak bluntly, you are one of the few men I know who is totally oblivious to his wealth."

Under his breath the duke said, "Were to God everyone shared that attitude."

Ah, Sir Robert knew, he had hit upon something. "Do I detect a note of bitterness? Has someone tried to bilk you? I thought you were impervious to that sort of thing."

Westermere looked up from his microscope, scowling. "Bilk me? You are absolutely right, Bobby, I've been gulled while indulging in the worst sort of stupid innocence. It's the classic story. Who else but a woman could do it?"

The other man was taken off guard. "Surely not the estimable Miss Fenwick, the Yorkshire vicar's daughter?" He looked his surprise. "Your pardon, Satch, but I would have sworn on a stack of Bibles that could not be so! How much did she take you for?"

Satch sat silent for a long moment before he said, "In terms of money and material things, nothing. Although, damn me, she tried hard enough." He got up abruptly and paced away from the table. "In this she was confoundedly insidious and clever. My fiancée never solicited gowns and jewels, the usual sort of demands, nor did she press for marriage. Another first for me, you may be sure. In fact she protested she did not want to be married, in order to increase my desire for a speedy tying of the knot! I confess to you, Bobby, I was outflanked, outmaneuvered and eventually decimated by these tactics. What she wanted, she told me, was a considerable part of my wealth to rectify alleged wrongs in some damned villages to the north I didn't even know I had. When she talked of mines and spinning mills, I thought she was babbling."

"Hmmm," Sir Robert said. "And you had them."

The duke ran his hand through his tousled black hair.

"Christ, yes. The solicitors tell me Westermere holdings are as thick as fleas up to the Scottish border. With mines, spinning mills, weaving towns, fishing villages, et cetera. For the most part they're run by companies of factors and managers. My father had little or no contact with anything except through the London solicitors' offices, and I know nothing of my grandfather's interests. You call me oblivious. I tell you, I was brought up in ignorance of all of it, and damn me, I would have preferred to keep it that way!"

He turned and strode back the length of the library, hands clasped behind him.

"You know the rest of it, no doubt city gossip has enlightened you," he growled. "Miss Fenwick threw herself into my coach pleading the case of the poor oppressed, as she put it, on Westermere lands, and demanding that I rectify the abundant evils thereof. I told her in so many words I had nothing to do with her accusations, and tried to throw her out of my coach. At that, she created a disturbance, threatening to blackmail me, and the upshot of it was that I took her here and sent for her father. By that time, surveying the havoc Miss Fenwick had wrought both to her reputation and mine, I told the father that I would put a good face on it and marry her."

"Ah, yes, she was your house guest for a while," Sir Robert said, diplomatically. "While you were readying the—ah, betrothal."

"What?" Lost in his thoughts, the duke turned to him. "Yes, house guest. You came to dinner several times, I recollect, when she was here."

"She made a delightful hostess."

"Umm, yes. She had the right social graces, I'll say that for her."

"In my opinion," Sir Robert drawled, "she was one of the most outstandingly beautiful young women I've ever seen." He paused. "Miss Fenwick is rather young, Satch. All of eighteen, did you say?"

The duke scratched his jaw, glowering. "Then she decamped in the middle of the night," he muttered. "Out of my bed like a shot while I slept, without so much as a note, or a message left with the servants. Nothing. A stupid move to make. I didn't tell her that after we were married I was going to settle ten thousand pounds a year on her. That should have been enough to clean up half a dozen miserable villages."

Sir Robert Peel considered all this. "Was she seized by sudden, inexplicable caprice, do you suppose? An irrational feminine whim?" He was beginning to feel this matter of the mysteriously disappearing fiancée was at the root of his friend's dismal funk. "Or had you done something to offend her?"

Katherine Deauxville

"I play a damned poor game of chess," the other admitted, "but hardly bad enough to drive anyone out of London. No, the thing's had me confounded. And don't ask, Bobby, for I will gladly tell you—few women have left my bed less than satisfied. I took particular pains with her, she was a virgin after all, and she was most enthusiastic. Exceptionally so. In fact she seemed blissfully happy, dammit, when I dozed off."

"Perhaps, being inexperienced, she took offense at that." Sir Robert didn't believe it, but he thought he'd put it in.

"Poppycock," the duke snorted. "She could have waked me, couldn't she, if she wanted anything? At any rate, now that I've found out about the suffering villages, I've sent some of my people north to open one of the Westermere houses and fix it up for my visit. I intend to go up to whatever the name of the place is—"

"Stokesbury Hatton," Sir Robert murmured.

"Yes." The duke scowled at him. "And have a look at the spinning mills and the coal mines and whatever. It can't be as bad as she would have me believe. I've seen the profit sheets and from the money I'm making there it seems to me the managers are running things fairly efficiently. If all were as bad as she contends, I'm damned sure that wouldn't be the case."

"And you'll see her," Sir Robert said, standing up to take his leave, and motioning for Pomfret to bring his hat and his cloak. At the duke's savage

226

look he added, "To demand an explanation, of course."

"Of course," Sacheverel de Vries, twelfth duke of Westermere responded. "What the devil else would I want to see that damned deceitful baggage for?"

Chapter Fifteen

Marigold, Penelope and Sophronia made their way down the street of the millworkers' cottages, carrying jugs of milk fortified with beaten egg and black West Indian treacle, and other food donations, including the remains of the Hortons' dinner. The twilight was turning chill, and there was a dampness in the air that magnified the special aromas of the area.

"Oh, I wish they wouldn't empty chamberpots into the ditch," Penelope complained, holding her nose.

The wheels of passing traffic straddled the open drain, but walking was hazardous. "They've got to put night soil somewhere," Sophronia said, "what else can you do with it?"

"They can build outhouses," the teacher's

daughter grumbled. "We have one, you know, and we are not rich. Da built it with his own hands. Sometimes I think people are right, and the poor in their sloth make things worse for themselves."

Marigold shifted her heavy parcels and looked at her friend in disbelief. "Sloth? I'm ashamed of you, Penny, to say such a thing. I know of no slothful poor in Stokesbury Hatton unless they are so sick and starved they can scarce take care of themselves."

"If the mill people had lumber to build out-houses," Sophronia reasoned wisely, "they would doubtless chop up the wood to use it for fires to keep their children warm."

They jumped the ditch, one by one, to cross over to the Cobbs' house. Johnny's mother met them at the door, wiping her wet hands on her skirt, as she took in washing and had not yet finished her day's work.

"Ah, bless you, young misses," she cried, when she saw the Cavaliers. "I see you carrying the jugs this week so I'm thinking you have some egg and milk." She stood aside to let the girls pass into the one-room, flagstone-floored hut euphemistically called a "cottage" by the mill company. "Nothing helps my darling Johnny more; it was a stroke of luck you could think of such a thing, young ladies so pretty and clever both."

Molly Cobb, a tall, broadfaced woman in her twenties with hair already turning gray, never showed, unlike some of the other mill people,

229

that she had heard of Marigold's disastrous venture to London. Molly continued to receive the girls more than warmly, certainly in part because she desperately needed the food they brought.

Five-year-old Johnny was lying by the fire on a makeshift bed of rags and old blankets, but he sat up and held out his arms when he saw the girls.

"Ah, how's my angel?" Marigold cried, sinking to her knees beside him.

The uneven flagstones cut into her kneecaps and she couldn't help thinking of the invalids' pensions in England's lake country that catered to consumptives. The sketches she'd seen of vast open porches overlooking magnificent scenery showed patients lying on couches in the sun, building their strength with fresh air and healthful food. Fair-haired little Johnny would not have such a chance at survival. Neither she nor Penelope nor Sophronia nor even their fathers had the resources to give it to him.

The child's body was bony and fragile as she held him in her arms. His skin never lost what the villagers called the "grave pallor," except for two hectic red spots on each cheekbone that were the telltale signs of consumptive lung disease.

"Give me your mouth, precious," Penelope said, holding the cup to his lips, "and drink up. When you've got the milk all down I've a bit of roast pork and boiled taties for you."

Johnny grimaced at the iron taste of the treacle in the milk. "Ma says good food will make me strong," he told Penny. "I asked her to say her prayers it wa'nt take too long, for I need to get up and work like me brothers Ben and Jimmy. Me ma needs help, or they're going to put us out."

Marigold got to her feet. "What is this you're saying?" She drew Molly aside, a frowning Sophronia joining them. "How can they put you out?" Marigold cried. "This is a mill cottage, your man was a good worker there before he died. I thought it was promised to you and the children for as long as you·needed."

Molly twisted her hands together, her eyes shifting away. "Ah, young missus, it's not putting me out, exactly. I won't lose me cot if I do what the company wants. There's naught in the mill for me, but Mr. Parham says there are jobs down in the mine, but the children must come and work, too." Her mouth twisted. "Even the little lad. I begged and begged, but Mr. Parham and the mine director, Mr. Hatfield, they came in and looked around and said I had a cottage all to meself with me children and didn't have to share with another family, which was more than I deserved, seeing how I was idle and not working. Mr. Hatfield said Johnny looked able-bodied enough and must work with me other children, too."

Marigold looked as though she were about to burst with indignation. "They looked at him and said he was able to endure the drudgery of the coal mine? The child is sick! Molly, you know Miss Sophronia's father examined him and told you Johnny has lung fever!"

"Oh, miss, don't shout so!" Molly looked

around, trembling, although there was no one to hear. "Spare me little family, I beg you, and don't make no fuss. We don't need no trouble, I don't see that we can do much more than bear our lot what the good Lord has given us, and do as Mr. Hatfield says. I can't let them put me poor children out into the street!" She lowered her voice and said, "You could call me fortunate, you know, for some of the other women on the mill street have another burden as well, if young Mr. Parham fancies them. And it's not just getting what he wants, neither. You're lucky, they tell me, if you don't come away covered with knots and bruises. He takes his pleasure very cruel."

Sophronia made a hissing sound under her breath. "Robinson Parham is molesting the mill women here? And they dare not resist his advances?"

Molly looked confused for a moment. "Molests them, yes, young misses, if you means does he take a girl up to his house and have carnal knowledge of her. Sometimes it's for more than one night, too, if he takes a particular fancy. He'll lock them away in his house until he's through with them, and it makes no difference to him what crying and begging goes on, either from them or their families, he takes what he wants. Parham fancies them young, that's the pity of it. Thirteen or fourteen's his favorite ages, although there's many a poor girl what has taken to the road and left Stokesbury Hatton, and her family urging her to go rather than have her maidenhead taken, and cruel-like, too, by that devil of a handsome beast."

"He needs killing," Sophronia said between her teeth. "A man like that ought not to be allowed to live."

The two women turned to her, one frightened, the other appalled. "Sophie," Marigold cried, "do not say such a thing! What if someone overheard you? The Parhams are most vengeful and powerful. They control the village, do they not? And you have told us he's already approached you with his evil intent."

"Lord, miss, you too?" Molly blurted. "And here I thought it was only the poor women that son of Satan preys on!"

"He will harass any woman," Sophronia said, darkly. "I see now Parham's nature is such that he will not hold back from any woman if he desires her. And we are agreed on what his loathesome desires are like."

Marigold put her hand on her friend's arm. "Oh Sophie, go no further, I beg you! You must put a check on your reckless tongue, or I fear we will draw suspicion that we are plotting against the Westermeres and their toadies. Then if anything happens, we will be blamed."

The other girl looked at her with her with strange lights dancing in her gypsy eyes. "And is anything going to happen?" she murmured.

Marigold shuddered. "Please, don't let's talk of it! We must avoid violence, or the appearance of it, at all costs. After all, we must not forget that we have our fathers and their livelihoods to consider as well as ourselves." But something had occurred to her even as she spoke. Just the smallest of ideas that seemed to flower, a quick inspiration that might become the most daring of plans.

She stood there, biting her lip as she watched Penelope sitting on the hearth feeding little Johnny Cobb bits of cold roast pork and boiled potato.

"We must go down into the mine," Marigold said, "and see the condition of women and children there. Otherwise no one will believe us, and call it hearsay when we testify to what's going on. If Westermere is coming here we must have something valid with which to confront him."

She quickly turned to Molly. "Rest easy, we are not going to ask you or the other women here to come forth, for we know you rightly fear the wrath of the Parhams if you should do so."

Molly blurted, "Ah, young misses, I'm sorry to say there's not a woman nor yet a man who would help you challenge Mr. Hatfield and the Parhams outright, for their vengeance would be so quick you'd never find out what had become of us!" She drew a deep breath, gathering her courage. "But we can help. If you wish to go down into the mines and witness for yoursel's what takes place there, we can find some what will do their best to get you into the galleries and out again."

Sophronia's face was fierce. "I'll do it, I'll go into the mines! If this is the way to bring Parham down, then I'll strike that blow for justice. Although I still think it would be better just to kill him."

"La, Sophie, if you continue to talk that way I fear for the success of our mission!" Marigold told her. "Besides, not one of us can go alone; we must all three witness, for it will make our story stronger."

Penelope had left Johnny to gather the other Cobb children and give them pieces of hardtack to chew on. Now she joined them. "What are all three of us going to witness?" she said brightly.

"We will tell you later," Marigold said, taking her arm as they gathered up their parcels and bade the Cobbs good-bye. "Outside, Penny, in a place where there is room enough for you to swoon when you hear."

Penelope laughed. "I am not going to swoon, you silly. There's nothing you could tell me that would make me act so, is there?"

But when Penny looked from Marigold to Sophronia and saw her friends' faces, her laughter died.

Three miles away, in the old dukes of Westermeres' house on Winston Lane, Mrs. Cawdigan walked through the newly cleaned rooms, giving them a last inspection.

Without old Pomfret under her feet and interfering, things got done in half the time. Certainly to take a house that hadn't been opened for twenty years and clean it, scrub it and even set the duke's porters to doing a bit of painting was no small job. And yet, as she walked through the rooms in the waning light, Mrs. Cawdigan judged herself satisfied. The rest of the furnishings, two more beds, a pianoforte, paintings, clocks, and bric-a-brac taken from the London place in Horton Crescent, and a few choice items brought by dray from the grand Westermere estate in Sussex, would arrive on the morrow.

Stopping in the dining room, Mrs. Cawdigan sniffed the air and looked about with a look of sheer pleasure. She liked the odor of newly cleaned rooms. Here the dining room floors had been newly waxed and smelled of it pleasantly. The chandelier had been lowered that afternoon and all its sparkling prisms cleaned, and at dusk a fine Hamadan carpet from Persia had been laid down. The room, dim in the twilight, waited now for the Charles the Second dining table and chairs to be brought in.

The present duke's grandfather had acquired the Stokesbury Hatton house from the local baronet when the duke had bought or confiscated most of the land north of the market town of Hobbs. But the old duke of Westermere had visited there but once, to inspect the mill and the mine, and then only overnight. Which was a shame, Mrs. Cawdigan couldn't help thinking. The house was far too fine not to be used.

The red brick two-story edifice, while not large in the grand manner of the London mansion or some of the great Westermere country estates, was a fine jewel in the Restoration-era style with its ornate plaster ceiling decorations and moldings, marble fireplaces, mahogany staircase, and a plentitude of long, French-style windows. The gardens had not been kept up, and out back were the untidy ruins of a boxwood maze that begged to be either cut down or set in order. But the porters and footmen had seen to the front shrubbery and the trees along the drive, cutting them back and hastily trimming until, all in all, The Elms presented a fairly inviting appearance.

The housekeeper picked up her candle and was about to leave the dining room when a sudden shadow startled her.

"The holy saints preserve us," she burst out, "you sneak up on me like that again, and no matter how big you are I'll give you a what-for with the back of me hand that will set your ears to ringing!" She paused, and put her hand over her plump bosom and racing heart. "What're you doing up here in this little village?" she demanded. "You're supposed to be in London!"

"Back and forth, back and forth," Jack Ironfoot said blandly. He removed his wide-brimmed coachman's hat and stood looking about, approving the freshly restored room. "I been going back and forth on errands in the four-in-hand coach. Today I bring His Grace's clothes as neatly packed away in boxes and trunks by the everworthy Mr. Timothy Cruddles. And how have you been, Mrs. Cawdigan? Will all be ready when His Grace arrives on Tuesday?"

The housekeeper's eyes narrowed. "Back and

forth is it? Prowling around is more like it, Jack Ironfoot! You don't put nothing past me!"

She herded him out of the dining room and into the downstairs hall and closed the door.

"You'll see me again in three days," the coachman said, studying her cautiously. "I'm bringing up His Grace's telescope in the big coach, with some of his scientific things he likes to have with him."

Mrs. Cawdigan snorted. "Ah, yes, that's all well and good, me boy. But if I was to guess," she said, wagging her finger at him, "I'd say you already been down to the village to have your look around, and out to them dreadful mill tenements, and given a look, yes, to the mines while you were at it. All the time having a sharp eye out for whatever it is you're looking for."

"Now Mrs. Cawdigan, me beauty," the coachman rumbled, taking her arm as she put down the candle on the hall table and snuffed it out. He held open the front door for her. "What makes you think I'm looking for anything, when I've got the pleasing distraction of your fine face and form so near in me sights?"

"Bah!" Mrs. Cawdigan retorted. She shook her arm from his grip. "None of your fish oil if you please, Mr. Ironfoot, I've no time for it." She took her ring of keys from her belt and locked The Elms' freshly painted front door. Then she turned to him.

"If you've his safety in mind," the housekeeper said in a low voice, "and I gather that you do, Mr.

Ironfoot, then you'd be best served to stick closer, like there in London with him. And not up here in this Yorkshire place where there's naught but poor folk and misery."

Jack gave her a long, thoughtful look. Mrs. Cawdigan could not see his face in the waning light and he had put back on the coachman's hat with its concealing brim.

"Ah, Mrs. Cawdigan, my rose," he said finally, taking her arm again. "You could not be more wrong. It's not London nor this here little grimy town where danger lurks. For the likes of him, fine brave young man that he is, it's everywhere."

Chapter Sixteen

The volunteers to take Marigold, Sophronia and Penny down into the mine were not men, but two barefoot women wearing shawls who stepped out of the shadows.

"Don't expect no names," Molly Cobb had warned them. "It's dangerous enough what they do, taking you young misses into the mine right under the noses of their bosses, for they risk losing not only their work but the food right out of the mouths of their poor families if they're caught. Anybody what's doing what they do will be drove right out of town, mark my word, and that's the least of it. Mr. Hatfield will see they're set on the road to starve. They know it, poor dears."

Now one shadowy figure said in a hoarse whisper, "You cain't wear no shoes."

The other shawled shape added, "The mine bosses will spot you for sure with them good leather shoon. Take 'em off and stick 'em under the bench, there."

The Cavaliers could hardly find the bench, it was so dark, but did as they were told. It was obvious the other women had eyes that had adjusted to darkness after working in it for so long.

The ground under their bare feet was freezing. Marigold tried to explain in a cautious whisper that they were eager to do as the other women directed; that they appreciated what was being done for them and realized the risks the others were taking, but the taller figure interrupted. "Shoes ain't the only things what you'll be shedding," she said, ominously.

There wasn't time to ask questions as they crouched behind some pens that were used for the mine ponies. The mine was running two shifts, one for the day and one for the night. The miners for the night shift were making their way toward the open mouth of a shaft that led at a steep slope downward to the underground workings. All the men wore caps with small candle lanterns in them, the tongues of light looking like so many fireflies against the blackness of the mine head. There were women and children, too, in the crowd, barefoot, indistinct shapes, with most of the women wearing shawls over their heads.

241

All three Cavaliers had been told to dress in their oldest clothing, but they could see they lacked the all-important layer of coal dust. Following the other women's whispered instructions, they gathered the cindery stuff from the pony pens and rubbed it into their clothing and exposed white skin until they began to look like the rest.

"We're a'goin' down number two gallery," one of the women told them. "That's the pit opening, over there. Tom Grandison is pit boss down number two. He already been told what you young missies want to see, and he give his permission, Tom did. He's a good man, he wants to see the poor miners' lot made easier. But he wants you to know the women and even the bairns don't want to lose their work, now. What little his lordship pays us is desperate needed to keep our families from the cold and hunger."

Marigold fixed her azure eyes on the two women. "Then what is it you want us to say?"

"Make the work easier," the other woman said promptly. "That's what we want you to tell 'im. And easier for the bairns, too."

"Take the little tads out of the mine altogether," the other snapped. "The work's hard, and only makes them sickly."

Evidently there was a disagreement between them. "Some of us needs the work they can do," the first woman said, turning her shawled head to glare at the other one. "But let the wee ones work short hours, so they's can come above

ground and see the sun sometimes. And don't
send them down so low, near the coal face. That's
hot and dangerous work down there."

"But don't take our work away from us, young
missies," the other woman repeated. She took Sophronia by the arm and hurried her toward the
crowd of workers around the mine entrance. "Remember that—not to take the jobs away entirely
from us poor folk, that's what you're to tell their
lordships."

That wasn't what the Cavaliers had in mind at
all, Marigold thought. They had planned to expose the shameful presence of women and children workers in the mines as something that
should be corrected. But it was no time to argue.
Perhaps some solution could be worked out, she
told herself, as they filed in among the miners going down to the galleries.

"I'm sure some of these people will recognize
us," Penelope moaned in her ear. She was answered by a sharp poke in the back from one of
their guides, and a muttered command not to
talk.

They found themselves in the midst of the night
shift going down to the number two part of the
mine. In spite of Penelope's worry, no one seemed
to notice them. Their concealing shawls and cam-
ouflage of coal dust seemed enough of a disguise,
at least in the dark.

The Stygian blackness was daunting. It was another world after one passed the mine's entrance.
Marigold knew that she, for one, would never get

used to it, no matter how long they stayed there. But the men and women and children shuffling around her seemed accustomed to the suffocating blackness; they walked with their heads down, hands guarding their candles against the stray drafts. It grew warmer as they descended. At one gallery a group of women and children left them to go to wooden pens with mine ponies and lines of coal carts waiting. They would tend the animals for the rest of the night.

Then the tunnel turned sharply and opened into a wide gallery where there was a wooden floor built above puddles of water that accumulated from constant seepage deep in the mine. There were wooden support beams in place overhead. Here the miners who were going to the coal faces below took off their clothes and hung trousers and jackets and shirts up on wooden pegs.

Marigold heard Sophronia's indrawn breath. The miners going to the lower galleries were clad only in underclothes so brief they were little more than rags. Another woman came up to the two women who had guided the Cavaliers into the mine. She wore only what a more genteel world called her "unmentionables," a pair of pantaloons and a torn underbodice, and every inch of her, including her hair, was covered in coal grime.

"Remember the wee children what's sick and are made to work down here," the apparition hissed. "You listen, you can hear them coughing with lung rot, the poor things. You tell that to the precious lords and nobles what get rich off our suffering!"

Some of the miners, hearing her shrill voice, looked in their direction. The two women quickly shoved her away. "She's mad," one of them muttered to Sophronia. "A bad one is Letty Fuller since she lost her husband to the black damp gas a time ago, and come down here to work herself."

"Always talking about the danger," the other woman put in. "As long as you is down in the galleries, young misses, stay away from her."

The two women had taken off their shawls. They wore dirty cloths knotted tightly over their hair. The girls stared as the others shed their woolen dresses and hung them up on pegs driven into the boards of the wall. Both were garbed in ancient, torn underbodices, and tattered pantaloons.

"Strip down, now, ladies," the taller woman said. "Where you're a'goin' you won't tolerate wearing them frocks a minute longer than you have to."

For a moment no one said anything.

"This is our noble cause," Marigold said, turning to Penelope and Sophronia. "We must stick to our good intentions and remember our spiritual leader, Mary Wollstonecraft." But her voice trembled. "At least when we divest ourselves of our frocks we'll be dressed—um, undressed—like everyone else."

"But Marigold," Penny whispered in an agony,

"there are men here, just look at them! I don't think I—"

"Sophie," Marigold said urgently.

Before Penny could utter another word Sophronia and Marigold flanked her and in a rather desperate flurry peeled off Penny's old tattered gardening frock and then their own clothes.

If we don't look at each other, Marigold was thinking as she and Sophronia and a shaken Penny hurriedly rubbed coal dust on their chemise tops and pantaloons, *it will be all right*.

The foremen and pit bosses had come into the gallery. Now they shouted out the work orders for the night. The pit gangs filed away into the dark tunnels, their voices echoing until they faded away. Wan, half-naked children led pit ponies dragging coal carts along the iron rails, the candles in the lanterns they carried flickering brightly.

Marigold and her group had backed into an alcove and were partly hidden. But a tall, almost completely naked miner found them and came over and addressed the two women in an undertone. Sweat glistened on his muscular body; the girls could not seem to drag their eyes away. The man was almost nude, but rather incongruously he was wearing heavy boots, as were the other men who worked on the coal face. As he talked, his teeth and eyes flashed whitely in his grimed face. This was Tom Grandison, the boss on the number-two coal seam.

"An hour or so, no more than that." He nodded

in their direction. "And then send them back up. No longer than that, the risk's too great."

The two women who had brought them down into the mine assented, and the half-naked, muscular man hurried off.

"Now we'll get you a cart," one of the women said in a low voice. "Where we're going, there's a plenty to see."

There was, indeed. If someone had told the three girls that they were about to glimpse a part of Dante's famous hell, they would not, of course, have believed it. But they pushed a coal cart down the iron rails at an incline so steep they had to dig their heels into the floor to keep it from running away with them. They juggled their precious lanterns at the same time, their straining eyes trying to see in the darkness. At one level they came upon wizened children on a ledge, little fellows of no more than five or six, sitting with their arms around each other like strange gnomes, waiting for the coal carts to come by and pick them up. In one of the tunnels there was an almost naked woman in a leather harness at least eight months pregnant, dragging a slag cart. And then there were the blind, bony little ponies that had spent most of their lives underground in the mine's darkness, plodding along pathetically.

As they went lower the heat and lack of air increased until the Cavaliers were gasping and soaked with perspiration. The gallery ceiling was low. They staggered down into the lower levels, almost on their hands and knees, dragging the coal cart to where men worked chopping blocks of coal from the gleaming face. By this time Penny was sobbing softly.

"For God's sake," Sophronia hissed at her, "be still! If little children can endure this, so can you!"

Marigold's eyes had found Tom Grandison, his body gleaming with sweat in the miners' flickering lights. He saw her, too, but his face gave no sign of recognition. All across the coal seam the miners attacked the black surface with their pickaxes, and women and children dragged away the chunks of fallen coal in carts. The three girls waited for their cart to be filled, then started back up the slope.

"Thank heavens we won't be coming back," Marigold whispered. "This is enough."

It was more than enough. Going up the slope toward the mine head was sheer torture. The wooden wheeled cart stuck where the rails had warped, and often veered to the right or left uncontrollably. They were soon gasping in the airless heat, and Sophronia developed a painful stitch in her side. Several times they came upon women and children lying by their carts, their tortured lungs struggling for air. "We must stop and help them," Sophronia gasped.

"There are too many," Marigold responded, grimly. "Our efforts would be futile, alas, and only reveal who we are. Besides, some of them are getting up again after having rested. Our duty is to get to the surface and make the horrors of this infernal place known to the world!"

The words were no sooner out of her mouth then there was the sound of running feet, greatly magnified in the close confines of the tunnel. The pony boys and the women dragging the coal carts scrambled to get out of the way of something coming down the slope.

"What is it?" Penny screamed a moment before she was seized, lifted by unknown hands and carried off.

The coal cart, left unbalanced by Penny's sudden departure, teetered crazily to one side, nearly pinning Sophronia against the tunnel wall. Suddenly a crowd of men filled up the dark.

"Who are you?" someone shouted. "What are you doing down here?"

A man in a tailored coat and shiny top hat, crouching under the low tunnel ceiling, placed himself in Marigold's way. Peering beyond the light from her lantern, she recognized Mr. Hatfield, the mine superintendant. "Seize them!" he cried.

Ahead of them, Penelope was being carried toward the mouth of the mine, screaming loud enough to be heard all the way to the village of Stokesbury Hatton.

The man dragging Marigold said, "Are you sure these are the intruders?" He turned to stare at Marigold in her grime-streaked underclothes. "They look like mine women to me."

So they didn't know who they were! Ahead of them, Superintendent Hatfield had connected with one of Sophronia's lethal kicks and was

249

limping slightly. "This will make a pretty tale," he shouted. "Strange women in the mine for God only knows what purpose. They might be spies, snooping about!"

They came into the night. The Cavaliers were half-dragged through the animal pens and coal carts to an open space where a crowd had gathered. Word had apparently traveled fast in spite of the late hour. A half-dozen men were waiting with lanterns.

"A fine lot," someone in the crowd said, laughing, "hiding in the duke's mine in their underdrawers! What were they hoping for?"

Marigold, Penelope and Sophronia were hauled forward to stand under a ring of lanterns the miners held shoulder high. Light spilled on the girls' coal-blackened faces, wild hair, and sweat-soaked underbodices. Their filthy pantaloons clung indecently to every outline of their lower bodies. Someone made a lewd remark.

Superintendent Hatfield came to stand before them, rocking on his heels and frowning. "Well, who are you?" he barked. "Why have my workers had to report that three bawdy trollops were trespassing in the mine?"

But it was another, familiar voice that answered. "Hatfield," it said loudly, "watch your tongue. If you look careful you will see one young lady is the vicar's daughter of this very town, Miss Marigold Fenwick. And if I am not mistaken the other two young women are her friends, Mistress Sophronia Stack, who is the daughter of the doctor, and the schoolmaster's esteemed offspring, Miss Penelope MacDougal."

There was a gasp from the crowd. All turned to stare at Jack Ironfoot, who stepped into the yellow lantern light.

"But of great importance, Hatfield, I'll have you know, is that Miss Fenwick is the betrothed of His Grace, the present duke of Westermere, proprietor of this mine and village and surroundings." The coachman was a towering figure in his black cape and wide-brimmed black hat, and the crowd shrank back to give him room. "It is far too late an hour for her and the other young ladies to be about these rough parts, in particular with no one to see to their protection."

The mine director recognized a member of the duke of Westermere's household, and quickly snatched off his stovepipe hat. But he peered at the barefoot, coal-blackened females before him with a face full of amazement and doubt. "Old Fenwick's daughter is the duke's betrothed?" he stammered. "Lord help us, which one is she?"

Jack Ironfoot gave the man a ferocious smile. "Hatfield, dismiss the matter from your mind, as no harm's been done. I am sure you will not object if I now, with your leave, take up the pleasant duty of escorting these young misses homeward."

Marigold and Sophronia hastily gathered up their clothes from under the benches and flung them on as best they could, anxious to be away from the place. Penny had cut her feet in several places while being dragged along in the mine by Robinson's henchmen. She did the best she could as she hobbled along to keep up, shoes in hand, following the tall figure of the duke's coachman.

Some of the crowd, still curious, followed, too, as they started down the hill to the town.

"Don't lallygag, young ladies," Jack Ironfoot cautioned. "One never can tell what some of these people up here in the north have in mind, sorry looking lot that they are." He looked over his shoulder. Then stopped abruptly. "Here now," he exclaimed, "what's happened to young Miss MacDougal?"

Sophronia had been helping Penny along, one arm around her shoulder. "I'm afraid we can't go any faster," she gasped. She knew Ironfoot was right about the mine people following them; their presence in the galleries that night certainly hadn't been explained. Goodness only knew what the grimy men and women, finding them routed out by the management, thought of it. "We were barefoot, and Penny's cut her feet." She looked back. "God in heaven, Penny, you're leaving a trail of blood!"

The duke's hawk-faced coachman whirled on them. "Can't have that. No need for Miss MacDougal to do herself further injury." He reached out and before any of them knew what he was about, swept Penny up in his arms. "I'll carry Miss MacDougal the rest of the way."

His long legs led them swiftly down toward the town. In a few minutes they had left the stragglers behind, and Marigold and Sophronia were running to keep up.

Penny put her arms around Jack Ironfoot's neck to hang on. Close up, the duke's war comrade appeared much younger than she'd expected, certainly not much more than thirty or so. There was no doubt he was strong: He carried Penny at a brisk jog and was not even breathing heavily. Still, she felt she should be polite.

"I would not overburden you, Mr. Ironfoot," she murmured as they turned toward the town green and the Fenwick parsonage. "Particularly as my father's house is quite a bit farther, on the other side of High Street. You have been more than kind, but I feel that if you put me down, I can walk now."

His grip tightened on her. "I have to ask, Miss MacDougal, although I freely admit it is none of my business, what prevailed upon you three young ladies to descend into a Yorkshire coal mine in the middle of the night and expose yourselves to considerable danger? It's something, if you'll pardon my saying so, that comes close to defying explanation, isn't it?"

Penny lifted cornflower-blue eyes to his face. "Mr. Ironfoot," she said softly, "I assure you that although what we did might look foolhardy and dangerous, it was through genuine concern for the terrible conditions, and the welfare of the women and children who are forced to work there. After some very reasonable deliberation, I assure you, we decided that our presence would establish some sort of testimony to the miners' misery."

He slowed to a walk, looking down at her. "Miss MacDougal, are you saying you and your fine young lady friends stripped off your—if you don't mind my saying so—proper clothes and even your shoes, and went down into the perils of a coal mine so as to testify to total strangers' misfortune?"

Penny managed to look reproving even as she clung to the big man with both hands. "Mr. Ironfoot, I am not a flighty, useless female, no matter what the oppressive dictates of our society in regards to women's role in life. It is my earnest desire to prove that I am an individual, a human being who, regardless of sex, is capable of much fortitude and—and—endurance! Which allows me to have active and fruitful compassion for those less fortunate than I. Now," she added, "you may put me down."

He studied her face silently for several strides, but did not stop. Behind them, Sophronia poked Marigold, who was trying to put her old gardening gown and her straggling hair into some sort of order before she got home.

"Look at his face," Sophronia whispered to her friend. "Have you noticed the duke's man is the picture of awe and amazement when he even so much as *looks* at our Penny?"

Marigold uttered a small moan under her breath. "It's not Ironfoot's awe and amazement that concerns me right now, Sophire but my own father's and yours and Penny's. Oh," she burst out, "what have we done? Who would have thought a perfectly sound idea, to be witness to the inhumanity of these dreadful working conditions, would cause us to be caught and escorted in our underclothes from the Stokesbury Hatton mine by Westermere's own bootlickers?" She was struck by a horrible thought. "Do you think it's not over, simply expelling us? Do you think they will still try to take some sort of legal action?"

It was Sophronia's turn to look somber. "I don't care. I'm glad we did it," she said, finally. She gave a defiant toss of her head. "Aren't you?"

Marigold didn't answer.

Chapter Seventeen

"Oh, lud," Marigold exclaimed with real horror, "we're notorious!"

Her eyes scanned the account in *The York Weekly Post* Penelope had just handed her, which began:

THREE WOMEN EJECTED FROM YORKSHIRE COAL MINE

Being an Account of the Mysterious Appearance of Three Females in the Depths of the Stokesbury Hatton Mine and Their Apprehension by Superintendent Mr. Hatfield

"I can't read any more," Marigold moaned, handing the paper back to Penelope. "Not with all that's happening today."

They were seated side by side on the settle in the vicarage parlor; Marigold, Penelope and Sophronia, dressed in their best frocks, their hair attractively arranged as for an important event, but fiercely holding hands, afraid to be parted for the few minutes required to go and claim more comfortable chairs.

It had been a trying afternoon. The three Cavaliers were so filled with poorly suppressed anxiety that they refused even the pleasure of a lunch of bread and butter and tea cakes Marigold had fixed for them. Instead they sat clutching each other while they waited to hear what was happening at The Elms, the duke of Westermere's residence.

Their fathers had been hurriedly summoned that morning to meet with His Grace, the Westermere agent Robinson Parham, and the mine superintendent, Hatfield. Through the long hours that had passed the three girls could only guess at what was being discussed, and the dire consequences that were no doubt brewing.

Sophronia put down the copy of *The York Weekly Post* and lifted her chin, her eyes defiant. "Whoever wrote this can make us out for fools, as indeed he has," she said, "but we know the abominable things that we saw, and will testify to them. That was the whole purpose of the trip into Westermere's coal mine, was it not?"

Penelope rolled her eyes. "Sophie, you know as well as I what has happened since then! That—that wretched writer put it down well when he accused us in the *Weekly Post* of being missish featherheads with fantastical imaginations. There were no poor, ill, suffering women and children in the mines when he went down to explore them. No indeed! Hatfield and that devil incarnate Robinson Parham had seen to their removal just in the nick of time before the duke arrived!"

"We might have known they would do something like that," Marigold muttered.

"Dear Da heard at once," Penelope went on "that the mine women and children have all lost their employment, just as they'd feared. Parham and Hatfield searched them out ruthlessly and sent them off with hardly the day's wages. Even the boss of the coal face, Tom Grandison, who is also minister to the Methodist chapel folk, was told to go and never come back. And he has four children and his aged parents to support! Oh," Penelope wailed, "I cannot tell you how the village people must despise us!"

Sophronia shook her head. "Not all of them. And do try to compose yourself, Penny. Tom Grandison came to the clinic and told Papa that he was not sorry we did what we did, only that we were caught. That he knew we had the welfare of the miners at heart when we went below to see their sufferings for ourselves."

Sophronia saw that Penelope was sitting with

head bent, dabbing at her eyes. On her other side Marigold was biting her lips, worriedly staring off into space.

She lifted her elbows and gave both girls a sharp poke in the ribs.

"Are you listening?" she demanded, when they jumped. "Westermere is here, is he not? Whether he finds women and children in the mine or even believes us when we try to tell our story is not so important when there is still misery enough everywhere for him to see! Parham cannot transform Stokesbury Hatton overnight. The three of us may be held up to ridicule and mockery, but let us take heart and regard it as only temporary. As for me, I want to see that black-hearted villain, Robinson Parham, get his just rewards! Preferably with my knife through his belly!"

"Ugh, don't be so bloodthirsty, Sophie," Penny said, shuddering. "You will get us all into trouble if anyone should overhear you talking so!"

But Marigold, who at the moment had been thinking only of facing the duke again, nodded. "Sophie is right, we have achieved our goal in bringing Westermere here," she said. "It is not the way we planned it, but he is here, and at least we have not had to blackmail him or threaten him with public scandal. At least—ah, not in the way we originally intended." Even Marigold could not overlook that the way things had turned out there had been scandal aplenty. "Well, Westermere would be a stupid, compassionless dolt," she went on bravely, "if he cannot see the injustices of Stokesbury Hatton right before his eyes!"

"Someone must make him see it," Penelope said, softly.

Sophronia added, "Marigold, do not forget, you are still betrothed to him."

Marigold jumped up. "Lud, are we back to that again?" she cried. "Here we sit, waiting for our fathers to come and deliver doom and punishment from the very lips of the great duke himself, and you still talk of my somehow exerting a benevolent influence upon that adamant, intractable, overbearing—"

She ran out of breath and words and stood for a moment, trying to gain her composure.

"Believe me, for I know him well," she finally continued, "if Westermere were in this room now, God knows what awful judgment he would inflict on all of us for daring to trespass on his glorious property. And exposing its true condition in the dreadful Yorkshire press!"

They heard carriage wheels in the driveway. Penelope turned in her seat and pushed aside the window curtains behind the settle. She gave a soft scream. "Oh, Heaven save us, dear friends, we are about to find out! It is the duke's carriage with our parents. Da is just alighting. There's your father, Marigold, and Dr. Stack. And there is the duke himself!"

Sophronia, too, peered through the window curtains. "Marigold, you did not tell me the archfiend was that handsome!"

At that moment Dr. Fenwick came in, followed

by the schoolmaster, Angus MacDougal, and Dr. Stack.

Marigold flew into her father's arms. "Oh, Papa dear," she burst out, "can you forgive me for causing you so much trouble? What can I do to atone for my terrible, headstrong nature?"

Dr. Eusebius Fenwick kissed his daughter on the forehead, and then gently held her away from him. The other girls were close behind Marigold, finding comfort in their fathers' arms. The broad-shouldered duke in black jacket, doeskin breeches and boots, entered the parlor.

"Shhh, dear heart, it is not as bad as all that," the vicar said. "But your young friends must leave now with their fathers. The duke's carriage will convey them safely home."

The Cavaliers took a teary-eyed farewell of each other. "Be brave," Penelope whispered, "like our mentor, the blessed Wollstonecraft."

As the door closed, the duke went over to the parlor mantel and, presenting his back, he busied himself examining a brass candlestick, a volume of Ovid's *Metamorphoses* and the small pot of dried flowers he found there.

Dr. Fenwick said to his daughter in a low tone, "His Grace wishes to speak to you, Marigold, and has asked my permission to do so in privacy. I shall be in my study."

Marigold clutched him. "Papa, don't leave me," she hissed. "If there is to be a punishment, in Heaven's name be merciful and don't leave me to face it alone!"

"Punishment?" The vicar raised his eyebrows. "Nothing of the sort. I have met with Westermere twice now, and His Grace appears to be a man of honor. And, I must remind you, he is your declared intended. He seems very firm on that point. Listen now to what he has to say, dumpling," her father told her. "Since I have heard Westermere's thoughts and find them eminently considerate of your own desires and ideals, I cannot think him unreasonable."

Desires and ideals? A cold chill ran down Marigold's back. Only the saints knew what Westermere had told him!

She groaned aloud as her father let himself out. She whirled to face Westermere at the same time he turned away from his studied inspection of the parlor mantel.

They stared warily at each other.

Marigold was uneasy to find herself with him in a small parlor, where his very size and looks seemed to render everything else insignificant. Those frowning black eyes now fixed on her were almost too much to bear. There was something else, too, she noticed nervously: He had cut his hair. The thick black mane was short, shaped in the "classical" style all the Ton had adopted. If anything, it made him even handsomer.

Marigold managed a stiff bow. She lifted her hand to indicate that he should take a seat, but no words would come out. Her throat seemed frozen.

He seemed not to notice. "You look very

pretty," he said, "in spite of that dress. I cannot conceive of any reputable textile establishment in the British Isles deliberately making cloth of that color."

He'd said nothing, Marigold thought as she stared at him, about her being found in the depths of the Stokesbury Hatton coal mine with Penelope and Sophronia. Nothing about the scandal as presented in Yorkshire periodicals that would doubtless make its way back to London. Nothing, even, of her flight from his house in the middle of the night without a word of explanation.

"It is my best blue frock," she said in a hoarse voice. "I—I—have one in green just like it."

His mouth thinned. "No doubt. But that soon will be rectified, as I have brought your wardrobe from London with me."

Marigold's vocal cords lost their paralysis. "I—I am not going to wear your c-clothes," she sputtered. "How dare you! You have provided for me like a common mistress! Enough of this! What I may have done in London no longer applies here. Dispense your vile punishment for whatever infractions you think I may have committed in your coal mine, and remove yourself from this house!"

His frown grew deeper. "You are not common or a mistress, Marigold, and I never wish to hear you speak of yourself in those terms again. You are my affianced, your father has given his permission, the banns have been read, certain—ah, intimate physical events of no small importance have taken place, and I consider myself bound to you."

Marigold put her hands over her ears. "Stop it, I won't listen to you! You're wasting your breath. I positively—positively—will not marry you!"

"That will not be necessary."

There was a pause. Marigold took her hands down. She glared at him a long moment. "What?"

"During the protracted conversation with your father this morning at my Stokesbury Hatton residence, I assured him that I would do no violence to your strongly held convictions on cohabitation based on Wollstonecraft's concepts of mutual affection and respect. I confess I have come to the conclusion myself that there is a certain merit in such views, considering the falseness and deception upon which so many marriages, particularly among the ruling classes, are based. I have seen many of my own friends succumb to much unhappiness because of a lack of initial truthfulness and trust between partners, and the breaking up of a marriage is particularly difficult where there are children."

The duke shifted his gaze to some point over Marigold's head. Although he looked as though he might be under something of a strain he said quite calmly, "Therefore, I accede to your wishes. Since I believe we have both demonstrated sufficient respect and affection in—er, past events, I am satisfied to meet your terms, and live with you without benefit of clergy."

It was a moment before Marigold could speak.

She could hardly believe what she was hearing standing there in her father's parlor. "My terms?"

"Yes, given to me repeatedly. How could I forget them? Once I explained this to your father, the vicar, he could see your objection to matrimony was a matter of sacred principal. And he admitted that he had encouraged this idealism and independence in you from an early age. Therefore, after some thought, he offered no resistance to your wishes."

The room seemed to whirl about Marigold. For a moment she swayed, dizzy and confused.

"Sacred principal?" She was stupidly repeating everything Westermere said but she could not help it; she could barely think.

"Your unwavering stand has only increased my respect for you," the duke said blandly. "Consistency is a prized trait in anyone, but most especially in a beautiful woman." He looked around. "You do not have much to take with you, do you? I had thought to give you an hour or so to collect your things and make your farewells to your father. Then my coach will bring you to our temporary residence in the village. I believe you know it—The Elms."

"I—I'm to go to live with you?" The room was reeling again. "Here, in Stokesbury Hatton?"

Black eyebrows shot up, sardonically. "For the time being, until my visit is completed. As you doubtless know, I have several residences in England, also a villa in Florence, a plantation—"

"But I can't live with you here!" Marigold

shrieked. "Good heavens, what will people think? M-m-my father is the vicar!"

"My affairs should be concluded within the week," he went on. "As soon as I am able to inspect the mill and the mine. Then we will return to—"

Marigold could not resist stamping her foot in sheer aggravation. "Oh, I cannot endure this!" she exploded. "You'll find nothing in that mine, you idiot—nothing! That degenerate monster Robinson Parham is no doubt at this very moment having the galleries swept out, coated with whitewash, and planted with flowers! And when you arrive at the spinning mill, all the women will be dressed like maids in a Christmas farce, doing a happy jig! While I—while I am living with you like some common tart, humiliating my father and his parishioners and wearing fancy clothes, helping to box up endless samples of rope and stupid specimens of clay every night!"

The duke studied her, his face unreadable. "I am only agreeing to your wishes as you have stated them to me, Marigold. Unless, of course, you wish to repudiate the estimable Miss Wollstonecraft and all her teachings and marry me."

"Never!" She couldn't do that. Marrying Westermere would be betraying Penny, and Sophia, and all their hard-won ideals, despite what her friends thought. Not to mention little Johnny Cobb and his poor, harried mother, and all the miners and mill people. "What will happen to Penny MacDougal and Sophronia Stack?" she demanded. "They were down in the coal mine with me. Have you imposed a suitably cruel punishment, too, on my friends and their parents?"

Westermere looked blank for a moment, as though he had forgotten all about them. As indeed he had.

"Oh, that," he said. "Actually, when they came this morning the doctor and the schoolmaster were interested in the achromatic microscope, which was just being unpacked. They'd never seen one, only in catalogue illustrations. And of course they wanted to see the other new instrument, a Belgian telescope. I demonstrated the microscope for them and ran a few specimen slides. The conversation was rather technical."

"You talked about the microscope?" She could not believe her ears. "Here Penny and Sophia and I have been eaten with dread, contemplating our fates, waiting in this very room all morning! We were wracked by torment, not knowing our fates! Do you know Mr. MacDougal even threatened to send Penny away to a women's charity school run by nuns in Aberdeen!"

"The fathers have promised to keep a closer rein on their girls in the future," the duke said stiffly, "and keep them out of the coal mine. We did not discuss anything in detail. My primary interest was to talk to your father, not the other two."

"You were not even interested in what was to become of my friends?"

He scowled, impatient. "I told you, MacDougal

and Stack have promised to keep their daughters out of the coal mines and the mill. And any other places they might choose to wreak their peculiar havoc. However, the removal of you as their acknowledged leader will do much, we all agreed, to improve the other females' deportment."

"Oh!" It was a cry of outrage. Marigold looked around the room as though searching for some way of escape. What Westermere proposed, that she live with him, was preposterous. Yet he had flung her own words and beliefs back at her, quoting Mary Wollstonecraft! There had to be some sort of compromise.

"I will agree to an—arrangement in London," Marigold said, suddenly feeling crafty. "I have not abandoned Wollstonecraft's teachings, you understand, I am still her devoted disciple. But neither will I allow you to connive to have me under your power this way. Since you insist that I defend my beliefs, I will live with you in London— with," she added hastily, "the proper respect and friendship. I insist on that. But we will not cohabit here, not at The Elms! Lud, what would people think?"

Sacheverel de Vries, Duke of Westermere, studied her for a long moment; then he sighed. "Alas, consistency—it did not last long, did it? I might ask how staunch and unshakable are your noble convictions, Miss Fenwick, if they are affected by mere geography?"

For the barest of seconds the duke's lips

seemed to twitch. "As for example, as a Christian would you feel compelled to practice your religion as a Musselman if you were transported to faraway Egypt? Or—"

"Oh, do be still!" Marigold snapped. She turned and paced up the room, the duke's black eyes following her.

When she finally turned to him, he saw glistening tears caught in the lashes. He could not know sheer vexation had put them there.

"This is my home," Marigold told him. "There are more things I would like to take with me for this—new mode of living, than can be done in an hour. I will have to ask you to send the coach for me in the morning. Say, at ten o'clock."

He thought it over, then apparently decided it was reasonable. "In the morning, then," he said. "At ten."

At the door he seemed to hesitate, as though he wished to come back, but thought better of it. The front door slammed as he left.

Marigold went to the fireplace and poked up the fire, and stood staring into the flames. In a quarter hour Westermere's coach would be well out of the village, mounting the hill to Winston Lane and his house. She had only to wait.

Then she would run to the hall closet and get her cloak and bonnet. Her father, deep in his books, would never know she had gone.

Penelope's house first, Marigold decided quickly, and then, with Penny, on to the doctor's.

Katherine Deauxville

In the Stack kitchen they would sit around the table and have a cup of tea just as they used to in the old days, before London, and Marigold would tell them what she was going to do.

Chapter Eighteen

"This may be the last time the Cavaliers will meet," Marigold said sadly.

She held up her cup so that Sophronia could pour her more tea. They were sitting in the Stacks' kitchen, with Penelope on the other side of Sophronia, their backs to a blazing fire that took the chill off the early spring night.

The firelight lit Marigold's troubled face as she said, "When I go to London this time I shall be far away from Stokesbury Hatton and my dear friends, living another life, one in many ways incompatible with all I hold familiar and true." She sighed. "But by that time let us hope we will have accomplished what we set out to do when we began our scheme these long weeks past."

"We have been led down some strange paths,"

Penelope agreed. "Stranger even than the one we chose to follow when we three left for London to accost the great villain Westermere face-to-face and wring justice from him."

"Do you think we will?" Sophronia said, cutting an apple into slices and offering it to the others.

Penelope took a piece from the tip of the extended knife. "Will what?"

"Wring justice from him," Sophronia said. "Westermere has his chance to set things to right if he has any sort of compassion for his people. After all, he does own them lock, stock and barrel—even if they are not legally slaves."

"Well, I for one never thought to end up pulling a cart in the depths of a coal mine," Penelope mused. "It was a very enlightening experience." She was struck by a sudden thought. "Oh dear, do you suppose Superintendent Hatfield and Robinson Parham will convince the duke of the falsity of their inhumane treatment of the mill and mine workers, so that Westermere will go back to London without even taking a look?"

Marigold snorted. "What good will it do him to look? The mine and the mill are miserable places, Westermere will expect that, for it is normal. But there will be no sick and overworked women and children, slaving long hours for a few farthings. Parham has dismissed them, every one."

Sophronia laid down her knife, turning dark eyes to Marigold. "But you have a plan—that is why we are meeting, is it not?"

"It is not my plan, but Penelope's." She turned

to Penny. "Remember how you admonished me in the duke's library that day you came to tea? That I should consider the mercenary aspects of a relationship with Westermere and make myself so indispensable to his lust that he would settle a large sum of money on me? Money that I could then use to help the people of Stokesbury Hatton?"

"Mercy, did I say that?" Penelope looked flustered. "Of course we were desperate after you jumped in his carriage and our plan did not work. That is, the duke took you instead to his London house and declared he wanted to marry—"

"He doesn't want that anymore," Marigold interrupted, frowning. "He has made that plain. I am to live with him, that is all, under what he deems the 'terms' I have laid down according to the tenets of Mary Wollstonecraft."

Sophronia looked up, eyebrows raised.

Penelope gave a small cry. "Oh, my dear Marigold, do you want that? I mean, no matter what Wollstonecraft says, our blessed guide never had to live in Stokesbury Hatton! And, heaven preserve us, if the duke has made you such an offer, it's insulting and degrading! It means that you will be regarded as no better than a wh—"

"Oh, I will do it," Marigold said shortly. "I have already made up my mind. Besides, nothing else works, does it? Westermere has laid down his ill-natured challenge thinking I will capitulate and agree to marry him. But actually I prefer things this way." She lifted her chin, daring them to disagree. "Proceeding according to his wishes makes it easier to carry out Penny's brilliant idea—seduce Westermere and enslave him in—um, sensual bonds and all that sort of thing so that he cannot resist settling a large sum of money on me. With a few jewels, and things like that," Marigold added. "While I'm at it, I shan't go cheap."

Sophronia looked skeptical. "La, Marigold, how do you plan to do this? I mean, render the duke of Westermere suddenly generous and open-handed through some sort of incomparable seductive arts?"

"Well, I—I have already had some small experience," Marigold said, blushing. Before the others could say anything she went on hurriedly, "And Westermere is satisfied enough to have followed me here, is he not? He does keep protesting that we are betrothed, even now!" She looked at Penny, then Sophronia. "Well, yes, it is a problem, I—I am certainly not as knowledgeable as I should be for the task, I confess. Oh, dear friends, when I was in London Westermere produced books of surpassing licentiousness, which he said were to instruct me in the erotic arts. I wish I had some of them to study now. Now that I look back on it, he was quite surprisingly conscientious, and tender and considerate—" Her voice trailed away.

There was a silence.

Then Penelope said in a small voice, "Marigold, sweet, if you want books, Da has a collection. I—er, am not supposed to know where they're hidden, I just discovered them recently when moving some volumes in Da's study to dust them, and found them concealed behind the collected works of Aristotle. It was quite a surprise. I suppose it is in the nature of a schoolmaster to acquire books on all sorts of subjects, but I admit the first time I opened them and read the contents, the shock was so great it took me days to get my poor addled thoughts back to their proper balance. But once one is used to them, Da's hidden cache is very interesting, and—um, instructive."

"You never told me about this!" Sophronia accused.

It was Penelope's turn to crimson. "Oh, please, Sophronia, I told you that I found the books hardly a fortnight ago!"

"What sort of books?" Marigold wanted to know. "Do they have pictures?"

"Not really. I think Da collected them when he was a young student at university. There are not a lot, three or four, but I remember one of them is entitled *Fanny Hill*."

"Oh, Penny, you are a darling. Anything will be a help, I'm sure," Marigold said. "I leave Papa's house tomorrow to go live with Westermere at The Elms. Then when he is finished here, we go on to London. Dearest friends, this may be our last chance!"

"Hah, Penny is not the only one who can contribute," Sophronia said, and stood up. "I have something. It is upstairs, in my room."

"Will your father—" Marigold began.

"He's asleep; he retires early. No fear, I'll be quiet."

When she came back down the stairs Sophronia carried a small painted wooden box. It could more correctly be described as a casket, Marigold thought, examining it as Sophronia put it down on the table. It had a high, rounded lid with brass fixtures and lock, and every inch of the wood had been painted with red, yellow and blue flowers, twining vines, and exotic tropical birds. Although it was quite old, the colors had not faded at all. In the dim light of the kitchen fire it was brilliant, foreign.

"Ah, how pretty!" Penny exclaimed. "What is it?"

"A gypsy box," the dark girl answered. "It was my mother's."

She released the brass catch and opened it. Inside was a tray with yellowed letters that Sophronia took out and set to one side. Underneath that was a layer of red gauze silk shot with gold that she lifted and shook out, the firelight catching the gleaming bits. Hanging it over her arm, Sophronia reached into the box and lifted what appeared to be a sort of harness of glass beads and leather decorated with a multitude of still-brilliant gold tassels.

Marigold could not believe what they were looking at. It seemed to be a costume. "Oh, don't tell me that piece of red leather goes where I think it does, Sophie!"

The other girl's face broke into a dark smile.

"This is my mother's dancing dress. Gypsy women will dance for village men, the *gadjos*, behind the wagons at fairs, if the *gadjos* pay a lot of money."

"How do you know this?" Marigold had delved into the painted box. There were silk scarves, brass leg and arm bangles, pots of rouge and eye paint and scent—the latter so heady that, even after years of being stored, the sensuous aroma filled up the kitchen. "Oh, Sophie, do you know how to use all this?"

"I never knew my mother, as she died when I was young," the other girl responded. "But I can guess. I have tried the costume on, it is not hard to imagine what goes where, when there is so little of it. The red silk veil is put on from head to toe over it all, to make you very mysterious." She grinned. "Then when the veil comes off there is underneath all the gypsy wickedness!"

Penny was bouncing up and down in her seat with excitement. "Marigold, you wouldn't! Look, there is no back at all to this lower piece with the tassels, it seems to fit into the indent in one's— well, derriere. And the beaded top is cut out for the breasts to fit through—I have never seen anything so depraved!" She suddenly squealed, "Dear heavens, what I would not give to be a fly on the wall to be there when you confront Westermere dressed in these!"

"Now you're being wicked," Marigold told her. "Think only pure thoughts, Penny, until we get to your house and I can borrow one of your father's

277

books. Did you say *Fanny Hill* was the one to read?"

"Yes, that's very appropriate," the other said, rather dreamily lifting a bangle and red tassel headdress and placing it on her forehead. "And *City of Love*, and *A Virgin's Tale*. They're all full of most ingenious ideas, you just can't imagine."

"Let us hope neither can the duke," Sophronia said dryly.

An hour later, just past midnight, Penelope and Marigold stealthily made their way down Stokesbury Hatton's back lanes to schoolmaster MacDougal's cottage, where Penny went in to find *Fanny Hill*, *City of Love* and *A Virgin's Tale*, while Marigold waited in the shadows by the back door.

Penny was back in a short time. "Good luck, dear friend," she whispered as she thrust the books into Marigold's arms. "You will find some way to get them back to me, won't you? Da will never forgive me if he finds them missing."

Marigold promised to do so and they embraced, the tearful schoolmaster's daughter murmuring that she could not believe that this was the last time they would see each other.

"It will not be, I swear," Marigold told her. "You will come to visit me. Westermere cannot keep the Cavaliers apart. I will see to it, even though he dares to object."

With Sophronia's gypsy box and Penny's books held tight against her bosom, she kept to the shadows under the trees. It was late and she was unescorted; if she were seen it would bring about more gossip, and heaven knows there'd been enough. In a few moments she rounded a bend in the lane by the miller's house and saw the spire of St. Dunstan's church in the moonlight and the smaller shadow of the rectory next to it.

She was home.

For only one last night, Marigold could not help thinking. But she was there.

Some miles away in Soldiers' Wood, the same moonlight illuminated the path that ran from the town of Wickham to Stokesbury Hatton, and a solitary horseman made his way at a slow canter upon a spirited, chestnut-colored horse. There was no other traffic on the road, and had not been since Robinson Parham rode out from Hobbs after taking a good dinner and several fine brandies in the market town's Golden Fleece tavern.

He was enjoying being away from Stokesbury Hatton for a few hours. Since the duke of Westermere had arrived, his junior agent had been walking a tightrope over the business of the mine and the mill that would have decimated the nerves of a weaker man. But he was almost in the clear, Parham told himself. Westermere would soon return to London. It was a matter of a few days more. And it could have been worse.

Parham had found the great duke of Westermere gratifyingly disinterested in his fortune, and not much inclined to look into the details of the workings of any of his industrial villages in the north. Although he had to admit Westermere seemed bright enough, certainly more so than the dense-brained aristocrats of Prince George's ton whom he had occasionally dealt with. At least this young duke understood the differences between claptrap moral issues and making a profit.

The Stokesbury Hatton mine was not a pretty place; neither was the mill. But with the help of Hatfield's hasty cleanup, both had presented a reasonable appearance. Also, the village magistrate, who knew which side his bread was buttered on, had seen to it that any delegation of miners or disgruntled mill people were kept out of Westermere's way.

So he had scraped by yet another time, Robinson Parham told himself. And it had been in spite of those damned interfering bluestocking girls, the vicar's daughter and her set.

Well, they were no threat now. The duke of Westermere had picked himself a nice piece of flesh for his pleasure in the Fenwick girl, and was taking her back to London with him. Once that was out of the way, Parham intended to press the matter of the doctor's gypsy daughter to his own satisfaction.

By God, the fire and hate in her face, spitting like a cat at him when he'd met her in these very woods, had sent erotic fantasies running wild in his head.

He could have any mill woman or girl from the mine; they were all afraid to deny him anything for fear he would take their employment and their miserable hovels away from them. But listening to them beg or weep was not half as exciting as picturing the scornful gypsy girl with her dark hair down from its braids, stripped naked and on all fours, surrendering, totally subject to his desires.

Parham's thoughts were interrupted when his horse shied at something. He touched Spanish Pete lightly with his heels. They were in the darkest part of Soldiers' Woods, the bright moon casting only narrow shafts of silver light through the still-leafless trees. A figure in a brightly colored cloak had stepped into the path. He could not see the face, for the hood of the cloak was pulled forward.

Parham was about to reach into his coat for his pistol when the figure pushed back the hood. The bright moon showed a familiar face.

"Oh, it's you," the agent said, visibly relieved. "What the devil are you doing here in Soldiers' Woods at this hour of the night?"

Chapter Nineteen

"Shall I help you dress for bed, miss?" Mrs. Cawdigan asked.

The housekeeper bustled about the dressing room that adjoined the duke's bedroom, looking in the wardrobes filled with Marigold's London clothes to make sure all was in order. The bedroom, wallpapered and redecorated in tones of pink and cream, was in perfect condition, and there was nothing to tidy.

Marigold lay on the velvet chaise longue reading a book. As the housekeeper had knocked and she'd called out for her to enter, she'd slipped *Fanny Hill* under the skirt of her robe. "No, thank you, Mrs. Cawdigan, I have already made myself ready for bed. What of the duke?"

She tried to appear properly casual, although

the housekeeper knew perfectly well that Marigold was waiting for Westermere to come upstairs and take her to bed.

"His Grace is still down in the library with his solicitor," the housekeeper answered.

Marigold tried to ignore the inquiring looks that Mrs. Cawdigan was directing at the velvet bed robe she wore, curious as to what was under it. The housekeeper had already seen Marigold's nightgowns, all accounted for, in the wardrobe.

"Mr. Broadus and the young man are just now doing the last of their business," Mrs. Cawdigan went on. "His Grace called for Pomfret to bring the nightcap, so they'll be leaving soon."

Marigold could not suppress a sigh. She was growing tired of waiting. The unexpected visit of Mr. Augustus Broadus and his law clerk from London had kept the duke sequestered in the library for the most of the day. Marigold had taken advantage of the rainy afternoon by reading schoolmaster MacDougal's forbidden books and looking over her clothes—some of them new— that the duke's household staff had brought from London. Among the new apparel were several pairs of walking boots for excursions into Stokesbury Hatton's countryside, a lightweight, waterproof cloak, as well as day and evening frocks. Marigold couldn't help inspecting them with a certain amount of irritation, remembering Westermere's rude and disparaging remarks about her blue dress in the vicarage parlor. She could just picture him barking orders to poor Madame

Rosenzweig about how swiftly everything was to be sewn and assembled in order to get them up to Stokesbury Hatton.

Marigold had worn one of the new frocks, a stiff silk brocade in a bright shade of rose red, when she joined Westermere and Solicitor Broadus and his clerk for dinner. But then she'd retired early to her upstairs dressing room, unable to wait any longer to finish up the astonishingly explicit *A Virgin's Tale* and begin *Fanny Hill*. The duke had gone back to the library with the lawyer or his assistant, closing the doors.

Now the hour, Marigold saw by the hands of the gold and ormolu clock on the mantel, was approaching midnight. "I won't require anything more, Mrs. Cawdigan," she told the housekeeper.

But the other woman lingered, fiddling with small tasks. Marigold had no doubt the staff downstairs all knew why she was in the duke's house, and they doubtless also knew that she'd spent a night of intimacy with him before she'd fled the city.

Too bad, Marigold told herself, that she could not satisfy Mrs. Cawdigan's curiosity. But one look at what she was wearing under her boudoir robe and she was sure the plump, bustling housekeeper would faint dead away.

Mrs. Cawdigan adjusted the candles in their holder and then fussed a bit with the small embroidered pillows while Marigold grew increasingly impatient.

Then, to Marigold's complete surprise, the

housekeeper impulsively reached out and patted her hand. "He was a lonely boy, he was," she burst out, "always reading and carrying about frogs and stones and strange bits he'd collected. And later it was the study of botany, that was his name for it. The grandsire adored him, I'll tell you, but the old duke was a stern man and didn't show that side of his nature easy. And of course the pa was always away in the army. The poor mother died young, she did, and it was a shame, for if ever a fine young lad needed the softness and affection of a woman, that one did."

Marigold could only stare. "Westermere? Is that who you mean, Mrs. Cawdigan?"

The other woman nodded, the starched pleats on her housekeeper's bonnet jiggling. "Yes, dear, His Grace, bless his heart. Them that knows him and has watched him grow up from a young lad has great affection for him. But you can see that for yourself, miss, you know the staff well enough by now. Besides, the duke's never brought a young lady into the house to live before. He's not that sort."

Marigold couldn't think of anything to say. The other woman looked around the room, distractedly. "But then you're his betrothed, and that's different, isn't it? And a vicar's daughter, too, that makes it sweet and proper. Bless us, we all want to see His Grace happy, that's all we ask!" Mrs. Cawdigan turned and almost bolted for the door. "If you say you've no need of me, miss, then I'll wish you a very good night."

As the door closed behind her, Marigold couldn't help thinking Mrs. Cawdigan's words were somewhat garbled, but the message was clear.

So Westermere was not in the habit of bringing women to his house? Well, the irascible duke certainly wasn't your typical London Ton Casanova; you had only to see him at balls and routs to be assured of that. Although women certainly pursued him.

It should make her task that much easier, Marigold told herself with something of a nervous shiver. Since scientific-minded Westermere was not a jaded rakehell, his senses were therefore more vulnerable. Certainly they had seemed vulnerable the last time they had gone to bed. Inexperienced as she was, Marigold had thought him in terrible pain. Which was, she knew now after reading the schoolmaster's books, a rather silly gaffe. One was supposed to learn the difference between real agony and the throes of passion, even if they did seem to be alarmingly similar.

Yes, things were quite different, she was thinking as she stood up, seeing herself full length in the pier glass. "Westermere," she told her reflected image firmly, "I want you to settle a large sum of money on me."

She frowned at the figure in the pier glass and it frowned back. No matter how she said it, the words had an unpleasant ring to them, but she could think of nothing else. The bald facts had to be said, sooner or later. The matter of when, too, was important.

Marigold let the robe slide from her shoulders. The demure image in the glass was instantly changed into one so startlingly erotic, so sensuously provocative, that even she had to blink.

At that moment there were footsteps in the hall outside, the heavy tread of footmen lighting the duke's way to his chambers.

Marigold picked up the gold-shot red silk veil that would cover her from head to toe and took a deep breath. She had a few moments to wait while Cruddles assisted Westermere in undressing, and prepared for his nightly ablutions. Then when all but a few candles were put out, she planned to enter from the dressing room by the connecting door.

She had rejected the idea of being in Westermere's bed, waiting for him, when he arrived; it seemed too gauche. Besides, she wanted to be standing up, in the best position to show off Sophronia's gypsy dancer's costume.

She dropped the glittering red silk veil over her head, pulling it down over her arms and hips until it covered the tops of her bare feet. The veil trapped the wonderful gypsy scent that she had rubbed into her skin. It rose up from her warm flesh into her nostrils, making her somewhat dizzy, almost needing to sneeze.

Standing before the adjoining door to the duke's bedroom, Marigold carefully rubbed her nose and waited.

* * *

Where the devil is she? Satch asked himself as Cruddles picked up the basin of shaving water and handed it to a footman to carry away. He was damned if he was going to ask his valet where his fiancée had gone to, as though he couldn't keep track of her. But from the way she'd bolted from the dinner table, he'd expected to find her waiting there in his room.

Satch had a sudden, unsettling thought. Perhaps his betrothed had turned fainthearted after all, given up the ideological struggle over Wollstonecraft, and returned home to her father, the vicar.

He didn't think she was capable of it, she was too stubborn for that. But assuming it was true, he was surprised at his knifelike sense of disappointment.

He leaned into the mirror, rubbing his jaw, frowning at the close-shaven smoothness. On the other hand, perhaps she hadn't run off to her father. But if not, where in creation was she? Sacheverel was not at all familiar with the Stokesbury Hatton house. There were two rather rambling, mostly empty wings and the place was full of doors and hallways; if he went off to search for her and got lost he would only make a fool of himself.

Behind him Cruddles made subtle motions in the air with a silver-backed brush, dabbing at his newly shortened hair. Their eyes met in the mirror.

"The new style is very becoming, Your Grace," the valet assured him. "Miss Fenwick will be greatly admiring, if you will allow me to say so."

The duke grunted. "She's already seen it."

The only thing to do was go to bed, he decided, read a book for a while, and hope that his betrothed appeared before he had to send someone to look for her.

Satch stood still while Cruddles stretched on his toes to lower the long white nightshirt over his head and fasten the neck and wristbands with their mother-of-pearl buttons. At the door, Pomfret made an appearance carrying a familiar-looking bottle of white wine and a plate of sugar cakes.

Satch picked up the bottle from the tray and looked at the label that extolled the virtues of the famous vineyard in France. He recognized it as the same wine. He could not help but remember an enchantingly tipsy Miss Marigold Fenwick, adorable and oh so seductive, in his arms the first time he had made her his.

And who had bolted, he reminded himself, from his bed as soon as he was asleep. By damn, he needed an explanation for that piece of humiliating idiocy, and would make a note to get it from her that very night!

Pomfret, hovering at his elbow, could tell the duke was not happy. "Perhaps I should bring up a nice claret instead, Your Grace?" the old man suggested. "The Monserrat usually travels well.

Or may I propose sherry? Several bottles of a good amontillado?"

"No, leave it," Satch said. Memory told him Miss Fenwick liked the French white; she'd swilled it down the last time like so much sweet cider.

He climbed into the big bed that had been very satisfactorily prepared by Mrs. Cawdigan with fine lace-trimmed sheets brought from London, and settled back against the pillows with his book, *A Study of Famous Criminals and Highwaymen in England's Eastern Counties*. Cruddles retired with the duke's boots and linen, wishing him a very good night. Pomfret went about the room extinguishing all the candles except those Satch was going to read by, and finally tottered off, softly closing the bedroom door.

Satch yawned, punched up the bed pillows to his satisfaction, then lay back to read a few pages of his book.

He must have dozed off. Rainy weather always made him logy, and he had spent a wearying afternoon closeted with Broadus and his law clerk and their records for Stokesbury Hatton.

He awoke with a start, though, when the leatherbound volume of *Famous Criminals* slipped out of his hand and landed on the floor beside the bed with a thump.

As he jerked awake Satch's eyes immediately located an ill-defined presence standing some distance away in front of an equally dimly lighted doorway that he had not, so far, been aware of.

Each and every nerve in Satch's body reacted with a trained soldier's sense of danger.

The thing in front of the doorway seemed to be veiled. It was vaguely red, amorphous. No semblance of human form showed at all.

For a moment the hair stood up unpleasantly on the back of his head. But the duke of Westermere was no believer in ghosts: He reached for the loaded pistol he kept under the bed pillows.

"Stand where you are," he barked, propping his weight on his elbow and leveling his firearm. "Or I'll put a ball through your heart!"

"Great heavens," a familiar voice cried, "don't do that! Not after all the trouble I've gone to get into this thing!"

Satch kept his pistol on target but his mouth dropped open slightly as the red, formless thing seemed to waver several times like a struggling bed curtain, then finally managed to cast off the scarlet mist.

"What the devil?" he said hoarsely.

He put the pistol down on the bedspread and reached for a candle to light several more. His fiancée—he recognized who it was now, but just barely—took some hesitant steps closer.

"La, Westermere," the provocative houri dressed in some outrageously naked and lascivious apparel complained, "I never thought you would try to shoot me or by the saints, I would have worn an old pair of drawers and a flannel underbodice! Do you always sleep with a pistol in your bed?"

Sacheverel had nothing to say. His eyes were too busy devouring a sight few men had ever seen except in their most wildly libidinous dreams.

The flare of candles showed a dazzling vision, a gorgeously wanton seductress with painted face, ripe, pouting red mouth, and flowing gold-brown curls festooned with gold coins that caressed her bare arms and shoulders.

On her upper body she wore the most shockingly abbreviated red leather vest Satch had ever seen. With stunned eyes he viewed places that were normally covered but were now cut out in the leather to allow her thrusting breasts to come through, revealing nipples boldly decorated with bright red rouge.

Below the vest there was an expanse of slender, silky abdomen, the belly button flashing a bright green glass jewel. Below that—

Satch's gaze was drawn with a sense of dread to a tiny triangle of red leather resting between his betrothed's thighs. This minuscule island of modesty was surrounded by floating red gauze strips that dangled down over her naked legs, which were complete with brass ankle bracelets and painted-toenail bare feet.

He recognized it all now. His fiancée, the intrepid Miss Marigold Fenwick, had not been daunted by the challenge of the social philosophy of Mary Wollstonecraft, nor had she abjectly surrendered to come live with him in humble Free Love.

No, she had taken it into her head to taunt him

dressed as a gypsy such as the most depraved of London's roues dreamed of in their debauched fantasies. The last time Satch had seen anything even remotely approaching the figure before him had been in a Romany camp outside Granada. Then it had taken him a whole week to get the rifle company back into some sort of physical shape, much less up to the mental order of military discipline.

Now what must be Lucifer's own favorite gypsy dancer sidled up to the bed. "Yes, do put away the gun," she told him, batting the lashes of her painted eyes. "I can't possibly think how we could use it. I brought ropes and a pot of honey we can do things with."

With that she yanked back the bedclothes. Taken by surprise, Satch clutched for them. It was too late; the covers were out of reach.

"Oh, you have on your nightshirt!" She sounded disappointed. "Never mind, there are really some very erotic ways of taking it off. First, I'm going to lift the hem up over your knees—" She did so, smiling at him roguishly. "—while I kiss each knee—" She did that. "—and then take your big toe and put it in my mouth and—um, suck on it!"

"The hell you say!" Satch jerked his foot away just in time. She grabbed for his other leg but he flung it upward, out of her reach.

That left him, he realized in a briefly confused moment, lying on his back in his own bed with both legs raised like some sort of expiring bug.

He also felt a slight breeze circulating around his exposed nether parts.

She looked at him thoughtfully from this new angle. Then she lifted her eyes. "Westermere, I had not intended to begin in exactly this way," she told him, "but it is obvious from what I see that you are not physically unaffected. Which makes it all the more mysterious that you object to having your toes sensuously ministered to!"

Satch swung his long legs over the side of the bed and sat up. He raked his hands through his hair, thinking she was right, he was not unaffected, he was as rigid and ready as the Tower of London. In that gypsy get-up she could twist his private part into a bow knot and he would still find it damned arousing.

"No toes," he said, ungraciously. "Kiss them if you will, but don't suck on them. It's a fancy I've never taken to."

He shrugged out of his nightshirt and tossed it out into the room, leaving her to stare at his body with even wider eyes.

She suddenly reached out and with truly reverent fingers caressed his muscular shoulder and then trailed them down his arm. "Oh, Westermere," the Devil's gypsy said faintly, "I had forgotten how magnificent you are. You really are a very beautiful man."

"Aaah," he growled, turning to her, eyes gleaming, holding out both arms.

But she slithered out of his grasp. "No, no," she insisted, "I am here to enchant you."

To show him, she put her hands on his shoulders and rubbed her rouge-tipped breasts against his nose and mouth. His lips followed her swaying bosom eagerly, but never managed to catch her.

"Marigold," he muttered into the warm surface of the gypsy vest, "enough of this. You know I want you. I will do anything to please you."

Gazing down at him, at his tempting mouth and unruly black hair, Marigold stiffened her resolve. It was so easy to succumb to Westermere—just a look from those smoldering dark eyes rendered her almost witless. Especially when they were in bed and almost naked, like this.

She had to remind herself that she was not there to surrender to him, but to conquer and enslave this arrogant man with her own skilled erotic strategies. A whole village depended on it. Westermere had laid down the challenge. Now, heaven help her, she was going to see it through!

Remembering *A Virgin's Tale* and certain parts of *Fanny Hill*, she used her fingernails to tease his brown nipples, making him start. Then she covered each in turn with her wet mouth, kissing, sucking and taking little bites at the sensitive nubs. At the same time Marigold slid her legs between his, pressing the daring little triangle of leather that held the gypsy skirt against his swollen privates, while rotating her hips sinuously. His lower body jerked and quivered, trying to pursue her elusive movements.

Meanwhile her naked breasts with their

roughed tips slid tantalizingly up and down his broad chest and, as she lifted herself on her knees, moved toward his lips. At that moment Marigold twined her fingers in his cropped, wavy black hair and held his face still while she kissed him deeply.

He made a hoarse, growling sound in his throat. His hands were busy behind her trying to undo the straps of the gypsy skirt.

"Marigold, I told you I would give you anything," the duke of Westermere rasped. He was trying to get the leather triangle pushed to one side without much success. "Take this confounded thing off. You can play gypsy games later. Right now I want to have you, damme, don't you realize I'm going mad with it?"

She shivered when he suddenly managed to catch her rouge-tipped breast with his mouth. Rivers of fire ran into her flesh from that nipping, passionate caress. And her own body responded convulsively.

"Ah," he cried, "you see? You cannot resist it, either. Sweetheart," he panted as he hauled her over his body, "where is the buckle or strap on this damned skirt? Can you reach it for me?"

Now was the time, Marigold knew, even while her own senses were whirling. Later, after they had spent their passion and lay in each other's arms, would be too tender and blissful a moment.

She managed to straighten up, a difficult thing to do as he was boldly trying to maneuver his lower body into a position to possess her.

"Westermere," Marigold said loudly, holding her disheveled hair back from her eyes, "are you listening to me? If we are to have this arrangement it is only fair that you settle a—a large sum of money on me!"

His hips stopped moving, even though the tip of his shaft was at her soft entrance and he had almost accomplished his goal. Nevertheless, he went very still.

"A large sum of money," he repeated.

"Yes, you know what I want it for," Marigold said, breathlessly. "I have already explained my aspirations for the village to you. And I understand a large money settlement on one's betrothed or—or—m-mistress is not uncommon, is it?"

Both his hands stole up under the gypsy skirt and stroked her bottom. "Not uncommon at all." His voice was devoid of expression. He paused, then said, "Tell me, Marigold, how much, in your estimation, would a 'large sum of money' be?"

She stared at him.

A large sum of money was—Well, it was a large sum of money, was all she could think.

Oh, woe! How was a vicar's daughter, raised in the most penny-pinching of frugal environments, to have any idea how much money the poor people of Stokesbury Hatton required? She suddenly realized the three Cavaliers had not planned this part of their endeavor well at all!

His hands had slipped around to her thighs where they had located the buckle to the skirt's leather triangle. Marigold winced slightly as she felt that part of the costume fall away. How much was a lot of money? she kept asking herself. Considering that she had agreed to live in the duke's house and sleep in his bed and indulge in the very things they were doing at that moment—surely that was worth a goodly sum! And she had told Penelope and Sophronia she did not intend to go cheap.

But what should she say? Five hundred pounds? Marigold dithered. A thousand? No one she knew had ever had that much money in their life!

"Ten thousand pounds," the duke said softly. "Would you consider that a great deal of money?"

For a moment the words didn't register. Marigold was distracted as the duke's fingers were doing wicked, incredible things to her tender flesh. She could hardly catch her breath.

On the other hand—

Ten thousand pounds? Is that what he'd said? Saints above, ten thousand pounds was a fortune!

"Oh," Marigold burst out as he held her hips in both hands and eagerly pressed her down on him, "t-ten thousand is a lot of money."

"A year," the duke said between his teeth. "Ten thousand a year."

Chapter Twenty

Ten thousand pounds a year was the exact sum the duke of Westermere had intended all along to settle on her, but Marigold couldn't know that.

The effect, though, was instantaneous.

"Oh, you are so wonderful!" She bounced up and down in a burst of sheer joy, at the same time inadvertently thrusting her hips so that he entered her. "I am quite sincere," she gasped, "I would admire and respect you even if you were not so excessively rich!"

Satch, shuddering at the unexpected but infinitely glorious sensation of intimate possession, could only seize her arms with both hands to hang on to her. "Marigold, my love," he managed in a strangled voice, "oh, my God!"

"Yes, isn't it lovely? You are still awfully large

for me, but once I have adjusted to it, it feels wonderful!" Kneeling above him, she rotated her hips enticingly. "Oh, you are so generous and understanding to allow me to make love to you like this! How liberating it is! If she were here, Mary Wollstonecraft would sing praises to your enlightenment!"

Satch blinked back the sweat seeping into his eyelashes. "She damned well better not be here," he croaked. "Marigold, sweetest, don't go any faster, I—"

But his words were lost as she unraveled the laces of the gypsy vest with one hand and threw it out into the room with a joyous whoop. At the same time her beautiful hips pumped enthusiastically over him.

The sight of his betrothed, with her tangled hair flying about them, her painted eyes and rouge-smeared lips, her bouncing breasts with red-tipped nipples grazing his nose, was too much for Satch. He threw himself, uncaring into the bottomless abyss of passion.

The bed creaked and bounced as he was ridden by a luscious, abandoned gypsy witch. She was the very picture of reckless desire, sending every nerve in his body into a sensual uproar. After all, the duke of Westermere had his erotic fantasies too. And this one, luckily for him, had just become enchantingly real!

But fantasies of such intensity seldom last long. He cried out as a convulsion of feeling made him seize her and drag her down against his gasping, heaving body. The force of his release propelled them both across several feet of the bedspread before it finally subsided.

"Marigold, my love." Satch shook his head to clear it, then felt about in the mounds of tangled covers for her. "Dear God, what a lout I am! Where are you? You must forgive the power of animal lust that made—"

"Westermere, don't be silly." Her head popped up beside him, and she freed one arm from a sheet. "I am quite all right, and I adore your animal lust. You were truly magnificent." She smiled a smeary red grin. "You must know I am finding I have quite a large animal lust of my own!"

He breathed a sigh of relief. "Forgive me if I say I am concerned that you have your pleasure, too." As she lay sprawled across his chest Satch stroked her sweaty hair with its net of gold coins. "It would haunt my dreams to think my beautiful, outrageous gypsy dancer had left my bed unsatisfied."

There was a long moment of silence while both attempted to slow their breathing. "Marigold, that is not why you left me in London, is it?"

She turned to look at him. So close, his eyes were like pieces of midnight. The gypsy rouge where he had kissed her breasts had spread over his face from nose to chin. She could not help giggling.

"It is nothing," Marigold murmured at his questioning look, bending down to kiss the tip of his nose. She smoothed back his unruly hair, tangling her fingers in it. "It is only that my nipple paint has rubbed off on you and made you look like a boy caught at the jam pot."

He thought that over. "Whatever put this idea into your head? The gypsy costume?"

Her laughter faded. "Oh, it is a very long story. The dancing dress belonged to Sophronia's mother." She leaned over him and said in a low, sultry voice, mocking him, "Tell me, Your Grace, that your poor gypsy entertainer brought you some moments of pleasure such as you may experience if you ever go and partake of the varied delights of faraway Spain—"

Her words were cut off as he grabbed her wrist, his face quite changed.

"You haven't answered my question, Marigold. Why did you leave me in London without a word of explanation, or tell me where you were going?"

"—and Egypt. . . ." Her voice trailed off.

"Is it because I failed to give you satisfaction?" he said harshly. "That you bolted from my bed in Horton Crescent because you abhorred your initial experience, and could not bear to repeat it with me?" He stopped, swallowed. "It would pain me deeply to think this was the case."

She looked away, sighing. "Oh, Westermere, could we not just lie here holding each other, savoring this moment, and talk of something else?

"No."

"Then do not punish yourself. That night I spent with you was sublime, I shall cherish it in my most precious memories forever."

Marigold could not tell him the real reason.
That after they had made love that first time, her
newly discovered emotion for the duke of Westermere had absolute, terrifying power over her.
As indeed, it almost did now.

Physical intimacy did not bring just mere
friendship and respect. It was a raging floodtide
of irresistible feeling that rushed one on, willy-
nilly, into the loved one's arms. She'd wanted
nothing more than to lie there in bed with him
that night and cover his body with kisses. To caress his unruly midnight hair and his adorable
ears, and trace his stern mouth and straight, com-
manding nose with her finger teasingly. Not to
mention nibble at those powerful, muscular
arms, and his broad chest.

She had suddenly adored his body. She adored
him! It had torn at her soul to have to leave him,
but she could not afford to compromise the village, her friends and family, everything, by surrendering to the enemy. She had known that
she'd had to escape.

Now, a month and a little more in Stokesbury
Hatton, thinking about it, had helped disperse
those burdensome, love-maddened thoughts, and
give Marigold a new perspective.

Perhaps the right sort of compromise had been
reached, after all, she thought. According to their
present agreement that the Duke of Westermere
himself had insisted on, she would live with him
following Mary Wollstonecraft's tenets. That is,

freely, without benefit of legal marriage, and if others wanted to think of her as a kept women, as his mistress, they would just have to do so.

Of course, it would be difficult to face the villagers and her own father and his parishioners, but she would have to put a good face on it. The benefits outweighed the drawbacks. She would have Westermere's powerful protection and his obvious passion for her, and ten thousand pounds a year.

That wonderful ten thousand pounds a year! she thought. First, she and Penelope and Sophronia would organize a Free Food Shop for the desperately needy, expand Dr. Stack's clinic and buy more medicines and equipment, and do something about the mine and mill workers who had been evicted from their cottages.

Heavens, how could she forget? They also had to do something immediately about the condition of the heath, and those terrible disease-ridden drains!

"Sweetheart, you have not answered my question," Satch said, cupping her breasts and bestowing a light kiss on his betrothed's rouged nipples.

"Ah," Marigold said. She was desperately trying to think of something to tell him, but what he was doing was totally, deliciously distracting.

How could she explain that her passionate feeling for him was so powerful she feared to lose herself to it? All he had to do was kiss her, fondle her as he was doing now, and she would give him anything! Good heavens, she wondered, was there no moderation to be found anywhere when one was in love? Or was it always a constant vigil to maintain a sturdy defense against someone as irresistible as Sacheverel de Vries, Duke of Westermere, so as not to be his helpless, craven love slave?

As it was, he had already imposed his will on her several times. The coach ride down the banks of the Thames. Instructing her in sex from his collection of erotic literature. And now by insisting that she live up to her beliefs as laid down by the great Wollstonecraft.

It was a good thing they were not to be married, Marigold thought sadly. She would likely be so ecstatically happy as his wife, raising their beautiful children, that she would probably have had no other goal in life.

"Marigold?" he reminded her.

She brought her attention back with an effort. With a choked sob she managed, "Oh, lud, I ran from your house in London because I was so madly besotted with the great duke of Westermere I feared I would become totally under your power! I was a virgin, I had never experienced the power of physical love before. And when I did, it was beyond my wildest imaginings! At that moment I found I loved you so much I was terrified that if I gave into this passion in the degree that my senses were demanding, it would render me a totally mindless, cringing, love-struck creature! And I did not want to become that!"

He immediately sat up in the bed, black eyes blazing. "Damme, Marigold, in all this blather are you saying you love me?"

"Don't shout at me!" she cried.

At that very moment there was a commotion in the hallway outside the bedroom. This was an occurrence so unusual in the duke's well-run household that he immediately turned, putting his finger to his lips to warn her, and reached under the pillows for his pistol. It took him a moment, in the disordered bed, to find it.

Then, stark naked, the duke of Westermere rose, cocked weapon in hand, and approached the door.

A voice that could only be that of the valet, Timothy Cruddles, said from the other side, "Your Grace, you must open up! I'm sorry to bother you at this hour but there's been a most lamentable incident. Sergeant Ironfoot is here to speak to you!"

The duke looked back at Marigold who, wide-eyed, pulled the coverlet up about her shoulders. Then he turned and unlocked the door and threw it open.

Cruddles the valet and the tall figure of Jack Ironfoot in his long black coachman's cape stood just outside. Several footmen hovered in the background, holding candles. No one seemed to find the sight of their liege lord, stark naked and pointing a cocked pistol while heavily streaked about his mouth and chin with red rouge, to be anything out of the ordinary.

The coachman said, "My apologies, Your Grace, but I would not disturb you this time of night without news of the most dire of events."

The duke lowered his pistol slightly. "It had better be at least murder, Ironfoot."

"That it is, that it is indeed," the other assured him. "Your agent, young Parham, sir, has been found dead in Soldiers' Wood about an hour ago by a farmer up early bringing his milk to Stokesbury Hatton. Cause of young Mr. Parham's death: stabbed with unknown weapon a number of times in the belly."

For a moment there was a silence. Then the duke cursed under his breath.

"Of all the damned—" The news was obviously an unpleasant surprise. "The magistrate has been informed? And Parham's father?"

Jack Ironfoot nodded. "The magistrate, yes. Someone from the mine office has been sent to tell the old man."

The coachman put one foot inside the doorway, his big body blocking the others from seeing as he reached out and clasped Sacheveral's hand, leaving something behind in his palm.

"This here, Your Grace," Ironfoot said in a low rumble, "you might want to take a look at under your magnifying machine, as I know such things are of great interest to you. It was what Parham had when they found him. I was the one to open his fist."

The duke closed his hand and indicated with a gesture of his head that Cruddles and Ironfoot and the rest could go below, and closed the door.

"What is it?" Marigold cried from the bed. She had not made out much of the conversation in the doorway, the voices were too low. But she knew something terrible had occurred. "What has happened? What did Ironfoot give you?"

By the dim light of the bedroom candles, Sacheverel stood staring at his open hand. Jack Ironfoot had laid several wispy strands of colored wool across his palm. Now he recognized them as yarn possibly pulled from the clothing of his killer as Parham was attacked and murdered.

Damme, he was thinking, he'd seen these colors or something like them somewhere. And not so very long ago.

Chapter Twenty-one

A heavy rain began at dawn and continued throughout the morning. At noon, when Jack Ironfoot took up his post behind a concealing yew hedge in the graveyard of St. Dunstan's Church, the downpour came through the branches of the old oak tree above him with such steady force that the tree, barely in early leaf, offered little shelter.

The duke's former sergeant was not of a mind to move to a drier spot. His perusal of the sky had convinced him that the weather was typical of the north of England and would probably linger for days. If the misbegotten little village did not have the river rise in spring flood it would be lucky.

As it was, he was well prepared to endure a soaking behind the yew hedge as long as he could keep an eye on the sacristy door. That was where the three young ladies had gone that morning for what was, no doubt, an urgent meeting inside the old church.

As well they might, he thought. The way things were going it was a fair bet that one or all of them would come before the magistrate to tell what they knew about Parham's murder.

Jack had followed young Miss Fenwick that morning as she'd left The Elms in a great hurry, just as soon as His Grace had retired to his study with his microscope. Somehow, it appeared, the duke's betrothed had arranged for the young ladies to meet her at St. Dunstan's just before noon. They'd been inside for over an hour, now, the pretty little Miss MacDougal, Miss Fenwick, and the gypsyish-looking beauty, Miss Stack, doubtless trying to think of some plan.

They were great ones for schemes, these three dauntless lovelies, as Jack well knew. The last episode had led them down into Stokesbury Hatton's coal mine, and only luckily had he learned of it in time to come extricate them from their predicament.

But, now, there had been a murder. And it was no secret in the village that young Parham had a fancy, if one could use such a term, for the doctor's daughter. It was said that he'd waylaid her on the road to Wickham to deliver his evil advances. Enough that, the gossips in the village tavern swore, Miss Sophronia had been heard threatening to kill him if he ever did such a thing again. More than one claimed to know that she carried a knife, and had sworn she would not fear to use it.

To stab Parham in the belly, not the heart, that was the interesting part, he told himself. Most young women would have said the heart, but in the belly was exactly how Parham's murderer had killed him.

On the other hand, to be perfectly fair about it, he'd learned that there was a not a good-looking woman in Stokesbury Hatton who hadn't been approached at some time or other by Westermere's young agent. Although it had not been Parham's usual style to bother any other than those who were helpless against him, such as mill girls or the poor drabs who worked in the mine.

He shifted his weight and kept his eyes on the door as he put his hands inside his greatcoat. His fingers touched the smooth walnut stock of the loaded pistol he always carried with him.

Parham was a fool to have gotten himself killed and Jack was certain that some woman had had her revenge on him. A knife was a woman's weapon, anyway; with a man it was a cudgel or a beating, or firearms.

Whatever, it always made him uneasy when blood was spilled. In that respect he was superstitious enough. Blood attracted blood. And the one he was always on the lookout for, the evil creature that he was, could smell it. Murder drew him like a bee to honey. It had happened before.

*　　*　　*

Inside the church, Marigold, Penelope and Sophronia sat in an alcove that held the baptismal font. The area off the nave was not only the darkest part of St. Dunstan's but the coldest, too: Penelope shivered and kept blowing on her fingers to warm them, and when any of them spoke, clouds of their breath hung in the chill air.

What they had come to discuss was not cheerful, either: Sophronia's scowl made her look like Mother Gloom, and Penny was downright terrified.

"Stop shaking, Penny," Sophronia said, poking her friend. "Be assured, Westermere can't have samples of all the wool fibers in England. And certainly not a piece from each of the millions of cloaks people wear. He's taken up a task worse than looking for a needle in a haystack."

"Stokesbury Hatton's a very small haystack," Penelope moaned. "Oh, I should never have listened to you, Sophronia, when you said you wanted to borrow my cloak to wear instead of your own when you went to the Widow McCandlish's for the eggs and bread."

"He does have a large collection," Marigold said, "it's his passion. I helped sort wool fibers for him in London, along with bits of rope and samples of clay."

Sophronia slid down in her pew, looking sulky. "I'm sorry you regret your generosity now, Penny. But you gave me the cloak willingly enough when I told you I wanted to disguise myself going through Soldiers' Wood so that the disgusting Parham would not accost me again."

Marigold peered at them through the shadows. "Oh, Sophie, I cannot help but agree with Penny. It wasn't a good plan, you should have realized that beforehand! If you'd consulted me I would have told you Parham would molest any woman on the Wickham road. Someone else's cloak would not have made any difference."

Sophronia, beleaguered, lashed out, "Marigold, you may consider yourself our mentor and guide, but that does not mean we are all in accord with your self-appointed leadership! I am quite capable of making my own decisions!"

"And Sophie, you threatened to stab him in the belly," Penny wailed, "remember? You said it right out loud more than once, I heard you and so did Marigold. Suppose someone else has overheard you?" A new thought struck her. "Merciful heavens, how will a magistrate know that it was not I, wearing my own cloak, who did the dreadful deed?"

"I'm glad someone killed Parham," Sophronia flung back at her. "He deserved to die!"

"Hush, please hush," Marigold begged. The Cavaliers were not only quarrelling, they were making so much noise that the verger might come, even though the old man was more than half-deaf. "Penny, I fear that Westermere may well be able to identify your plaid cloak. It is Scottish-made and quite—distinctive." She had a good idea of the duke's opinion of Penelope's wardrobe. "That places all of us in great difficulty. You say you lent the cloak to Sophronia. And even if Sophronia says she never wore it because someone in her father's surgery waiting room took it from its hook, she cannot prove that, either. It makes it worse if Sophie tells even more—that she wanted your cloak to deceive Parham and escape his unwelcome advances, because then she is admitting she might have had a reason to murder him even defending herself."

Penny could hardly wait for her to stop speaking. "You must do something, Marigold," she cried. "Oh, do you wish your dear friends to be tried for murder and hanged? You must go to the duke at once and tell him to stop his experiments before he discovers it was my cloak the murderer wore! Surely he will do this for you, since you have him under your sensuous spell now. Did you not tell us that last night he promised to settle ten thousand pounds on you?"

There was a silence. In it they could hear the rain beating on the slate shingles. "Is that what you two think?" Marigold's face was in shadow. "That Westermere is my love slave now, and because I have thoroughly seduced him he has given me ten thousand a year?"

"A year?" Penny gasped. "Marigold, did you say a year?"

"Well, was that not what he was supposed to become?" Sophronia demanded. "After all, Marigold, I gave you my mother's gypsy dancing dress to bedazzle him. From what you tell us it worked surpassing well!"

Marigold shook her head. "Oh, Sophie, Penny, consider what we have done! Yes, Westermere did agree to settle ten thousand a year on me, but ensnaring him sounded so much more—well, nobly intended—before we went to London than it does now." She sighed. "We were so sure we had a sacred cause, and that any means were justified to achieve our glorious end!"

"Ten thousand a year," Penny was still murmuring.

"But he would have settled it on me anyway," Marigold continued, "when we were married. Sacheverel—the duke—told me so last night."

Sophie cried, "Hah, when did Westermere say that, in the throes of passion? Or after you twisted his arm?"

"Sophronia, how can you speak to Marigold that way?" Penny demanded. "She did get his promise to settle the money on her, so the plan worked. Surely the word of a duke is eminently trustworthy?"

Marigold surveyed her friends rather coldly. "I believe his word is his bond. That's the mark of a gentleman, is it not?"

Sophronia scowled. "Now who has seduced whom, Marigold? Have your wits been addled by Westermere's masterful passion?"

"Lud, what do you want?" she cried, exasperated. "Is ten thousand too much for a mere vicar's daughter? I did not know my friends had placed a limit on it! But I do know we have been mistaken about him. For one thing, Westermere asked for a report from his solicitors while he was still in London. They told him of holdings he didn't know he possessed, including the mill and mine villages here in northeast England. Once he had their surveys in hand, he assigned a Mr. Broadus of London, a financier and solicitor, to investigate Parham and Parham and the duke's other agents. From what he told me last night it was not long before Broadus exposed the Parhams' exploitation of the Stokesbury Hatton workers in order to return a great profit. But what was uncovered was not only the injustices we know so well and which Sachev—the duke assures me he will promptly correct, but Mr. Broadus and his clerk discovered a great deal of dishonesty and chicanery throughout the Westermere empire. The first order of things, after their meeting yesterday, was the decision to dismiss Robinson Parham and his father and bring criminal charges against them." She paused. "But as we know, someone saw to it that young Parham was conveniently murdered."

Sophronia cried, "Westermere told you that he was not at fault abusing his people, that his managers were? And that he intended to set things to right after he'd fired the lot of them? Marigold, has the villain cozzened you!"

Marigold opened her mouth and then shut it.

She wanted to blurt out that the wonderful man who had held her in his arms as they talked into the night was indeed to be believed and trusted. The duke of Westermere had told her that the night after he had arrived in Stokesbury Hatton he had disguised himself and secretly gone down into the mine with that somewhat mysterious jack-of-all-jobs, Jack Ironfoot. The two men had seen for themselves the conditions there. So whatever the Parhams had told him, or shown him afterward, had only reinforced the duke's opinion of them as liars and charlatans. Since then Westermere had been biding his time, waiting for solicitor Broadus to bring him the final evidence from London.

But Marigold only said, "He is not a villain as we thought, he is a hero who fought bravely under Wellington in Spain. And I do not care whether you like it or not," she announced, lifting her chin, "I find I have fallen madly in love with him!"

The cries of outrage and disbelief from Sophronia and Penny did bring the St. Dunstan's verger to see what all the racket was about. He peered at them from the back of the church, then shuffled away.

"How can you be such an idiot?" Sophronia snapped. "Really, Marigold, is Westermere's story now that he was ignorant of the misery that has been going on here for years? I for one don't believe it!"

"But it's true, I swear. I've listened to him. I still don't think the man knows how rich he is. Or exactly what he owns."

Penny made a huffing noise. "Marigold, in spite of your great strength of character, I believe you have been deceived and misled due to—well, Westermere's talent for—ah, physical intimacy. Really, I must agree with Sophronia. How can anyone so rich and powerful be oblivious to all the evil he's caused?"

"He didn't cause the evil, the people who worked for him did!" she protested. "Besides, he was away in Spain, fighting a war!"

Sophronia snorted. "The Westermeres' ruthless reign has been going on for generations. The duke of Westermere is responsible for Robinson Parham being here, isn't he? If he hadn't been blind, as he maintains, to what was going on in Stokesbury Hatton, men like the Parhams would not have had the power to molest women and ruin the workmen's lives and abuse starving children. Nor would Penny and I," she cried, raising her voice, "now be in danger of hanging!"

"Oh, fiddlesticks, you're not going to hang, Sophronia," Marigold shot back. "What an absurd idea! And neither is Penny. I won't let you."

Sophia laughed, bitterly. "You won't let us? How do you intend to stop it, dear friend?"

"I know how," Penny said, suddenly. "Marigold will simply have to go back to bed with him and withhold her—er—passion until Westermere has agreed to stop trying to identify the murderer by examining the fibers from my cloak."

There was a long moment while Marigold stared at both of them.

"Are you mad?" she managed, finally. "Do we, the once brave and bold Three Cavaliers, have no other solution to our problems than to supposedly inflict sensual frustration on the duke of Westermere until he gives us something?" When they didn't speak she went on, "I tell you, I am not sure I have succeeded in making him that much a slave to my charms. On the contrary, what has happened is that *I* have somehow fallen wildly in love with *him*!"

"That's not important," Sophronia said brusquely. "You would know how inconsequential so-called love is, Marigold, if you refreshed your memory by reading Wollstonecraft again. What is important is that this is a matter of life and death. We could all be hung for Parham's murder."

Marigold muttered, "Oh, the devil with Mary Wollstonecraft," and listened to her friends' shocked gasps.

But Sophronia's words had a chilling effect.

Perhaps it would be a good idea to lay the whole matter before the duke and straighten out the ownership of the cloak, and see if he had any good advice for their terrible dilemma. That seemed a much better plan to Marigold than trying to wheedle him away from his microscope.

Besides, she doubted anything, perhaps even the wildly erotic delights of their bed, could do that.

* * *

The freshening downpour had driven Jack Iron-foot inside after all, to stand in the shadows under the arch by the sacristy door. In spite of the now thunderous drumming of rain on the church roof he could hear the young ladies' voices, and he listened with interest, especially to the details of their several plots over the past weeks to bring the duke under the spell of the lovely Miss Fenwick. From time to time he moved out of the shadows just enough to get a glimpse of them before he quickly shifted back again.

The one his eyes always fell upon was the schoolmaster's daughter, Miss Penelope, that angelic little thing with her big eyes and blond curls; she quite fascinated him. He couldn't forget that night he'd carried her in his arms, and the feel of her soft young body against his; he was quite surprised at his own reaction. Girlish and spritely as she was, pretty Miss Penny MacDougal made a man want to hover near and protect her, and see that she lacked for nothing. On the other hand, she had spirit and courage. It was a tantalizing combination. More than once, contemplating her from a distance, he'd found his thoughts wandering to retirement from an active life of intrigue with the duke, and settling down on the considerable land his family owned in the west. However, this was not yet quite the right time. He sighed.

It seemed to him at that moment that the other two were not quite sympathetic enough to Miss Penelope's terrors in spite of the fact that, with her generous nature, she had gladly lent her cloak to the gypsy girl, not thinking at all of her own peril, and that they might get their identities mixed by some careless witness.

There was no doubt about it, Jack decided, this time these young ladies were in a fix. He doubted even Miss Marigold could stop His Grace from what he was determined to do. That is, use his precious microscope to find the evidence to discover Parham's killer.

But who was the murderer?

Even Jack Ironfoot, the duke of Westermere's longtime spy master, could not hazard a guess.

And when it came to that, where was little Miss Penelope's plaid Scottish cloak?

Chapter Twenty-two

"Odds fish," Reginald Pendragon exclaimed as Pomfret helped him off with his sodden cloak, "I thought we would never get here, Satch. The coach had a bad enough time on the roads coming north, but the wagon could not make two miles without bogging down. I had to get out several times and help dig in the mud myself. If you don't believe me, look at my boots! It's a solid deluge north from Doncaster, and no better here, is it?"

"Um, yes, I suppose it's been raining quite a bit," the duke said indifferently. "Come into the study, Reggie. I want to show you something."

The surgeon followed the duke of Westermere into the big salon now serving as his laboratory.

"I heard the news—that your agent's been murdered," he said, as he looked around for a place to sit among stacks of specimen cases and scientific periodicals in various languages. "That's a rum bit of luck. Do you know yet who did the foul deed? On the road we heard there might be a workers' uprising, and there was talk of the militia being called out."

The duke grunted. "That's rubbish. No one's going to call out the militia unless I tell them to. But Parham's dead, all right, stabbed to death on the Wickham road where, no doubt, he was up to no good. I would say the odds are slight that the villagers had anything to do with it, although there was no doubt the man was universally hated. As well as being, with his father, as I am discovering, an embezzler of major proportions of my assets. Now." He pushed the other man toward the study table where the microscope had been installed. "Look into that," he ordered, "and tell me what you see."

The doctor looked around, hopefully, for a sign of Pomfret and his tray of brandy, much needed by a man who'd been travelling in rain and mud for several days. But the ancient butler was nowhere to be seen. He leaned over the microscope with a sigh.

After a few long minutes Reggie said cautiously, "Microscopic life of some sort?" He looked up. "Ah, you've discovered something in the depths of the coal mine, Satch, and are going to name it after me?"

The duke was in no mood for levity. "What the

devil are you looking at?" he growled, pushing the young doctor away. "Those are fibers, man, fibers. And a damned precious clue, now that I've identified them."

"You've identified them? I can't believe it. You mean this contraption has proved its worth?" Pomfret had finally made his appearance. The doctor greeted him and his tray of spirits with relief. "More to the point," he said, tossing back the brandy the butler poured for him and holding out his glass for another, "will it stand up in a court of law?"

"Um," the duke said. He waved Pomfret and drinks aside, and got up to pace to the fireplace. "We're not that far along. There's a small imbroglio, it would seem."

The doctor, considerably refreshed, unbuttoned his slightly mud-spattered jacket and settled himself in a chair. The journey by coach and wagon from London to bring supplies to some doctor's clinic in Stokesbury Hatton had not been easily accomplished. Reggie was dog tired. But he could see there was an air of tension about his friend. The duke had wanted the medicines in his usual precipitous way; now that he was there, it was obvious he was under considerable pressure. Where, Reggie wondered, was the irresistibly lovely fiancée, the vicar's daughter, Miss Fenwick?

"What sort of imbroglio, Satch?" he said, cautiously.

The duke concentrated on poking up the fire.

With his back to the doctor he said, "The wool's Scottish. It was no great feat to identify the clip of their blackfaced stock, it's common enough. But I hardly needed the knowledge. Parham had enough of a death grip on the garment to tear it, so the specimen was plain enough: five broken green, yellow, black and red strands. Presuming that from the texture and thickness the attacker was wearing it as an outer garment, such as a cloak, one has only to ask oneself where in the name of all that's holy would one find such a preposterous mix?"

The duke turned to glare darkly at his friend. Reggie blinked, not quite sure what to answer.

"A tartan?" he offered, hazarding a guess. "Er, a Scottish cloak made of somewhat—ah, loud-colored plaid?" When Sacheveral stood staring at him, Reggie said, "Well, at least one doesn't see many of those hereabouts."

"No, even in Yorkshire they've a better eye for dress than that," the other growled. "Once I saw the colors up close, of course, I needn't have gone any further. I realized I'd viewed the confounded thing myself at least once. How could one forget it?"

Reggie stroked his chin. "And the problem?"

The duke paced the room, hands behind his back. "Have you noticed, Reggie, in the short time you've known her, how mayhem and disaster seem to hover in the wake of my betrothed, Miss Marigold Fenwick, despite her obvious charms and unchallengeable beauty?"

"Um, well now that you mention it," Reggie said, "perhaps. The lady *is* adorable and ravishing. By the way, has she returned to her home village here, and her father the vicar? Have you had the pleasure of calling on her?"

"She's living here with me," the duke said shortly. "Miss Fenwick is a follower of Mary Wollstonecraft and a believer in free love."

"Oh, I say," Reggie said, looking somewhat nonplussed. "How fortunate for you. I mean—" He caught another glare from the duke and subsided, confused.

"Yes, fortunate for me," Sacheverel grunted, "six to eight hours of the night when I am in bed and have her in my arms, and at least know where she is and what she is doing. The rest of the time is becoming pure hell. For I recognized the cloak the murderer was wearing as soon as I saw the colors under the microscope, I hardly had to go forward to confirm the Scottish origin of the wool. The cloak belongs to one of Miss Fenwick's friends."

The doctor looked surprised. "Zounds! One of Miss Fenwick's lady friends is the murderer?"

"I'm not sure." Sacheverel paced back down the study again. "I would sincerely doubt Miss Penelope MacDougal has the stomach to murder anything larger than a fuzzy caterpillar, if that. On the other hand the doctor's daughter is an interesting specimen, half-gypsy, of doughty character, and there's a rumor Parham attempted to approach her and was rebuffed. Miss Stack from all reports did not take their encounter lightly. She's supposed to have carried a knife after that."

Reggie stirred, uncomfortably. "Hard to fault a woman, Satch, for wanting to protect herself from a ruthless cad such as you describe. Besides, it wasn't the gypsy girl's cloak, was it?"

He appeared not to have heard him. "Then there's my own betrothed," Satch was saying, "who has a valiant spirit and a burning desire to correct the world's injustices, as I can well attest. In addition, she possesses a strong, well-made physique. I have thought it over for long hours and I still cannot say if passion would drive the woman I'm enamored of to murder." He stopped his pacing and considered it. "But then a jury probably could not, either."

"Damme, Satch," Reggie cried, "that's pretty cold-blooded!"

He shrugged. "On the contrary, you know me better than that. Words cannot express the depths of my feeling in this matter. Miss Fenwick is my betrothed, my future duchess and intended bride."

"Well, it was not Miss Fenwick's cloak," Reggie said. "You must consider that."

"I have." Satch rubbed his fingers across his eyes and sighed. "And I am reminded from observing the females in my own family how they constantly borrow each others' clothing. And, in the eternal manner of their sex, reinforce each other fearlessly like flocks of irate geese when they feel they are assailed. Reggie, if I were to command Miss Fenwick and her friends to present themselves to me in the company of the local magistrate, I know they would all three declare they were wearing the abominable plaid cloak the night of Parham's murder. Even my own betrothed, whose testimony is virtually unassailable, as she was lying in my bed, in my arms, all of that very night after having engaged in the most intimate and satisfactory of physical relations, would undoubtedly swear she was on the Wickham road wearing the damned cloak, out of loyalty to the rest."

The doctor swallowed several times before he could speak. "What do you plan to do?" was all he could say.

But the duke had turned away. He made no answer.

Sacheverel returned to his microscope and Reggie Pendragon retired to take a hot bath and a rest before dinner. Several hours passed before Marigold, who had stopped to pay a visit to her father at the parsonage, entered the downstairs hall of The Elms. She was surprised to find a delegation of miners waiting, including Tom Grandison, once the pit boss of number two gallery. Now, Marigold saw, the tall miner, who was also the chapel pastor, had assumed some sort of leadership since the dismissal of Superintendent Hatfield and most of the foremen.

Mrs. Cawdigan came bustling out to take Marigold's wet things. "They're waiting to see His

Grace," the housekeeper whispered, indicating the miners with a jerk of her head. "I wouldn't have let 'em in but they said it was desperate, like something terrible about the mine. But I daren't disturb the duke, miss, those were His Grace's orders. Not to interrupt him when he was working with his magnifying machine."

Marigold turned to face the muddy, coal-blackened miners, many of whom, she was sure, remembered her from that night she'd been dragged from the mine by Hatfield and his minions in her torn and ragged pantaloons and underbodice.

"Something terrible about the mine?" She took a step toward the man she knew. "Tom Grandison? Are you and the other men waiting to speak to the duke?"

He pulled off his grimy cap. "Yes, miss." If he remembered Marigold in her underclothes his face did not show it. "It's the rain. Since Superintendent Hatfield has been removed, and we thank the good Lord for that, there's no one to take the water into account. But we fear what will happen with what's already fallen."

The door to the study opened and the duke came out into the hall. His cropped hair stuck up in tufts where he'd run his fingers through it, and his black-browed face looked tired.

"What's all the commotion?" He stared at the miners as though the last thing he expected was to find a half-dozen of them grouped uneasily in The Elm's elegant entranceway. His eyes found

Marigold. Then he said, "Mrs. Cawdigan, what do these men want?"

"Yer pardon, milord," Grandison spoke up, "but we ha'an't no authority in the mine to take action now that the superintendent's gone, and the situation grows perilous. So we come to you."

"It's the water," a miner's voice in the back added.

Westermere frowned. "Water? What drivel is this? Surely you don't need any water with the heavens pouring down this way!"

The men looked puzzled for a moment.

Then Tom Grandison said, "Your lordship couldn't know it, as it's been more than fifty years by now, but the river was dammed up on orders from your grandsire so's the galleries in the mine could be dug on out under the river bed. That's what them earthen dams up the valley are for. But when it rains like this, there's danger of flooding in the mine."

The duke looked the miner up and down piercingly. "Who the devil are you?"

"Tom Grandison, sir, was acting foreman of number two gallery." While the others shuffled their feet and looked uncertain Grandison went on, "We come to ask yer permission to close the mine down, as the men below are in some danger if water comes in."

The duke stroked his jaw. "You mean they are in danger of drowning."

Grandison's blue eyes did not waver. "That's it in so many words, if your lordship will pardon my saying it. We had it happen once before when my father was a young man working the north gallery seam. He was one of those lost. Now the men ought to be pulled out of there within the hour in my opinion. There's no time to dally."

The corners of the duke's mouth twitched. Abruptly, he nodded. "Then get to it! I'll send a paper down to the mine office at once."

The miners looked at each other, and there was a muffled sound of surprise, and gratification. As they turned and started toward the front door, Mrs. Cawdigan bustling ahead of them to open it and almost shoo them out into the rain, the duke called out.

"Grandison?" The other man stopped, and turned. "Was this your idea," Sacheverel said, "to bring a delegation of men up here and present yourself for my attention at my very door?"

Grandison's face went blank, as though he saw what was coming. "It was my idea, your lordship," he answered.

The duke studied him for a moment. "My guess is there was something else you wanted to tell me."

Tom Grandison's face showed relief; the blow had not fallen, after all. He looked away. "It's not something your lordship would want to hear. In all these years I've found that nobody does. God knows the miners've tried often enough to talk to Mr. Hatfield about it and your agents that was, the Parhams." He shrugged. "The valley's always in peril, anyway, as long as them old earthen work dams are the way they is."

There was a moment's silence. Then the duke ground out, "Good God, man, are you telling me what I think you are?" He seized the miner by the arm, steering him toward the door of the study. "I want to hear more of this. Can you write? Can you draw a diagram of Stokesbury Hatton?" When the other man nodded, he looked over his shoulder at the housekeeper. "Mrs. Cawdigan, where the devil is Pomfret? Find him and send him with a tray of—ah, beer, for Grandison here."

Mrs. Cawdigan was closing the front door on the last of the muddy miners. She looked over the remaining one with an audible sniff. "Tom Grandison don't drink beer, Your Grace, he's the chapel preacher. All the Methodists are abstainers."

"Interesting. Very interesting." The duke of Westermere examined the other man keenly as he pushed him into the study. "A pot of tea, then, and a plate of cheese and bread. Make enough for two."

The door slammed. Mrs. Cawdigan sighed, and turned away to go to look for the butler. Marigold stood staring at the freshly painted panels of the door to the study.

Westermere had looked straight at her and had not even acknowledged her, she thought. Not even a nod. Now there was the trouble with the mine, and he was preoccupied with Tom Grandison. It was evident he saw intelligence and leadership in the tall miner.

But all this did not make what she urgently had to tell him any easier.

Chapter Twenty-three

One of the footmen came in as Pomfret was supervising the serving of the port trifle. He whispered into the butler's ear and then discreetly retired from the dining room.

Pomfret promptly caught the duke's eye. "Your Grace," he intoned after the duke had nodded his permission to speak, "the magistrate regrets he will not be able to take dinner with you as planned, as he has decided not to chance the village bridge. At last report the river was up and flowing over it to a depth of half a foot."

Reginald Pendragon leaned to Marigold and said behind his hand, "The magistrate may stay on the other side of the river for all I care. They say he is a spineless toady and crony of the recently departed Hatfield and Parham, junior and senior. Do you know him?"

Marigold gave the doctor a nervous look. "No, why should I know him? I-I've not been charged with anything." It was not quite the right thing to say. She glanced down the table where the duke of Westermere, elegantly attired for dinner in blue velvet coat with gold buttons, high white stock and scarlet weskit, was rapidly dispatching his dessert.

Before the trifle was served the conversation had been about the duke's approval of the pit boss, Tom Grandison, whom he considered to be remarkably superior in intelligence and potential.

"The magistrate was to come to dinner this evening," Marigold rattled on, "to discuss the m-murder, was he not?"

"Was he?" Pendragon gave her an interested stare. "I have no idea, Miss Marigold. I had not discussed the magistrate coming to dinner with His Grace, at all. Although with this weather, I hardly think his presence was seriously expected."

Marigold gave a little shudder. Whatever the reason, she was glad to have been spared the magistrate's presence. At least until she had a chance to talk to the duke in the privacy of his bedchamber. The hands of the clock over the fireplace seemed to turn excruciatingly slowly. Westermere and his friend the doctor had been discussing the possibility of a flood in the valley at length.

"Here, Reggie, have you seen the map Grandison drew?" the duke said, wiping his lips with a linen napkin at the same time he pushed a sheet of paper down the table. "It's amazingly clever, everything drawn to scale. The man's got a talent for abstracts and is very observant." He reached over with his dessert spoon to direct the doctor's attention to certain points. "Here are the old earthwork dams at the head of the valley that have received little or no attention since they were built by my grandfather, and are assumed to be in dangerous condition. Here's the valley itself with the river drained down to one tenth of its former size so as to accommodate expanded mine excavations. The pressure of water in the river bed when it is full leaks through the rock strata and into the mine below, as Grandison warned us. It has drowned some of the miners before. But the real danger is here, at the dams."

The doctor had leaned forward to study the map. "There is no way, now, even at this late hour, to send men up to reinforce them?"

"In this deluge?" The duke frowned. "Even timber braces would wash away, if they could be got in place at all. I have seen something of engineers' work in Spain, and I do not think any one of them would advise trying to shore up a dirt dam in this rain. No, what Grandison proposes is the best scheme. Get the men out of the mine first, and if the river continues to rise, direct the villagers to take shelter on these high points surrounding Stokesbury Hatton: the hill of St. Dunstan's church, the old common pasture which covers a respectably elevated knoll on this side of the river, and the land surrounding the house we're in now."

Marigold, leaning on her elbows, had been following the spoon as it traced across Grandison's neatly drawn map of the valley.

What her eyes saw was a forecasting of terrible disaster. If water from broken dams swept through the valley it would create a swath of unimaginable destruction. Virtually all of the village of Stokesbury Hatton lay in the path.

"It's not going to happen, is it?" she murmured. "It can't! The village would be wiped from the face of the earth and the mill—even the coal mine would be flooded, wouldn't it? Dear heavens, everything would be swept away!"

"Except that which is on the high ground," the doctor reminded her. "The Elms, where we've partaken of such an admirable dinner tonight, would still be here. And your father's church, St. Dunstan's, and the rectory would be spared."

She stared at him. Did they think she was worried about her father's church? She was thinking of the mill people, and the miserable hovels of the miners' heath.

She looked down the table at the duke. "Your Grace, would not the miners volunteer to go up the valley and work on the dams? They are very skilled and daring." She remembered them in the colliery, working on the dangerous coal face. "They would not be daunted, either, by the weather, for the mine and all that they have is at stake."

His look was impassive. "Yes, no doubt they would volunteer to go. But it would be a good way to drown brave men."

"Yet Miss Fenwick is right," the doctor put in. "Remember the sappers we had at the siege of Santa Rosa in the war? They were Welshmen, as I recall, out of the mines there, and a stubborn, valiant lot. Wellington put them to work excavating galleries under the outer walls of the castle." Pomfret had come in with the brandy, a signal for Marigold to retire. "Talk about brave men— the sappers went down into black, airless holes I would not go into for all the gold in the Bank of England."

With a sigh, Marigold rose and the men got up from their seats with her. Both bowed, lifting their glasses in polite salute, as she took her leave. She knew they wanted to talk of the old days and the peninsular war, as they frequently did when together. The handsome doctor was a gifted storyteller.

She thought of going into the parlor to do a bit of needlework and knew that if she did it would be a solitary occupation. Westermere and Reggie Pendragon had often sat up for hours in the house in London, drinking and telling war stories; she doubted she could count on them to join her any time soon.

The sound of the rain outside did nothing to lift Marigold's spirits. If only it would stop, she told herself. Doom seemed to hang in the stifling air.

She picked up a candle from the hall table, waved aside the young footman stationed in the hallway who fairly leaped to assist her, and turned toward the stair.

She would bathe, she decided, get into her bedclothes, and while she waited for Westermere, try to compose her thoughts to appeal to him concerning her friends' plight.

Great heavens, Marigold thought, they already had Parham's unresolved murder hanging over them, and now there was the danger of losing Stokesbury Hatton to a great flood! In addition it was her unlucky task to have to throw herself on the mercy and understanding of Sacheverel de Vries, whose manner had recently become rather unexpectedly distant and ironical, and ask for his help. Things could not be worse.

Outside the village, on the road that led from the south, a limping figure made its way through the ankle-deep mud carrying a battered valise. The wind was up, lashing the rain against him and tearing at his cloak, making walking difficult, but the traveler's gaunt, pallid face and sunken eyes showed little but stoic indifference. He had left the Edinburgh coach at the crossroads, fully prepared to walk the remaining four miles into Stokesbury Hatton in spite of the weather and the hour which was now swiftly approaching midnight.

There'd been a murder here, he reminded himself as he stomped to the top of a rise and looked down into the black abyss of the night and the sheets of rain that were scouring the valley. He'd read about the killing in the Edinburgh papers of an agent for the dukes of Westermere, who'd been stabbed and his body dumped in the woods.

It was that news which now brought him to Stokesbury Hatton. Below, lamplight still shone in a few houses; the watery, pinpoint glow was the only sign that a town existed. Still, he knew he was in the right place. Death, as always, pointed the way.

He would find a shed, he told himself, or an abandoned byre, and crawl in to take shelter for the night. It was not the first time he had lived so, like a beggar or a vagabond, sleeping in hedgerows and barns and wherever else he could hide. It had been a long time since he had slept in a bed safe and protected under silk sheets in the manner of the vast wealth he'd been born to.

But all that would soon be changed, he told himself. Discomfort was forgotten as he hobbled forward on his misshapen leg down the descending road, the valise banging against his thigh.

He was getting closer to his goal now, after long and frustrating delays. It was ironic that what he would do would no doubt avenge the death of Robinson Parham, whoever he had been, at the same time.

* * *

Marigold had gone to sleep in a chair reading a book borrowed from Westermere's shelves, the title of which was *Being an Account of Vampires and Other Forms of the Demonic Undead*, by a Countess Irena Tszagne, who lived in a castle in deepest Transylvania.

Not unexpectedly, Marigold was in the middle of a turbulent dream about clouds of bloodthirsty bats that were sent through the air by a dreadful, cadaverous figure in a black cloak, when a noise wakened her.

She sat up in the chair with a barely muffled scream on her lips. It was only Westermere, she saw, who had come in. He had evidently tried to be quiet, but it was the sound of his shaving and washing that had wakened her.

Marigold was terribly glad to see him. In fact, she would have stumbled across the room to embrace him out of sheer relief, considering that the Transylvanian bats and their horrid master had proved to be only a nightmare, but he had already removed his shirt and was toweling off, vigorously rubbing his wet hair.

As she straightened her lavender silk peignoir Marigold was struck anew by the sight of Westermere, who was such a wonderful-looking man. She'd noticed that generally he seemed oblivious to the effect of his virile beauty on others, although men's eyes quickened, appraisingly, when they viewed his powerful torso. And women continually sighed over his black hair and eyes, his tall figure's natural grace. If the duke of Westermere reacted at all, it was with an almost testy impatience that others had even taken note of it. And of course, with his notorious meticulousness about his clothes.

"Is there something amiss?" he said, lowering the towel. "Why are you looking at me like that?"

"I am not—" Her lips tightened. It was going to be a difficult hour or two; she could sense that already. "Good evening, Your Grace," Marigold said, and dropped him a small curtsy. "I hope you have had an entertaining time with your good friend, Dr. Pendragon."

He put the towel on the wash stand and studied her. "Now, my beloved," he said, "enlighten me as to what you have on your devious mind."

"My mind is not devious!" Well, perhaps it was, just a little. And it had become more so dealing with him. Good heavens, she realized; had he called her his beloved?

Marigold took a deep breath. "Westermere, I want to speak to you about the mystery of the murder of your agent, Robinson Parham." She saw his eyebrows lift, sardonically. "But I beg you to keep an open mind, as I most desperately must appeal to your sense of fairness!"

He pulled up a chair and sat down on it, crossing one booted leg over the other. "Fairness? This sounds worse than I thought. Pray, do continue."

She watched the muscles in his biceps swell as he crossed his arms over his naked chest. Distracted by the sight, she blurted out, "You must help because my friends and I find ourselves in a most unfortunate position, and we do not want to be hanged!"

His expression did not change. "Yes, I have known few people who have expressed enthusiasm for the process." As Marigold stared blankly at him, he went on, "Yes, I cannot recall having heard anyone say that they could not wait to be hanged by the neck until they were dead."

Oh, how could he not be serious at a time like this? "What is the matter with you?" she cried. "This is no time for gallows humor!"

As soon as she said it she saw his lips quirk. He covered it with a choked cough. "Perhaps, sweetheart, you should tell me what you want of me."

Marigold twisted her hands in some distress. She'd certainly not been wrong about this being difficult. For a brief moment she wished that Penelope, Sophronia, the dead Parham and the miserable cloak would just go away. But of course things did not happen like that.

"Westermere, the fibers you are examining come from a cloak belonging to my dear friend, the schoolmaster's daughter," she began, "Penelope MacDougal. Who lent it to another friend, Dr. Stack's daughter, Sophronia. She wanted the cloak to wear rather than her own, when she went to Wickham to the Widow McCandlish's to get our regular weekly donation of eggs and hardtack for Stokesbury Hatton's children who do not get enough to eat. But Sophronia claims that she hung Penny's cloak upon a hook in the waiting room of her father's surgery while she was helping him with his patients, and someone stole it. We do not know who has it now," she ended breathlessly, "but we implore you to find it through your knowledge of scientific techniques."

He had followed all this with a bemused look. "Tell me," the duke said when Marigold had stopped, "did your friend the gypsy girl kill Parham?"

Marigold recoiled.

"I-I don't know," she stammered. "He—Parham—had accosted her before in the woods, you know, and Sophie—alas, she did say she would kill him if he attempted it again, but that was only to Penelope and me in the confidence of our long friendship! But I swear that was her passionate gypsy nature speaking, and nothing more." She met his gaze with her chin lifted. "I believe Sophie when she says she did not kill him."

For a moment admiration gleamed in his black eyes. He stood up. "Now you wish me to find the real killer."

"W-why, yes. You are brilliant, everyone agrees. Dr. Pendragon says you are a genius, and Sir Robert Peel calls you *un homme formidable*. Westermere, you can do it, can you not?"

"Hmmm." He was close enough to take the ribbon ties of the lavender peignoir between his fingers. "How do you like this color? That fat modiste howled her head off at the sight of it and said it was not suitable for a genteel betrothed female, but I had thought it would become you."

"I am not overly fond of purple," Marigold admitted, pulling his hand away, "and there is certainly an excess of ribbons as one does not expect to find them all around the hem, but yes, it does suit in a way. Westermere, can you find Parham's murderer?"

"The color is lilac," he murmured, pulling the neck ribbons loose and baring the scandalously low-cut bodice under it, "not purple, my dear vicarage-raised heathen. And the fabric is Lyons tissue silk."

As he slid the peignoir from her shoulders he said, "Thanks to the microscope I had already matched the yarn taken from Parham's clutch with a Scottish fabric, and then remembered that damnable penchant your friend has for wearing loud colors. I could not forget the cloak she was wearing when I brought MacDougal and Stack to the vicarage to pick up their girls. I was waiting for you to tell me the story." His eyes swept over her, noting the way the translucent lavender silk clung to her body and revealed her breasts. "Frankly, I had expected more."

"M-more?" Marigold breathed, as his hands caressed her waist and hips, then pulled her to him.

"Of course," he said, kissing her ever-so-lightly on the mouth and chin and forehead so that she gasped, and eagerly tried to follow his lips with her own. "Whenever I am with you, dear Marigold, I gird myself as I would for a bill to be debated in the House of Lords. Tilting with you has taught me there is always some grand maneuver, some artful argument, even some scurrilous threat or other, before you propose whatever it is you propose. What is it this time?" he said, slipping the straps of the gauzy nightgown down over her arms and baring her rosy-tipped breasts. "And most important, what is it going to cost me?"

Marigold shuddered, and pushed him away. "Artful argument? Scurrilous threat? That is hardly the truth! What really happens is that you so confound me with—uh, temptation—that the weaker side of my feminine character is subdued and subverted! It's not fair! You expect me to surrender all to you!"

"By God, yes," he growled. "If this is what you are offering me to rescue the misses MacDougal and Stack from the gallows, then do it now!"

He lifted her and carried her to the bed as she struggled.

"Westermere, cease and desist!" Marigold cried. "You do not even know what you are bargaining for. Do you simply wish me to be intimate with you? If so, for how long?"

"As long as you can stand it," he muttered, dropping her into the bed. "We have all night."

"No, no," she protested as he pulled the lilac silk up and over her head and tossed it to the far corner of the room. "Westermere, are we agreeing to weeks or mon—"

"My name is Sacheverel," he said in her ear. "I wish you to use it. And there will be no more haggling, my love, even at the cost of total destruction of your 'weaker feminine character.' Which, frankly, I doubt exists. The weaker part, anyway." He held her down, his black eyes blazing, while he bestowed kisses on her throat and breasts. "When I was a young man my grandfather warned me that, with the immodest extent of the Westermere wealth, it would be a rare thing indeed if I found anyone who loved me for myself. That all those about me, alas, would be corrupted, and offer loyalty and affection only when influenced by my money."

He lifted her hand and kissed each finger, biting the last, her thumb, rather sharply. "I must admit I have certainly found this to be true of you, sweet Marigold," he murmured. "However, I have become reconciled to your venality, and excuse some part of it as not only your infatuation with Wollstonecraft's nonsense, but also the life you have led as a vicar's daughter raised in pious poverty." When Marigold jerked her hand away, he smiled. "Although when I think on it, it is a great challenge. I fear our life together will be one long thieves' market, with bargains offered at every nightfall."

"How can you insult me so?" Marigold whispered, as he took her in his arms and moved his big body over hers. "I am not venal! Fagh, West—Sacheverel, it is easy to criticize when one has all the money in the world! And I did not bargain with you, I only asked that you help my friends!"

But it was too late. His mouth had already

seized hers with the fieriest of kisses, his plundering tongue opening her lips. And with a thrust of his hips Sacheverel de Vries, Duke of Westermere, possessed her.

The night of their lovemaking had begun.

Chapter Twenty-four

Marigold woke to the sound of church bells. In the last few moments of sleep she'd been dreaming that she was being wed to Sacheverel de Vries, Duke of Westermere, in her father's church, St. Dunstan's. The sun was shining, a glorious day, and the whole village of Stokesbury Hatton had turned out to see her alight from a coach—a golden vehicle so splendid it could have come straight from the tale of Cinderella—to be greeted by her own dear father at the church door.

My, the bells were loud, she couldn't help thinking as she lifted her crystal-and-pearl embroidered skirts to mount the steps of the porch. In the distance there was the insistent, frantic blatting of horns. But in her dream she saw Sacheverel, unbelievably handsome in beige jacket and new-style long trousers, holding a top hat in his hand and waiting for her just inside the church.

Marigold sighed, thinking it was certainly flattering to be praised for successfully living up to Mary Wollstonecraft's concepts of free love, as the duke himself had done in the intervals between their passionate lovemaking during the night. But it was also wonderful to think of getting married.

After all was said and done, she now knew that in her heart every woman longed for the ultimate happiness of the wedded estate. Why, hadn't Mary Wollstonecraft herself finally married the bookseller and writer William Godwin?

It was too bad, the dream was fading. She had to open her eyes.

Sacheverel was not there beside her, she saw. After a moment's disappointment, Marigold stretched like a cat, arms above her head in the tumbled bed, smiling but noting a certain soreness in overused muscles. It had been a marvelous, ardent, burningly passionate night, and Westermere a constantly surprising, tireless lover. She would never forget a moment of it.

But Marigold frowned.

What was that racket outside? Those were church bells ringing! She knew at once from the sound of them which were St. Dunstan's. But this was Tuesday, not Sunday; they shouldn't be ringing. Nor should the others.

Alarmed, she sprang out of bed, snatching up

her peignoir from the carpet, and went to the window to pull back the curtains. Unlike her beautiful wedding dream the sun was not shining; it was still raining. And those were horns, right enough; they sounded as though they were down in the village.

Marigold pressed her nose against the window glass. Crowds of villagers were coming up the drive. There were all sorts of wagons with whole families in them, even carts pushed by hand. And hundreds more on foot, some of them already setting up makeshift shelters under the trees.

The church bells, St. Dunstan's, Catholic St. Anne's, the tinny clamor of the Methodist and Baptist chapels, rang ceaselessly. That could only mean one thing. The alarm had been given. The plan that the duke and Dr. Pendragon had discussed, to get the population of Stokesbury Hatton to high ground in the case the valley was flooded, was now proceeding.

Lud, they expected the dams to give way!

Marigold did not bother to ring for Mrs. Cawdigan to come help her dress. She doubted if the housekeeper could be found, anyway, judging from the uproar coming from downstairs.

She hastily combed her hair and washed up, putting on her warmest clothes and new walking boots, and picked up the new blue cloak, flinging it over her arm. Coming down the stairs Marigold had to squeeze past footmen carrying blankets taken from the upstairs cupboards out to the refugees. A stream of servants came and went by the front door, some guiding shawled mill women and their infants off to the kitchen. Mrs. Cawdigan bustled past Marigold, her arms full, then stopped with a cry and turned back.

"Bless you, I'd almost forgotten about you!" the housekeeper panted. "You'll be wanting your breakfast." She shouted to a footman and he dropped his blankets on the hall settle and left at a run. "You can see what we're about here, can't you, miss? Half the town's moved in, on His Grace's orders. I've been doing me best to keep the poor cold, wet wretches outside and only let in the babes with their mothers. Otherwise this fine house, which has just been fixed up and painted, would be ruined with mud and squalling humanity."

A footman in impeccable scarlet livery came hurrying up with a tray with a silver pot of hot tea and several pieces of toast. Marigold took the tea and toast from him hungrily.

"I'm sure the duke would say well done," she tried to tell the housekeeper as another group of mothers and small children came in. She recognized them as mill workers. Most of them knew her. "Where is the duke, Mrs. Cawdigan? And Dr. Pendragon? Have all the miners come out of the mine?"

"The duke's gone, miss," the footman answered, "he didn't even stop to tell Mr. Ironfoot nor none of the others. It was His Grace who carried the rope across the bridge this morning, so's they could get down to the people still in the heath. If it hadn't been for His Grace's strength, which is more than any other man in the village save for a few like Tom Grandison, none of them would have had a hand line to get across.'

He stopped, abruptly, aware that Mrs. Cawdigan was glaring at him.

Marigold thrust her empty teacup at him. "What are you saying? The duke crossed the bridge in the village? But there is a current running over it—the river is flooded! The magistrate wouldn't chance coming across last night because of it!"

"Hush now," the other woman told her hurriedly, "there's no need to worry just because some young pup I won't name can't keep his wagging tongue in his head!" She shot an angry look at the footman, then took Marigold's arm and steered her toward the stairs. "Now miss, you go back up and rest, and I'll bring you some breakfast proper with eggs and a bit of a mutton chop, and a glass of stout."

"Thank you Mrs. Cawdigan, but I'm no longer hungry." She seized the footman's arm as he was trying to lose himself in the crowd. "Tell me what you know," Marigold ordered. "Don't be afraid, the duke of Westermere will be far more stern with you if he finds you have overset me by not telling me anything. Why did His Grace go back to the village, and who went with him?" He shot a look of appeal to Mrs. Cawdigan, but the housekeeper's disapproving face said, *Do as you like, I wash my hands of it.*

353

"I can tell you there was not anyone here who wished His Grace to go, miss," the footman told her, "as it is exceedingly dangerous. Dr. Pendragon shouted and ranted, he did, but not even he could dissuade His Grace from it. It is just as you said, miss, the bridge is underwater. Even with the ropes the duke and Grandison swam across with, it's chancy to get over there, much less come back."

For a moment Marigold could not seem to visualize it. When she did, it made her shudder. "Dear heavens," she moaned, "have they all lost their senses? Why are they crossing the river at all? Are the dams not about to break? Isn't that what the church bells are ringing for?"

"Aye, that they are," the housekeeper put in. "And when the dams go, a flood will sweep everything below to perdition. That's what them people in the heath were told by the mine office, but still they won't budge."

She was shocked. "There are still people in the heath?"

The other woman nodded. "Aye, there are those what believe that if they leave their cots the company won't let them back, such fear as they have of being homeless. They'll sit over there until the good Lord sends the water to sweep them away." Mrs. Cawdigan gave a sniff. "Not that it wouldn't be for the better, stinking, nasty place that it is. There's many what would say good riddance."

Marigold was staring at her. "Dear God, little Johnny! He's there, too! Mrs. Cawdigan, before they left did anyone mention Molly Cobb and her family? Did anyone say the Cobbs were among those who refused to leave?"

There was an outcry in the kitchen, followed by a chorus of screeching babies. "I'm sure I wouldn't know, miss," the other woman said, lifting her voice. "If 'twas me, I wouldn't say my Christian charity was such to take me down to a cold river with a danger of being swept away in a terrible flood, to try to save those what don't really want to be saved." Mrs. Cawdigan gave a sudden, tearful sniff. "If I am praying for anyone, I'm praying for His Grace, that dear, brave wonderful boy I used to hold in me lap when he was a lad, and save the treacle pudding for!"

The housekeeper threw her apron over her head to hide a new outburst of tears, and rushed off to the kitchen.

At that very moment Penelope pushed her way through the front door.

"Marigold!" the blond girl shrieked, "have you heard what has happened? Westermere has swum the river with the miners, and gone down to the heath to bring out the people who still remain there. But one of the dams has already broken through, and they are saying the rest will go at any time!"

Marigold sat down on the settle. She did not feel that she could stand up any longer. The tea and toast she'd taken were suddenly like a painful stone in her stomach, and she had a feeling she might be sick. Behind them the kitchen full of screaming babies was almost deafening.

"If the dam breaks," she heard herself saying, "they will all be trapped over there."

And drowned. But she could not bring herself to say it aloud.

The water was thigh-deep going across Stokesbury Hatton's bridge. Several times the current drove Sacheverel and Tom Grandison against its downstream stone sides, pinning them there until they could struggle free.

"Another foot," the miner shouted over the roar of the water, "and it will pick us up and drag us over the top!"

Satch nodded, grimly. They both knew it would be a devil of a task returning, not forgetting that the seeping earthworks above the valley could break at any time. God knows the old stone bridge could not stand any more water tearing at it. It had stood for centuries but if the flood surge hit it, it would go, too.

When they reached the far side Grandison staggered to his feet in the mud and began to haul in the line attached to a heavier rope that would make a handhold for the half-dozen miners to come across.

"Keep going," Satch shouted to him when the heavy rope was finally secured, "no time to wait!"

Grandison led the way through what he said was a short cut around the tenements and backs of the spinning mill. The flood water was not so deep there, but the mill people had wisely evacuated their dwellings anyway. It was only the impoverished women and children of the heath who were terrified of leaving what little they had.

Satch began to smell the odor even before they reached the turn in the road that led down to the hovels. The rest of the miners had joined them, except for the two left to secure the lines at the bridge.

"There's nobody here," one of the miners shouted.

Rain beat down in a curtain. The heath was a running river, ankle deep, and looked deserted. The cottages were stubbornly shut, doors closed. But even above the sound of the rain they could hear faint voices and children crying.

Westermere, the military man, raised his arm to signal. He'd evacuated villages before.

"Door to door," he shouted, "rout them out and get them down to the bridge. Make them hop to it!"

A few doors swung open at the sound of his voice. Barefoot women, clutching children, peered out, goggling as they recognized the duke of Westermere himself splashing along in the flood.

The sight of him seemed to mesmerize the heath people. Some of them came out into the street just to stare. But a few men were ready to defend themselves and their families from being evicted, as they saw it. Some put up a fight as the miners dragged them out.

The duke stepped in between Grandison subduing a man whose wife had joined in, swinging the leg of a broken chair, and took a smart blow on the forehead for his pains.

"Are you all right, sir?" The miner had to step close and shout in Satch's ear to be heard. A new sound, an ominous rumble, had joined the roar of the river and the pouring rain.

Satch nodded. He mopped at his bleeding head with the first thing he could find, the tail of his sodden shirt. He gestured urgently to Grandison to go onward. A pathetic group of women and children had been rounded up in the middle of the street, and now were swiftly being herded down the road to the bridge. Only two cottages remained, their doors tightly closed.

Satch put his foot against the door of the nearest one and kicked it in.

The water had put out the heath fire, and the place was full of choking smoke. Through it he could barely see a woman clutching the hand of a little girl. The dark shadows of other children seemed to lurk in the corners.

"Come, woman," Satch ordered. Groping around, he found a boy of about eleven in the murk and pulled him to his feet. "You can't stay here, you and your brood will be drowned! How many of you are there?"

He looked around, counting five. The woman retreated, her face contorted in terror.

"I know you, devil that you are," she shrilled. "It's the duke of Westermere himself, here to see that what's left of us in the heath is dragged from our poor homes and set on the road to starve!"

"Nonsense!" Satch bellowed. He took the woman by the arm and was struggling to drag her out, when Grandison filled the doorway. The children had gathered around Satch, hitting him and screaming.

"Let me handle this, sir," the miner shouted. "It's Molly Cobb, a poor widow. She used to work in the mine."

Deftly, Grandison took Molly by both arms and pushed her toward the door.

"Johnny!" She looked back, frantic. "Bastards! Fiends! You're taking me away without me poor little lad!"

Another miner stuck his head inside. "For God's sake, Your Grace," he shouted, "hurry! The water's up—if another dam's broke we may not make it back!"

One of the Cobb children threw herself at Satch's legs and managed to bite him. "Leggo me ma!" the little girl screamed. "You canna take us! You're leaving me brother here!"

He pried her away with some difficulty and handed her over to the miner. "Damme, there's another child somewhere about," he shouted. "Go on! I will be right behind you."

He turned back. Of course he could not see a confounded thing inside the hut. There was little furniture, although the dirt floor was covered with rags. Cautiously, he bent over and poked about with his hands. Almost immediately his fingers found something.

Satch dropped to one knee to excavate a sickly-looking child who'd been buried in some indistinguishable ragged stuff that seemed to pass for a bed.

"Lord, boy," Satch breathed in relief, "what were you afraid of, hiding from me like that?"

The child was shaking with fear. Satch picked him up and got to his feet, seeing that underneath the rags the boy was wrapped in something bright and woolly. Satch paused to examine it. Not a blanket or a bed covering, he told himself. It had a hood. He stared at it.

A cloak.

A damned plaid cloak, filthy by now, but he would recognize it anywhere. Miss Penelope MacDougal's hideous Scottish tartan of red and green and black and yellow.

Satch did not have time to consider the matter. He peeled the thing away from the boy and threw it into the smoking hearth. Damn the woman, she had caused them all an incredible amount of trouble! This was the best he could do. If the thing didn't burn it was to be hoped it would be swept far downstream by the flood.

As for the child and himself, they had to put their minds to getting out of there. If they could.

Satch took off his own jacket and wrapped the Cobb boy in it and made his way back down the flooded street. The odorous water was somewhat higher than when they had come in. The news that the miner had relayed, that no doubt another dam had broken, did not make their chances for getting back across the village bridge any better.

Carrying the child, too, was not easy. It interfered with his balance and the mud under the flood waters had deepened. It sucked at his boots like some demon determined to seize and hold him there.

Satch came stumbling at full speed down the last few feet to the bridge where Grandison waited.

He saw the heath's people had been herded across in good time considering the children and some of the women had to be lashed to the men's backs. No doubt when they realized their dire situation the heath dwellers had finally come to their senses and cooperated.

"I was about to go back for you," Grandison miner shouted over the river's roar. "I see you've found the lad."

Sacheverel shoved the boy into Grandison's arms. From the look of the river they barely had time to make it. And from the looks of the straining rope he knew they had better not put the weight of more than one man on it at a time.

"Take him across," he bellowed. "I'll wait until you are on the other side."

The miner balked. "Ah, Your Grace," he shouted back, "you don't think I'll leave you here by yerself, do you? It's a hero now you are! If anything should happen to you, they'd hang me at Hobbs at the next assizes!"

"Don't babble, man." He gave the other a shove

361

so that he slipped down the bank into the water and had to grab for the handline. "Take him across, Grandison," Satch ordered. "I will follow as soon as you make the far shore."

He saw the miner hesitate, but knew he understood. "Don't linger," the other shouted back.

Satch nodded. He wrapped the little boy in his coat and, cutting off a piece of the line, tied him to Grandison's shoulders.

"Keep your head up, lad," he told the white-faced child. "And don't swallow any more water than you have to."

He watched Grandison start back across the bridge, chest-deep now in raging floodwater. Several times the miner was thrown up against the stone abutments, the river tearing at him, trying to take him over the side.

Most of the heath people had run for higher ground, but a small group of spectators had come down to the bridge, ignoring the obvious danger. Among them was the schoolmaster, MacDougal, Jack Ironfoot, scowling with worry, and Reggie Pendragon. The widow Cobb stayed with the miners attending the rope, lending her anguished screams to the noise of the flood.

Molly Cobb fell upon the boy as soon as Grandison came within reach, nearly knocking both of them down. She began at once tearing at the ties that held the child to him. Ironfoot and the schoolmaster managed to drag her away and hold her until the miners could get Grandison free.

Satch didn't wait a moment longer. Grasping

the handline, he lowered himself into the icy water.

The river seized his lower body and legs. He fought it with all his considerable strength, inching himself hand over hand along the rope. The water was rapidly rising, filled now with debris. More dams, perhaps the last of them, had given way.

Then it happened. The roar increased like that of an oncoming earthquake. The miners waiting on the shore pointed upstream, their voices drowned in the noise. Over his shoulder Satch saw the flood surge coming down in a wall of brown water, carrying trees and lumber and the body of a sheep in its teeth.

He was midway on the bridge, in the middle of the river. He fought to get to the other side with desperate fury but the wall of water hit him.

He experienced the shock of total immersion, of not being able to breathe, the rope that he clutched breaking and flying away. The flood surge itself knocked him head over heels. Then something in the water struck him, perhaps a piece of lumber or a tree limb. The world turned black.

Chapter Twenty-five

By late afternoon the rain had stopped, and a chill wind was blowing in an overcast sky. The living of the village of Stokesbury Hatton gathered on the three points of high ground: the hill of St. Dunstan's Church, the old common on the valley's northeastern ridge, and the land surrounding the Westermeres' mansion, The Elms.

Dr. Stack, with Sophronia acting as his nurse, had gone to tend the refugees on the knoll of the old common pasture, as there were pregnant mill women there without even trees for shelter.

Marigold's father had sent word that, thanks to his parishioners, he had an abundance of help at the church. The refugees were settled inside the sanctuary with the overflow in the parish hall and the vicarage.

But there was no doctor at The Elms to help Mrs. Cawdigan and Marigold and Penelope. A frantic Reggie Pendragon, along with Jack Ironfoot and most of the coachmen, had gone off with the search parties looking for the duke, who by now everyone knew had been swept from the bridge and into the flood while rescuing the people from the heath. Or, as many had begun to refer to it behind their hands, the search parties had gone off to scour the river and its banks to look for the duke's body.

Marigold could not bear to think of it. He must be alive, she told herself, as she struggled with Penny to bring an iron pot out into the front lawn to fix hot porridge for the crowd.

Yet the outlook had not been good. Too many had been on the spot to witness Westermere going under in the midst of trees and debris uprooted by the dams' breaking. And most dismal of all, they had not seen him surface farther downstream.

But there was always hope. Marigold had been raised to believe that. She wished her father were there; the vicar was a tower of comfort and strength. That's why the village—and his daughter—loved him.

But her father had his own duties at the church. Marigold knew he would expect her to stay where she was, and do her best to help. Of course it didn't make it easier that poor Mrs. Cawdigan gave way to tears every few minutes and, apron over her head, collapsed into the nearest chair as though they had already received news of the worst.

Meanwhile, The Elms' lawn continued to fill up with villagers fleeing the flood. The miller and his family had unwisely decided to stay with his house and mill; it was feared that they'd all drowned. The town bailiff had gone to help a man with a wagon stuck in the mud and had been swept away, only to miraculously crawl ashore, both of them, just below the bridge.

Many of the townspeople on the lawn had brought their own food, but the majority had waited until the last moment before leaving their homes, bringing little but the soggy clothes on their backs. And what the more prudent villagers had provided would probably be gone soon; many had given portions of their own food for the babies and nursing mothers who had been put up in the mansion's kitchen.

Drinking water, the duke's servants reported to Marigold, was growing scarce, too. The ground around The Elms had two wells, one near the kitchen and one at the stables, but the water was beginning to show an ominous tinge that might be seeping mud.

The young footmen and the duke's porters proved to be the most helpful. Even old Pomfret stayed stoically calm in spite of the pervasive gloom growing around them, and helped get the refugees settled on the cold, soggy lawn. And of course there was Penny MacDougal who, in spite of her petite frame, hauled water and carried an astonishing number of heavy pots and pans while remaining in unusually brave spirits.

"He's alive," she told Marigold as they set the iron kettle over a fire the porters had fixed, and emptied a bucket of water into it. "You love him with all your heart, don't you? Well, you must trust to God to keep Westermere safe. You mustn't let your mind dwell on anything else, for you know Mary Wollstonecraft would say that it is woman's destiny to be a haven of strength when all around her languish with despair."

Listening to her friend, Marigold could not hold back a sigh. There was hardly anyone at The Elms who hadn't approached her to assure her that somehow they knew the duke of Westermere had not drowned but was safe somewhere. No doubt they wanted to be kind, but she was beginning to feel that if another person uttered cheerful words, she would scream.

Penelope went off to the main house to get a footman to fetch a sack of meal for the porridge. Marigold was left standing by the fire, waiting for the water to come to a boil.

Out of the corner of her eye she saw a strange figure limping across the lawn, wending his way in between the makeshift shelters and groups of bedraggled villagers. He was no one she knew or had ever seen before. He wore a great black cloak with shoulder capelet, the hood thrown back to reveal the most cadaverous face Marigold had ever encountered. The crippled man's complexion was gray, the feverish eyes rimmed with the dark circles of chronic ill health. Lank black hair was cropped close to his skull. If he had ever been handsome—and there was a faint, ghostly air that still clung to him—it had given way long ago to this ravaged shell.

He came up quickly in spite of his lurching walk and stood close enough to stare into her eyes.

He looked foreign, not like any of the Yorkshire villagers. Marigold regarded him uneasily.

"What do you want?" When he didn't answer, only kept staring, she said, "We will have hot porridge soon." Heaven knows he looked as though he could use a meal. She hesitated. "Are you ailing, sir? If you wish, one of the footmen will take you into the house, where you may rest out of the wind."

To her surprise his face contorted with mirthless laughter. "The duke of Westermere is alive," he said in a hoarse whisper. He pointed at her with a muddy finger. "You, his *puta*, will see all this, that they cannot kill him, when they bring him back. I will wait—I have not come this far for nothing."

While Marigold stared after him, openmouthed, the crowlike figure hobbled off and quickly disappeared into the crowd under the trees.

As the gray daylight waned and there was no word from the search parties along the river, some of the miners came together to sing. The men's songs were chapel hymns and leaned heavily on suffering and the Lord's salvation in the midst of a sinful world. The sort of hymns, Marigold couldn't help thinking, one sang at a funeral. Tired as she was, even their harmonious voices grated on her nerves.

She and Penelope had been dishing out hot porridge, but the crowd around the fire was beginning to thin. Marigold thought longingly of the quiet of the duke's bedroom on the second floor of the mansion, and the wonderful relief of stretching out on the bed for some time alone. Several times she'd found tears running down her cheeks, and would not have known they were there except for the sympathetic looks of the villagers.

She put down her ladle, and was about to tell Penelope that she did not think she could stand on her aching feet one moment longer and that she was going into the house to take a short rest, when a low, moaning sound broke like a wave from the refugees below, and drifted up the lawn to them.

"Dear God!" Marigold froze where she stood, knowing what the sound meant before she saw men making their way up the hill, six of them carrying something large in a blanket slung between them.

With a cry, she hurled herself through the crowd and plunged down the slope.

Reggie Pendragon carried a corner of the blanket. She saw his white, anguished face and then, in a blur, a man's hand that she knew so well, dangling over the blanket's edge.

He was dead. She could tell by their faces. "Put him down!" Marigold screamed.

Jack Ironfoot was in front. Grimly, he called out to the others to stop. They bent and lowered the Duke of Westermere carefully to the ground.

"He's so cold," Marigold heard the surgeon say. Poor Reggie looked destroyed. "God, he's like ice. I have tried and tried, but I can't find a pulse."

Marigold dropped to her knees beside the body. The duke was naked, his clothes, even his boots, stripped away by the raging currents. There was a great knot on his head that had stopped bleeding. Still and pale as marble, he had never looked more beautiful to Marigold.

With a low cry she threw herself flat against him. The doctor was right. His big body felt like ice. She was holding a corpse in her arms.

"Oh, Westermere, how could you die!" The words came out of her in an anguished wail. "I can't tell you how foolish I have been! I would have loved you deeply, passionately, truly, if you had been the lowliest of paupers! Oh, Heaven forgive me," Marigold sobbed, "now I know I would have followed you barefoot on every road in England, I would have borne your children in a hovel and begged shamelessly in the streets for you!" She took him by the shoulders and tried to shake him, but he was too heavy. "Sacheverel, do you hear me?"

Desperate with grief, Marigold lowered her

mouth to his in a fervent kiss. It was like embracing stone. Someone groaned. A large crowd was gathering. One of the muddy rescue party reached down to pull Marigold away, but Jack Ironfoot hauled him back.

At that moment Marigold lifted her head and gasped. She stared down into the face of the duke.

As she kissed him it seemed that there had been the faintest of breaths whispered against her lips. She looked up at Jack Ironfoot.

He knew at once. "A mirror," the big coachman shouted at the crowd. "Stop your infernal gawking and fetch us a mirror!"

Several people ran off, but it was a mill woman in the crowd who produced a broken piece of looking glass from her jacket pocket and thrust it into the coachman's hand.

"Let me do it," Reggie Pendragon said, coming out of his grief-stricken paralysis. He took the mirror and threw himself on his knees to hold it to Westermere's mouth.

For a moment the crowd was absolutely silent, so still the cold moan of the wind in the trees could be heard. Then the surgeon pulled the glass away, and stared it as though he could not believe it.

"There's nothing." He peered again. And then again. "No, by God, there is! It's so confounded slight—"

The coachman leaped forward. "Haul him up," Jack Ironfoot ordered, "and give him air! He's not drowned, he's stunned from that blow on the head." He turned on the crowd. "Make way, there, you fools!"

The duke was hauled to a sitting position, his head lolling, rattails of black hair hanging in his face. Those closest to him saw the convulsive movement of his bare chest, the triangle of his diaphragm fluttering.

"Cover him up!" Marigold cried. "Dear Heaven, get him warm!" She reached for the blanket. Some of the others were trying to push back the crowd as the man they were holding seemed ever so slightly to try to lift his head.

It was at this very moment that a figure, black cape billowing, darted out of the crowd with a pistol in his hand.

No one saw him. The attention of the rescue party was directed to lifting the duke of Westermere to carry him into the house. But as if alerted by a sixth sense, Jack Ironfoot turned just in time to throw himself in between as the wild-eyed man in black fired the pistol directly at the duke.

The coachman took the ball and reeled. The men lifting the duke looked up, surprised. Marigold could only stare as Jack clutched his arm, bright blood spurting.

"Get His Grace out of here," Jack Ironfoot shouted. He staggered away in pursuit of the man in the black cloak, who was running across the lawn toward the house, trying to reload his weapon.

Penny MacGregor had just filled a large pot with steaming porridge to be taken to the kitchen to feed the babies and smaller children. Quicker than anyone around her she took in the running man and his pistol, and Jack the coachman lurching after him holding his bleeding arm, and realized what was happening.

Her eyes widened.

"How dare you shoot Mr. Ironfoot!" the smallest and youngest of the Three Cavaliers cried.

As the man in the black cape tried to veer away from her, Penny stepped in front of him and, with a wild swing, hurled pot and steaming porridge at his head.

The man in the black cape fell as if poleaxed, his pistol flying out of his hand to lie some distance away on the grass. Jack Ironfoot lurched up just in time to pick it up. Then he fell to his knees and toppled over in a faint. Penelope dropped to her knees beside him and put her hand on his forehead.

"Dear Mr. Ironfoot," she said, somewhat weakly, "please don't be terribly injured. Great Heavens, I don't care what Mary Wollstonecraft says about feminine strength and fortitude—I swear, I don't think I can stand any more excitement this day!"

Chapter Twenty-six

"It will take a year or more to pump out the mine," Tom Grandison said, "maybe twice as long. There's no way of knowing, Your Grace, as it's never been done before. That is, not the whole mine." He looked uncomfortable. "There'll be no jobs for the miners, meantime, and many of them has lost their cots, in particular the folk in the heath. The river made a clean sweep of the place."

"Hah, it won't be missed," Sacheverel responded. He touched the huge bandage that swathed his head from eyebrows up, and his fingers twitched. "The damned river may have done its best to drown me, but it was on God's side when it swept the heath out of this world. I've never found an area so disgustingly odoriferous, even in the worst souks in Egypt."

Enraptured

Since he was confined to bed on Dr. Pendragon's orders he had turned it into a field of operations with a walnut lap desk, notepad, pen, and a bottle of ink that frequently overturned, much to Mrs. Cawdigan's despair, and stacks of books. Now he dug among sheets of paper, looking for something.

"In any event," he told Grandison, "we'll begin right away constructing new cottages and rebuilding the improved tenement blocks. The solicitor, Broadus, must have my notes. You'll have to seek him out later and tell him to turn them over to you. However, the rebuilding will occupy a work force in the village until we have sufficiently organized the railroad factory."

There was a pause while Tom Grandison gave the duke a cautious look. "A railroad factory, Your Grace?"

"Hand me that cup of tea, Grandison, and pour yourself some," Sacheverel told him, "and help yourself to the pickles and cheese." As the other man obediently turned to the table at bedside, he went on, "They have one at the Killingworth colliery, northwest of Newcastle, and are extolling its virtues. But it's a matter of record Welsh miners had concocted something similar half a century ago, when they made flanged wheels to run on iron rails in their mines. They used ponies and human labor for locomotion, just as the mine here has done. Now there's a chap, Stephenson, who's put together a machine he calls a 'steam locomotive' to pull the cars. Not just in the colliery, mind you, but outside, on iron rails that would run all around England. Better than canals and canal boats, is the argument, and far better than horse-drawn coaches and drays. Broadus informs me there's a syndicate at work to propose a system of English railways in Parliament. The opportunity's there, man," he said enthusiastically, "to supply this proposed railway company from a factory here, since Stokesbury Hatton's been building mine rails and coal carts for decades."

Satch put a piece of cheese and a pickle between two slices of bread and held it up to study it. "The earl of Sandwich said he invented this," he observed. "Debauched old windbag. People have been eating bread and cheese this way since the Druids were here."

"Your Grace," the other man protested, "your confidence in me is greatly appreciated, but I know nothing about railroads, if you will pardon my saying so. Now if you was to hire a proper engineer for any sort of factory you—"

Satch bit into the bread. "Stuff and nonsense," he said, his mouth full, "the whole idea of railroads is damned interesting, and worthy of your talents, Grandison. Don't underestimate yourself, man, we've faced death together, remember, and I can testify that you are smart as paint and uncommonly resourceful. God knows you're head and shoulders above those lecherous thieves, my former agents. You'll do a fine job as my general manager in charge of production of railroad equipment, and we'll hire you a good staff to do the rest."

"Your Grace," the miner began, "I am not unaware of the honor, in fact I am greatly flattered that you would consider me for such a fine opportunity. But—"

"Good," Sactch said, "then it's done. You'll report to me from time to time about the Stokesbury Hatton railroad equipment factory, and I shall have the leisure to devote myself to the pursuit of my scientific applications in the field of criminology."

"Your Grace," Grandison said, making one last stab, "I do have a congregation of chapel folk, it's my ministry here—"

"Excellent," Satch said, giving him an approving look, "I had forgotten about that. I shall contact the bishop myself personally. Methodists have bishops, I believe?"

"Yes, they do," the miner sighed.

"I shall inform your bishop of your new duties and suggest he appoint you a suitable ecclesiastical secretary. I shall endow the position, of course, adding one hundred percent above whatever is the current church allotment for such jobs. You'll have plenty of applicants. And I must make a note to tell the bishop about your contribution to the living conditions here in the past and the town's future economic development through the factory."

For the first time, Grandison brightened. "Ah, that would please him very much, Your Grace, as the condition of England's workers has always been a foremost Methodist concern. If you—"

"Yes, and that reminds me," Satch told him as the door opened and Cruddles came in to get him out of bed and dress him. "My betrothed, Miss Fenwick, whom we shall see shortly, has made an excellent suggestion about the emigration program. It was she originally who made me aware, now that the valley is flooded, that there are those who know their chances for future employment remain discouragingly low, and therefore wish to consider alternatives such as emigrating to the United States, Canada, or Australia. Consequently, a fund has been set up, Broadus and his clerk are supervising it for those Stokesbury Hatton people who wish to take advantage of the opportunity of moving to another country."

"That is very kind of you, Your Grace," Grandison said, beaming now. "Bishop Jones will appreciate that, too."

The valet got on one side of the duke and signaled the miner to take his other arm, and they helped him out of the bed and onto his feet.

"Hmm, doubtless he will." Satch was finding he was still somewhat shaky. "One of the Campbells is doing something of the sort for his tenants in Scotland. Although I can't say the altruism, and especially the expense, is all that popular with my fellow peers."

He lifted his arms and swayed as Cruddles stripped off his nightshirt. "Bother, that crack on the head did me little good," he muttered, leaning on both men. "I'm glad Pendragon is not here yet to fuss." But he had turned quite pale.

"It looks like no full morning kit for me, Cruddles, I can't go the course of boots, jacket and all that. We'll have to settle for bedclothes and the dressing gown."

"An excellent choice, Your Grace," the valet told him, whipping away the shirt and trousers, and snapping his fingers for fresh night garments to be brought. "I recommend the robe of Venetian plum velvet with gold tassels and matching slippers. Just the very thing, if I may say so, Your Grace, for a wedding before noon."

Satch steadied himself with one hand on the bedpost. Naked, his body was still magnificently graceful, but more injuries were revealed: Large bruises extended down the left side of his rib cage, one knee was discolored and had what appeared to be teeth marks above it. Also, he was as covered with scratches from his passage through Stokesbury Hatton via the river Stoke as though he had fallen into a bramble patch.

"And Grandison," Satch continued as Cruddles selected an embroidered Irish linen nightshirt and slipped it over his head, "about the list of villagers for emigration. Make sure there's one name that receives special attention—put her at the top, the widow Molly Cobb and her six or seven children. Suggest Australia, it's the farthest of the lot. Did you make a note of that?"

"Yes, Your Grace," Tom Grandison said. Molly was on his list, too. "I'm attending to it now."

Katherine Deauxville

He wrote down next to Cobb, Molly, and family: *Australia.*

Down the hallway in a large guest chamber Marigold, too, was being helped to dress by Penny and Sophronia and Mrs. Cawdigan and two upstairs maids. The pale pink wedding gown with its embroidery of crystal beads and pearls had been brought from London with Westermere's effects before his arrival, but she had never seen it.

Now, as Mrs. Cawdigan did the laces of the bodice in back, Sophronia and Penny stepped away to view her.

"It would look better with a train," Sophronia said, critically. "If one must be married there's no error in being in the best of style. And trains are very elegant."

"Mary Wollstonecraft married, you know," Marigold calmly reminded her. "She wedded William Godwin. So it is not all that great a sin."

"Ah yes," Penny sighed, "and this is so nobly romantic, Marigold, I don't care what Sophronia says. Did not the duke declare, as he was being swept away by the terrible flood, that his heart was full of remorse that he might die without having married you, and making you his own beloved? La, the marvel of it is that he survived, and was not wounded by the Spanish madman thanks to Mr. Ironfoot, who so bravely sacrificed himself! And now what could be more affecting that, in a few minutes, Westermere will rise from his bed while still severely injured, to wed with you, with your own dear father officiating?"

"You have not given yourself due credit, Penny," Marigold said as Mrs. Cawdigan settled an antique Westermere tiara of topazes and diamonds upon her hair. It had taken all morning for the housekeeper and two maids to arrange Marigold's coiffure, which looked delightfully dégagé with its cascade of honey-brown curls in back, and teased locks in the Greek style before each ear.

"You are our true heroine," Marigold told her friend. "Penny, if you had not had the presence of mind to stun the lunatic with the porridge kettle he would have escaped to pursue the duke as relentlessly as he has since Spain. And then Jack Ironfoot would have had to resume his dutiful surveillance and not been free to declare for you."

Mrs. Cawdigan and the maids looked up. "Is that true, miss?" one of the girls cried. "That Mr. Ironfoot has asked for your hand?"

The schoolmaster's daughter turned an even deeper shade of crimson. "My father," she murmured. "Mr. Ironfoot has spoken to my father, to tell him that he owns land and is by title a squire in Shropshire, the Ironfoot family being anciently settled there and of old Saxon extraction. Of course, my dear Da then told me about Mr. Ironfoot's offer, so that I could—consider the matter."

"He's a brave man, dear," the housekeeper said promptly, "and a bit of a rogue, I warn you, they say he was His Grace's spy master when they were in the war together. But he does cut quite a manly figure, and likes a bit of dancing and gambling, as do all men that were in the military. But I daresay you can manage that in your own sweet, ladylike way."

"He is intelligent and kind," Penny said, thoughtfully. "We have already discussed the philosophy of a great woman I admire, Mary Wollstonecraft, and Mr. Ironfoot was very impressed. He said that from what I had quoted she reminded him greatly of his mother."

"And how about you, Miss Stack?" one of the maids inquired pertly of Sophronia. The girls giggled. "Both your friends is married, now, you can't lag behind, can you?"

Sophronia was, like Penelope, attired in her best Sunday gown of russet silk, and wore a wreath of ivy and jonquils. Both wore their hair down and flowing, and looked like spring wood nymphs attending the bride.

But Sophronia only gave them all her enigmatic gypsy smile. "I'm going to wait for the Romany to return," she told them. "This year I'm going to Soldiers' Woods to meet my mother's people. Then we'll see."

"Soldiers' Woods," Mrs. Cawdigan said, and shuddered. "You couldn't get me there now, not for a hundred pounds. It's haunted, it is! I suppose we'll never know who killed young Mr. Parham."

"That devil," one of the maids muttered. "Whoever done him in did the world a favor."

Marigold lifted both hands and settled the tiara

somewhat more firmly upon her upswept curls.

"Yes, it is a real mystery," she murmured. Marigold knew everything; the duke had told her all about it. It had come as no surprise that poor Molly, driven to distraction by the thought of being turned out of her home, would attack what she saw as the source of her misery. Although the duke, who had a rather deep bite on his knee inflicted by one of the Cobb children, was less sympathetic.

Someone knocked on the door. "His Grace the duke of Westermere inquires if you are ready, Miss Fenwick," a voice said.

They met in one of the guest bedchambers where Jack Ironfoot had been placed to recover from his wound. Marigold's father, Dr. Eusebius Fenwick, was already there, along with Dr. Stack, schoolmaster MacDougal, members of the duke's staff such as Manuel the coachmen, old Pomfret, Mrs. Cawdigan, and of course Ironfoot himself, propped up on pillows and looking remarkably like a tamed but very pleased hawk.

Coming down the upstairs hallway Satch had persuaded Reginald Pendragon to cut away the cumbersome head bandage, in spite of the surgeon's protests that compression was needed to bring about complete recovery. With the helmet of gauze gone, he gingerly combed his flattened hair with his fingers.

All irritable thoughts fled, though, when he saw his bride.

*   *   *

Her husband-to-be looked so pale Marigold wanted to put out her arm to support him. But some sixth sense told her such a gesture would not be acceptable to one of Wellington's most fondly regarded heroes. Especially in front of so many of his former comrades.

Yet it was because of this very heroism that she had come so close to losing him. She'd been so ignorant of any peril. The duke of Westermere had not even hinted all these months, and neither had his faithful and formidable watchdog, Jack Ironfoot, that his life was in danger every moment that he lived it.

Marigold had at last learned that his murderous nemesis was the marques Fernando de Alba y Garcia, a nobleman of the most noble family of Spain, whose estate and family had been destroyed in an English bombardment during the war.

Alba y Garcia's only son and heir had been killed, along with his wife and three small daughters. The marques himself had sustained severe injuries and had nearly lost his leg. Ruined, nearly destitute, the Spanish nobleman blamed the young commander in charge of the British troops, Captain Sacheverel de Vries, who had given the order to Wellington's cannoneers to fire on the town. Afterward, a madman's Spanish pride had dictated that the marques devote his life to finding the destroyer of his family, and killing him.

Enraptured

The vicar, Dr. Fenwick, took his place before the windows but near to the bed where Jack Ironfoot lay, Penelope standing at his side, and beckoned the bridal party forward.

Marigold felt a slight nudge. When she turned to him, the groom whispered, "Make sure Ironfoot has the ring."

She relayed the message in a whisper to Penelope, who told the man in the bed. With a grin the best man nodded.

"Dearly beloved . . ." Dr. Fenwick began.

Marigold hardly heard the words of her wedding or her own responses, so busy was she with her thoughts. It was wonderful to have Penelope so near, her eyes like stars as she gazed down at Jack Ironfoot, but hard to realize that the Three Cavaliers would no longer be together. Sophronia was quite serious about seeking out her mother's people, the gypsies, this summer. And she, Marigold, had perhaps embarked on the biggest adventure of them all as the new duchess of Westermere.

Once or twice during the ceremony the duke took her arm and leaned rather heavily on it. She gave him a worried glance but those black eyes reassured her. I will go through any sort of hell, even this damnable never-ending ceremony, his expression said, for I am determined to have you.

Inwardly, Marigold sighed.

Penny might think the duke's anguish over leaving his beloved alone and impoverished and

385

unwed as the flood swept him down river was terribly poignant and romantic, but there was another side to it, as Marigold well knew.

Not that Sacheverel de Vries, twelfth Duke of Westermere, didn't love her—she knew now with all her heart that he did. But one had to acknowledge the scientific and practical man, too.

What Sacheverel de Vries had said to her later as Marigold sat by his bed in the candlelight, holding his hand and putting warm cloths on his battered brow, was that while he had been in the process of nearly drowning, being dragged along by debris and tree branches churning in the flood, he was not only struck by the horrifying thought of losing Marigold, his betrothed, and never looking on her beautiful face again or even knowing if she already carried his child, but also the realization that the line of the Westermere dukes would automatically transfer, should Satch die without legitimate heirs, to his Aunt Bessie's loathsome and totally unsuitable son, Neville.

At that he had been galvanized to even greater effort, and managed against all odds to swim through the raging currents to a muddy bank where, unfortunately, he had been hit in the head by an oak log on its way downstream just as he hauled himself to relative safety.

It was a laudably honest confession, Marigold supposed. The thought that she might have his bastard child in dire poverty had of course torn at him, but Marigold also knew she would be dealing for the rest of her life with a loved one who spoke the unembellished truth. Which was not all that bad, one supposed; it was more than many women could expect from their husbands. No doubt Mary Wollstonecraft would have approved.

And she did love him, she thought, turning to look at him. There he stood beside her, Sacheverel de Vries, Duke of Westermere, so tall and handsome in his plum velvet dressing gown, his shaggy black hair not quite covering the swollen knot on his forehead, that Marigold quite impulsively reached up to put the back of her hand to his cheek.

He immediately turned to her and without a word swept her into his arms, his mouth covering hers with a fervent passion.

"The ring, please," Marigold's father, the vicar, said to the best man in the bed.

Jack handed the gold band to a beaming Penelope, who passed it on to her father, who handed it to Dr. Fenwick. Who prodded the duke to get his attention.

"Take this," the vicar of St. Dunstan's said, "and repeat after me—with this ring, I do wed—"

"I do love you, sweetheart," Satch said to the woman in his arms.

"Yes, dear, I know," Marigold breathed.

But it was all she wanted to hear.

Epilogue

1851

A slight, sandy-haired young man in his thirties, holding a well-worn beaver hat in his lap and with his two young sons beside him, sat in the downstairs reception hall of the duke of Westermere's estate in Sussex, watching what could only be regarded as an extraordinary flow of domestic traffic.

First there had been a pair of uniformed maids carrying picnic hampers, following in the wake of two ravishing young ladies of about thirteen with armfuls of books, parasols and three King Charles spaniels at their heels.

The twins had greeted the man and his children as they passed with cordial smiles. One dazzling sylph with red hair had turned to say over her shoulder, "It won't be long, sir, don't lose patience. Someone will be with you shortly!"

Not five minutes elapsed before an elderly woman in starched cap and black bombazine, obviously the housekeeper, appeared with four footmen carrying what appeared to be equipment for a sick room: kettles, basins and towels, as well as a bottle of champagne in a silver bucket of ice and a tray of fruit.

The housekeeper stopped to look over the young man, and inspect the two little boys with him. "Ah, you're the new assistant, aren't you?" she said. "His Grace will be glad enough to know you've arrived. I heard him only yesterday say how you come highly recommended. From Sir Robert Peel himself, isn't it?"

The young man got to his feet, the two silent, well-behaved little boys following suit. "Yes," he answered, "I am indeed fortunate to have Sir Robert's testimony, since I've been assistant to the general manager of the Oxford constabulary division—"

"Sit down, sit down," the housekeeper interrupted, waving the footmen toward the staircase. "Someone's been sent for—they'll be with you shortly."

She bustled off up the stairs with the servants. They were no sooner out of sight than three god-like youths ranging in age from about sixteen to twenty-one, carrying wicker creels and dressed to go fishing, followed by four rambunctious foxhounds, appeared from the rear of the house.

"I say, get down, Hercules!" the youngest of them shouted. The dogs, tongues lolling, tails wagging, made for the little boys. The youngest god managed to grab the collar of the nearest hound and pull him away. "Damnation, you, too, Hecate!" he ordered.

"I'm sorry," the oldest god apologized, smiling, "it's the children, you know, the dogs want to romp. But they're filthy, as we've been down to the river. I sincerely hope they didn't dirty you."

"Stout lads," the middle one said, giving the boys a pat on the head. "Weren't frightened of the dogs at all, were you?"

The oldest had been studying the man keenly, as he once again got to his feet. "You must be father's new assistant. How long have you been waiting? Is someone coming to see to you?"

The other nodded, saying, "Thank you, sir, I've been told someone will be with us shortly. A wagon is bringing up our household effects from the station. Could I ask—"

"Good!" "Smashing!" "Nice to meet you!" the young gods chorused.

Shouting for the dogs to follow, they took off down a hallway to the left.

With a sigh, the man sat down again. One of the children giggled. Without looking, he gently shook his head, and the sound subsided.

On the far wall of the reception room hung a recent portrait of the master and mistress of the house, the duke and duchess of Westermere—he renowned for his experiments in deductive science, particularly the criminal field, and she for her philanthropy and studies of the effects of heredity in female lawbreakers. They had jointly endowed the famous college of criminal medicine in Leeds.

The man studied the painting, thinking the family resemblance could not be missed. The twin beauties of thirteen, the godlike young males could not be other than Westermere offspring. The duke, an imposingly fit figure of the military man, was Olympian in his mature good looks, a few strands of silver showing in his black hair. He was painted in full dress uniform with decorations of the Napoleonic wars, his hand resting on the shoulder of the seated duchess.

She was as lovely in her early fifties as she had doubtless been as a much younger woman. Glossy gold-brown curls framed her face, the tight bodice above a full crinoline revealed her still-youthful form, and dazzling azure eyes full of laughter looked out at the world.

"Have you been waiting long?" a voice said.

A young man in his twenties came quickly down the staircase followed by a young woman almost as beautiful as her mother.

"I'm terribly sorry," the handsome young man said, shaking the other's hand. "You're the new assistant, aren't you? I'm Osbert de Vries, and this is my sister, Lady Alicia. My father will be delighted to know you've finally arrived. Unfortunately, His Grace is down with the quinsy, an affliction that attacks him infrequently. So my mother is reading to him, something he enjoys very much. My sister and I will be seeing to your arrangements, if that's agreeable."

Lady Alicia showed them her enchanting dimples. "Your cottage is ready, Ozzie will take you down himself, and see that you and the children are settled in. I know you will like working with my father. Papa fancies himself as something of a dragon, but he really has a dear, soft heart."

The young man gave her a grateful look. Like working with the duke of Westermere? This position was the fulfillment of all his dreams! He did not care if the famed theorist of the Lamberton murders was a fire-eating ogre—there was not a laboratory assistant in all of England who would not drop everything to work for the duke of Westermere and the privilege of being in close proximity to that brilliant mind. His wife and partner, the duchess, was fully his equal. Her paper on the study of poverty and the abnormal mind, published in the Cambridge Journal of Criminal Law, had set new standards for the field.

"What lovely children!" Lady Alicia dropped to her knees in front of the boys, smiling as she looked into their solemn faces. "I know they will be happy here. There's an excellent school in the village, as Papa has doubtless informed you, and when they are a bit older I have no doubt that if they are interested they will be allowed to poke about in the laboratory and learn what they can there, too. What are their ages?"

Enraptured

"They are aged five and eight, Lady Alicia," their father replied. "And bright boys, if I do say so. And thank you, they will be quick to pick up any learning they can, you may count on it."

She looked up at him. "And their names?"

"The oldest is Mycroft, milady," Robert Holmes said. "And my youngest boy—here, stand up, lad, and give her ladyship your hand. My youngest is Sherlock after his grandfather. Sherlock Holmes."

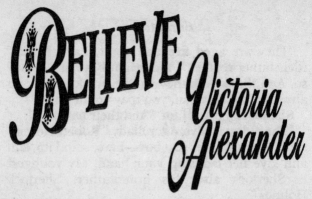

BELIEVE
Victoria Alexander

Tessa thinks as little of love as she does of the Arthurian legend—it is just a myth. But when an enchanted tome falls into the lovely teacher's hands, she learns that the legend is nothing like she remembers. Galahad the Chaste is everything but—the powerful knight is an expert lover—and not only wizards can weave powerful spells. Still, even in Galahad's muscled embrace, she feels unsure of this man who seemed a myth. But soon the beautiful skeptic is on a quest as real as her heart, and the grail—and Galahad's love—is within reach. All she has to do is believe.

___52267-5 $5.99 US/$6.99 CAN

RECKLESS HEART

MADELINE BAKER

They play together as children—the Indian lad and little Hannah Kincaid. Then Shadow and his people go away, and when he returns, it is as a handsome young Cheyenne brave. Hannah, now a beautiful young woman, has never forgotten her childhood friend—but the man who sweeps her into his powerful arms is no longer a child. He awakens in her a wild, erotic passion she has never known. But war is about to erupt in the Dakota Territory, a war that will pit the settlers against the Indians. Both Hannah and Shadow know that the time is coming when they will have to choose between happiness and hatred, between passion and duty, in a conflict that will test to the limit the steadfastness of their love. . . .

___4527-3 $5.99 US/$6.99 CAN

Dorchester Publishing Co., Inc.
P.O. Box 6640
Wayne, PA 19087-8640

Please add $1.75 for shipping and handling for the first book and $.50 for each book thereafter. NY, NYC, and PA residents, please add appropriate sales tax. No cash, stamps, or C.O.D.s. All orders shipped within 6 weeks via postal service book rate. Canadian orders require $2.00 extra postage and must be paid in U.S. dollars through a U.S. banking facility.

Name_____
Address_____
City_____State_____Zip_____
I have enclosed $_____ in payment for the checked book(s).
Payment <u>must</u> accompany all orders. ☐ Please send a free catalog.
     CHECK OUT OUR WEBSITE! www.dorchesterpub.com

Fairest of Them All
Josette Browning

A true stoic and a gentleman, Daniel Canty has worked furiously to achieve the high esteem of the English nobility. Therefore, it is more his reputation than the promise of wealth that compels him to accept the ninth earl of Hawkenge's challenge to turn an orphan wild child into a lady. But the girl who's been raised by animals in the African interior is hardly an orphan—and his wildly beautiful charge is hardly a child. Truly, Talitha is a woman—and the most compelling Daniel has ever seen. But the mute firebrand also poses the greatest threat he has ever faced. In the girl's soft kiss is the jeopardy which Daniel has fought all his life to avoid: the danger of losing his heart.

___4513-3 $5.50 US/$6.50 CAN

Lady of the Night — Cordia Byers

Manacled to a stone wall is not the way Katharina Fergersen planned to spend her vacation. But a wrong turn in the right place and the haunted English castle she is touring is suddenly full of life—and so is the man who is bathing before her. As the frosty winter days melt into hot passionate nights, she realizes that there is more to Kane than just a well-filled pair of breeches. Katharina is determined not to let this man who has touched her soul escape her, even if it means giving up all to remain Sedgewick's lady of the night.

___4404-8 $5.99 US/$6.99 CAN

Dorchester Publishing Co., Inc.
P.O. Box 6640
Wayne, PA 19087-8640

Please add $1.75 for shipping and handling for the first book and $.50 for each book thereafter. NY, NYC, and PA residents, please add appropriate sales tax. No cash, stamps, or C.O.D.s. All orders shipped within 6 weeks via postal service book rate. Canadian orders require $2.00 extra postage and must be paid in U.S. dollars through a U.S. banking facility.

Name_____
Address_____
City_____State_____Zip_____
I have enclosed $_____ in payment for the checked book(s).
Payment <u>must</u> accompany all orders. ☐ Please send a free catalog.
CHECK OUT OUR WEBSITE! www.dorchesterpub.com

PRETENDER'S GAMES — LOUISE CLARK

James MacLonan is in desperate need of a wife. Recently pardoned, the charming Scotsman has to prove his loyalty to the king by marrying a woman with proper ties to the English throne. Thea is the perfect wife: beautiful, witty, and the daughter of an English general. And while she can be as prickly as a thistle when it comes to her undying loyalty to King George, James finds himself longing for her passionate kisses and sweet embrace. Thea never thinks she will marry a Scot, let alone a Jacobite renegade who has just returned from his years of exile on the Continent. Convinced she can't lose her heart to a traitor of the crown, Thea nevertheless finds herself swept into his strong arms, wondering if indeed her rogue husband has truly abandoned his rebellious ways for a life filled with love.

___4514-1 $4.99 US/$5.99 CAN

JAGUAR EYES

Casey Claybourne

Daniel Heywood ventures into the wilds of the Amazon, determined to leave his mark on science. Wounded by Indians shortly into his journey, he is rescued by a beautiful woman with the longest legs he's ever seen. As she nurses him back to health, Daniel realizes he has stumbled upon an undiscovered civilization. But he cannot explain the way his heart skips a beat when he looks into the captivating beauty's gold-green eyes. When she returns with him to England, she wonders if she is really the object of his affections—or a subject in his experiment. The answer lies in Daniel's willingness to leave convention behind for a love as lush as the Amazon jungle.

___52284-5 $5.50 US/$6.50 CAN

Dorchester Publishing Co., Inc.
P.O. Box 6640
Wayne, PA 19087-8640

Please add $1.75 for shipping and handling for the first book and $.50 for each book thereafter. NY, NYC, and PA residents, please add appropriate sales tax. No cash, stamps, or C.O.D.s. All orders shipped within 6 weeks via postal service book rate. Canadian orders require $2.00 extra postage and must be paid in U.S. dollars through a U.S. banking facility.

Name_____
Address_____
City_____State_____Zip_____
I have enclosed $_____ in payment for the checked book(s).
Payment <u>must</u> accompany all orders. ❑ Please send a free catalog.